Queen of Broken Hearts

Also by Cassandra King

Making Waves

The Sunday Wife

The Same Sweet Girls

Queen *of* Broken Hearts

❧ ❧ ❧ ❧ ❧ ❧ ❧ ❧ ❧ ❧ ❧ ❧

CASSANDRA KING

HYPERION

NEW YORK

Excerpt from "What Lips My Lips Have Kissed" by Edna St. Vincent Millay. From *Collected Poems*, HarperCollins. Copyright © 1923, 1951 by Edna St. Vincent Millay and Norma Millay Ellis. All rights reserved. Used by permission of Elizabeth Barnett, literary executor.

Library of Congress Cataloging-in-Publication Data

King, Cassandra
    Queen of broken hearts / Cassandra King. — 1st ed.
      p. cm.
    ISBN-13: 978-1-4013-0177-4
    ISBN-10: 1-4013-0177-0
    1. Women—Southern States—Fiction. 2. Divorce therapy—Fiction. I. Title.
    PS3568.A922Q44 2007
    813'.6—dc22   2006049697

Hyperion books are available for special promotions and premiums. For details contact Michael Rentas, Assistant Director, Inventory Operations, Hyperion, 77 West 66th Street, 12th floor, New York, New York 10023, or call 212-456-0133.

FIRST EDITION

10 9 8 7 6 5 4 3 2 1

To Nancy, who lived through it and came out even stronger. You make me proud, baby sister.

And to Patrick, who made me believe in happy endings.

Acknowledgments

To Marly, Leslie, and Ellen: I couldn't have done it without your encouragement, help, patience, and perseverance.

To the family and friends: I love each of you more than I can say, even if I weren't known as Helen Keller.

To the people of Fairhope, Alabama: It is a privilege to set my story in your unique and enchanting town. Please forgive any poetic license I might have taken.

And especially to Margot Swann and the women of Visions Anew, the wonderful real-life organization that inspired the fictional Wayfarer's Landing. Please visit them at VisionsAnew.org.

Thus in the winter stands the lonely tree,
Nor knows what birds have vanished one by one,
Yet knows its boughs more silent than before:
I cannot say what loves have come and gone,
I only know that summer sang in me
A little while, that in me sings no more.

Edna St. Vincent Millay

Queen of Broken Hearts

Chapter One

❧　❧　❧　❧　❧

At the exact moment the cash register dings and I open my change purse, the chain of bells on the front door of the coffee shop bangs together with a brassy clatter. I hear the sound of voices raised in greetings, a loud and hearty hello in response, and the bells jangling again as the door closes. Curious to see who's making such an entrance, I glance over my shoulder. When I see that it's Son Rodgers, my face flames and my heart pounds. On top of everything else that's happened today, I go to the coffee shop for lunch, and who do I run into? One thing for sure: I have to get out of here before he sees me. It would be embarrassing for me and him and the dozen or so other folks enjoying their afternoon coffee. Instinctively, I duck my head and pull my arms close as if to make myself invisible.

Barely turning my head, I look over my shoulder again to determine the distance between me and the front door. No way I can get out that way without him seeing me; I'll have to exit through the bookstore. Now I wish I'd driven to town instead of walking, even though it would've been ridiculous to drive so few blocks. But my getaway would have been easier. I could have gone through the adjoining bookstore, gotten nonchalantly into my car, and put the pedal to the metal. Instead, everyone in both stores will see me running out of the coffee shop right after my best friend's husband has walked in. I can only imagine the talk that will follow, since our small town has talked of little else all summer except what's gone on in the Rodgers household. I can hear it now: "Did you know it's gotten so bad that Clare sneaked out of the coffee shop to avoid Son? Poor Dory!"

Making my getaway is turning out to be more difficult than I thought. The lethargic, bespectacled teenager behind the counter is new—his first day, he told me proudly—and he doesn't know the ropes yet. He takes his time wrapping the two slices of carrot cake in parchment paper, placing them in a flat white box, then bringing the edges of the box together. When I see him searching for tape, I say, "It's fine. Don't bother taping it," and hope that my voice doesn't sound as flustered as I feel. But he shrugs me off and says no problem, it's no trouble at all. He rings it up wrong for the second time, muttering, "Oops." After canceling out the sale, he punches in the numbers again, glances at me over the top of his glasses, and mumbles, "Uh, that'll be eight fifty-three."

It hits me that I used all my change by counting out the exact amount for the veggie wrap and iced tea I had for lunch, plus a tip; I left the money on the table, anchoring my ticket. On my way out, I decided on impulse to take a couple pieces of carrot cake with me, and I stopped at the counter to place my order. I have nothing but a twenty to pay with. Another glance over my shoulder, and I toss the twenty-dollar bill at Pokey. In a low voice, I say, "If you could hurry, I'd really appreciate it. I'm running late for an appointment." Of course, I speak too softly, trying to keep Son from hearing my voice, and Pokey tilts his head sideways to say, "Ma'am?"

"Hurry with the change, please," I hiss.

From the corner of my eye, I see that Son is working the room like a politician running for reelection, slapping backs and grinning like the Cheshire cat. His greetings are met with cries of "Hey—look who's back in town!" and "Son! How was your trip? When did you get home?" I watch him lean over to kiss the cheek of a plump, white-haired lady who coos and giggles and puts both hands to her face in something resembling the ecstasy of Saint Teresa. He then joins a couple of businessmen from the bank who get to their feet to shake his hand and pound his back with great vigor, buying me a few seconds. Son throws back his head to laugh at something one of them says, which gives me a chance for a furtive study of him. I haven't seen him all summer, the longest span of time since he and Dory married, and that was twenty-five years ago.

Son is casually dressed in crisp, pressed jeans and a white oxford-cloth shirt, the sleeves carelessly rolled up to reveal brown, well-muscled arms. Usually he's in a shirt and tie, as befitting such a highly regarded and important hotshot. I guess he hasn't yet gone back to work in his real estate business, since he and Dory have been home only a couple of days. Even though he has a hand on the shoulder of one of the businessmen and appears to be listening with great interest, I notice that his eyes occasionally search the room to make sure he's kissed up to everyone there. When his gaze comes my way, I turn my head quickly, almost dropping the bills and change that Pokey is counting into my outstretched hand. When he miscounts and starts over, I'm tempted to tell the poor fellow to keep it, even if it would make me the biggest tipper in town. He'd probably be so surprised that he'd ask me to repeat myself yet again, and I'd end up getting caught by Son after all.

With his scrutiny of the coffee shop, it's unbelievable that Son hasn't recognized me yet, even with my back to him and the counter located at a helpful angle. It occurs to me that he hasn't seen me since I've had my hair cut. From the first day we met, Son has gone on and on about what great hair I have. It's nothing but his usual empty flattery, the only way he knows to relate to women. The truth is, my long, heavy hair has always been unruly and difficult. After struggling with it all my life, I gave up and had it chopped off a few weeks ago. Everybody tells me I look like a different person with my mass of hair gone, which must be true. Even so, I'm not taking any chances, not with the way Son keeps looking everyone over, so I drop the change into my briefcase instead of in my purse. Thankfully, the door of the adjoining bookstore is only a few feet away.

I've taken a step away from the counter when the young man clears his throat and says in a loud voice, "Uh—ma'am?" My cheeks burning, I turn to see him holding out the box with the carrot cake in it. I yank it out of his hand so quickly that his eyes widen in surprise and his Adam's apple jerks up and down. I feel bad for him, but not as bad as he would feel if Son saw me and caused a scene in the crowded shop. It would *not* be a good way to end his first day at work.

In the Page and Palette bookstore, a glance assures me that the salesclerk is helping a customer in the back, so I step behind a revolving display of paperbacks in order to peer into the coffee shop, making sure I got away without being seen. To my relief, I've escaped: Son is still standing with the two businessmen and running his mouth, with a big grin on his face. The three of them bend their heads together as he relates something, and they all laugh appreciatively, slapping backs again. Satisfied that I've escaped undetected, I sling the strap of my briefcase over my shoulder and tuck the box of carrot cake under my arm, then head toward the front door.

Once I'm outside, I'm surprised to find the sidewalks still crowded with shoppers and sightseers, which is unusual for early fall. Anxious to get away from the coffee shop, I mutter my apologies as I make my way through, wondering if there's a tour bus in town. Although off the beaten path, Fairhope is becoming more and more of a tourist attraction, and it's not unusual to have several tour buses in town during the summer, but not this time of year. In an effort to avoid a cluster of people blocking the sidewalk in front of one of the street's many art galleries, I cut through a group of charming and colorful little shops that make up the area known as the French Quarter. And that's where I run into Rye Ballenger, quite literally.

If I hadn't been hugging the bakery box so close, carrot cake would have gone flying.

"Clare!" he exclaims at the same time I gasp, "Rye!" Then both of us say together, "What are you doing here?"

I link an arm into his and continue my walk, pulling Rye along with me down the brick-paved lane. Out of the corner of my mouth, I say to him in a low voice, "I'm trying to get far enough away from the coffee shop so I won't be seen by a certain person who just walked in."

Rye plays along with me, matching my stride. "Who is it?" he whispers dramatically, looking around in mock terror. "An ex-husband of one of your clients?"

"Actually, you're close," I say with a groan. "It's Son."

"Son!" Rye comes to such an abrupt halt that I almost trip over a protruding brick. "Did he say anything to you? Tell me the truth."

"He didn't see me, thank God. I hightailed it out of there as fast as I could. Something tells me I'm not on his list of favorite people right now."

With a frown, Rye studies my face. He disengages my arm in order to take my hand in both of his and squeeze it tight. "Why don't you go back and confront him, sweetheart? I'll go with you, by God. I don't like the idea of him bullying you, and he needs to hear that."

"Your problem is, you're much too gallant," I say with an affectionate smile. "Charging in on your white horse and defending the honor of the poor maiden."

He snorts with indignation, his color high. "I've never been on a horse in my life, and have no intention of ever doing so. But I hate missing the chance to give Son Rodgers a piece of my mind."

"All I want to do is avoid him," I assure him. "I'm not interested in a confrontation at this point. Especially now, with him and Dory back together."

"Still no idea how that miraculous event came about?" Rye asks, watching me curiously.

I shrug. "None whatsoever. But I'll see Dory tomorrow at the group meeting, and she's promised me that we'll talk beforehand. Have you—"

Before I realize what's happening, Rye has grabbed me by the shoulders and pulled me out of the way of a large gray-haired woman who barges past us, then turns back to scowl at us for blocking the sidewalk. As we watch her walk away, I send up a thank-you to whatever gods were responsible for sending Rye strolling through the French Quarter at the very moment I turned the corner. From the first day I arrived in Fairhope, the sardonic and irreverent Rye Ballenger has been one of my dearest friends, and there's no one I'd rather see now, after the near miss with Son. Certainly no one else understands my history with Son better than Rye does.

He and I move to stand under the jasmine-entwined arbor of a café, then Rye leans toward me to whisper in my ear, "Lord God Almighty, would you look at that! How ghastly." He nods toward the retreating woman, who's clad in a hot-pink T-shirt with flowered capri pants stretched way too tight across her very ample rear end. "I can promise you that she hails from north of the Mason-Dixon line."

"What gives her away?" I ask with a grin, pushing my sunglasses on top of my head. "The camera hanging around her neck or the Gulf Shores T-shirt?"

Brow furrowed, Rye shudders and says, "Come on, Clare. No self-respecting Southern belle would be caught dead wearing white socks with sandals, and you know it. It's a disgrace, that's what it is. If they are going to run us off our lovely streets, the least they could do is dress properly."

"You're such a snob," I say fondly. "But you know what? I think you love it. You work hard at being the biggest snob in Baldwin County, don't you?"

Pretending to be offended, he pulls back and drawls in his melodious, honey-toned voice, "I just happen to have my standards, is all."

When I first met the courtly Ryman Ballenger, a cousin of my former husband's, I thought he had to be putting me on. He has the most pronounced Southern accent I've ever heard, and on the Eastern Shore of Alabama, that's saying a lot. It suits him, though, just another of his many charms. In addition to being the most breathtakingly handsome man I've ever had the pleasure of knowing, Rye is also the most elegant. He's always seemed out of place in this offbeat, artsy little town. He should be strolling the lavish grounds of an English estate instead, trailed by a bevy of manservants and Cavalier King Charles spaniels.

"It's strange that I ran into you just as I was running out of the coffee shop," I say, gazing up at him. Rye is one of those people I enjoy just looking at, in the same way I might stop by an art gallery and admire a painting. "Don't tell me you walked to town." In all the years I've known him, I've never seen him walk anywhere. He'll get into his big old silver Mercedes to drive a block.

He looks at me as though I've lost my mind. "Me walk to town? In this heat? I should hope not." With a nod, he indicates a place across the street. "My car's over there. I almost never found a parking place in this damn mob." He points out a small shop on the corner. "I came down to pick up a print that Lou framed for me. But the mat didn't suit me, so I had her redo it."

"Not up to your standards, huh?" I tease him.

Rye studies me through long dark lashes, and his fine gray eyes go soft. "I can't tell you how happy I am to see you. I called your cell phone not five minutes ago."

With a grimace, I admit that I turned it off when I left the office. "You know how hard it is for me to close shop on Friday afternoons. Etta had to stand in the door to keep me from returning for some unfinished paperwork. If I'd kept my cell turned on and one of my clients called, having a crisis, I would've had to go running back to meet them there."

He clucks his tongue in reproach. "Ah, Clare, what am I going to do with you? You promised me that you'd stop giving your private numbers to your clients!"

"I know . . ." My voice trails off, and I look up at him helplessly.

He places a hand on my shoulder. "When you didn't answer your cell, I got concerned about you, after what happened this morning."

"You concerned about *me*? That's a switch, since I'm officially the one who gets to worry about everybody else. It's in my job description."

"You can worry your pretty head off about whomever you want, my dear Clare, but I'm in charge of you."

"How very touching," I say, trying to keep my voice light. "I assume you're referring to a certain letter in this morning's paper?"

"So you've seen it?" With a worried frown, Rye reaches into his pocket and pulls out a clipping. "I have it with me, so if anyone dares to say anything about it, I can tell them what a bunch of hogwash it is."

"I've seen it," I tell him dismally. I arrived at my office early this morning, bringing the local paper to read while waiting for my first client. Like most weeklies, *The Fairhoper* is the perfect antidote to the grim headlines of the national news. Unless we've had one of our infamous hurricanes, the articles are full of small-town dramas that can be heartwarming but are more often unintentionally comic. Dory and I will call each other to read some of the more priceless ones aloud. Her favorite remains the obituary written about a certain Mr. McMillan, who is said to have died in his sleep so peacefully that it didn't wake him or Mrs. McMillan, either one. The human interest stories are usually pretty good, but last month I was embarrassed to find myself named Fairhope's Citizen of the Month. To my further embarrassment, one of this morning's letters to the editor, which I read in dismay, referred to my award:

This letter is written to protest your choice of August's Citizen of the Month, a self-proclaimed divorce "coach." The honor was based on the national attention that has come this woman's way, praising her innovative methods of divorce recovery. I have to wonder if those retreats of hers, held right here in our own conference center, actually do more to promote divorces than to help people get over them. Surely if folks were encouraged to work on their marriages instead, the disgracefully high divorce rates in our country would go down. I hope next month's choice will better reflect the ideals of our community and country. The letter was signed by Oscar T. Allen, a "concerned" citizen whom I'd not had the pleasure of meeting, fortunately.

Rye stands with his hands on his hips, scowling. "I can't tell you how furious I am. And you've got to be, too, though you won't let on. I know how you operate. In spite of all your degrees, you hide your feelings like the rest of us."

"You know better than that." I can't resist adding with a sly smile, "I'd never hide my feelings from you."

"Ha!" he scoffs. "You could've fooled me."

"You've lived here all your life, and you know everyone in town, so tell me who Oscar T. Allen is."

"He's a damned nitwit, that's who he is. The good thing is, no one will take him seriously, because we all know he's batty."

I let out a sigh of relief. "Well, I have to say I'm glad to hear that he's a crackpot. It could've been a pretty damaging indictment otherwise. The reference to the conference center makes my work sound sleazy, like those fly-by-night operations that breeze into town and rent a seminar room at the Holiday Inn. Calling me a divorce coach, which I've *never* been, implies that I find confused, unhappy women and teach them the secrets of pulling off a successful divorce, feathering my nest in the process."

"It's ridiculous," Rye agrees, his eyes blazing. "But don't even think about it harming you professionally. You're too highly respected for that. The newspaper allowing the letter to be printed is what made me so mad."

"To tell you the truth, I'm surprised that this is the first attack I've had."

"I don't like anyone going after my girl," he says gently. "As soon as I read the paper, I called Clyde Ayers and gave him a piece of my mind. I'm sick of him giving voice to every ignorant Bible thumper who picks up a pen. Clyde proceeded to lecture me on First Amendment rights. Me! Can you imagine? I reminded him that I have a law degree from Ole Miss, then hung up on him."

"Oh, Rye." Frowning, I put a hand on his arm. "You and Clyde Ayers have been buddies forever. I don't want you losing any friends on my account. It's not that big a deal."

"Just as I thought. You're trying to blow it off."

"I'm not!" I tell him, giving his arm a shake. "As soon as I ran into you, so to speak, I knew you'd make me feel better, and you already have."

He regards me for a long moment, then says in a soft voice, "You know I'd do anything for you."

"You're such a dear friend." It's difficult to meet his gaze without blushing like a fool. In addition to everything else that went on this past summer, Rye and I had a rather unsettling evening that neither of us has mentioned since. We need to discuss it at some point, but I chicken out every time I see him.

"And then there was the other thing, in Miss Dingbat's column," Rye goes on. "I can only imagine what your reaction was to that one."

"After the letter, I didn't read any further," I admit. "What's she done this time?" The society column, "Fairhope's Fairest," is penned by a woman who uses the moniker Ernestine Hemingway, apparently with no idea that it makes her sound like a drag queen. Guess she figures it gives her more literary credibility than her real name, Ima June Hicks.

"Oh, her column was worse than usual." He glances around before taking my arm and pulling me closer to the shelter of the little café. "While Dory and Son were in Europe, he sent a postcard to Ernestine, and she quoted it in her column. It was all about

Fairhope's favorite couple spending the month of August on a second honeymoon in France. Ernestine went on to say that they were taking in the sights but mostly gazing into each other's eyes. It was beyond nauseating."

"Oh, Lord!" I wail. "It's pure propaganda on Son's part. No, I take that back. 'Propaganda' is much too long a word for his vocabulary."

Rye regards me sternly, his head tilted to the side. "I've told you, Clare, that Son will get the best of you if you keep dismissing him by claiming he's not very bright. It's all a part of his good-old-boy act. He's crazy like a fox. Have you seen Dory since they got back?" When I shake my head, he lowers his voice conspiratorially and says, "I ran into the happy couple last night, having dinner at the Yacht Club, and she seemed fine, in spite of all he put her through last year. She looked more beautiful than ever." His gray eyes are suddenly dreamy. "But Dory always does, doesn't she?"

"I'm sure Prince Charming was working the room, kissing ass all over the place, just like he was doing a few minutes ago at the coffee shop."

"Even worse," Rye says in disgust. "With Dory back by his side, he was beaming like he'd just scored the winning touchdown in an Alabama–Auburn game. He held on to Dory's arm and didn't let her out of his sight all night."

"Hovering over Dory? That's so unlike Son," I say sarcastically.

"When I approached their table to welcome them back, he did something that really surprised me."

"Told you that scientists have discovered someone with a lower IQ than he has?"

Rye sighs in exasperation before telling me, "He jumped to his feet and hugged me like a long-lost brother."

"Oh, please!" I groan. "Thank God I wasn't there. A performance like that would gag a maggot."

He regards me with a troubled expression. "I know how disappointed you were when they got back together. Both of us were."

"After the last stunt Son pulled, I thought for sure that she was through with him. Dory may be perfect in every other way, but her taste in men leaves something to be desired."

"You expect too much of people, my dear. Of all of us. You always have." Rye says it casually, without censure, but it stings anyway.

"Maybe I do," I reply weakly.

We avoid each other's eyes until I say, "Listen, I've *got* to go. Dory's coming to the group tomorrow morning, and I'll let you know how it goes, okay?" Before putting an arm around his shoulder and kissing him goodbye, I add with real regret, "If only she'd had the good sense to marry you, instead of Son, when she had the chance! You wouldn't still be looking for the one who got away, and Dory would've had a good man instead of a pain in the butt like Son."

With a seemingly nonchalant smile, Rye shrugs. "You're right about one thing: I've spent my life searching for the right woman." We fall silent, then he says wistfully, "Why don't you change your mind and come to the party with me tonight? Be good for you."

"I wouldn't do that to you," I say breezily. "Think what it'd do to your social life to be seen with Fairhope's most notorious homewrecker."

"It'd be worth it."

"I'm busy tonight and couldn't go even if I wanted to. Which I don't."

He takes me by the arm as though to lead me to one of the wrought-iron tables of the outdoor café. "Let's sit down," he says. "I need a smoke bad." At my expression, he flinches. "No lectures, sweetheart. Eventually I'll honor my promise to quit, but not now. Smoking calms my nerves."

"You've been saying that for years, Rye! You ought to have the calmest nerves in the state of Alabama. I'll put that on your tombstone: 'He died of calm nerves.' "

"Okay, okay. I won't have a cigarette, then—we'll get a glass of sherry instead."

"I can't. I've *got* to get home." Twisting my wrist sideways, I look down at my watch. "Oh, Jesus, I'm running late as it is."

He eyes me suspiciously, tilting his head. "You're two-timing me, aren't you, Clare? Running off with your new boyfriend, that Yankee sea captain. He's the real reason you won't go with me tonight, isn't he?"

"I told you why I didn't want to go," I say flippantly. "If I had to get all dressed up, then make small talk with that snooty crowd you hang around, I'd jump off the municipal pier."

"You're not only heartless, you have no manners, either." Following my lead, Rye goes back to his playful bantering. "It's rude to say that you don't want to go. You should make up an excuse that won't hurt my feelings."

Leaning over, I brush his cheek with my lips, laying a hand on his shoulder. "Oh, phooey. Nobody in their right mind *likes* going to cocktail parties. Well, except you, maybe."

Returning my kiss, he smells delicious, his shaving lotion like rare spices. Holding me close for a minute, he whispers in my ear before releasing me, "You're not fooling me, you know. On my way into town, I drove by your house. Your sea captain is already there. That god-awful vehicle he drives is parked out front."

"Good. We're going to the Landing, and as you well know, we'll need the Jeep. I'm leaving now, my friend. Have a good time at your snotty party tonight. Oh—and by the way, you don't fool me, either. I'm sure you won't be going to the party alone."

"Anytime I'm not with you, my dear girl, I might as well be alone." He says it with that devastating smile of his, the one that's left a trail of broken hearts all across the South.

"Oh, God," I groan. "With that corny line, I'm definitely leaving. See you later, okay?"

At the corner of the alley leading out of the French Quarter, I turn to wave goodbye. Rye's still standing on the sidewalk, his hands thrust into the pockets of his straw-colored trousers as he watches me leave. When I wave, he mouths, "Two-timer," and I chuckle, rolling my eyes before turning onto Church Street, toward my house.

On my walk home, I avoid the sidewalks and walk the shady little alleyways, thinking I'll be less likely to run into anyone I know. I've had a couple of calls this morning about the letter to the editor, but too many things are vying for my attention for me to worry about it. I wonder if Dory's seen it yet, and if she's been trying to reach me. She knows I'll fret over it a while, then blow it off, if I practice what I'm always preaching about troublesome things like that. I tell my clients that three of the most important and powerful words in the English language are "Let it go." Pick your battles, decide which are worth putting your energy into fighting and which aren't. Seeing Son at the coffee shop, the letter to the editor . . . those are things I have to let go before I get home. My days are always full, but today even more so. The next thing on my agenda is the all-important trip out to the Landing with Lex; if I hurry home, we'll have time for a few leisurely moments, maybe even a glass of wine beforehand.

Walking the alleyways was a good decision: I don't see anyone, and I've escaped the tourists. Although I dutifully join in the complaints against them, in truth I can't blame anyone for coming here. I fell in love with this little town the first time I saw it exactly twenty-five years ago this summer, when I came here with my new fiancé to meet his family. Fairhope has a way of casting its spell on everyone who spends any time here. It's such a quaint and picturesque town, with its historic waterfront and beach, but the beauty is only part of it. Seeing it initially, I was enchanted with the quiet, unpaved streets meandering under overhanging limbs of towering oaks and huge magnolias. Almost all the little cottages and stately old homes are hidden from view, which makes them seem sheltered and safe, as though nothing bad could happen to anyone fortunate enough to live in them. A foolish illusion, of course, as I know better than anyone.

The unique, even mythical history of the town is as much a part of its appeal as its beauty, and I'm still astonished that such a place exists in Alabama. Fairhope was founded around the turn of the twentieth century by a group of idealists who dreamed of creating a utopia. Even the name reflects their ideal: The story goes that one of the founders remarked that their project had a "fair hope" of succeeding. I'm surprised they gave it that much of a chance, actually. A group of Midwestern idealists establishing a freethinking colony founded on the principles of social and economic justice in the middle of the Deep South is a pretty radical idea even now, but especially for that day and age. The founders left their comfortable lives and homes to venture into the unknown, putting everything they had into building a new and perfect society. When I first started conducting the retreats, the idea hit me to draw an analogy between that adventure and the journey of the participants. It's still one of the most popular parts of the retreats. Handing out material on the history of Fairhope, I compare the way the colony was established to the way each of them will be beginning her new life. Like the first settlers of this community, each newly divorced woman is charting an unfamiliar course, setting out for the unknown.

To reach my home, I have to pass the stuccoed, tile-roofed cottage that houses my practice. Because it is not only the home of a therapy practice but also Spanish in style and decor, the locals have nicknamed it Casa Loco. At first I was unamused, but over time the whimsical epithet has served me well. Everyone in town knows its location, and new clients who are directed to Casa Loco almost always arrive smiling. I stand outside it now and wonder if I should go in and get the casework I didn't complete this morning. Then I scoff at myself. Even if I had it with me, when would I have time to work on it? I take a few steps away, then pause. Maybe I should check my messages. Won't take but a minute, and one of my really distraught clients might have called. But no. No, no, no! I pick up my pace and refuse to look back at Casa Loco. Like Lot's wife, I'm liable to be turned into something horrible if I do, and it won't be a pillar of salt. More likely it will be a stack of paperwork.

Going around the curve and arriving at my house, I see that Rye wasn't joking—Lex's beat-up old Jeep is indeed out front. I'm getting here later than I'd told him to expect me, but he would've made himself at home. Over the past few weeks, he's gotten more comfortable about coming and going in my house. It started even before, in mid-July, when I gave him a key so he could keep an eye on things while I was out of town for a conference. On returning, I asked if he'd keep the key in case I needed him again. There are times when neither Etta nor I can free ourselves from work, and I don't mind calling Lex and asking if he'll stop by the house while he's out and let in the plumber or whatever. Unlike me, trapped in Casa Loco seeing clients all day, Lex is constantly coming into town from the marina, making regular runs to the hardware store or post office or bank.

Funny, me having two men in my life now. I'm equally fond of both Rye and Lex and often find myself juggling my time between them. Our choice of friends can reveal our needs, I think, and that's proved true with those two. I give Rye credit for introducing me to the joys of dancing, since he takes me out dancing whenever I need a mental-health break, which is fairly frequent in my business. Then Lex was the one who insisted that I get my work obsession under control. When we first became friends, he was appalled at my hours, not believing that I often stayed at my office for hours after my last client left. One day this summer he barged in and demanded I get a *life,* for Christ's sake.

Lex and I met on an unforgettable night at the beginning of the summer and hit it off instantly. I enjoy his company in much the same way I've always enjoyed Rye's, though I wouldn't put it that way to either of them, since each teases me about the other. No two men could be any more opposite in personality, temperament, and appearance than Lex Yarbrough and Rye Ballenger. Rye is witty, glib, and urbane, while Lex is playful, outgoing, and full of mischief. With his looks, charm, and courtliness, Rye is adored by women and envied by men. Being neither seductive nor flirtatious, Lex cares nothing for adoration or envy. What you see is what you get with him. He's blunt and no-nonsense, yet he has more sheer magnetism than any man I've ever met.

I'm aware that everyone in Fairhope assumes Lex and I are lovers, but I'm used to that; people have made the same assumption about me and Rye for quite a while now. Pushing open the door of my house, which feels blissfully cool after the long walk from town, I find myself chuckling. Well, if certain people think my job is coaching women on the fine art of leaving their husbands and destroying their families, it's not much of a stretch to see me as a woman who'd sleep with two men at once. How disappointed they'd be to know the truth! Setting my purse and the cake box on the table in the foyer, I see that Lex brought in the mail and stacked it neatly on the table. The only piece separate is *The Fairhoper,* and since it's refolded in a crooked manner, I know he's read it. I wonder what his reaction will be. Although laid-back and easygoing to a fault, Lex is not a man I'd want to cross.

"Hey, where are you, Lex?" I call out, heading toward the back of the house. One thing for sure, he will be in either the kitchen or the backyard, his two favorite hangouts here. Not finding him in the kitchen, I lean over the sink and look out the double windows. Yep, he's in the herb garden, knee-deep in thyme. I wonder why it is that the sight of him tending a garden never fails to surprise me. I can't help myself; seeing a man like Lex Yarbrough in my garden makes me think of a story I loved as a child, one about a bull who would rather smell flowers than fight the matador. What was his name, Ferdinand? Kicking off my low-heeled sandals, I push open the back door. It's been a stressful day thus far, but I've learned one thing in my business: Never, ever assume that things can't get worse.

Chapter Two

❧   ❧   ❧   ❧   ❧

O nce I'm outside, the day's heat from the flagstone pathway forces me to make a run for the shade of the wisteria arbor. Standing on the cool, mossy ground under the arbor, I cup my hands around my mouth to call out to Lex again.

His back is to me, and I realize he can't hear me because of the sprinklers, which are humming like little helicopters. Kneeling among the herbs, shears in hand, he's snipping off dried brown clusters of the pale green thyme, which is supposed to be a border but has almost overtaken the beds. The lemony smell drifts my way, along with the heady scent of the Confederate jasmine that covers the entire fence around the backyard. "Hey!" I raise my voice over the whir of the half-dozen sprinklers watering the flower beds. "I'm here."

Turning his head to find me standing under the arbor, Lex gets heavily to his feet and wipes his hands on the seat of his jeans, then brushes the dirt off his knees. Like me, he's barefoot. The two of us have this in common: We consider shoes superfluous and take them off at the first opportunity. Lex removes the Red Sox cap he's rarely without and fans with it as he walks toward me. Damp with sweat, his dark hair is plastered to his forehead except in the back, where it sticks up like a boy's cowlick.

"Hey, doctor lady! Didn't hear you come in," he says cheerily when he reaches the arbor. His ruddy face is flushed and shiny, glistening with sweat, and I frown. Seems to me he shouldn't be working in this heat. His doctors have encouraged his new interest in gardening, but still. Some things are just common sense.

"I hollered at you, but the sprinklers were too loud. Sorry I'm running late. It's been quite a day."

"Yeah, I figured it would be. You've seen the paper, then?"

I nod and roll my eyes. "I have indeed."

Lex grins a wicked grin. "The divorce coach all of Fairhope is talking about. Anybody say anything to you?"

"Well . . . I got a couple of calls." I'm careful not to mention Rye, since Lex claims to be jealous of him, just to aggravate me. "And then someone told me about the other crazy thing, what Ernestine wrote about Dory and Son in her column. Did you see it?"

"Yeah, but it didn't make a damn bit of sense to me. Let me go wash up, then I want to hear everything that's going on in this potty place. Fairhope Loco." Replacing the baseball cap, Lex turns and heads toward the house, moving much slower than I did over the hot flagstones of the pathway. I tease him by saying his big old feet are callused and tough, while mine, like all Southern belles', are delicate and tender.

When he opens the screened door of the back porch, I call out to him. "Bring us a glass of wine, okay? I need one bad," and he salutes me with his cap.

I should go inside and change into something cooler, but I flop down in a willow chair instead. My outfit has wilted even more now, and even the long strand of flat turquoise stones around my neck feels hot and heavy. I pull it over my head and place it on a nearby table, along with the matching earrings. The hazards of early fall in the South. Although I've lived in it all my life, it still gets to me, saps my energy. "It's the South, supposed to be hot," my granddaddy used to say. "You want cold, move to New York City." Granddaddy never set foot in the Big Apple but loved referring to it, always calling it New York *City*.

Sprawled in the lounge chair, I watch Lex coming out the back door, pushing it open with his hip, a glass of wine in each hand. I study him for signs of fatigue or weakness, but he appears fine, the same old Lex. Having washed off the grime and sweat of the garden, he looks cooler now, thank goodness. It's too early for our cocktail hour, but what the heck. As Lex is apt to say with a wink, it's five o'clock somewhere. Cocktail hour in Fairhope is actually six o'clock; has been since I've lived here. Even though Fairhope is considered artsy and nontraditional compared to other places in the South, it's as set in its rituals and customs as small towns everywhere. Not a native, Lex bristled at its conventions when he first moved here, but he soon adjusted his Northern ways to fit in. Like other transplants to the Fairhope way of life, he has become more of a Fairhoper than the rest of us.

"Cheers." Lex hands me a chilled glass of pinot grigio as he settles himself into the chair next to mine. Since he's allowed only one glass of red wine now, he uses the largest goblet he can find and fills it to the brim with a hearty cabernet. "Tell it, sister," he says, raising his glass to me. That phrase has become one of our buzzwords since I told him another story about my grandfather. When I was a child and visited my grandparents in the foothills of northern Alabama, he would always embarrass me in their country church. Whenever the minister said something Granddaddy liked, he'd thump his cane on the floor and cry out, "Tell it, brother!"

I sip the sharp, icy wine, sighing. "Oh, God, that's *so* good. I don't know where to start. Things went pretty well this morning, considering I had two suicidal clients, a referral from the courts, and an abused wife whose husband is stalking her with a gun."

Lex takes a big gulp of his wine. "Another fun day in paradise, huh?"

"Pretty typical. At precisely one o'clock, Etta pushed me out the door like she'd promised to do. She took her task literally."

"Etta pushed you?" he says with a chuckle. "I'd love to have seen that. I've about talked her into leaving R.J. and running off with me. I can tell she wants me."

"If anyone could straighten you out, it'd be Etta."

"Shows what you know. The other day I told her if she didn't keep her hands off me, I'd be forced to tell R.J. how bad it's gotten."

Struggling to keep a straight face, I say sternly, "You'd better quit messing with Etta like that! I'm surprised she hasn't clobbered you, the way you pick at her. Etta's of the old school. She's in her sixties, a staunch Southern Baptist, and not used to your foolishness."

"So she got you out by one o'clock, huh? Damn. Guess that means I can't marry her after all. Anyone who can get you away from that precious office of yours is too much woman for me."

"Would you be serious for once in your life? I'm trying to tell you how my day went."

With a twinkle in his eyes, Lex grins at me over the rim of his wineglass. "You think you've had a tough day? Ha. I get here at two o'clock—when you said you'd be home, if you recall—but no sign of the esteemed doctor lady. I decide to read the paper while I wait. Bad idea. I find out that the woman I thought was a highly respected therapist is in truth nothing but a homewrecker. Does this mean she's going to have to give back her Citizen of the Month plaque? I wonder. She'll be devastated."

"The award didn't come with a plaque," I remind him.

"Minor detail. They can demand that you rescind the title." He pauses to take another gulp of his cabernet. "After the shy, demure, and sane inhabitants of our quiet little town read the paper, your phone started ringing. So I spent the rest of the afternoon answering it and doing damage control."

"Answering my phone! You did not."

"Naw, I'm teasing." His look is pure mischief. "I'd never answer anyone else's phone."

"You're such a shameless liar, Lex Yarbrough. You've answered mine plenty of times. Remember the rector's secretary called last month, when they were updating the church directory?"

At least he has the grace to look sheepish. "Oh, yeah. Forgot about that. You accused me of shocking her."

"You told her I hadn't been to church in so long that I couldn't pick out Father Gibbs in a police lineup! Of course she was shocked."

"So you've told me a hundred times, which really hurts my feelings."

"Bull. It's impossible to hurt your feelings."

"This time it wasn't the secretary, it was the big man himself."

"God called me? I'd never have allowed Father Gibbs to have my home number if I'd known he'd give it to just anybody."

"Not that big. Go a step down. It was the good Father himself. When I heard his voice, I picked up and told him I was waiting here to comfort you once you saw the paper."

"And you've done such a great job, too, Lex. Next time I need comfort, I know where to find it."

He ignores my sarcastic tone and goes on blithely. "Father Gibbs said that since you were a member of St. John's—though not a very *active* one, ha ha—he was calling to tell you that the old fruit-cake who wrote the letter was a well-known crackpot. He assured me that he knew you were doing the Lord's work with your retreats. I couldn't let him get by with that."

"Oh, no. Please tell me you're making this up. You didn't really say anything to him, did you?"

He tries his best to look innocent. "He added that he also knew you believed in the sanctity of marriage."

"And how did you respond? she asks with dread."

"Here's all I said, and I quote: 'On the contrary, Father. Clare doesn't believe in the sanctity of marriage at all. If everybody got married and lived happily ever after, she'd be out of business.' "

"Lex! Poor Father Gibbs. Bless his meddling old heart."

The look he gives me over the rim of his glass is a sly one. "Bless his heart, my ass. You're such a hypocrite."

"Guess that's why we're such good friends, then. I'm a hypocrite, and you're incorrigible." We click our wineglasses together, then I say, "Listen, do you want to hear this or not? I was getting to the thing in the gossip column about Son and Dory."

Lex raises his eyebrows. "You told me they'd gotten back together, and Son took her all the way to Europe to get her away from you."

"I'm sure that's what he's telling everyone," I say glumly.

"Now that I've seen the paper, I don't blame him. I wouldn't want my wife palling around with a divorce coach, either."

I rub my eyes wearily and sigh. "I got really nervous when I saw Son at the coffee shop, but thank God he didn't see me. As I was telling Rye when I ran into him—"

It slipped out, and Lex pounces on it. "Rye? Where'd you run into him, at the beauty parlor? Was he having his hair or his nails done?"

I glare at him and say huffily, "Not funny. I ran into him downtown, right after lunch."

He tries to glare back but can't quite pull it off. "Yeah, sure. If you had lunch with another man, just tell me. My heart will be broken, but I'll survive. I still have Etta."

Rather sheepishly, I confess that Rye was the one to tell me about the pukey item in the society column, then add, "It's such an obvious ploy on Son's part, letting everyone know he and Dory are back together."

Lex jerks his head up. "Forgot to tell you. A couple of your calls were from Son."

"That can only mean trouble," I groan. "Guess you talked to him, too."

"Naw. Maybe I should've, found out what he's up to. All he said was for you to call him as soon as you got in. I deleted his messages, by the way. Didn't want them to put you in a bad mood."

"I hope he doesn't hold his breath until I return his call," I say in disgust.

"Me, too. Might cause brain damage."

"Yeah, right. Not a chance of that." I take a sip of my wine and stare absently at the garden, hot and heavy with hundreds of blossoms. "You know, when Dory left me a message saying she'd taken Son back because she truly believed he was a changed man, it surprised me how bad I wanted to believe it."

Lex eyes me skeptically. "How long have you known Son?"

I count silently, squinting in the glare of the late-afternoon sun. "Hmm, let's see. I met him and Mack and Dory at the same time, the second semester of my freshman year at Bama. God, that was over twenty-eight years ago. Long time, huh?"

"And didn't you tell me it took you a while to see through him, but he's the same guy now that he was then?"

"I believe the way I put it was, he's the same cocky, overbearing, arrogant jerk he's always been. Your point is well taken. But in my business, I have to believe that everyone is capable of change, and that includes Son Rodgers. With him, however, it will happen only if someone perfects the science of brain transplants, evidently."

Lex chuckles, then regards me with a puzzled expression. "So if Son knows how you feel about him, why does he bother calling you? Doesn't make sense, does it?"

"This is Son we're talking about. The operative word is *sense.*"

For some reason, this strikes Lex as funny, and he lets out one of his great big infectious laughs. I lean back in my chair and laugh, too. Somehow I knew that once I got home, Lex would be able to make me forget about the letter and Dory and all my other concerns. It's impossible to stay gloomy around Lex. Dory's the only other person I know who has a laugh as irrepressible as his, and hers used to have the same effect on me. I always felt good, happy and carefree and lighthearted, when I was with Dory. I reach into the pocket of my skirt for a tissue to wipe my eyes and wonder for the umpteenth time what Dory will say when I see her tomorrow, the first time in over a month.

"You're not crying, are you?" Lex asks in surprise.

I shake my head. "Just wiping my eyes. Lex, what on earth is on that table?"

One of the small willow tables holds a copper watering can with a surprisingly artful arrangement of flowers, pink zinnias, and purplish-blue hydrangeas mixed in with stalks of lavender. "I believe they're called flowers," he says dryly.

I look at him in wonder. "*You* arranged those?"

Even though he scowls, it's obvious that he's pleased with himself. "Me putting pink and purple flowers together. If my old navy buddies could see me now."

"You did good." The sprinklers make a hypnotic noise as they whir round and round, throwing out silver droplets of water in ever widening circles, a sound that's oddly comforting. "Oh, look," I say, pointing, and he turns his head to watch a pair of yellow-and-black butterflies stagger among the daylilies, drunk with nectar.

Lex is quiet, savoring his wine and watching the butterflies, and I study him a minute before asking, "Hey, you're feeling okay, aren't you?"

His eyes are playful as he turns toward me. Lex has great eyes, green as grass, a startling contrast to his sunbaked skin and dark hair. His craggy face reminds me of the maritime maps hanging on the walls of his marina, full of many lines and markings but simple to read and follow, if you make the effort.

"With everything else going on, I didn't want to worry you," he says, "but . . ." With a dramatic cry, he clutches his chest and drops his head forward, face contorted in apparent agony.

I grab a cushion from the chair next to me and throw it at him. "Stop it! That's *not* funny, you idiot."

Catching the cushion midair before it hits his coveted glass of wine, Lex grabs it, laughing. In spite of my aggravation with him,

I smile and shake my head. "God, you're awful! I don't know why I put up with you."

"Can't accuse me of being heartless, though," he says with a grin. "It may be broken, but at least we've seen proof that I have one."

"I really don't like you joking like this. Just as I got used to having you around, it looked like I was going to lose you." I resist adding that I'm dead serious.

His expression is playful, impish. "Aw, Clare, how sweet. Would you miss me if I croaked?"

"Of course I would, fool. You scared the daylights out of me."

"Ha. Didn't scare you enough to get you to marry me, did it?"

"*Marry* you?" Wary, I put down my wineglass to stare at him.

"On my deathbed, I said I wanted us to get married, remember?"

"You said a lot of crazy things in the emergency room."

"Like what?" He regards me suspiciously.

I laugh. It's my turn to tease him. "You cracked the nurses up. Actually, it was the head nurse you proposed to, not me. Remember her, the one with the mustache and shoulders like a linebacker?"

He finishes off his wine and shakes his head. "Not true. I remember everything that happened, and I definitely remember asking you to marry me. I've gotten tired of our friendship, and the best way to end it is to get married. That way we'll never have to be nice to each other again."

"Lord Jesus, you are one crazy man." I sigh, then get to my feet and stretch widely. "Enough of this. I'm going inside and change into something cooler, then we have to go. George Johnson is meeting us in"—I look at my watch—"about half an hour."

Lex picks up the cushion I threw and places it behind his head, leaning back lazily. "We could have our wedding out here. I'll do the flowers, and your priest can officiate. Prove to everybody once and for all that you do believe in marriage."

When passing his chair, I stop and look down at him, my hands on my hips as he grins up at me, as mischievous as a little boy. "Is this the same man who swore that he'd never get married again? Even if Miss Universe got on her knees and begged?"

"Yeah, but that was before I realized how much you lust after my body." He closes his eyes and turns his face to the sun. "I saw you looking at me when the nurses put me in that skimpy hospital gown." He opens one eye to leer at me. "Got a glimpse of something that changed the way you feel about me, didn't you?"

"Oh, please." I laugh, scampering across the flagstones to the back porch. "You wish."

"Hey, bring the binoculars when you come back, okay?"

I stop suddenly and raise my voice so he can hear me over the sound of the sprinklers. "Lex? Seriously now, you sure you feel up to going? You don't have to, you know."

In spite of our bantering, it's hard to keep my voice light, but my anxiety is far from unwarranted. The weekend before last, when Lex didn't show up for our first scheduled meeting with George Johnson, I went to his office at the marina and found him slumped over and clutching his chest, pale and gasping for breath. He was furious at me for calling 911, but the emergency crew said if I'd waited a few more minutes, he might not have survived. Getting him to the hospital so quickly allowed them to insert a stent before a full-fledged heart attack did irreparable damage. Since then I haven't hesitated to remind him that I saved his sorry life.

"I'm dying to go. Naw, that was last time. Hurry up with those binoculars, would you?" He points a finger toward the herb garden. "One of those ruby-throated hummingbirds in the pineapple sage."

I go into the house, shaking my head at Lex's relentless foolishness. He's such a crazy man that when we first met, I stayed confused, not sure how to take him. I later admitted to him that I had the absurd notion Yankee men were humorless, unlike the rowdy Southern boys I was raised with. His being a native of Maine only made it worse, because I pictured people from Maine as particularly austere and dour. Since relocating to Fairhope, Lex has become yet another of our many colorful characters, a distinction earned with his "Men of Maine" story. That story has become his trademark, so folks here refer to him as the Man of Maine. When he first moved to town, he told everyone about his great-great-grandfather, a survivor of one of the most famous battles of Gettysburg, where the legendary Men of Maine, a ragtag regiment of lumberjacks and fishermen, defeated the mighty 15th Alabama, a much more highly trained and skilled regiment. Although I recalled the battle from my American history class, I questioned Lex's great-great-whatever being in it until he showed me the documentation. He goes around declaring that the Men of Maine could still beat the wimps of Alabama, over 140 years later. The first time I went with Lex to a local waterfront bar for a beer, he threw open the door and shouted, "Rednecks of Alabama, the Men of Maine have arrived!" I was petrified, imagining a brawl, until the patrons raised their beers in a salute, laughing. The locals love getting Lex to tell the Gettysburg story, cheering when they hear how the 15th Alabama, though defeated in the end, fought the 20th Maine until the last gray-clothed soldier was down.

After changing into a loose T-shirt and cropped pants, I pick up the binoculars and start toward the back porch. On the kitchen counter, I see the photograph I'd put by the door so I wouldn't forget to take it to Zoe Catherine, and I pick it up and carry it outside to show Lex. The first time he came to my house, he picked up photos of my family members and studied them, asking who was who. When he came across an old picture of my brother and me together, arm in arm, he asked if the man in the photograph was my former husband. I'm not sure which of us was more surprised when I said in a choked-up voice, "No. I still can't bear to have pictures of Mack around." To cover my embarrassment, I moved quickly to show him the most recent pictures of Haley's children, Abbie in a pink tutu at her dance recital, baby Zach taking his first steps.

Outside, Lex is standing for a closer look at the hummingbird, and he takes the binoculars out of my hand. "You and Zoe Catherine are going to become big buddies," I say as he adjusts the viewer, squinting. "The Bird Lady and the Man of Maine."

During his recovery from the heart attack, Lex took up not only gardening but also bird-watching. Restless and unable to go back to work, he reluctantly followed my suggestion to use my backyard gardens as part of his healing process, rather than spending his days holed up in his small quarters above the marina. It was there that he began to notice the many varieties of birds drawn to my feeders and birdbaths, and started jotting down observations about their habits. One night last week, he stopped by after attending a meeting of the Audubon Society. The program was about shorebirds, he told me, eyes bright with excitement. A guy from the Weeks Bay Reserve showed slides.

"Did you know that the male oystercatcher bows his head to the female oystercatcher as part of the mating ritual? Lots of birds do mating dances to attract females," he said, then added, "maybe I ought to try it." Lex couldn't believe how much I knew about birds until I explained it was due to Zoe Catherine. For years she has rescued injured birds that aren't able to return to their habitat and kept them in the shelter she founded at the Landing.

"All species of cranes do mating dances," I told him. "Some of them pick up a feather or twig while dancing and throw it in the air to impress a prospective mate."

"Hey, they've got a covered-dish supper next week," Lex said. "Want to go? The Audubon Society is furnishing the main dish—roasted ivory-billed woodpecker in cream sauce—and we're bringing the rest."

I couldn't make it because I was too far behind with my paperwork, I replied, realizing too late that I'd hit a sore subject with Lex. I'd gotten behind by helping him during his recovery, and it had caused somewhat of a strain between us. Like most men, he'd been a difficult patient, cranky and embarrassed and ungraciously insisting that he didn't need or want my help.

Lowering the binoculars now, Lex asks, "Time to go?"

I look down at my watch. "Yep. Can't wait for you to be out there at sunset. It's a sight you'll never forget."

"I've seen plenty of sunsets," he says as he puts the caps back on the lenses.

"Not like this, you haven't," I reply with a knowing smile. "I can promise you that. Oh, wait—let me show you this picture first. Remember the time you came to the house and I said I'd packed up all the photos of my former husband? Well, looks like I was wrong. Last night I moved a stack of books and found one."

I hold up the photograph as Lex pats both pockets of his jeans until he locates his reading glasses. He frowns in concentration, studying the picture, then peers at me over the top of the rims. "Hmm. When was this taken?"

I shrug. "I'm not sure of the exact date, but it's Christmas several years ago. And I'm pretty sure we're at the yacht club. One of Fairhope's many holiday parties, is all I can tell. You'll see—you'll be invited to a dozen this year, now that you're eligible. Lots of single women need dinner partners."

In the snapshot, Zoe Catherine and I, our heads thrown back in laughter, hold flutes of champagne in our hands, and we're dressed in seasonal finery, bejeweled and sparkling. I wonder what happened to that beaded green jacket, the one I wore to every Christmas party for years. Must have finally worn it out. I remember those unusual earrings of Zoe's: folk art, long dangling Santas of hand-carved wood, very Zoe. Bright-eyed, she looks festive with her shoulders draped in a claret-colored shawl, her startling white hair pinned up and glowing in the light of the holiday candles. Zoe Catherine hardly ever attends Fairhope parties; it's her presence that makes me recall the occasion. Hosted by Dory, the party had doubled as a fund-raiser for Zoe's bird sanctuary.

Haley stands next to us, but it's not an especially good picture of her. Her eyes are half closed, the camera having caught her at the wrong moment, as cameras have a way of doing. In spite of that, she still looks like the princess in a fairy tale, with her pale blond hair falling over her shoulders, pinned back from her face with sprigs of holly. It's obviously before the kids were born but after she and Austin married, even though he's not with us. As young as Haley looks now, at age thirty, she looks shockingly young in the photo, almost like a child. I wonder why Austin isn't in the picture, then realize he's most likely the one taking it. Every family get-together, Austin has a new camera, it seems. He's one of those men enamored with gadgets, always tinkering with the latest one.

Lex glances at me curiously as he points to the photo. "That's got to be Mack." I nod as my throat tightens. In the picture, Mack, too, is smiling, a glass of champagne in hand, slouching slightly. He's standing next to us, the women of his life, but also apart, a couple of steps away. Always apart. Funny, when I found the photo, I didn't notice how it captured so many things about Mack. For one thing, it's beautiful, as he was. Not many pictures ever caught that dreamy, faraway look of his, a look that set him apart from any man I've ever known, before or since. It's a fairly dark photo, taken at night in a room lit by candles, and each of us is illuminated by the yellow flash of the camera in a strange sort of way. It makes us look ghostly, unreal, frozen in the moment. It's as though I'm looking at people who lived years ago, people I don't know, long dead. It's a ridiculous and fanciful notion; except for Mack, we are all here, the same as we were when the picture was taken. God, Mack looks so young!

"Jeez, Mack looks younger than I expected," Lex says, echoing my thoughts. "How old was he?"

"In the photo? Or when he died?" Without waiting for an answer, I blurt out, "He died a few days before his forty-sixth birthday." With trembling hands, I take the photo from Lex. "Funny, Mack once said he hoped he'd die young. He said he wasn't sure he could face old age."

"No kidding." I can tell that shocks Lex, a fairly unshockable man. He's a few years older than Mack would have been, having had his fifty-fifth birthday this year. He's told me often that he likes being in his fifties, that he hated the insecurities of youth and the uncertainties of middle-aged angst.

Feeling Lex's curious eyes on me, I say "What?" somewhat testily.

"Couldn't face old age? Sounds kind of wimpy, you ask me."

I don't know why I feel a need to defend Mack, but I say that of course it's more complicated than it sounds. Mack was a complex man, I tell him, with a host of issues.

"Issues." Lex snorts. "God, I hate that word. It's so self-indulgent." Putting his glasses back on, he reaches for the photo again, lifting it high for another look. "I've heard folks say that Mack Ballenger was a good-looking fellow, but I can't judge other men. Tell me the truth, now—don't worry about hurting my feelings—he couldn't hold a candle to yours truly, could he?"

"Not even in the same league," I say dryly.

"Naw, it's obvious what you women would like about him." He squints, pulling the photo closer. "In addition to those Robert Redford looks, he has that other thing women go for."

"I cannot *wait* to hear this."

"He has sort of . . . you know . . . a faggy look about him."

I can't help myself. I laugh in spite of the lump that's forming in my throat. "No one ever said *that* about Mack."

Lex frowns and scratches his head. "Okay, not faggy, exactly. More— Aw, hell, what's the word?"

"Sensitive? You're trying to say 'sensitive,' aren't you, a word that's not even in your vocabulary?"

"Yeah, that's it! Sensitive. Mack looks like the kind of guy women go for because he'd always be telling them how pretty they are and stuff. Right?"

"Actually, you're onto something. Mack could be quite a charmer."

"Someone just the other day told me that Mack was a star pitcher at Bama and had started a pro career when he threw his shoulder out."

"He had trouble with that shoulder until the day he . . ." I stop to clear my throat. "Right up until he died. The funny thing is, baseball wasn't his passion, really. Most men would've been devastated by an injury that ended a promising sports career. But as long as it didn't keep Mack from fishing or hunting, it didn't seem to bother him that much."

I catch myself, realizing what I just said, and I look at Lex helplessly. I've told him all about it, so he knows what I'm thinking. It was almost five years ago, the day Mack drove his truck to a remote cove near the bay and got out with his rifle in hand to go hunting in the nearby swamp, as he did so many times during our marriage. Something went terribly wrong that day, though none of us will ever know exactly what it was. Although an expert hunter, Mack tripped over a tangle of vines and the gun went off, killing him instantly. Or so the coroner assured me later, when I almost went crazy imagining him lying there as his life ebbed away those long hours before Son and Rye found him.

"Well!" I say briskly. "Enough happy memories for one day."

Lex raises an eyebrow when I put the photograph in the pocket of my pants. "You taking that with you?"

"I'd planned on giving it to Zoe Catherine." At his obvious surprise, I have a moment of uncertainty. In trying to put my life back together after Mack's accident, I'd boxed up every memento and locked all of them away, but not before asking the other family members what they wanted. At the time, no one could bear to look at any of them, especially not Haley, our only child, and both she and Zoe were satisfied to leave them in my attic. But for some reason, when I found the photo last night, I'd decided to take it to Zoe Catherine when we went to the Landing today. I look at Lex. "You don't think I should, do you?"

At first he shrugs dismissively, then he rubs his chin. "I don't know her well enough to say. But it seems like . . ." He stops himself, shrugging again, and his green eyes darken. "Even if she wasn't on good terms with him, I'd think a picture of happier times would upset her."

"Yeah, you're right. Maybe I need to think about it." I'm quiet for a long minute, then say, "Let's get going, okay?"

When we go through the house on the way out to Lex's Jeep, I stop by the foyer table to pick up my purse and the carrot cake, then open a drawer and drop the photograph in. What was I thinking, I wonder as I step out on the porch, where sweet-smelling jasmine hangs like clusters of grapes from the latticework of the arched entryway. A carefree, smiling picture of Mack, taken long before the day that changed all of our lives forever, disturbs me so much I can hardly stand to look at it. Why would his mother want those painful memories revived just as she's beginning to heal from her terrible grief?

❧

As I'd told Rye when I ran into him downtown, Lex's Jeep is perfect for getting to Zoe Catherine's place, which is located on the banks of a meandering, marshy creek several miles south of Fairhope, near Weeks Bay. We bump along the washed-out road so roughly that I grab the door handle and hang on. Lex glances my way to ask, "Didn't forget my notebook, did I?" I release my death grip on the door and pick up the clipboard and attached pencil, holding it aloft for him to see. "Good," he says, maneuvering the steering wheel to avoid the worst of the potholes. "Write this down. Number one, get the damned road paved. You'll lose half your customers before they can get out here. Though I warn you, paving it's liable to cost you a pretty penny."

"Not really. I've talked to the county about doing it with

crushed oyster shells. I'm using native material as much as possible." The briny smell of Weeks Bay blows in the open window, and I inhale it, closing my eyes in sheer pleasure.

"Oyster shells. Hey, that's good." Lex grins his approval. He has the same appreciation of the wild beauty of this coastal area as I do. "Does Swamp Woman know I'm coming with you?" Although he knows Zoe Catherine's name among the locals is the Bird Lady, he won't call her that because he says it's an insult to birds the world over.

"She's been anxiously awaiting your recovery so I could bring you out," I assure him. "She couldn't be more pleased that you'll be helping me."

Although I, too, am pleased by Lex's input into the process of turning the property Zoe is giving me into a retreat center, I'm a little nervous about throwing two strong personalities like Zoe Catherine and Lex together. Both of them are so strong-willed and opinionated that they're bound to clash. Zoe has always said exactly what was on her mind, regardless of the consequences. The first time she met Lex, a week or so before his heart attack, I invited the two of them to dinner, since she'd pestered me to death about meeting this man I'd become such close friends with. Before dinner, however, Lex's beeper went off and he had to leave. The dockmaster at the marina had called with a bit of an emergency, something about a leaking fuel line on one of the boats. As Zoe Catherine watched Lex walk out the gate, I knew what she was going to say before she opened her mouth, and she didn't let me down.

"So that's your Yankee boyfriend, Clare," she said, leaning so far out of her patio chair that she almost toppled over. "Good-looking fellow, isn't he? And I can tell he's good in the sack, too. Guess you have to be on top, though. You're so little, he'd squash you flat as a pancake otherwise. Myself, I'd rather be on top anyhow."

Before I could open my mouth, aghast, she continued nonchalantly, wagging a finger my way. "Glad to hear him say he was a linebacker in his college days at the naval academy. Stick with the defense, I always say. Best lover I ever had was a lineman at FSU. Been way over fifty years ago, but I won't ever forget his blitz. And honey, could he cover a zone."

"I've told you, Zoe Catherine, that Lex and I aren't lovers. We're just good friends," I protested. "*Not* that it's any of your business."

She hooted at that. "Oh, bull. No such thing as being friends with a man. They're only good for one thing, and it ain't being your girlfriend." She straightened up in her chair and eyed me suspiciously. "Don't tell me he's queer."

"You're too smart for us. Truth is, he only hangs around because he wants to redecorate my house."

She shook her head, her dark eyes thoughtful. "Naw, he couldn't be a fairy. Nobody from Maine is queer."

I stared at her in astonishment. "That is one of the most outrageous things I've ever heard from you, which is saying a lot."

"It's true! There are no fairies in Maine. You can look at them and tell. All the men up there look like moose. Or mooses, meese, whatever you call 'em."

"You've never been to Maine, Zoe Catherine Gaillard!"

She tossed her head and snorted. "Shows what you know, Miss Priss. Papa Mack and me, we went to Niagara Falls for our honeymoon. Then we drove up and down the East Coast and visited Kennebunk, Boston, Cape Cod—all sorts of Yankee places. So don't tell me I don't know what I'm talking about."

Recalling that conversation now, I catch myself sneaking speculative looks at Lex as he drives, observing not for the first time the unexpected grace of his large body, the span of his wide shoulders. He's fit and well muscled for a man of his age, and he takes pride in not working out in a gym but staying in shape with hard work, the way he's always done it, he brags, having come from a long line of lobster fishermen. Though rough and callused, his hands on the steering wheel appear not only competent but also gentle, and I suspect he'd be a thoughtful lover. Blushing, I look down at the notebook I'm clutching, aggravated at myself for allowing my mind to wander in such a direction when I've been so determined not to think of Lex that way. Damn Zoe Catherine—it's her fault.

"You've gotten awfully quiet," he says, startling me out of my musing. I turn to him guiltily, hoping my expression won't reveal my salacious thoughts. He pulls the Jeep under a low-hanging live oak next to the creek and turns off the ignition.

"Well, well," he says as he looks around in wonder. "So *this* is the famous Landing."

Chapter Three

❧ ❧ ❧ ❧ ❧

Although the Landing is now a bird sanctuary and nature preserve, at one time it was a popular fishing camp, built by Albert Gaillard, Zoe Catherine's father, a man even more eccentric than his daughter. Zoe earned her nickname because of her passion for and work with birds; Albert was famed throughout the Gulf Coast for his skills as a fisherman. The Gaillard family came to this area in 1817 as French exiles, no longer welcome in their country after the fall of Napoleon, whom they'd supported. Our government gave the exiles land grants, and though many failed to prosper and eventually returned to France, the Gaillards stayed. Blacksmiths in their native country, they expanded the smithy to manufacture much needed tools, making a fortune in the process. A few generations later, Albert Gaillard preferred fishing to managing the family business, and he allowed the business to fold, losing the family fortune. According to Zoe Catherine, her father had gotten himself trapped in a miserable marriage with the daughter of another French family from Mobile, and he was branded a ne'er-do-well and failure by all the relatives except her. In a pattern ironically repeated years later by his daughter and only heir, Albert gave up wealth, privilege, and prestige to spend the better part of his life at the fish camp. He named the place the Landing because of the way a bend in Folly Creek, a tributary of Weeks Bay, formed a secluded inlet and a natural boat landing, where he'd built a dock and boathouse for his many fishing vessels.

In addition to building a small breezy cabin near the boathouse—Zoe's residence for several years now—Albert Gaillard also constructed a rambling building of rough-hewn cypress planks and river stones that served as the main part of the fish camp. Albert's lifelong friend and business partner in running the fish camp was an old Cherokee called Jubilee Joe, who was legendary in the Fairhope area for his ability to predict Jubilees, a fishing phenomenon occurring in only two places in the world, one of them being Mobile Bay's Eastern Shore. During the unusual conditions that cause a Jubilee, which might occur once or twice during a summer or once or twice a lifetime, hundreds of blue crab, shrimp, and all sorts of fish suddenly appear along the shoreline, as though waiting to be scooped up.

Zoe's current boyfriend, a wild man with the improbable name of Cooter Poulette, is not only a descendant of Jubilee Joe's, he also boasts the ability to predict Jubilees. Zoe says his gift has appeared only since she took up residence at the Landing. The way she tells it, on Jubilee nights when Cooter is bedded down with her, old Joe appears to him in a dream shortly after midnight, and Cooter promptly wakes her up with the news. They place a few strategic phone calls before leaving the Landing and hightailing it to Mobile Bay (evidently Cooter has some sort of mysterious radar that sends him to the right spot). Then the two of them send out the cry of *Jubilee!*, a call that spreads up and down the coastal area, from Point Clear to Daphne. The anticipated herald brings people out in droves, toting buckets, coolers, nets, and lanterns, to gather the gifts from the sea, which magically appear in the shallow waters in such numbers that all you have to do to fill a bucket is reach down and scoop them up.

With such a colorful history, it is impossible not to be affected by the Landing, and I watch Lex in amusement as he stands outside the Jeep with his hands on his hips, looking around. Even though it's time for our appointment, no sign yet of the builder, George Johnson.

After I climb out of the Jeep, my slamming of the door is the only sound disturbing the late-afternoon stillness. Even Zoe's peacocks are nowhere to be seen, although normally their raucous cries provide the background music for the peaceful setting. With a rush of excitement, it hits me anew why we're here, and I throw my arms above my head and shout, "I'm getting my own retreat site!" My cry shatters the stillness, and a snowy egret at the creek's edge lifts his wings and rises high, landing in the branches of a dead tree to glare at me.

Lex raises an eyebrow. "You scared the shit out of that poor bird."

"Just saying hello," I mutter as I walk around the Jeep. It's difficult to keep my excitement under control, though, and I resist the urge to throw up my arms again and dance a jig. The setting of the Landing is one of heart-stopping beauty, made up of moss-draped oaks, towering palm trees, acres of yellow and green marsh, and a lazy, brackish creek with sandy banks fringed in cattails. Beyond the creek lies the dark and mysterious swamp. We've parked near the dock, where Zoe keeps an assortment of canoes and sloops and rowboats rocking on the gentle waters of Folly Creek. Albert's old boathouse holds a jumble of fishing equipment, and I figure that's where Zoe is, on the creek fishing for her supper. I know she's here: Her truck is parked by one of the many outbuildings clustered around the boathouse. Cooter Poulette's pickup isn't there, so she's alone. Thank God. I adore Cooter, but he and Zoe together can be a tad overwhelming, to put it mildly.

Shading my eyes from the glare of the yellow sun, which will soon sink into the treetops on the other side of the creek, I walk down to the sandy bank. To my left is a bend that disappears into the foliage overhanging the creek, and even though I lean as far as possible without falling in, I can't tell if a boat is there or not. A silver mullet jumps into the air, startling me, then turns a couple of back-flips before plopping back into the water with a splash. I once remarked to Zoe that no one knows why mullet jump like they do, and she said that's not true: They jump for the pure joy of doing so.

"Swamp Woman's not on the creek?" Lex calls out to me, and I walk back to stand beside him, shrugging. He's still looking around with wide eyes. Zoe Catherine's cabin is hidden by a thicket of sweet-smelling tea olive bushes and sheltered under another of the magnificent oaks that dominate the property like monoliths. The low-hanging branches of the oak seem to cradle the weathered house like a mother holding a child in her arms. Because of Zoe's assortment of birds roaming everywhere, on the grounds and roosting in the tree branches, the quiet is unusual. She allows them free rein, except for the ones that won't stay put, and for them she's provided screened pens, aviaries the size of an average room, furnished with branches and stumps for roosting. Nothing too good for Zoe's birds. Several of her black-and-white guinea hens are scattered about the yard, pecking the sandy ground, but they are noiseless as their little heads bobble up and down in their search through the scraggly grass.

"She'll be along," I say. "While we're waiting for Mr. Johnson, I'll show you the nature preserve, then the fish camp. We won't have time to walk the trails today, but next time you're here, I'll take you through them."

The entirety of the Landing covers almost fifty acres, some of it swamp. Zoe set up the bird shelter and nature trails in a sparsely wooded area to the south of the creek and her cabin, to provide her some privacy from visitors. As Lex and I walk down the driveway toward the sanctuary, I explain how Zoe established it as a non-profit organization several years ago, and used to lead visitors through the trails herself. When she was in her prime and able to devote herself full-time to running it, it flourished, a hot spot for school field trips and bird-watchers. Over the last few years, Zoe has pretty much let it run itself. It hits me that the badly washed-out road indicates how she's had to let go of it. She still gets a few injured birds, though, which a retired veterinarian cares for and Zoe houses. When we enter the fenced-off area, I point out the cages.

"These are for permanently injured birds, mostly hawks and owls, that aren't able to survive in the wild anymore," I tell Lex. "Only a few of them are left now, but she used to have dozens of them." We stop before a huge cage built around two trees and housing a one-eyed owl, and Lex reads Zoe's carefully printed sign, describing the bird's native habitat, feeding habits, and injury.

"Pretty impressive," he says, putting his glasses back into the pocket of his jeans. "So Zoe Catherine is the real thing, huh?"

"Well, she's just an amateur ornithologist, but it's been a lifelong passion." I point to the trail and the cages placed at intervals among the trees, each of them with a handmade sign describing either the bird in the cage or the kinds of birds likely to be spotted on the trail. "The trail wanders around an acre or so, then returns to this spot. Let's go to the fish camp now, and I'll show you what I hope to do with it."

I lead the way from the sanctuary back to the creek, then take the path to the original fish camp, the structure that Zoe has given me to turn into a retreat site. Perched at the edge of the creek, it's a large building on stilts, the cypress-plank walls having weathered to a silvery color that blends like camouflage into the surrounding Spanish moss and dried marsh and grayish sand. Although it's badly outdated, fortunately for my budget, the building comes equipped with all the things necessary for running a retreat: a serviceable kitchen, a sizable gathering room, two separate bunk rooms, and concrete showers. "Rustic" is much too kind a word; although it has the air of a summer camp, it's rough and unfinished and will need a *lot* of renovation. Lex and I climb the river-rock steps leading up to a porch overlooking the creek, and I stop by the front door.

"What do you think so far?" I ask, hoping for some encouragement before leading him to the part of the project that's so daunting.

Lex takes his time before replying. "It's certainly a spectacular piece of property," he says cautiously. "That's a plus. Folks are bound to be impressed with how pretty it is out here, and how peaceful."

I look around the grounds, trying to see it as others will. "Yeah, I really want its beauty to be part of the healing process. And even if I were designing a retreat from scratch, I'd want it to be rustic. But getting this place from just plain shabby to shabby chic is going to be both horrendous and expensive, don't you think?"

"Didn't you tell me that you only have to finance the renovation? That Zoe Catherine is deeding it over to you free and clear?"

"It was her idea, too. I would've never thought of it. I'd mentioned in one of the articles that my dream was to have a permanent site for the retreats one of these days, and Zoe Catherine called to say she had the perfect place. It was to go to Mack on her death, becoming Haley's one day, of course. Haley was thrilled for me to have part of the property, and she'll inherit the rest of it. Don't worry; our lawyers made sure all of that stuff's worked out."

Lex props himself against the porch railing and folds his arms across his chest, pen and clipboard in hand. "One thing's for sure. It's going to take a small fortune to get this old place up and running." He scans the building with a critical eye, taking in the state of disrepair and disuse. Both of us stare in dismay at the tin roof, which is rusted and sagging in places.

"I'll find out when George Johnson gets here." I'm more worried about expenses than I've let on, but I'm trying to quell my panic. I can't let a lack of funding stop me from doing this, though I have no idea how it will happen.

Lex is regarding me with a speculative look. "Hell, if I'd known you were so loaded, I would've been a lot nicer to you."

"Believe me, I'm not," I say with a laugh. "Mack would've been, but he and his father were always fighting, and Papa Mack would cut him out of his will only to reinstate him when they made up. As luck would have it, Mack's father died during one of their bad times, and the wicked stepmother walked off with the Ballenger dough. Mack was too blame stubborn to take it to court, like Rye . . . ah . . . some of his relatives begged him to."

A thrifty New Englander, Lex frowns. "Then how are you planning to do this, Clare?"

"Dory's talking about a fund-raiser, and I'm doing a lot of bartering."

"Bartering?"

"Don't look at me like that. I've been doing it for years. The woman who cleans my house on Thursdays? She can't afford therapy otherwise. I've done similar things with gardeners, handymen, caterers, hairdressers—works well for all of us."

He takes off his cap and fans with it. "What you're saying is, if the construction guys have marital problems, you'll be in good shape, huh?"

"One can only hope." I turn my head at the sound of an approaching truck. "We're about to find out—here comes Mr. Johnson."

When George Johnson parks his truck in front of the fish camp and gets out, throwing us a wave, Lex says in a low voice, "While you're going through the place with this fellow, why don't I sneak off to his house and make a play for his wife? Naturally she'll prefer a virile stud like me to an old fart like him, so he'll be in dire need of a therapist. Who knows, you might get the whole place done for free."

"Hush—he'll hear you. Don't forget, I'm counting on you to do a lot of the work as well. You promised!"

He grins. "Damn right I'll help, now that I've found out about your system of bartering. Except it's not therapy I'll be wanting in return."

I poke him with my elbow, hard, then turn to greet George Johnson, who holds the fate of my retreat site in his hands.

Standing on the porch of the fish camp, estimates in hand, I watch the cloud of dust behind George Johnson's truck as it disappears down the road, and realize that the whole time we were making up the list, I held my breath, figuratively if not literally. My once unattainable dream of a permanent retreat site is actually going to happen, and I can't quite take it in. At first it looked impossible, and my heart sank. George Johnson shook his head sadly as we walked through the building and I pointed out what needed to be done. Although he said nothing, I could tell he was appalled by the condition of the camp. After the walk-through, we stood on the porch, and Mr. Johnson went over his notes as I studied him nervously. On impulse, I blurted out what I intended to use the building for, unable to hide my despair at the thought that it wouldn't happen. When my voice trailed off, Mr. Johnson stared off into the distance for what seemed like forever, scratching his head thoughtfully. I dared not glance at Lex, who scribbled in his notebook as he awaited the verdict.

George Johnson is a gruff, uneducated black man who worked for Mack before leaving to open his own construction business, which prospered once the building boom hit the Gulf area. I'd never have imagined him swayed by his emotions, but he turned to me with watery eyes and said, "My youngest girl is going through the worse divorce you ever seen, Miz Ballenger. It's 'bout to kill her, and the wife and me, too. Maybe if she had somethin' like them retreats of yours . . ." I jumped on it, saying quickly, "Oh, I'm *sure* we can work something out, Mr. Johnson. Matter of fact, I'll be glad to exchange therapy, retreats, whatever she needs, as part of our dealings." He thought for a long moment before nodding, then offered his hand, saying, "We're gonna make this happen. I'll give you a good estimate, and we'll work out a payment plan to suit both of us." I shook his hand formally, even though I wanted to throw my arms around him and plant a big kiss on his cheek.

I can't help myself: After the truck disappears, I'm so relieved that my eyes fill with tears. I wipe them with the edge of my T-shirt. Turning my head, I see that the sun is disappearing behind the dark silhouette of treetops, and the waters of Folly Creek have become fiery red. Beyond the bend in the creek, I spot a familiar shape.

"Lex!" I call out. My and Mr. Johnson's bartering must have inspired him, because a few minutes ago he returned to his measuring. "Finish what you're doing and get out here—you've got to see this."

He sticks his head out the front door, a pencil behind his ear. "What on earth you yelling about?"

"Hurry." I grab his arm and begin pulling him down the steps. "This you've *got* to see."

"Whoa, woman," he groans as he stumbles behind me, almost losing his footing. "The sunsets around here are something, granted, but not worth me busting my ass on these loose steps. Remind me to add them to the list."

"It's not the sunset I want you to see. It's Zoe Catherine."

Lex stops in his tracks. "She's sure not worth me busting my ass."

I roll my eyes in exasperation. "Trust me, okay?" I hurry across the driveway, making my way to the creek as I look over my shoulder and motion for Lex to follow. Grumbling under his breath, he rambles behind me, and when I reach the creek, he comes to stand next to me, huffing and puffing in an exaggerated manner.

"This better be good—" he begins, but I hold up a hand.

"Hush! You'll have to shut your big mouth to get the full effect."

An old wooden canoe comes into sight, rounding the bend in the creek. It's what I had spotted from the front porch, way off in the distance. Zoe Catherine is seated at the helm, grinning at me as I stand there waving, Lex beside me with his hands on his hips. When Zoe dips the oars into the sunlit waters of the creek, it looks as though she's dipping them into molten lava. I'm tickled to see that she's in all her glory this afternoon. When she came to my house for dinner, she was pure Southern belle, in an antique white dress that looked like something she'd snitched from the wardrobe of a Tennessee Williams production. Today she's decked out in army fatigues, and with heavy boots laced almost to her knees, she looks like an extra from an old World War II movie. Her white hair is in a braid down her back, and before docking the boat, she removes a wide-brimmed hat that's tied on at a rakish angle. After a spry leap, she secures the boat to a post and removes a bucket of fish and her fishing gear, placing them on the dock. Zoe heads our way as though to greet us, but instead she stops and places two fingers at the corners of her mouth, letting out a sharp, loud whistle.

"Watch this!" I say, clutching Lex's arm again.

In response to Zoe Catherine's whistle, we hear the rustle of hundreds of wings, and the once quiet setting comes alive with the sound of birds. From the trees, droves of silver-gray doves descend on Zoe as though part of some ancient biblical ritual, called forth by the Almighty Himself. The cattails sway as they release scores of ducks, which scramble up the creek bank, waddling and quacking as they make their ponderous way toward the figure in fatigues, calling them to their supper. From the yard, the guineas gobble joyously as they hurry down to the creek, their pear-shaped, awkward bodies rocking from side to side. Even the penned birds join in the cacophony, fluttering their wings against the confinement of their cages as they squawk. Then the magnificent crescendo—the peacocks and peahens, crying their terrible but majestic cry as they strut toward us, the peacocks dragging their great long tail feathers behind them. Zoe pulls out a covered metal can kept in the lean-to next to the dock and begins to scatter their feed far and wide, the motion causing the doves, which have perched on her shoulders, to lift their wings and float downward, cooing as they land at her feet. She stands poised among her beloved birds like some unholy statue of Saint Francis, decked out in boots and army fatigues by pranksters.

I turn to see Lex's expression, and it doesn't let me down. "Holy shit!" he says, eyebrows shooting straight up. His eyes meet mine, and he raises his voice to be heard over the deafening clamor. "Guess that's why she calls this place the Landing, huh?"

Even though it's still hot outside, the twilight air heavy and damp, neither Lex nor I utter a word of protest when Zoe Catherine insists on our staying for a visit, then leads us to a bluff overlooking the creek bank, underneath the low-lying branches of a live oak. She wants to hear every detail of my meeting with George Johnson, since she missed it after losing track of time fishing. I'm so grateful Zoe hasn't read the paper yet that I'm tempted to slip into her house and hide it before she has a chance to. At least we'll be long gone then. I know Zoe Catherine well enough to know that she'll pitch a fit when she sees the letter to the editor, and I don't want to be in her presence when she does.

Fortunately for us, a strong breeze blows across the creek, bringing the taste of salt as it scatters the mosquitoes and gnats that could make sitting outside impossible, no matter what time of day. This little bluff is one of Zoe's favorite places, and she's assembled a seating area of twig chairs out here, nestled under the sweeping branches of the oak as though they sprang from the tree and obligingly formed themselves into chairs for our pleasure.

"Y'all sit tight till I get back," Zoe says. "I'm gonna run inside and get us some of my scuppernong wine to go with that carrot cake you brought." She's her usual frisky self this afternoon, black eyes shining mischievously, and I'm also grateful that I didn't bring the photograph. Again I wonder what on earth I was thinking. Zoe shuts down whenever Mack is mentioned, her eyes blank and her normally expressive face stilled, frozen in a mask of unresolved grief. She and her only child were estranged on and off for years, and death robbed her of any chance of reconciliation.

Zoe Catherine pauses by Lex's chair and nods toward a huge peacock that seems intent on exploring Lex's feet. "Don't you mind Genghis Khan," she says. "He won't hurt you." The rest of her birds are still near the dock, searching the grounds for the last of the feed Zoe scattered. When Lex leans over as though to pat Genghis, Zoe slaps his hand away. "Watch it! He'll peck the pure-tee shit out of you if you touch his head."

Lex blinks up at her, and I stifle a giggle. "You just told me he wouldn't hurt me," he reminds her.

"Figured even a Yankee had sense enough not to pet them. They ain't dogs." Zoe unties the floppy hat that she's let fall down her back and tries to shoo the peacock away, but he merely blinks his beady eyes at her indignantly before resuming his peck, peck, pecking at Lex's work boots. The old bird is as large as a turkey, with his plumed train trailing at least five feet behind him. "Guess you've stepped on some of his food," Zoe muses. "Either that or he's gotten so old, he's gone blind and thinks your shoe is his feeding dish."

"It's certainly big enough," I say with a laugh. Zoe Catherine keeps flapping her hat at the impervious Genghis even after Lex swears to her that the bird isn't bothering him.

"Ah! Here comes my namesake, Catherine the Great. Maybe she'll distract him," Zoe says, watching the approach of the peacock's mate, a mousy, bedraggled peahen almost as old as Genghis. Zoe swears he's been with her almost twenty years, though most of them live ten years at best. She names all of the birds and never loses track of them, which amazes me. The peafowls she calls after the more exotic historical figures, Gandhi, Marco Polo, Marie Antoinette, and the latest, the resplendent Queen of Sheba. Zoe renamed one Jesus Christ after he appeared to be dead one night only to revive at sunrise. Her lovely but less spectacular birds, the pheasants, she names for literary characters: Falstaff, Madame Bovary, David Copperfield, Rhett Butler, and Scarlett O'Hara. The ducks are politicians, Harry Truman, Huey Long, Strom Thurmond, and Big Jim Folsom, a colorful Alabama governor Zoe was close to.

When Zoe Catherine disappears into the house to fetch the wine, Lex leans forward in the small twig chair where he's wedged, watching her depart. Both the Queen of Sheba and Catherine the Great have not only failed to distract Genghis Khan but have now joined him in pulling on the laces of Lex's boots as though they're fat, juicy worms. As soon as Zoe is out of sight, Lex stomps his feet heavily and hisses at the birds, "Get lost, you pesky bastards."

"Lex!" First I try to grab Catherine the Great, then the Queen of Sheba, both of whom flap their wings and squawk in terror. I've seen Zoe hold them like babies, but the peahens elude my grasp and run away to the other birds clustered near the dock. Genghis backs away from Lex, who reaches down to retie his shoelace, muttering to himself. Just as Zoe appears with a tray of wineglasses and the carrot cake, a rustling sound comes from Genghis, and I clap my hands like Abbie does when one of the peacocks begins his display.

"Hey, look, Lex." I smile. "Genghis is showing off for you."

Genghis Khan's magnificent iridescent plumes spread slowly upward as he cocks his small head to one side, beady eyes fastened on Lex for his reaction. Once the plumes are fully fanned out behind him, Genghis shivers and lets out a screech that always startles me, no matter how often I hear it. He then begins his dance, moving ponderously from one side to the other on his heavy white legs.

Zoe Catherine straightens a little table with her foot before putting down the tray, then she hands Lex and me our glasses of wine. Lex, however, is so entranced by watching Genghis that she has to pry open his hand to place the glass in it.

"What's wrong with you, Man of Maine?" She grins, looking my way and winking. "Never seen a peacock before?"

❧

On the ride home, I'm so excited that I blather on and on about the work on the retreat site. Only when Lex makes a mock snoring sound do I stop myself, putting a hand to my mouth. "Oh, Lord, I'm getting to be such a bore."

"*Getting* to be?"

"And it's too late for you to be out. We shouldn't have stayed for supper."

I feel guilty; I was sitting in the hospital room when the cardiologist specifically told Lex that for the next month, he should be in bed by ten, even if just to rest. "Sit up and read awhile," the doctor suggested. "Rest is an important part of a full recovery." As is diet, yet Lex glared at me tonight when I asked Zoe if she could broil the fresh-caught speckled trout she and Lex had cleaned, instead of frying them. Zoe looked at me as if I'd asked her to smother the fish in crème fraîche and serve it over a bed of arugula. She's never prepared fish any way but deep-fried, with hush puppies and onion rings bobbling in the hot grease next to the cornmeal-coated fillets until everything is golden-brown and glistening with cholesterol. With her fried fish, Zoe serves coleslaw so thick with mayo, it's hard to detect the presence of shredded cabbage. I tried to compensate by selecting the smallest fillet, one hush puppy, and a tablespoon of the rich coleslaw, then grimaced to see Lex pile his plate high, grease-deprived after two weeks of a heart-healthy diet.

Good thing was, no need for me to have worried about Zoe

Catherine and Lex hitting it off. Once I got her to describe how she trained the wedding doves, she had him in the palm of her hand. Part of the way Zoe supports herself is with her ceremonial white doves. They are in great demand at outdoor weddings, where she releases two dozen of them from a golden cage. No matter how far she's traveled for the wedding, the doves always make it back home, she's trained them so well. Or the way Zoe tells it, she has yet to lose one, even to an overzealous, camouflage-dressed redneck eager to flush out a nice covey of birds for his supper.

"Tell me the truth, Lex," I say. "The inside of the fish camp has to be totally gutted. Do you think the renovations will be ready so I can schedule the first retreat for early spring?"

Lex nods solemnly. "Should be, if the weather holds out and Mr. Johnson starts next week, like he promised you. Sounds like he's got a good-sized crew, so shouldn't be any problem there. Hey— you still want me to get the guy who did the sign for the marina to do yours?"

"Yep. I don't want folks going to Zoe's cabin by mistake."

"You'd have to start a whole new retreat for them to recover from the shock. But you'll need two signs, won't you, one for the building and one at the turnoff from the highway? Cost you twice as much, natch."

"Oh, God, I hadn't thought of that. No one will find it unless I have a sign on the highway, will they?"

Even in the darkness of the Jeep, I can see that Lex's eyes are full of mischief. "What will your sign say—'Devastated, Depressed, and Divorced? Follow the Arrows.'"

"Very funny." I think about it, then shake my head. "On second thought, Zoe already has a sign at the turnoff. The stuff going out to the participants will include directions to the Landing Bird Sanctuary off of Highway One, so I won't need my own sign. Matter of fact, some of the participants wouldn't want our sign at the entrance anyhow."

Lex looks startled. "You mean they're afraid their exes might track them down? Do things like that really happen?"

I glance at him to see if he's serious, then realize that, like most people, he has no idea. He'd be shocked at the number of restraining orders, the 911 calls, and the subpoenas that are an everyday part of my professional life.

"It happens all the time. Jesus, you've seen for yourself how crazy folks act when they're going through a divorce. Main reason I'm calling the retreat site Wayfarer's Landing is, the name reveals nothing about the nature of it. Could be a gathering of boaters or something."

"What the hell is a wayfarer, anyway?"

"Once I started doing the retreats, I had to call them something, so I decided on Wayfarers. It works for either gender, and I plan to start some all-male retreats eventually, as you know. Besides, it's metaphorical, something your unromantic brain can't comprehend."

"Bull. I'm the most romantic man you'll ever meet. What you're saying is, you don't know what a wayfarer is, either."

"I most certainly do. It's a poetic way of calling someone a voyager. The original meaning was to travel on foot, I believe, but basically it means any kind of traveler."

"Ah! I'm a sea captain, so that makes me a wayfarer, right?"

"Yeah, but that's literal, not figurative. You're also a wayfarer in life. We all are."

Lex wrinkles his nose. "Too touchy-feely for me. Remind me never to come to one of your retreats."

"I'm signing you up for the first one. God knows, you need it."

"Oh, no, you don't. You won't catch me dancing in a circle or taking part in those weird ceremonies or any of that other bullshit you've told me about. No way."

"When you attend one, it'll be such a great experience, you'll sign up as a volunteer for the future ones," I say, smiling. "Just you wait and see."

"Yeah, right. That'll be the day."

"You do know what Dory named my corps of volunteers, don't you?"

"No, but I'll bet it has something to do with circles." Dory makes no secret of her obsession with circles, which she believes have magical properties. She's always been fascinated with symbols and mythology, too, and finds meaning in numbers, colors, sizes, and shapes, something that amuses Lex to no end.

"They call themselves the White Ring Society," I tell him. "Or mostly the White Rings."

"They're all white women?"

I hoot, shaking my head. "Of course not. Jesus, you're hopeless! Here's what it means. When you divorce, first thing you do is remove your wedding band, and what does it leave? The imprint of where it was, a faint white circle around your finger." I roll my eyes when Lex raises his left hand above the steering wheel to look at his ring finger. "Have you always been such a literalist? The white circle doesn't last—it's not like a brand or something."

One way I've financed the retreats—which have been held at the local convention center, as today's paper so helpfully pointed out—is by using volunteers, participants from previous retreats. The volunteers identify themselves with name tags, which they've come to regard as badges of honor. The name tags are made by Dory, small wooden rings that she paints with their names and all sorts of weird symbols based on what she knows about each one; then she hangs the rings from a cord so the women can wear them around their necks and be easily spotted by the retreat participants. I imagine that once again Son will try to talk Dory out of working with the White Rings. After their youngest left for college, he tried to convince her that she'd spent her life giving to others, and now she had the opportunity to focus on herself. Naturally I translated that as focus on *him*.

Lex turns the Jeep down Fairview Street to my house, and I experience the lift I always do at seeing my street at night, its overhanging oaks dappled in moon shadows and the muted glow of streetlamps. I fell in love with this street and the house the moment I laid eyes on them, and that feeling has never left me, in spite of everything. The house belonged to a maiden aunt of Mack's, and Papa Mack bought it for us as a wedding gift on the condition that we renovate it. Although it was a great old house with what had once been widely famed formal gardens in back, it was almost falling down when we moved in, a young couple in our twenties with no idea where to begin either our lives or the renovations. But ultimately it was the project that got Mack into the business of preserving old houses and, more indirectly, pushed me toward what was to become my career path.

"It's a lovely sight, isn't it?" I murmur. On Lex's initial visit to my house, he had the same reaction I did on seeing it for the first time. He stood in the entrance hall, hands on hips, then removed his baseball cap reverently. "I'll be damned," he said with a whistle. "So this is what you guys mean by Southern Gothic." Technically it wasn't, since Fairhope wasn't founded until the 1890s, and the houses built by the single-tax colony were plain and austere rather than Gothic. But our rambling old Victorian, built a few years later, seemed grand in comparison.

When we reach the end of the street and my house on the corner lot, I see a car parked out front. I look over for Lex's reaction, and he groans.

"Well, well. Look who's here," I say as he pulls the Jeep behind the silver Lexus and grinds to a halt.

With a wry grin, he says, "Why don't I just drop you off and haul ass?"

"Leaving me to face her alone? Oh, no, you don't."

I open the passenger door and take a deep breath before getting out. This is all I need after a day that has included not only the letter and Son's appearance in the coffee shop but also the anxiety over my meeting with George Johnson. A woman is standing on the front portico of my house, partially hidden in the riotous jasmine covering the latticework. She hears the sound of the Jeep and starts down the steps, her head lowered. The faceted-glass bulb of the lamp over the curved front door shines down like a spotlight and turns her silver-blond hair the color of moonlight. I straighten my shoulders and start toward her. Elinor Eaton-Yarbrough, Lex's ex-wife, who has been nothing but trouble since the first day she and I met.

⸙

It was about this time last year when I saw that Elinor Eaton-Yarbrough was on the list of my afternoon appointments. I'd been surprised to see her name; when we'd first met, she'd hinted that she might be coming to see me, but I hadn't expected her. As a therapist, you develop a feel for potential clients, and Elinor did not strike me as a serious candidate for therapy, especially the kind that I do. I rarely have success with anyone who refuses to follow up with group work, and she had let me know in no uncertain terms that kind of therapy did not appeal to her.

At one time Lex and Elinor Yarbrough's (or Eaton-Yarbrough, the name she uses professionally) move into Fairhope would have been the talk of the town, and they still created quite a stir. Over the last few years, however, Fairhope has become such a hot spot on the Gulf Coast that the appearance of new people is more commonplace, and our population includes several nationally known writers as well as Nall, a world-famous artist who studied with Salvador Dalí. Although everyone in town was talking about the retired naval captain who purchased and would be running the new marina, it was when his wife appeared and opened an expensive boutique downtown that the tongues really wagged. Actually, it was Elinor Eaton-Yarbrough herself, rather than her upscale boutique by the name of My Fair Lady, that attracted the attention of the locals. Everybody was going in just to catch a glimpse of her.

A few weeks after My Fair Lady opened, I'd gone in, too, but not out of curiosity. I desperately needed a suitable outfit for a presentation I was giving at a conference in Chicago, and I was willing to splurge on it. The initial article on my work with divorcing women had just come out in a magazine; I'd been on national TV, and it was the first time I'd been asked to be the keynote speaker at a prestigious conference of my peers. I'd never been one to pay much attention to my appearance, but I wanted to look as confident and put together as I could for the occasion. I was surprised when Elinor herself waited on me. Since I've always been hopelessly fashion-challenged, she listened intently when I said I needed a couple of smart outfits for a conference I was attending, one for the talk and one for a reception the day before. What I didn't tell her was, if I didn't dress the part and feel confident in myself, I'd give myself away, and everyone at the conference would be able to tell I was terrified.

I'd already heard all about the glamorous Elinor Eaton-Yarbrough, and she didn't disappoint. She was everything I expected and more. Had I met her on the street, I would've figured her to be European, French maybe, because her obvious sophistication was so out of place among the laid-back population of Fairhope. Although I'd already heard from the town gossips that Elinor was in her early fifties, she made the lovely young college girls she hired in the boutique look unformed and insipid in comparison. She was absolutely stunning, a statuesque blonde with high cheekbones, ice-blue eyes, and the confident carriage of a runway model. Fairhope had never seen anything quite like her. The men of town looked at her as though a goddess had landed in their midst, and the women jealously speculated on everything from the color of her pale eyes (surely that color could be obtained only with contacts!) to her flawless skin (did the credit go to the shock-ingly expensive creams she sold in the boutique or to a face-lift?).

Elinor's personality turned out to be as intimidating as her looks. Used to bubbly, overly friendly Southern women, shoppers were made uncomfortable by the inscrutable gaze of the Boston-bred Mrs. Eaton-Yarbrough, and most reported that they felt they were being evaluated and found wanting. Even though I'd thought myself immune after the various types I'd encountered in my business, I, too, felt uncomfortable under Elinor's cool scrutiny. Her disdainful look told me how little she regarded my sense of style, and she couldn't hide her horror at my loose, rumpled linen pants and top when I discarded them to try on a black suit she'd picked out for me.

"You *have* to wear black," she retorted when I asked for something a little less . . . severe. Truth of the matter was, I almost fainted when I saw the price tag—more than I made in a month. Naturally, the black suit turned out to be so perfect that I would've mortgaged my soul to own it. The black-and-bronze heels cost almost as much as the suit, but they made the outfit, and Elinor pointed out that since they also matched the bronze silk pantsuit necessary to make my wardrobe complete, I saved money by not having to buy another pair of shoes. At this bit of logic, I caught the eye of the young salesclerk helping us and winked, but I ended up buying everything I tried on. Hand it to Elinor: In spite of her disdainful attitude—or maybe because of it—she was very good at her job.

The only time I elicited a flicker of warmth from Elinor was when, as she questioned me about the occasion for the new clothes, it came out that I was a therapist specializing in divorce recovery. The salesclerk overheard us and pointed out that I'd gotten a lot of attention based on the innovative methods I was developing. "Dr. Ballenger was on *Good Morning America* not too long ago, Mrs. Eaton-Yarbrough," she added breathlessly, and one of Elinor's perfectly arched eyebrows shot up as she regarded me.

"Oh? I've never heard of a divorce therapist, even in Boston. You're not a marriage counselor, then?" she asked me, tilting her head to the side curiously. I explained that I didn't work with couples, only men and women who were having problems dealing with a separation or divorce, and that a lot of group work was involved.

"I'm not interested in group work or baring my soul before strangers," she told me with a sniff, "but if you see patients on an individual basis, I'll make an appointment." Her pale blue eyes darted around the store to make sure no one was listening, and she confided in a low voice, "I'm planning on asking my husband for a divorce, and I might need some help because he'll go berserk when I do. Will you see me?" Before walking home with my arms full of packages and my bank account depleted, I handed her my card and explained where Casa Loco was located.

Elinor Eaton-Yarbrough's session was as close to a disaster as any I'd ever had, and she never returned. Hostility radiated from her like a bad sunburn, and none of my usual tactics worked with her. At that time I hadn't met Lex, but I knew from the talk around town that Elinor was married to the man who ran the new marina and had charmed the locals with his hearty good nature and zany humor. He sounded like the last person on earth to be married to a woman like her. But one thing I'd learned in my practice: The old adage about opposites attracting must be engraved on God's golden throne. Still, though I thought I'd become immune to the unlikely matches that people made, the Yarbroughs took it to a whole new level. During her session, Elinor echoed my thoughts.

"None of my family nor friends understood why I married Lex," she told me, crossing her long, shapely legs and fidgeting with a silver cigarette case, flicking it open and shut, open and shut. She'd been appalled by my no-smoking rule, snapping, "How like you uptight Southerners! If you can't smoke in your therapist's office, then where?" How about most places in New York City, I thought, but kept my silence.

"Tell me what it was about your husband—Lex, right?—that attracted you," I suggested. That was my usual opening gambit, since most of my clients were disillusioned with their spouses, and it helped for them to remember the days before hurt and bitterness set in. I'd heard almost everything in response, but rarely had I seen anyone struggle for an answer like Elinor did. I felt, then quickly suppressed, a flicker of sympathy for the man unlucky enough to have married her. Elinor finally told me that she'd most likely married Lex because her parents were so opposed to the match. She and Lex had met when she was "slumming" in a bar in Boston (her phrase), and he was a young officer assigned to the nearby naval base.

"He was boisterous and raw-boned and hilarious, so very different from the Ivy League boys I'd been dating," she mused. "He won me over when a brawl broke out, and he took charge so masterfully, then made sure I got home safely. I felt protected or something, like he rescued me. My knight in shining armor. Ha! I was such a wide-eyed innocent back then."

That image was certainly difficult to conjure, but I proceeded with my usual follow-up question: What was it that had held them together through the years? There was no hesitation this time. "Mostly it was our daughter," she said simply. "I've wanted to leave a dozen times, but even when she went away to college, Alexia couldn't stand the idea of her parents not being together. Not only is she named after her father, she dotes on him, and he on her."

As the session went on, I realized with a sinking feeling that Elinor was one of those clients who blames everything on the other partner and goes to a therapist only seeking verification of her position. She scorned my oft-repeated adage that she could not change her partner, only herself. She haughtily informed me that *she* wasn't the one who needed changing. She admitted that she'd agreed to move to Fairhope as a last-ditch effort to save their marriage, and even then only because their daughter had begged them to give it one more try. When Lex had retired from the navy and decided to fulfill his lifelong dream of running his own marina, Elinor had agreed to move from their home in Baltimore to Florida, had even been eager to live in a warmer climate. Earlier in their marriage, they'd spent a few years at the naval base in Pensacola, she told me, and she'd been surprised to like it so much.

"But of course, Florida is not really the *South*, is it?" she added. However, they soon found the cost of purchasing a marina any-where in Florida prohibitive. The one in Fairhope, not all that far from Pensacola, was the only one remotely affordable, and Lex had snatched it up. Elinor had never been to Alabama—never wanted to, she assured me—but had been so taken with the charm of Fairhope that she'd decided to stay and open a shop like the one she'd had in Baltimore. In the short time they'd been here, both the boutique and the marina had flourished, but not the marriage. She'd decided to ask her husband to move out for a trial separation, she told me, then she'd file for divorce once he had some time to adjust. The reason she had come to me, she repeated, was for ad-vice on the best way to make sure everything went smoothly.

"So your husband is not going to want a divorce?" I inquired, and Elinor looked at me in astonishment at such a question, since any man would surely be broken up at the thought of losing her.

"He'll go ballistic," she assured me.

"Are you afraid of him?" I asked anxiously, and Elinor rolled her eyes.

"Afraid of *Lex*?" She snorted. "Hardly. Oh, he rants and raves and carries on, but it doesn't mean anything. Plus, he adores me too much to harm me. He's going to be so devastated when I finally leave him that I worry about what could happen. And I don't want Alexia to take his side if he runs to her for sympathy."

My usual practice during a first session was to urge my clients to preserve their marriage if at all possible, so I suggested that rather

than rushing into a divorce, she spend a week or so keeping a journal, writing down the pros and cons of her marriage in order to
make sure this was what she really wanted. To my utter astonishment, the suggestion outraged Elinor. She stormed out of my office, saying all she wanted from her marriage was *out,* and she'd
counted on me being more supportive. I sent her a follow-up letter,
urging her to return so we could continue the session and discuss
her options. When I heard from the local gossips that she and her
husband had separated, I wasn't surprised. Neither was I particularly surprised to hear that she was bad-mouthing me all over
town. But when Rye said she was telling the high-society crowd
she hung with that *I* was the one who'd talked her into filing—that
she hadn't wanted to because of her daughter—that did it.

I returned to My Fair Lady and asked Elinor if I could speak to
her in private. With a huff, she showed me to her office and closed
the door. I told her that I had no control over her conversations
with her friends, but if I heard again of her saying I'd been the one
to urge her to file for divorce, I'd have no choice but to contact my
attorney. "Don't think I don't know what you're doing, Elinor," I
said tightly, my voice trembling. "You're shifting the blame because you're afraid to tell your daughter it was your idea, aren't
you?" She denied it, of course, but I stood my ground, refusing to
let her intimidate me. After I left her shop that day, the gossip
stopped.

Now here I am, facing Elinor Eaton-Yarbrough on my own
front porch. Who would have thought that, long after the disastrous session in my office, her husband and I would become
friends, and as a result, she'd decide she wanted him back, out of
my clutches? Lex appears to have no idea that's what she's up to,
but it's obvious to me. Doesn't take a therapist to see it, either, just
another woman.

"Elinor? Are you looking for us?" I ask her, admittedly not the sharpest of questions. *Oh, no, Clare, I'm standing on your porch at eleven o'clock at night for the hell of it.*

Her pale eyes are cool as she stares at me, but she forces a smile. "Oh, hello, Clare." Elinor and I forged an unspoken truce when Lex was in the hospital, having no choice but to be civil to each other. "Are you okay, dear?" she coos, wrinkling her lovely brow in concern.

"Why wouldn't I be?" I say rather sharply. I know where she's going, but I'm not about to give her the satisfaction of showing it.

"That awful letter from that awful old man!" She turns to Lex, the look of distress on her face worthy of an Academy Award. "Did you see *The Fairhoper* today, Lex? I felt so bad for Clare."

Without a moment's hesitation or a flicker of remorse, Lex flat-out lies to her. "Naw, I never read that rag. Nothing of interest in it, anyway."

"You won't say that when you see the editorial page," she tells him with a shudder, then looks my way. "But don't worry, Clare. Everyone in town is talking about it now, but it'll blow over in a day or two." Having gotten her usual dig in, she's finished with me, and she turns back to Lex. "Surely you can't be aware of the time! I went by your place to check on you," she adds breathlessly, "and I was worried sick not to find you there. When I couldn't reach you on your cell, I came over here to see if Clare knew where you were. I couldn't call, since all of Clare's numbers are such highly guarded secrets."

Yeah, and it'll be a cold day in hell before you get one of them, Mrs. Eaton-Yarbrough, I think, but manage to keep my face expressionless.

Lex retrieves his phone from his front pocket and frowns down at it. "Damn," he mutters. "Hadn't even noticed it needed charging. Sorry, Elinor. And you're right. We must've lost track of the time."

He told me that he'd made a promise to her in the hospital when he thought he was on his deathbed. He'd given his word that he would make more of an effort to maintain a friendly relationship. As Elinor had predicted, Lex had not wanted the divorce, and he'd been bitter and angry afterward, refusing to even be in her presence. The local gossips—especially Rye, naturally—had a field day when he made a great show of leaving after the two of them turned up at the same place. Even better was the way he crossed to the other side of the street when he was in town and happened to see her entering or leaving her shop. I have hopes that he'll eventually find healthier ways of dealing with her. Lex thinks I'm kidding about enrolling him in one of the retreats, but I'm not. Although he's told me that he loved Elinor and didn't want their marriage to end, he either shrugs it off or jokes about it when I've tried to get him to talk about his feelings. The anger he displayed afterward is a typical male reaction, I've told him, but he needs desperately to go through the rest of the process. I've tried to make him see his heartbreak as manifesting itself in a literal manner, with the heart attack coming not too many months after their divorce was final. (Apply your literal-mindedness here! I argued.) It's obvious to me that Lex has yet to deal with the emotional devastation that a divorce causes for everyone involved.

"Alexia tried to call you earlier this evening. She's the one who thought I should come over here to check on you," Elinor tells him, her whispery voice provocative. When Lex was hospitalized, I also met Alexia, who's a student at Boston College and a willowy blonde with Lex's grass-green eyes. It was painfully obvious that her mother had done a number on her, since she masked her love and concern for her father with a studied nonchalance. After nodding a polite but cool greeting, she pointedly ignored me, and I knew Elinor had told her about me as well.

Elinor's cool blue stare would cower anyone, so I can't really blame Lex for not looking her way as he mutters, "Yeah, it's gotten pretty late, hasn't it?"

She takes him by the arm as though he's a naughty child caught playing hooky, and starts down the steps. "You should talk to Alexia, don't you think, and assure her that you're all right? Let's get you home and call her from there."

He turns to me questioningly, and I give him a nod. "Elinor's right, Lex: You need to be home. Thanks for your help this afternoon. I really appreciate it."

With a wave of his hand, he brushes off my appreciation, but it's difficult to say more with Elinor practically dragging him down the front steps. I go inside quickly so I don't have to witness her manipulation. Why can't Lex see what she's doing? Funny, how we allow the people we love to pull our strings like that. I see it all the time. It's obvious in Dory's reunion with Son.

When I enter the kitchen, I see that the message light on the answering machine is blinking furiously, like the malevolent red eye of an angry god, and I press it with dread. What now? The first one appears to be a hang-up, but before I can delete it, a falsetto voice comes on. "Is Fairhope's one and only divorce coach there? I need someone to help me get rid of my sorry-ass husband." Rye laughs appreciatively at his own humor before he says, "I missed you tonight, sweetheart. Call me, and I'll tell you about the party."

The next one is Dory, her voice soft and gentle. "Clare? I wish you were in so we could talk. I doubt you let that letter bother you, but I wanted to let you know that I'm thinking of you, honey." There's a pause, then she adds, "I can't wait to see you in the morning. I'll bring the refreshments early so we can talk before the meeting starts, okay?"

I rub my face wearily before listening to the final message. Upon hearing Son's voice, I flinch and reach for the delete button. Lex deleted Son's previous messages, so it's a new one. "Hey, Clare, it's Son," he says, as though the nitwit thought I wouldn't know his voice. I even recognize the tone. It's Son's cajoling, I'm-so-charming-no-one-could-possibly-resist-me voice. "Just trying to figure out why the hell you haven't called me back, since I've left you so many messages," he says with an indulgent chuckle. "It's real important that we talk, Clare. *Real* important. Let me hear from you—"

Hitting the delete button with a sigh, I decide it's time to call it a day.

Chapter Four

❧   ❧   ❧   ❧   ❧

Before Dory gets to Casa Loco on Saturday morning, bringing refreshments for the ten o'clock group meeting, I pace the floor, unable to keep from peering out the windows every time a car drives by.

It's difficult when someone we love marries someone we don't love. When my clients lament their lack of affection—or worse—of a stepparent, an in-law, or a friend's spouse, my advice is always the same: You're stuck with having them in your life, so make the best of it. Decide if voicing your opposition is worth losing a loved one, since that could be the outcome. Whatever you do, don't put your loved one in the position of choosing between the two of you. I've had to follow my own advice with Dory. When I first met Dory Shaw, she was engaged to Son, and they were the golden couple on campus. All the girls thought Dory was lucky to have landed Son Rodgers, no doubt because he was wealthy, charming, and drop-dead gorgeous. Even though I thought he was the one lucky to have Dory, I, too, was taken with Son at first, but I was as unworldly as a wildflower then. I mistook his arrogance for self-assurance, his brashness for pride, and his jealous possessiveness as proof of his deep love for Dory. By the time I saw his true nature, she was in too deep to heed my warnings.

It was then I experienced something that had been only a theory up until that time. When forced into an intolerable situation, we find a way of making it tolerable: the Serenity Prayer in action. Dory loved a man I found unlovable, but she was my dearest friend, and if she was to remain so, I'd best learn to live with it. Son was also Mack's best buddy; the four of us were constantly together; and when the Rodgerses' first child came along, Mack and I were named godparents. As the old saw goes, God granted me the wisdom to accept what I couldn't change. Son and I often clashed and sparred, but over the span of twenty-five-plus years, we learned to tolerate each other. There were even times when I became almost fond of him and tried to convince myself that he'd mellowed. Our relationship sat atop a fault line, though, and the ground beneath us could shake at any moment.

This past year the rumblings began, and the earth shifted. Dory and Son faced the empty nest when the youngest of their two boys, Shaw, left for college. Having always been something of a domestic goddess and earth mother, Dory had dedicated her life to her family and flower gardens. She was a certified master gardener, and gardening was the great passion of her life, even more so than Son was. (Or so I told myself.) The empty nest provided the perfect opportunity for her to start a business in landscape design, a life-long dream. Son, however, had other ideas. Her passion might be gardening, but his was, and always has been, Dory, and he was finally getting her all to himself. He cut way back on his work hours and purchased a small yacht for the two of them to use for the many trips he planned. In what he considered the ultimate thoughtful gesture, he even hired a full-time gardener (whom Dory promptly fired). Without her consent, Dory's days and nights were all mapped out, leaving her little time for her gardens, much less starting up a business. The resulting tension caused the first serious problems in their marriage, and last year was a stress-filled and miserable one.

Son pouted and flung fits and carried on like a bigger jackass than usual.

At the first of the summer, when the inevitable blowup came, it was so ugly that Dory, much to my astonishment, kicked Son out. I found myself walking a delicate line between supporting her decision and hiding my joy that she'd seen the light at last. Until I was convinced she was really through with him, however, I kept a low profile. I knew Son would be looking for someone to blame—it couldn't be his fault, after all—and I was a perfect target. In much the same way Elinor Eaton-Yarbrough had done, Son went around telling everyone that I'd talked Dory into leaving him, as he'd feared since she started her volunteer work with me. Hanging around all those divorced women whining about their exes would naturally cause Dory to look for his flaws, he said, hoping his listeners would assure him that she'd have to look long and hard. Dory surprised me even more by sticking to her decision, seemingly content without Son as she got serious about starting the business. Since she planned on working out of her home, she was consulting with Rye on the legalities of licenses and zoning laws. During that time I let her know I was there for her, but I stepped back so she could, at long last, have her own life.

I'll always wonder if I made the right decision. This past summer was a viciously hot one, with thick, waxen days melting into sweltering, sleepless nights. Every afternoon in July, ominous black thunderclouds rumbled in over the bay and teased us with the promise of relief, only to retreat to the Gulf, leaving the air heavier than ever. It left everyone edgy, tense, and expectant, waiting for the inevitable storm to hit. It held off until the last day of July, then roared in with a fury, turning the bay into a cauldron and leaving mighty oaks cowering in its wake. But it broke the heat, and August promised better things. The next morning I called Dory early to ask if she wanted to join Lex and me for a celebratory sunset boat ride, complete with a bottle of champagne. On my return home from work, I played my messages with no premonition of what was to come: Dory, her voice tremulous yet joy-filled, saying that she'd be gone by the time I got her message. Something wondrous, even miraculous, had happened, she'd said breathlessly, and she and Son were driving to Pensacola to hop on a plane to Europe. They'd be away for a month, but she'd explain everything when she returned.

When Dory arrives at Casa Loco, backing into the door of the conference room laden with bags and baskets, my greeting is friendly, cheerful, and upbeat, as though nothing unusual has happened since I last saw her. I don't want her to pick up on my bewilderment, curiosity, or disappointment about her reconciliation with Son—not until we have our talk, anyway. Putting an arm around her and pulling her close, I kiss her cheek and say with a hearty smile, "Hey, Dory! It's great to see you. Welcome back." With her arms full, she can't do much more than return my greeting and kiss my cheek in return, at which point I pat her back so enthusiastically that she almost trips. Way to go, Clare, I think as I grab some of her baskets. You've paced the floor waiting for her anxiously, she finally gets here, and you knock her down before she can get into the room.

"It's great to see you, too, honey," is all she says. In contrast to the sappiness of my greeting, hers seems unusually reserved. But it's hard to tell with Dory: One of the things I admire most about her is the air of tranquillity she's always worn like a majestic cloak.

"The table's in place, but everything else I left to you," I say cheerily as I lead her to the narrow table I pushed against a wall to hold her refreshments. "Want me to put the basket here?"

"Ah . . . yeah. Sure. Anywhere is fine," she replies absently. By her bemused expression, I can tell that she finds my enthusiasm a bit much. Even though I, too, cringe at my Pollyanna routine, I can't seem to stop it.

"Do you need anything?" I ask as she places her tote bag and basket on the table, and she shakes her head solemnly.

"Think I brought everything with me, but if not, I know where to find it." Dory glances around the room with what appears to be only the mildest of curiosities before turning back to me with a serene smile.

I force myself to ask the question and get it out of the way. "So, did you have a good trip to Europe?"

It's a relief when she answers casually, with no details. "We spent most of the time in France, which is beyond fabulous. You and I must go one day. There's so much I'm dying to show you."

"Umm. I'd love that." I stop myself from asking her about the gardens she saw, always the main focus of her trips. The questioning can wait until she finishes the refreshment table.

With a rueful grin, Dory says, "So, how's the divorce coach this morning?"

Standing with my hands on my hips, I roll my eyes to the ceiling. "What a crock, huh?"

She regards me for a moment, then says in a gentle voice, "I knew you'd have no problem handling it. But it sure pissed me off. I'm trying to decide whether to write a response or not dignify such idiocy with a reply."

It touches me that she'd want to defend me. "Everyone assures me the guy is a loon, so I've decided to leave it alone and let it blow over."

"One thing for sure, you don't have to worry about it hurting your business. The waiting lists for the retreats are a mile long, and the groups fill up as fast as you post them." Dory stops herself, her eyes falling away from mine. "Which is really sad, when you think about it. So many people in so much pain."

"The retreats fill a need, evidently," I agree. Then, to lighten the mood, I turn again to the refreshment table. "Boy, something smells good! Don't tell me you brought your orange-blossom sweet rolls."

"Yep. Knowing they're your favorites, how could I not?"

"Oh, no," I groan. "I can't resist them, and the last thing my fanny needs is a few more pounds. You've gone to way too much trouble, as usual."

She shrugs it off. "Not at all. Just threw some stuff together at the last minute."

"Yeah, right," I say with a hoot. "It would've taken me a week to do all this."

"I love doing it, hon; you know that." To kick off a new group, Dory makes a big production of the refreshments, which never fail to dazzle the newcomers. At first I protested, saying it was unnecessary and maybe even distracting, but I shut up once I saw the magic it works on a group of tense, unhappy women. Arriving to such a welcome, they relax and chat among themselves before having to deal with the emotionally fraught business of group therapy. Afterward, I vowed that Dory was a genius and I'd never argue with her again.

"I was putting the handouts together when you got here," I tell her, "so let me get back to them and leave the refreshment table to you, okay?"

Situated a few feet away from her, I busy myself with the handouts while Dory turns her attention to the refreshments. At one point, feeling my gaze on her, she stops and turns to smile at me. Her hands full of flowers, she remarks that she's lucky to have late-blooming roses in her garden. I would've stuck them in a glass jar, but Dory arranges the heavy-headed pink roses as if she planned on entering them in a garden show. While she sets up the table, I count the handouts to make sure there's enough for the number of chairs I've set up in a circle. On each of the well-worn cushions, I place a stack that deals with the concerns of the meeting: finding the best legal advice; avoiding custody battles; ensuring financial stability; and fighting depression and loneliness.

Frowning in concentration, Dory unwraps her cinnamon-fragrant orange rolls and arranges them on a pottery plate. I wait for the touch that will make it uniquely hers, and sure enough, she brings out a cluster of yellow and purple pansies. As she edges the plate with the sweet-faced blossoms, she murmurs, "Guess I shouldn't put them on the rolls in case someone eats theirs. They're perfectly edible, though. I eat my flowers all the time."

"You shouldn't tell me that, girlfriend. I'm obligated to have you committed now. One of the perks of my profession."

She bites off the head of one of the pansies, then widens her eyes in appreciation as she munches. "Umm," she says with a mouthful of pansy. "This one's unusually good. Brisk and woodsy, with undertones of . . . potting soil. Want a bite?"

"I'll pass."

She smiles. "Tastes just like chicken."

"How would you know?"

"In case you've forgotten, I'm now a recovering vegetarian."

"In case *you've* forgotten, I've never liked chicken."

"Oh, yeah," she murmurs. "You've always had appalling taste, Clare."

"Really? And what does that say about my choice of friends?" Suddenly it's a struggle to keep my voice light, and I catch myself stacking folders next to my chair as though the fate of the world depends on my getting them in the right order.

With a grin, Dory makes an imaginary mark in the air—her way of saying "Score one for you," which goes back to the early days of our friendship. She still laughs because the first time she did it, I thought she was swatting flies. "The basil in my garden was so pretty that I put it in the dip instead of parsley this time," she says while anchoring a cluster the size of a baseball on a bowl of goat cheese. Catching my look of longing, she fixes me a cracker and holds it out, and I cross the room eagerly.

"Umm! That's delicious." I gobble up the cracker and a sweet roll, then reach for a napkin only to groan when I see it. "Oh, no! What have you done this time, girl?" Not only does Dory bring refreshments for the groups and retreats, she's amused herself and the participants by bringing napkins with outrageous sayings printed on them. Everywhere she goes, she searches for them. The ones today say, *If it comes with wheels or testicles, expect trouble.*

"I love the way you spoil us," I tell her as I lick the cinnamon sugar off my fingers. "If it weren't for you, I'd bring plain old napkins, donuts, and Maxwell House or Lipton. None of your fancy teas. What do you have for us today?"

She unscrews a tin of herbal tea and holds it under my nose. Dory's flower and herb gardens are famed far and wide, and she does unbelievable things with her harvest, creating teas and sachets and potpourri and unique arrangements.

"Lemon verbena and rose hip. From the batch I made at the end of May—" She stops herself in time, but I know what she almost said: *before the night Son came home drunk and, in a jealous fit, threw out all of the things in the workshop I created for my projects.* What he didn't expect was to land among them once Dory saw what he'd done.

There's an awkward silence, then she turns to fiddle with an old coffeemaker rigged up to brew her tea. I steal curious glances at her, amazed that she's behaving so normally, as though she hadn't left me a mysterious message that I've wondered about for a month. She's cool and put together and lovelier than ever. As Rye so wistfully said, Dory's looking great these days and has been since her separation from Son. During that time, her unique and understated beauty seemed to ripen and blossom like one of her roses. Today her translucent skin is so radiant it appears lit from within, and her fawn-brown hair, pulled into a long braid down her back, is silkier and more lustrous than ever. But for me, it's always been about her eyes. Dory has the largest, most expressive eyes of anyone I've ever known, the color a gold-and-green mosaic; they're so luminous they almost glow in the dark, like a cat's. I've always been able to read Dory by searching her eyes.

"So, what's the verdict?" she says, startling me.

"W-what?"

"Come on, Clare. What did you think, that I wouldn't notice you staring at me ever since I got here?"

"I was *not* staring at you," I say with a forced laugh. "Jesus, you're such an egomaniac."

"And you're such a bad liar."

"Not true. I'm an expert liar. Quite helpful in my profession." The tea has brewed, and I take my mug from the rack and fill it with the pale liquid, fragrant with lemon and roses. "This smells heavenly."

Dory watches me knowingly. She's dressed with her usual flair, in snug jeans, wedged espadrilles, a loose, embroidered top that must have come from some exotic place on their trip, and dangling earrings of polished sea glass, looped in thin circles of silver. "I must look like shit," she says, glancing down at herself suspiciously. "This top makes me look fat, doesn't it? I put on a few pounds in France. French women may not get fat on all that butter and bread and cream sauce, but you can't say the same about us."

"Dory! That's ridiculous. You look great, as usual." Instead of sipping the tea, I gulp it down, burning my mouth. "If you gained an ounce, I can't tell it." Dory's blessed with one of those willowy, fine-boned bodies that she claims is due to not just her yoga but also all the bending and stooping she does in her yard. She never diets.

She tilts her head suspiciously. "Liar."

"I'm not lying, I swear! It's just me. As you're always reminding me, I'm the same uptight worrywart I've always been." Both of us look away from the other, Dory fiddling with the perfectly set table again, me studying the pattern of the wide-planked floor. Finally I raise my head, swallow hard, and say, "Ah, Dory?"

This time she doesn't look away when our eyes lock. "Yes, Clare?"

"I'd made up my mind to play it cool this morning until we had a chance to talk," I confess.

Reaching up to rub the back of her neck, Dory smiles wryly. "Yeah. Me, too. We didn't quite pull it off, did we?"

"You did a better job than me. I decided not to ask you about . . . what happened with you and Son, or your trip, or anything. I was waiting to take my cue from you. That's why I've been watching you, not because you look bad or put on weight. I don't want you thinking that."

After a moment she asks, "You've finished setting up, haven't you?" When I nod, she says, "The refreshments are ready, so let's find a quiet corner and talk."

"Want to go to my office?"

Dory's expression changes to one of exasperated amusement. "No, Dr. Ballenger, I don't need a therapy session. Well, I'm sure I do, but let's go to the courtyard instead."

"Perfect! It should be more pleasant now that the mornings are cooler. Get yourself a cup of tea and bring it with you, okay?"

It catches me off guard. She picks up her favorite pottery mug with her fine, long-boned fingers, and memories sweep over me: My eyes sting with tears. I turn my head away but not fast enough. "Oh, honey," Dory says, sighing.

When she reaches out for me, I wave her off, unable to speak, and I move quickly toward the door that leads outside the building. With my back turned to her, I blink away the unexpected tears and take a deep breath, pulling myself together. I go through the door so quickly it slips out of my hand and almost slams in Dory's face. "Whoa," she says with a startled laugh. "I'm right behind you, fool, carrying a cup of hot tea."

Calling the back area a courtyard is a joke between us. When I opened my therapy practice in Casa Loco, an odd U-shaped cottage built at the turn of the century to house a doctor's clinic, I could afford to rent only an office and a reception room. As my practice expanded, so did my space, and took over the whole house, turning the front into the reception area and space for Etta; one of the wings into a consultation room and my office; the other wing into rooms for group meetings. When I got in a position to buy the property, the owners wouldn't sell but offered an extended lease to include what they called the "courtyard," a grassy space between the two wings and walled off in the back from the alley. Dory saw my irritation at them calling the useless area a courtyard and charging extra for it, so she went into action. Treating the nondescript space like a blank canvas, she transformed it into what she calls our Zen garden, where any of us, staff or clients, can go for a few minutes of peace and serenity. After constructing several trellises in her workshop, she secured them around the plain stucco walls, almost to the roof. With utmost patience, she trained morning glory vines to climb them, and the ugly space was soon cocooned in blue flowers. Against the cement wall that blocks off the back alley, she added a concrete fountain surrounded by feathery ferns, its recirculating water a soothing melody to drown out the street noises. A white-pebbled pathway leads to the fountain, with benches on either side.

When she and I sit on one of the wooden benches, I reach out and touch her arm. "Dory? I started thinking about all we've been through over the years, and it got to me. That's why I teared up."

Her eyes fastened on the gurgling fountain, she nods, a small smile on her lips. "I figured that's what it was. I've been thinking about the past a lot lately, too—I guess with all that's happened this summer."

"It's been quite a year, hasn't it?"

She takes a sip of her tea and glances my way. Her eyes soft, she says, "You're one cool customer. If I'd gotten a message from you like the one I left, then you'd disappeared for a month, I would've died of curiosity."

"You think I didn't? I've tried to keep busy so as not to obsess about it. Your postcards helped, though. At least I knew you hadn't flipped out."

"Ha. You might change your mind when you hear what I have to say," she says with a wry smile.

"Okay, let me amend it to say that your postcards convinced me you weren't loonier than usual."

Mack always teased Dory because of her seemingly insatiable interest in what he dismissed as all that "weird crap." I, on the other hand, saw her experimentation in the occult and the unknown, mythology, Jungian psychology, Zen, and other such things as evidence of Dory's search for meaning in life and her attempt to understand the natural world she loved so much. Each of us has to find her own path, and Dory's has always been a different one.

"Several times I thought I should write or call you from France," she says, "but I decided I needed to see you in person instead."

I nod. "As badly as I wanted to know what was going on, I resisted the urge to try and track you down, for the same reason."

She glances at me, then clears her throat. "It's really important to me that you understand the reason I took Son back."

"Don't tell me you're pregnant?" I say lightly, and she hoots, clapping her hands together.

"Yeah, right. One for the tabloids! 'Forty-eight-year-old woman who had her plumbing removed almost twenty years ago shocks the medical community.'" We smile together, and the tension eases. "Actually, here's what happened. The night before Son and I got back together, I think I had a nervous breakdown. Maybe my terminology isn't right, but whatever happened was pretty awful. I'd never gone through anything like it before."

"Dammit, Dory—why didn't you tell me? I could've helped you."

She cringes, biting her lower lip. "I was going to call you, I swear. And I'll explain why I didn't." She glances at me reluctantly, then says, "Before I do, though, I need to say this: I'm not strong like you, Clare. I want to make that clear from the beginning."

"What are you saying? That's absurd."

"No. It's true. Your strength amazes me, and I've envied it more than you'll ever know. After all the heartaches in your life, with the babies, and Haley, and Mack, you're still standing."

"You say that as though I had a choice." I try to say it flippantly, but my voice sounds tight and strangled.

"Of course you do. We all do. Falling apart is an option for any of us, at any given moment," she says simply. "When Mack died, I was afraid you might, too, you were so torn up. More than anyone else, I know how you loved him."

"He's the only person I've ever loved like that," I agree. "Or ever will."

"Yet when you lost him, especially in such a god-awful way, you didn't go to pieces like I would have. I don't think anyone knew how bad you were hurting. It got so I could barely stand to be around you because you were trying to be so damn brave. I never could've handled it as courageously as you did. If Son hadn't held me up at Mack's funeral, I couldn't have stood, and I wept so much I made myself sick, literally. It was the same when your baby died all those years ago. Surely you remember how I fainted at the cemetery, seeing that tiny white coffin waiting to be lowered into the ground." She shudders, her eyes filling with tears, and I grab her hand and hold on tight.

"All those awful memories, Dory—that's what got me earlier."

Wiping her eyes furiously, she goes on. "I know. And I'm going somewhere with this, if you'll bear with me. When Son came home drunk and trashed my workshop, after he'd been such a turd all last year, something changed in me. I didn't want to see him again. And you know Son's been a major part of my life since I was a child. I grew up loving him, and it was as natural to me as breathing. I know how you feel about him, and I understand why." She pauses and shrugs. "You think I'm blind to Son's flaws, but that's not true. I love him in spite of them, and I haven't been able to stop loving him, no matter how much I've wanted to at times. But in spite of that, and the passion we share, and a lifetime spent with him, having his kids—suddenly none of it mattered anymore. I just wanted him gone. I wanted him out of my life."

I nod. "I could tell. You've said you were through with him before, but this time I was sure you meant it."

"Because I did! When he first left, it was heaven without him hovering over me, demanding my attention, never giving me any space." She pauses. "But here's what I didn't count on. I had *no* idea how lonely I'd get, and how terribly lost I'd be living alone. I've never done it before, remember, not once. Even with you, and the kids, and my friends, and a full life—there's never enough time for all the stuff I do!—I was surprised to find myself miserable in that big empty house haunted by the ghosts of our times together as a family. Thinking about the good times hurt as much as remembering the bad ones. I was much more miserable than I let anyone know. Especially you, since you'd been so strong when you lost Mack."

"God, Dory, I could kick myself! I thought you were doing great, and I purposely backed off until you had time to adjust. You didn't let on, so I thought you were adjusting and doing it well. Dammit to hell and back! I should've known better."

She lays a hand on my arm. "Stop it, Clare. I won't let you blame yourself. You lost the only man you've ever loved, but you didn't fall apart. So I wasn't about to tell you how bad I was feeling about the loss of one I claimed not to love anymore."

"But that feeling—it's the most common thing you battle after the breakup of a long-term marriage. Learning how to deal with the loneliness is the whole point of the retreats, and one of the things we talk most about, remember?"

"Yeah, but it's all talk until you experience it. You can't imagine what it's like to cry yourself to sleep, night after night, in a bed you've shared with someone for so many years."

"*I* can't imagine that? Don't you think it's happened to me, honey? So many times since Mack has been gone. There were times when I've missed him so bad I didn't think I could stand it another minute. So please don't think that I'm unsympathetic."

She says cautiously, "Maybe so, but you're stronger than me. That's what I'm trying to tell you. You didn't give in to those feelings."

"Christ, Son was gone what, not even two months? If you're telling me that you took him back out of loneliness, I understand, okay? I'm not going to lecture you or anything. Take it from someone who knows, the loneliness is almost unbearable at first, but it does get better. You didn't give yourself enough time. Mack's been gone almost five years, but I've learned how to live with it and go on with my life."

She shakes her head. "It wasn't the loneliness, Clare. It was something else."

"Something else?"

Lowering her head to stare into her cup of tea, she says, "You know how Son begged me to forgive him and give him another chance, sending me flowers and writing notes, making the boys ask on his behalf, the usual crap he's done when we've had arguments in the past and I've threatened to leave his sorry ass. But this time I wouldn't see him or talk to him or anything. It was the only way I could make it, I thought. Then one night, a little over a month ago now, after we had that big storm, something happened to me. I went through a really bad time."

"And this is the nervous breakdown you mentioned?"

She nods, deep in thought. "It was late, way after midnight, and I woke up confused and lost and alone. I started crying and wasn't able to stop. It was like a psychic meltdown or a panic attack or something. Or maybe all the tension of the past year accumulated, I don't know. Whatever it was, I started hyperventilating, unable to catch my breath, and it scared me. I got up to call you, stumbling around in the dark because I was sobbing so hard I couldn't even find the lamp, and all of a sudden, Son was there."

"There? You mean, in your bedroom?" Dory nods, and a shiver runs down my spine. "He broke into your house?" The night Son trashed the workshop, Dory told him to get out of her sight. Whenever they'd had fights in the past, he'd gone to his parents' summer cottage several miles away until they both cooled down. Within a day or two, he'd return, they'd make up, and soon everything would be lovey-dovey again. This time Dory astonished me and shocked Son speechless when he returned—she'd had the locks changed. Not surprisingly, Son stormed and wept and banged on the doors and windows until Dory called their oldest son to come get his dad, or she'd be forced to call the police. Then she had her numbers unlisted.

Dory shakes her head. "That's just it, the weird thing. He didn't break in. He didn't have to. Later he told me that he was sound asleep in his old bed at his parents' cottage when something woke him. All he knew was something was wrong, and I needed him. He drove to the house to check on me, and the back door was unlocked. What's so strange is, I checked it before I went upstairs. I'm *positive* it was locked, because I'd gotten so obsessive about checking all the doors since I'd been living alone. Son swears it was open, which has to be true, because he couldn't have gotten in otherwise. As soon as he came in, he heard me crying. And that's when he found me."

"And you let him stay," I say in a tight voice.

"It was true, I needed someone—anyone—at that moment. You know I'd never call you during the night unless I had to, but I was freaked out, like I was coming unglued. I was heading for the phone to call you, but there was Son instead. Don't you see, Clare? It was a sign!"

I eye her skeptically. "And you're convinced that he didn't break in?"

"Absolutely," she repeats.

"What about . . . I don't know . . . could he have bribed the locksmith and had a key cut, maybe?"

She shakes her head furiously. "Think about what you're saying. Son bribes the locksmith at two in the morning? And even if he did, how could he have timed himself to arrive at the exact moment I got up to call you? What do you think, that he'd been hiding in the bushes under my window every night until the right moment presented itself?"

I snort. "I wouldn't doubt it."

"My bedroom is on the third floor," she reminds me.

"I wouldn't put it past him to stand on stilts," I say petulantly.

She smiles. "Neither would I, before. But the man who came to my room that night wasn't the same one I'd thrown out of my house and my life. Our time apart had shaken him to the core. He saw that I could stop loving him if he drove me to it. Both of us ended up crying, and he was so different that night, so tender and sweet. And so repentant for all he'd done to make me unhappy. That's when I agreed to give him another chance. We decided the only thing to do was go away and see if we couldn't patch things up. Son already had tickets to Europe that he'd planned on surprising me with on our anniversary, so that's why we left so suddenly." She pauses for my reaction. "Do you understand now how it happened?" Before I can reply, she adds hastily, "Oh, I knew what you thought. You assumed I'd had a moment of weakness and let him in my bed, didn't you?"

"Ah . . . the thought did enter my mind," I admit. When Son

and Dory are together, the charge between them is almost palpable. From the beginning, I've understood it as a major factor in their attraction for each other. As little as I like Son Rodgers, to give the devil his due, he radiates such erotic energy that most women melt like hot butter in his presence.

"But that wasn't it, I swear. You know I've always believed in signs and magic circles and all that other stuff. Son appearing like he did, well, it was clearly a sign, whether it makes sense to you or me or anyone else. Somehow, from several miles away, he felt my need, and he responded. And it changed him, I swear it did. It was almost like a conversion experience."

Imagining Son as Saul of Tarsus, converted into Saint Paul on the road to Damascus, is more than I can take. My mind is spinning, trying to figure out how he could've arranged this amazing experience, a foolproof way of getting a believer like Dory to give him another chance. I wouldn't put anything past Son and whatever stands in the way of what he wants. And one thing I'll give him, if nothing else: What he's always wanted is Dory. All these years, and she's still the great obsession of his life.

"Clare?" I realize that Dory's calling me, and I turn toward her guiltily. "I'm sorry I left without telling you all this, but I was in a daze at the time. I'm not using that as an excuse, just to explain how it happened."

"I see why you wanted to wait and tell me in person. It's an amazing story."

"The most amazing part of it is how it's changed Son. I swear it has. I don't know if I can make you see that or not—" At my look of skepticism, she stops herself. "No, guess I can't. He'll have to prove himself to you, won't he?"

"Son doesn't have to prove anything to *me*," I say shortly. "It's not me I'm worried about. My only concern is for you. I've tried not to say much, because you know Son and I have our differences, so I can hardly be objective. But . . . I just hope you're doing the right thing."

"There's no doubt in my mind." As she raises her hands to push away the silky strands of hair that are always slipping out of her loose braid, her eyes fall on her watch, and she grimaces. "Oh, crap, it's time for the group. I'm not going to stay today, but don't fool with the refreshment table. I'll come back afterward and clean up."

"Don't be silly. I'll take care of everything, since you're bound to have a lot to do, being gone a month."

"But I wasn't through talking with you. There's something else that we need to discuss face-to-face."

"Oh, Lord," I say with a groan. "Don't tell me Saint Son had another conversion experience?"

We get to our feet, and Dory's expression remains serious. "No, it's not that. I'll go ahead and tell you so you can be thinking about it, okay? You're not going to like it, but promise me you won't say no until you give it a lot of thought."

Wary, I watch her. "Sounds fair, though rather mysterious. What is it?"

"This past June fifteenth was Son's and my twenty-fifth wedding anniversary, remember?"

"Of course I do. The week before would've been Mack's and my twenty-third." Although their wedding was a few weeks after Dory and I graduated, Mack and I didn't marry until I finished my master's degree. "But you and Son were separated then, so you had to cancel the party plans." It occurs to me what she wants to say. "Oh! You're planning to have the party after all, huh?"

After a moment's hesitation, she says, "It'll be at the Grand Hotel on the fifteenth of October. The boys will host it, though we'll foot the bill, naturally."

"If you're asking whether I'll attend, honey, there's no need. I wouldn't do that to you—not show up at your party—even if I'm less than thrilled about you and Son getting back together."

"What I'm asking isn't about the party, except indirectly. Son has gotten it in his head that we should make a public statement of our reconciliation. It's important to him." When I widen my eyes, startled, she holds up a hand. "Please, Clare! Just hear me out for now, then I'm leaving so you can have a few minutes to yourself before the group arrives. I want you to think about something, okay? Son and I are talking about having a ceremony at the church before the party. A renewal of our wedding vows."

"A ceremony?"

"The opposite of the one at our retreats, I guess," she says with an ironic smile. "Believe me, when Son suggested it, my first reaction was pretty much like yours. But you're the one who's taught me the importance of ceremony."

"Oh, Lord," I say. "I should've known it'd come back to haunt me."

Dory rushes on before I can interrupt again. "The more I thought about it, though, the more I liked it. A renewal ceremony for a twenty-fifth wedding anniversary feels *right* to me. I decided this morning that it was a great idea. Partly because Son brought me breakfast in bed, presented me with some lovely primroses, and wrote me the most unbelievable poem."

"Whoa. Evidently middle age causes deafness, along with everything else. I could've sworn you said Son wrote you a *poem*. As I recall, if you hadn't written his essays for him, Son would've flunked every English course he took."

A flush suffuses Dory's face with high color, and her eyes shine. "Can you believe he's writing poetry now? That's what I'm trying to tell you—this experience has turned him into a different man."

"If Son Rodgers has turned into William Shakespeare, the world is a scarier place than I ever dreamed it to be," I say with a snort.

"I'll make a copy of the poem and leave it in your mailbox, then you'll see what I mean. It's not only appropriate for us, it's so beautiful." Then he plagiarized it, I think, but keep that unkind thought to myself as Dory continues breathlessly, "I decided the poem would be perfect for him to read at the ceremony. Right after breakfast, Son called Father Gibbs, who's coming over after church tomorrow so we can plan everything."

With a sharp intake of breath, I say, "And you're telling me this because . . . ?" I have a sick feeling about where she's going.

"You were the maid of honor at my wedding. I want you to stand up with me again."

I turn away from her blindly, putting my hand on the bench to steady myself. "Oh, Christ, Dory, don't ask me to do that . . . please. Not that."

Dory and Son had a spectacular wedding in their hometown, Mountain Brook, and after the wedding reception at the country club, Dory tossed her bouquet of orchids right into my arms. Had I not caught it, her and Mack's carefully laid plan would've backfired. I wasn't as surprised by catching the bouquet as I was to see something odd dangling from the white ribbons, something that caught the light from the chandelier overhead. Before I could figure out why Dory had thrown me what appeared to be her ring, Mack stepped forward and took the bouquet from my hands. To the surprise and delight of everyone present, especially me, he untied the ring and said as he slipped it on my finger, "It was Dory's idea to do it this way. Guess she was afraid you'd turn me down otherwise." Everyone applauded; Dory squealed and hugged me, and I embarrassed myself by bursting into tears.

"Oh, honey," Dory whispers. "I'm so sorry. I shouldn't have asked you. Really. Don't even think about it, okay? Forget I said anything."

Standing behind me, she puts both her hands on my shoulders, then leans her forehead against my back. I long to turn around and put my arms around her. I want to tell her how much I wish I could feel good about what she's doing. I'd give anything if I could stand up at the renewal ceremony in front of her family and our friends and show my support of the vows she'll be saying. Before I come up with a response, Dory has squeezed my shoulders and scurried down the white-pebbled path, pulling the door shut behind her.

≫

The group meeting goes unusually well, a blessing since I'm distracted after my talk with Dory. In my business, I can't afford to show it; no one wants to spill his or her guts to a therapist whose mind is a thousand miles away or, worse, who responds with a yawn or a vacant stare. I needed some time to process Dory's story but didn't get a chance to; the meeting was abruptly on me. My suspicions are that Son somehow manipulated the whole thing, taking advantage of her loneliness and confusion. Or could Dory have done it herself unintentionally? Maybe she'd gotten overly upset and called Son, and her emotional state caused her to remember the outcome the way she described it to me. Ever since I first met Dory, Son has been her Achilles' heel. I don't suppose I'll ever understand it. Not that I don't know what she sees in him, the hold he has on her, but that's a different thing altogether. It astonishes and amuses me now to think of my first days as a therapist, the way I was convinced that I'd finally see all the things I'd never understood before. What a fool I was! If anything, I understand even less now. After years of extensive study and a doctorate on the subject, I know quite a bit about what makes us tick, what motivates us, and what causes us to behave the way we do. But when it doesn't happen the way it's supposed to, I'm as perplexed and confused as I was before becoming a so-called expert in human behavior.

I think about it, looking around the women gathered here today, the beginnings of a new group of broken hearts, as Dory calls them. All of the women are going through the process, their divorces not yet finalized. Most of them will finish up by attending a retreat, since the primary focus is on recovery and the rebuilding of lives. For the retreats, I take not only my clients but also referrals from other therapists, though the groups are primarily made up of my clients. Today these women are all mine. I know their stories, but they don't know one another. I watch them size one another up, glancing around the circle curiously as they balance their plates laden with Dory's goodies. I see that Joanna Stuckey is talking quietly with Helen Murray, the oldest with the youngest, though it's doubtful they know that about each other. Or maybe they do. Joanna, in her late sixties, no doubt would have spotted Helen as being the one closest to her daughter's age, and she probably sat next to her for that reason, even if subconsciously. With that thought, I take a sip of my tea to hide a smile. Dory would laugh if I said that aloud, since she teases me about those kinds of observations. "Better watch out, folks, Madame Freud's at it again," she'll say.

As I think of Dory and her revelation, something strikes me. How many of the women here today would do the same thing she's done? I've sat through session after session with them, listening to their stories of devastation and heartbreak, and it occurs to me for the first time that they'd go back to where they were before if they could. Surely not Joanna, I think. But am I right? I had my doubts about Joanna ever recovering from the shock of discovering that her husband of forty-five years has had another family in another state all this time, but as I watch her chat breezily with Helen and Helen's friend Sissy, it seems she's on her way. Yet I wonder if she wouldn't take her husband back if she could. In spite of her hurt and humiliation, all of Joanna's life has been dedicated to her family. It's all she's ever known. She'd go back, I think, dizzy with the realization.

The others I don't know well enough yet. Joanna I've seen twice a week for four months, but the others have just started coming to me, and summer appointments are always more relaxed, dependent on vacations, visits from relatives, and school starting back, among other factors. Helen Murray, talking with Joanna, is the one I've been most concerned about. Of this group, she's the shakiest. She's been in an abusive relationship for years but has lacked the courage to break free. As I pick up my material and take a seat in order to get the group started, I'm sure my epiphany was correct: Just as Dory has done, most of the women here today, if given the opportunity, would take their husbands back.

Chapter Five

❧ ❧ ❧ ❧ ❧

Over the muted sobs of Helen Murray, I hear a commotion in the reception area down the hall from the consultation room I use for client sessions. I look up from my chair, placed strategically across from the love seat where Helen sits. Helen, pale and haggard, was sitting on the front steps of Casa Loco when I arrived this morning, and she and I have just started our session. She was in the midst of telling me yet again how she's having to fight the desire to return to her husband. Not once have I heard her use the word "love"; rather, she's terrified to be on her own. When Helen confessed to her friend Sissy that her husband's abuse had gone beyond verbal and into pushing and shoving, Sissy got her away from him as fast as she could. Helen had gone directly from an overbearing father to an equally overbearing husband, a young partner in her father's law firm who was like the son her father always wanted, Helen told me. It's becoming obvious that she's a daddy's girl who married her father's choice in an effort to please him. I've seen hundreds like her, women who've always been so pampered and sheltered that they become helpless and frightened without a man in their lives.

Removing a soggy tissue from her eyes, Helen tilts her head in bewilderment at the racket, but I urge her to continue, raising my voice to be heard over the clamor. What on earth can be going on?

Etta is not the kind to allow anyone in the waiting area to bully her into giving out an immediate appointment, to insist on seeing me, to demand to know where his or her spouse is, or whatever else could be taking place out there. Through the years we've had numerous incidents, but Etta has remained victorious.

Before I can speculate further, Etta's booming voice comes from the hallway right outside the consultation room. "Hey! Don't even *think* about opening that door, you hear me?"

I jump to my feet, the pad I'm holding spiraling downward, papers fluttering. On her last visit, Helen finally admitted that her husband's temper tantrums had gotten so bad she was more frightened of staying with him than of leaving. When the door is flung open, I expect to see him there, having tracked her down in a rage. While I don't know Mr. Murray, I do know how to handle this. As the door flies open, I cry out, "Call the police, Etta—*now*!" Calling the police is the last resort for us, since it disrupts the entire day; usually Etta or I can handle the disturbance and get the offender calmed down and out of Casa Loco by ourselves. This is the first time anyone's gotten this far past Etta.

When I recognize the man standing in my doorway, his hand on the doorknob and his face dark with anger, I'm too stunned to move. It's Son Rodgers, and he points a finger at me.

"You, Clare!" he says in a loud voice. "We're gonna have our little talk, and we're gonna have it now." Son's blue eyes are blazing, and his full-lipped mouth is twisted into a snarl. Behind him, I see Etta lumbering down the hallway and turning the corner to the phone on her desk as she mutters to herself.

I swallow hard as a flush scalds my neck and face. "How *dare* you come barging into this room! I'm with a client now. Please leave immediately."

Son jabs in the air with his finger, pointing it at me like a weapon. "Who the hell do you think you are, refusing to return my calls?" he cries. I'd received other angry messages from Son, including one this morning before I left for work. He said it was urgent that he talk to me about Dory; figuring it was another of his ruses, I decided to give him time to cool down first. "Guess you don't care that Dory's so upset she almost had another breakdown?" Son shouts.

I glance over at Helen, who's staring at him with wide eyes. "I will not discuss Dory or anything else with you now, Son," I say between clenched teeth. "I repeat, you need to leave here immediately. I'll call you when I finish with my client."

"I'm not going anywhere until you hear me out." Son's lips curl into a sneer. "I've known all along what would happen with me and Dory once you started all this stuff." He makes a sweeping motion with his arm, and his gaze falls on Helen Murray huddled on the love seat and blinking at him in a kind of daze. "Sure hope you're ready for your marriage to end, young lady," he says to her. "Because I can promise you, this woman here"—he points at me again—"will try and talk you into it, just like she did my wife. Next thing you know, you'll be going to those retreats of hers, then you can kiss everything goodbye."

Etta comes to stand in the doorway, mouth set in a firm line and eyes flashing with fury as she glares at Son. "Police on the way," she announces. To me she whispers tersely, "Sorry he slipped past me. I thought he'd left."

"You can call the police all you want to, Etta," Son says, glancing her way, "and they can drag me away, but I'll be back." He turns from Etta to me. "I'll come here, or I'll come to your house—Mack's house, I should say—until you hear me out."

"Then you better get a restraining order when the police get here," Etta says, standing with her arms folded across her chest as she blocks the doorway. If Son decides to make a run for it before the police arrive, he'll have to get past her. Towering several inches over my five-foot-three frame, Etta is a formidable African-American woman built as solid as a tree trunk. Today she wears one of her flowing batik shifts in a startling pattern of yellow, green, and black with a matching scarf wrapped like a turban around her head, which makes her appear even taller. Although Son keeps himself in good shape, Etta would be the last person I'd want to push out of my way, if I were him.

I have to make a snap decision before the police get here. I cut my eyes from Etta to Son to Helen Murray before taking a step forward to address Etta.

"Would you call the police back and tell them not to come, that I have the situation under control?" Etta opens her mouth to protest, but I hold up a hand. "And could you show Mr. Rodgers into my office? He'll wait there until this session is finished." Without glancing Son's way, I add, "At that time I'll give him five minutes to explain himself."

I've called Son's bluff, and he hesitates as he returns my stare. Finally he shrugs elaborately, and instead of waiting for Etta to escort him, he stomps out of the room and heads down the hall toward my office, yanking the door open.

I lean in close and say quietly to Etta, "Check on him. Make sure the door stays open, okay?"

"I'm not sure this is a good idea," Etta mutters. I know she wants to say more but won't in front of a client. She hesitates before leaving but at last turns and follows Son to my office. She let him fool her once; he won't pull anything on her again, if I know Etta.

After I finish the session and Helen Murray leaves, more composed now in spite of the disturbance, I take a deep breath and walk down the hall to my office, wondering if Son stayed after all. The answer's obvious when I see Etta standing guard outside the door. I suppress a smile. She's not happy about my seeing Son, I can tell, but she leaves without protest. Taking a deep breath, I go into my office, where Son is pacing the floor.

As soon as I enter, he walks over without a word and slams the door shut. I experience a slight shiver of fear but brush it off. I am not afraid of him. He's dramatic and volatile and impulsive, but he's not dangerous. In spite of his display of anger, I know Son too well to think he'd harm me. He's never touched Dory or the kids; if anything, it's the other way around. A couple of times Dory's gotten so frustrated with him that she's lost her cool, rare for her. Once she clobbered him with a hard loaf of French bread, swinging it like a baseball bat. And we still laugh about the time she flung a book at him and almost knocked him out, because it was her book on Zen meditation that he'd made fun of once too often. On neither occasion did he fight back or go after her. Although Son and I have always clashed, we go too far back for me to fear him.

I fold my arms and say, "All right, Son. You have exactly five minutes to tell me what's going on with Dory."

My calmness seems to infuriate him even more. "You think you're hot shit, don't you?" Again the sneer on his face, the blue blaze of his eyes. "You think you've got *all* the answers."

"Yeah, I do. Now that we've established that, let me repeat myself: You've got five minutes to tell me why you're acting like a bigger fool than usual. You come bursting in like a maniac; you scare one of my clients; then you almost get arrested by the police or punched out by Etta. Whom I wouldn't mess with if I were you, by the way. You'll be lucky if she lets you leave here without knocking your block off. She takes pride in protecting me and my clients, and she's not happy that you slipped past her."

Son waves his hand in the air as though brushing aside a buzzing fly. "Etta Young knows where her bread is buttered. I'm the one who got R.J. his job at the Ford dealership, in case you've forgotten. She won't push me too far."

"What an important man you are, *Andrew*." It's an old barb, and I experience a surge of satisfaction when he flushes. As a child, Andrew Jackson Rodgers, Jr., was nicknamed Son by his indulgent family. But I've always teased him, saying he couldn't have a better namesake than the ruthless Andrew Jackson, who's known in these parts for his heartless treatment and displacement of the area's Native American tribes.

As we glare at each other, it hits me that I've fallen back into an old pattern established by Son and me soon after I married Mack. I'm most likely the only female Son Rodgers hasn't been able to win over by soulful looks from those soft blue eyes, or to charm with his winsome boyishness. His family's position in this state, his wealth and privilege, his shocking good looks and smooth charm, all those things have always bought him everything he's ever wanted, won over everyone he's encountered, including Dory. That I'm not impressed has always bewildered him. A man used to being fawned over by women, Son is both puzzled and threatened when he encounters anyone who's indifferent to his charms. Our mutual animosity comes out in different ways, hidden in various guises, but it's always present. This time it's about Dory. Or maybe, I realize with a shock of understanding, it always has been. Either Dory or Mack, whom both of us loved, and neither wanted the other to have.

"I've got no argument with Etta," Son snaps impatiently. "My beef is with you."

"Then spit it out. Before you do, please know that normally I'd never reward such preposterous behavior. The only reason I'm hearing you out instead of having the police haul you off—"

He interrupts, pretending to wring his hands in fear. "Yeah, right, I'm shaking in my boots. In case you've forgotten, the sheriff is married to a cousin of mine. One of his deputies played baseball with Mack at Bama, and the other lives in one of my houses rent-free. My contribution to law and order in our lovely city."

Ignoring his interruption, I continue, raising my voice. "The only reason I'm doing this is for Dory. I have no doubt you've got the whole police department in your pocket, Mr. Big Shot, but they'd have no choice except to haul you out of here, regardless of who you are. As much as I'd love to see you embarrassed—and God, how I'd love it!—you've put Dory through enough. More than enough. And you pulled one over on me, didn't you? You said that about her having another breakdown because it was a sure way to make me hear you out."

"Of course, Clare. Whatever you say, Clare. You're always right, aren't you, Clare?" When I start toward the door to open it and push him out if I have to, he stops me. "Wait! I wasn't lying about Dory. She got all upset after seeing you Saturday, and that night she had another of those crying episodes. Okay, maybe it wasn't a breakdown, but it still scared me. Strange, isn't it, that everything was going great until she saw *you,* and now she's upset and confused again?"

"I'm sorry to hear about her having a bad time. But to say *I'm* the one who upset her is ludicrous, as you well know—"

"She was so happy on our trip, and doing so well! She comes back here *one* time, and she's all torn up again." He waves his hands high, and I take a step backward. "You claim you want the best for her. Huh! That's a bunch of crap. Being with me is what's best for her. She was so miserable when we separated that she went to pieces."

"No. She went to pieces because of all the trauma you'd put her through previous to that. Tell me the real reason you and Dory separated. I want to hear you say it."

To my surprise, both guilt and sorrow cloud Son's expression, but he quickly recovers. "I admit that I behaved like an idiot last year. I thought it'd finally be just me and Dory, and I didn't handle it well when she had a different idea of how she'd spend her time."

"That's putting it mildly. You were constantly in her face, demanding her attention and pouting when you didn't get it. You made last year a nightmare for her."

"All right, I'll admit it. I acted the fool, and I drank too much. Is that what you want to hear? Do you feel better now?"

"Acted the fool and drank too much?" I echo in disbelief. "What's missing? What part of the story are you leaving out?"

He says in a petulant voice, "You know damn well what it is. You just want me to say it, don't you? It's what I did to her workshop, okay? It was wrong of me, but I can't undo it now. I did all I could to make it up to her. I apologized, I sent her notes and flowers and—"

"Ha. Ironic that you'd send flowers to make up for trashing the workshop where Dory works on her garden stuff, isn't it?"

Son hangs his head and shuffles his feet before saying softly, "I was a goddamn idiot to touch that place, as much as she loves it, and I still don't know what made me do it. Sure, I was drunk, but I've been drunk plenty of times and never done anything like that. I'll regret it till the day I die."

I study him. This remorse is the closest thing to humility that I've seen in Son, and it takes me a minute to process it. "At least you're no longer blaming it on being drunk. Drinking was no excuse for your despicable behavior, nor did it explain your going into a jealous rage. But you haven't admitted that part of it, have you? Have you asked yourself why you trashed Dory's workshop rather than, say, the gardens she spends so much time on? Why not take a weed-eater or sling blade to the plants and flowers she loves so much?" When he flushes darkly, I move in for the kill. "Wasn't it also about your jealousy of Rye?"

He shakes his head and snorts. "My jealousy of *Rye*? If that's your theory, it's beyond stupid."

"Oh, really? It was a sheer coincidence, then, that you tore up her workshop the very night that Dory met with Rye about starting her business?"

Son's gaze is unwavering and cocksure. "You think I'm jealous of Rye Ballenger? Bullshit. Ever since we were kids, he's panted after Dory like a dog in heat."

"How like you to put it so crudely. I'm sure you prefer not to remember that Rye fell in love with Dory that summer you spent at Bama, making up all the courses you failed by partying so much your freshman year." I don't add that I suspect Rye's still in love with Dory, though he pretends otherwise. I've always thought he'd be quick to admit it if Son were out of the picture.

"Maybe so, but he sure hauled ass when she made it clear she preferred me to a wimp like him, didn't he?" Son says with disdain. "I'm not jealous of him or any other man, so you can forget that. But I've admitted to Dory that I was jealous of her time. I didn't want her starting a business, and I did everything I could to stop her."

That admission is so much more than I expected that I'm quick to agree. "You certainly did."

Son stares at me, long and hard. "I've made some mistakes this past year. Okay, I made a *lot* of mistakes, then my tantrum disgusted Dory so much that she threw me out. Is that what you want me to say? But Dory is willing to forgive me. She loves me in spite of my faults and always has. The problem is, she loves you, too. She values your opinion way the hell too much and always has. I've never thought it was good, the way she keeps running to you about everything."

"I don't care what you think. Dory's my best friend, and any time she asks for my advice, I'll give it to her. If you don't like it, too bad. As for her well-being, these prolonged crying jags aren't good for her or anyone. They're brought on by too much stress."

Although Son's anger has dissipated, his hostility hasn't, and he stares at me balefully. "If it hadn't been for Father Gibbs, it would've been even worse."

"You called Father Gibbs?" I ask in surprise.

Son shakes his head as he runs his fingers through his curly hair. "Of course not. Father Gibbs came home with me after church yesterday to talk with us about the renewal ceremony." He glances at me sideways, but I won't give him the satisfaction of reacting.

"When Dory told Father Gibbs that she wanted you to stand up with her, like you did at our wedding—"

"And like she did at mine and Mack's," I murmur.

He goes on as though I haven't spoken. Son rarely mentions Mack; he's never dealt with the shock and grief of Mack's tragic accident. "Dory told Father Gibbs that she didn't think you'd do it, and he said he'd talk to you."

"That won't be necessary," I snap. "I don't need him sticking his nose into something that's between me and Dory."

Yet again Son continues as though he hasn't heard me. "Father Gibbs asked if he could talk with Dory alone, so I went out to play golf. When I got home, he'd helped her feel better, and they had made plans for the renewal ceremony, which was his suggestion in the first place."

On hearing this, I struggle to keep my face expressionless. When Dory told me yesterday that the ceremony was Son's idea, I was skeptical, since Son's not imaginative enough to come up with something like that. I figured someone was behind it but couldn't think who it might be. Why hadn't I thought of Father Gibbs? After all, Son is one of St. John's biggest contributors, as well as being head of the vestry and no telling what else. Considering all the therapy sessions I've conducted with the parishioners of well-meaning but blundering pastors or priests, women torn apart by guilt and the notion that God demands they keep their families together regardless of the cost, it should've been obvious to me that Father Gibbs was behind it.

Son startles me out of my thoughts by saying in an awed voice, "When I told Father Gibbs about the night me and Dory got back together, he said it was definitely a sign from God."

Again I don't reveal what I'm thinking, that I suspect Son contrived it somehow. If nothing else, he's using it to his advantage. "Dory told me that was the night she thought she'd had a nervous breakdown. Those kinds of episodes can be quite scary, but it wasn't a breakdown."

He glares at me. "You weren't there, so how do you know?"

"It's my business to know," I snap. "Dory had a particularly bad episode of grief and loneliness, which is common during a separation, but nothing like a psychotic breakdown. I'm going to urge her to see a counselor." I let the last part slip; I tried to get Dory to someone all last year, with no success, because she prefers less orthodox methods, all her meditating and other malarky.

With his scorn for both me and my occupation, I figure Son will pounce on that notion, but he surprises me one more time. "I promised myself that if Dory took me back, I'd see somebody who can help me get my head on straight, and I'm going next week. Maybe I can get Dory to come, too." I don't dare ask who he's seeing. He adds, "I'm determined to show her that I'm a changed man."

"Oh, really? You could've fooled me."

Son falls quiet as he regards me. Finally he says, "You might hate me, Clare, but Dory doesn't. She loves me as much now as she ever did. Always has, always will."

"Of course I don't hate you." We're back to where we were when he came bursting in to disrupt my day. Same old, same old. "After the way you behaved, I thought Dory did the only thing she could, leaving you. I've said it to her, I've said it to you, and I've said it to your kids. And I hoped she'd give herself enough time to see if that's what she really wanted. When she didn't, I wasn't happy about it, I'll admit. But I'll support her decision to take you back, whether I agree with it or not."

Instead of being pleased, he makes a face. "You know how to make it sound that way, don't you, with all your highfalutin psychobabble! But it's what you *do* that counts. Saying you'll support Dory is one thing, and doing it something else. Well, you have a chance to show it. Stand up with Dory at our church ceremony.

That will be the statement she's looking for from you. If you love Dory like you claim, then you'll do it for her."

I take a trembling breath, determined not to let Son stare me down. "I'll discuss that with Dory," I say tightly, "but not with you or Father Gibbs or anyone else. That's something for Dory and me to work out. And now your five minutes are up, and you need to leave. We've said all that can be said. Both of us know that whatever it is between the two of us will never be resolved, don't we?"

He looks taken aback. He knows that I'm talking about more than Dory. Although neither of us has brought up Mack except indirectly, his presence is between us and always will be. Son might forgive me for Dory but never for Mack. Almost five years later, Mack is still the unquiet specter who refuses to stay in his grave, to allow us to exorcise his ghost and get on with our lives. No matter where we go or what we're doing, none of us who loved him will ever be free of him. Like a tenant who vacates a house but leaves his possessions behind, Mack left us with too much of what once belonged to him.

After Son leaves, his anger tamped down but not dissipated, with nothing really resolved between us, I have to endure Etta's looks of disapproval until she forgives me for letting Son disrupt our morning. She's right, of course. I should have let Son's cousin-in-law and his freeloading renter haul him off to jail instead of trying to be the appeaser, the together, above-it-all mediator with all the answers. My face burns when I wonder with a shock if that was indeed what I was doing, if I've fallen into that old trap again. Son has always given me the impression that he didn't consider me good enough for Mack or worthy of taking the prestigious Ballenger name as my own. After all these years, am I still trying to prove him wrong? The thought disgusts me, but if I've learned anything as a therapist, it's that an unpleasantry about yourself can't be dealt with until it's acknowledged. Name it, and it's yours.

"Half an hour before your next appointment," Etta informs me briskly, coming into my office. Then she softens and puts an arm around my shoulder. "Sit down, Clare, and let me bring you a cup of tea."

I don't argue with her. I sink into the chair at my desk and say weakly, "Oh, Etta, what would I do without you?"

Relenting, she smiles her warm, forgiving smile. "That's something you're not gonna find out anytime soon, I promise you. Now, kick off those shoes and put your feet up. I'll be right back with the tea."

Shamelessly, I let Etta wait on me, brew me a cup of tea, but she doesn't ask what's going on, nor why Son Rodgers came here raving like a lunatic. The truth is, Etta knows more than anyone, even me, about what really goes on behind the pretty facades of the households around here, what happens when the bedroom door is closed and the lights go out. But she never asks questions or makes judgments, even when clients have to be let in the back door, eyes swollen shut from crying or faces too bruised to be seen by others. I give her a grateful little wave when she slips out the door, leaving me to savor the cup of tea, pale with milk and sweet with honey.

❧

My unlikely friendship with Dory Rodgers began almost thirty years ago, the second semester of our freshman year at the University of Alabama. Looking back, I can understand why Dory thinks of destiny, or fate, as such a determining factor in all of our lives. Unlike her, I've always been practical, down-to-earth, and of a scientific mind-set, not especially interested in the unknown or prone to give much credence to the unexplained. Still, considering how our friendship came about, I can see why she insists that fate brought us together. According to her theory, it takes only a small, insignificant thing to change the entire course of one's life. Maybe she's right; that Dory and I ended up in the same Chemistry 102 class was a coincidence all by itself. Although I was enrolled in the scholastic honors program, I couldn't schedule an honors chemistry class, and I had a choice between taking the only one available that semester or waiting until the next year for the one I was supposed to take. What if I'd decided to wait? But I was a psychology major, eager to get into some meatier courses on a subject I'd become fascinated with while taking a basic psychology course as a high school senior. So I unwittingly signed up for the same course Dory was in.

Even that fortuitous happening wouldn't have necessarily thrown Dory and me together, since the class was held in an auditorium with more than a hundred students. Another twist of fate worked in our favor: During those days, freshmen at UA were often assigned to study groups, and I found myself, Clare Skidmore, assigned to a group with others whose last names also ended in S. With no notion, of course, that destiny was at work, I picked up my assignment sheet with annoyance. For students like me, the study groups were a waste of time, but I was such an uptight little rule-follower that it never would have occurred to me not to attend, unlike most students in the class. Sure enough, at the group's first meeting, a girl named Isadora Shaw and I were the only ones to show up. Otherwise, I can't imagine how I ever would have met Dory, or Son, or Mack.

The previous semester that I'd spent at UA was my first time away from home, and I'd been lonely and scared, overwhelmed by the vast campus and hordes of milling students. I shared a cramped dorm room with a quiet, studious girl who was nice enough but stuck with her own group of friends and left me alone. Although I hung out with students I'd met in various classes, I wasn't really close to any of them. I spent my time either studying or engaging in my favorite pastime, people watching. Like a scientist researching a strange and fascinating new species, I amused myself by analyzing the various types of students on campus, a hobby that would later come in handy in my profession. At the University of Alabama in the mid-1970s, the class system was as rigid as that of Victorian England, and each entity tended to stick closely to its own kind. I spent hours observing the rowdy fraternity boys and beautiful sorority girls; the Neanderthal jocks; the flamboyant yet aloof theater people; the weird art majors; and the serious science students. The group I fit most closely into, which I fondly called intellectuals, would one day be given the unflattering label of nerds or geeks.

When Dory and I met in the assigned cubicle of the science library that first night and smiled at each other in greeting, I tried not to look too surprised, or too pleased, either. Of all the students in my chemistry class, Isadora Shaw, seated a row down from me, was the one who'd fallen under my microscope because she both mystified and intrigued me. As my eyes roamed over the classroom searching for my next specimen to analyze, they landed on her because she didn't fit any of my classifications. She doodled in her notebook, or crossed her long, shapely legs restlessly, or sighed in boredom, and I observed her curiously. I couldn't figure out where she belonged or what made her so different from the other students. To my delight, our first study session provided the opportunity to observe her up close and personal.

For one thing, Dory Shaw didn't look like the rest of us. Though she was one of the most exquisite girls I'd seen on a campus famed far and wide for its beauties, even her kind of beauty was unusual. With her fluid grace and the long fawn-brown hair falling like a silken curtain down her back, Dory moved as though suspended in moonbeams. Almost all the girls on campus, including me, either ironed our hair or tortured it into hot rollers to style the hairdos of our day, but not Dory. Her look was as natural as sunlight. She didn't dress like other coeds, either. Even I, who knew or cared nothing about fashion, spent a lot of time studying others before purchasing my meager wardrobe, not wanting to be seen in anything that would set me apart from my peers. It was obvious Dory had no such qualms. One day I stared in amazement when she showed up in class wearing Chinese pajamas of a deep garnet silk, stunning with her flawless ivory skin. Another time she swept in decked out in a vintage dress of the sheerest lawn, worn with lace-up granny boots that must've come from an antique store. But what made her stand out was not her beauty or style; it was the incredible smile that lit up her face and made her kitten eyes glow golden. Neither before nor afterward have I met anyone with a sweeter smile than Dory Shaw.

The dreaded study sessions proved to be the bright spot in my lonely week, and I discovered that Dory Shaw was not merely an interesting specimen for my observation, she was warm, lighthearted, and funny. Although a bright student with decent grades, she was so baffled by chemistry that she'd barely passed the first semester and was terrified of failing the much more difficult 102. It constantly amazed her that I got it. Once she realized that I was good at explaining complex principles she thought were beyond her comprehension, she latched on to me and wouldn't let go. "I feel *so* much better now that I've met you, Clare!" she said after our first night spent in the stuffy study cubicle going over the properties of elements. "If we keep on studying together, I might even make a good grade in this course."

Once I assured her I'd continue attending our study sessions (in truth, I wouldn't have missed them), she suggested we go to the Krispy Kreme for a cup of coffee. Licking our fingers as we devoured donuts hot from the oven, Dory and I sat in a booth and talked for hours. She indulged my obvious curiosity about her with good humor, flattered that I found her life so intriguing. She thought it neat that I planned on becoming a therapist one day, and claimed she was making her contribution to science by allowing me to practice my skills on her. I was as thrilled to find myself spending time with her as an archaeologist might be, uncovering a hidden world.

There was a lot in Dory Shaw's habitat to intrigue me. Because of her self-assurance and exquisite looks, I wasn't surprised to hear that she was a "Brookie," what Alabamians called the residents of Mountain Brook, the oldest and wealthiest suburb of Birmingham. But I never would have pegged Dory as a sorority girl. With a shrug, she admitted it was a good thing she found life in the sorority house tolerable, since she was a legacy. "It was simple. If I pledged my mama's sorority, all expenses would be paid to dear old Bama," she explained. "If I didn't, I'd be flipping burgers to put myself through school." When she described some of the strange and archaic rituals and conventions of sorority and fraternity life, I had a glimpse of a world I wouldn't have seen otherwise. I was astonished to learn that she was a home economics major, yet another way she refused to fit any of my classifications. "But . . . I thought home ec majors were prissy!" I blurted out, and Dory scoffed. My passion was the studying and analyzing of others; hers was flowers, plants, and gardening, an interest instilled in her as a child by her beloved grandmother. Since her science skills weren't strong enough for a major in horticulture or landscape architecture, home ec, with its gardening component, was the best she could do.

After a couple of our late-night sessions at the Krispy Kreme, Dory and I got around to discussing guys. Although I'd had the usual crushes, I'd never really been in love, but Dory was and had been for as long as she could remember. She was pinned to her childhood sweetheart, a junior named Son Rodgers. They were already planning their wedding, a few weeks after her graduation, her future all mapped out. Both of their well-to-do families had vacation homes in Fairhope, on the Eastern Shore of Mobile Bay, where they "summered." She and Son liked the area so much they'd decided to live in Fairhope after their wedding.

"Is it a part of the Redneck Riviera?" I inquired. Born and raised in Panama City, Florida, I didn't know a lot about Alabama, even though my maternal grandparents lived in the northern part of the state. I'd ended up going to college in Tuscaloosa because my high grades and SAT score earned me an academic scholarship. Unlike Dory's, my family background was strictly working-class and blue-collar. While some of my classmates thought that being raised in a resort town like Panama City was an exotic and endless romp in the sun, I knew better. My parents worked long, tiring hours in the seafood joint they owned and operated downtown, where I spent my sunny summer days running the cash register. For all we saw of the famed Gulf of Mexico, we might as well have lived in Podunk, Kansas.

Dory's and my lifelong friendship began during those hours spent at the Krispy Kreme following our study sessions; we talked and laughed and drank coffee until closing time. We'd leave the Krispy Kreme and stroll across the moonlit campus, still talking, until Dory had to sneak into the sorority house and me the dorm because we'd lost track of time and stayed out past the freshman curfew. Spending so much time with her, I was bound to meet her boyfriend, Son Rodgers. And it was just as inevitable that his best friend, Mack—Macomber Hayden Ballenger III—would be with him.

I'd heard almost as much about Mack Ballenger from Dory as I had about Son, since the three of them were close friends from their summers together in Fairhope. Dory told me that Mack was not a summer person but was fortunate enough to live in Fairhope, on the bay next to the Rodgerses' summer home. I listened wide-eyed when she described the Ballenger house, which she claimed was a big old Victorian mansion full of secrets and skeletons and all sorts of delicious Southern Gothic intrigue. Of course I was fascinated, but when I pressed for details, she was pretty hazy, saying Mack never talked about his family, like most guys. She knew that his parents had divorced when he was only two years old, and his father had married another woman, rumored to be his mistress, right afterward. Even though his real mother was nearby, Mack lived with his father and stepmother and rarely saw his mother, an unusual arrangement in those days. But Dory wasn't sure why, except it had something to do with his mother being "weird," an old hippie or something, who had given up her only child to live in the swamps and raise birds. That was the official Ballenger version; it would be years before Dory and I would hear the truth from Zoe Catherine herself.

Dory confessed that as a little girl, she'd had a crush on both Mack and Son, although she begged me not to tell Son, who was the jealous type. As a teenager, she said, she'd settled on Son after having a kissing contest between the two boys. I'd laughed and asked if that meant Son was a better kisser than Mack.

"Noooo, it wasn't that," she replied, eyes bright with remembrance. "Mack's plenty hot. You'll see when you meet him. But even at the tender age of fourteen, I had better sense than to fall for someone like Mack Ballenger. He scared the daylights out of me."

Scared her? Aghast, I asked what that meant. Did he torture small animals or pull the wings off flies or something? Dory threw back her head and laughed her infectious, bubbling laugh, which always made me laugh, too. "No wonder you're a psychology major!" she said before assuring me that Mack was actually much nicer and sweeter than Son was. Pressed to explain her fear of him, she thought about it a long time before saying, "Mack is one of those guys you could lose your heart to and never get it back. You know what I mean?"

I didn't, but little did I know that I was soon to find out. As an overly serious girl more interested in books and my studies than going out, I'd dated little in high school and not at all so far at Bama, so I had no experience with boys like Mack or Son. Then Dory said something that I've never forgotten. Later, I was to reflect on her comment and realize that it is not always how we feel about another person that's significant; more often it's how they make us feel about ourselves.

"Son may be dumb as dirt," she told me, completely serious, "but he's good-looking, funny, and sexy. Most of all, he seems to adore me, and shallow as it sounds, I've found that I adore being adored."

And then one night in April, when everything green was exploding into flower, and the air had turned as soft and sweet and fragrant as a newly mowed field, Mack Ballenger appeared and turned my orderly life upside down. Dory and I were heading toward the Krispy Kreme after our study session when she casually remarked that Son and Mack were going to stop by later on. She'd talked about me so much, she said, that both of them were just *dying* to meet me. Although I doubted it, I was more intrigued than I let on. An hour later, when they walked in the door and headed toward our booth, I recognized them immediately by the many vivid descriptions I'd cajoled from her. The grinning, curly-haired Son was even better-looking than Dory had described him, and watching him walk our way, I understood why she was so taken with him. If you were looking for a boy toy, she'd found the perfect candidate.

But Mack Ballenger—he was a different matter altogether, and I couldn't imagine how anyone, especially a girl as sharp as Dory, could've chosen the brash, brawny Son over someone like Mack. With his classic looks and elegance, Mack appeared to have stepped out of the pages of an F. Scott Fitzgerald novel. He even looked like the photograph of the delicate-featured author on the back cover of *The Great Gatsby*, a book I'd just discovered in my American lit class. Later, I was to realize that I'd fallen in love with Mack the moment our eyes met, but I didn't have enough sense or experience to know it at the time. All I knew was, something happened that threw me off course like a small planet hit by a massive meteorite.

At first I was nervous and self-conscious, but both Son and Mack were so gracious to me that I relaxed and enjoyed the evening. Originally Son was all charm, his way with every woman he met, and his flattery had me laughing and blushing at the same time. Mack, too, was funny and captivating and quite attentive to me. I was perfectly content to admire him from afar, though, and not dream beyond that. In the past, I'd tried to pass off my social awkwardness as a sort of intellectual aloofness, but the truth was, I had no idea how to go about winning over someone like Mack. I considered myself a plain Jane, having no idea how to dress or apply makeup or make the most of my best features, the heavy caramel-blond hair that fell in unruly waves around my face, or the brownish eyes that could turn to amber in the right light. Inexperienced as I was, I was way out of my element with Mack, who had celebrity status as a star pitcher for Bama's baseball team. That in itself would have made him a magnet for every girl on campus, but Mack—with his easy elegance and long, lean-muscled body, his fair hair and dreamy gray eyes—proved to be as sweet and sensitive as Dory had said. If only he'd been as cocky as Son, I would've come away with my heart intact.

As the night went on, Mack surprised Dory and Son—but most of all, me—with his apparent interest in me, and later, with his relentless pursuit. Sitting across from me in the booth over coffee and donuts, Mack ignored his closest friends in order to engage me in long, intense conversations. His silver eyes, glowing like the fire of opals, never left me. But Mack wasn't the only one staring. Son,

under the mistaken impression that I was so wide-eyed and innocent that I'd be malleable and easily influenced by him, beamed at
me, winking knowingly whenever I happened to meet his eye. The
irony would come when I realized how he'd been such an ally at
first and encouraged Mack's interest in me. Dory, on the other
hand, watched me nervously, chewing a fingernail. Finally she could
stand it no longer, and she dragged me off to the restroom. Pushing me inside, she whispered, "You and Mack are scaring me, Clare!
Don't go falling for him, you hear? Don't you remember what I told
you about him? He's a heartache waiting to happen."

I brushed her concerns aside, saying there was no way he could be
interested in me, but Dory shook her head. "I've never seen him look
at anyone like he's looking at you, and I've known him all my life,"
she said. "Christ, I feel so guilty! He'll end up breaking your innocent little heart, and it will be my fault for introducing him to you."

Dory was soon to forget about me and Mack, though. It wasn't
long before she and Son were entwined, unable to keep their hands
off each other. The eroticism they gave off was like another presence at the booth, and I stole fascinated glances their way, unable to
help myself. When I caught Mack regarding me with amusement,
I colored hotly. Smiling, he inclined his head toward the door and
said, "Come on, Clare. I don't think the lovebirds will miss us."

It was Mack who walked me home that night, rather than Dory.
With his hands thrust in the pockets of his jeans as we strolled
across campus, he talked as freely and easily with me as if we'd been
friends all our lives, like he and Dory. And a strange thing happened to me when I was with him. I forgot to be self-conscious and
nervous, and I found myself laughing breezily, countering his light
banter with clever, witty comebacks I had no idea I was capable of.
He and I sat in the moon shadows of a tree near my dorm and
talked for hours. Even though I tried to go in several times, he
begged me to stay, his shining eyes intense as he took my trembling
hand in his and held on tight. In spite of all that, when I at last

reached the safety of my room, I convinced myself that this couldn't be happening. Surely I had better sense than to imagine—to hope against hope—that someone like Mack could be attracted to a nobody like me. I refused to let myself relive how I felt when I was with him because I knew I was in for a huge disappointment if I did. Drifting into a troubled sleep, I told myself that I was *not* going to fall in love with him. I couldn't! Dory was right: If I were foolish enough to do such a thing, then I'd deserve the heartache that was sure to follow.

When Mack stopped by my dorm the next day to ask if I'd like to come to ball practice with him, I turned my head so he couldn't see my face light up, and I prayed he didn't notice that my knees had turned to water. "Oh, I just *love* baseball!" I gushed foolishly. The truth was, I knew nothing about baseball or any other sport, which made me even more of an oddity on a campus where sports were more like a religion than a pastime. I had no way of knowing then that what happened at ball practice that day would be what sealed Mack's and my fate.

At the ballpark, I sat in the bleachers and watched the field intently in an attempt to figure out what was taking place out there. What was taking place *off* the field became much more obvious, and I kept my eyes straight ahead, mortified. Since Mack and I had arrived late, everyone had watched us enter. The girlfriends of the players huddled in one section of the bleachers, laughing and gossiping. I'd been too shy to join them, so I sat apart but within earshot, unfortunately. As soon as I sat down, a buzzing erupted from the group.

"Well, well," I heard someone say. "Mack's got a new one today." After much whispering, another voice reached my burning ears. "Think he's just trying to make Amy jealous?" More giggles and whispers, then I heard, "What else could he possibly see in *her*?" They stopped their whispering long enough to yell and clap when their boyfriends appeared on the field, then bent their heads together to continue their careless chatter. Finally I couldn't stand it any longer and, trying to be nonchalant, glanced their way casually, hoping for a friendly face. Instead, several pairs of eyes glared at me malevolently, though I had no idea what I'd done. Evidently it was that I'd invaded their territory, unwelcome and uninvited. During my brief glance, I was sure I recognized some of the girls from Dory's sorority. As I turned my head away from them, it struck me anew how strange it was that Dory had befriended me, and I felt a surge of affection for her. The barriers between us were as obvious as the chain-link fence around the ball field and as impregnable as the distance between me and the gaggle of giggling girls who sat behind me.

I tried to put them out of my mind as I watched Mack on the field, his graceful pitching movements as finely choreographed as the steps of a ballet, which brought a chorus of wistful sighs from the girls behind me. What was I thinking, being here with him? Dory had been right to be alarmed last night, and the gossiping girls were right, too—I didn't belong. I was way, way out of my element. If I had any sense, I'd get away while I still could, before I fell any harder for Mack Ballenger than I already had. Although I could feel the stares of the girls like laser beams on my retreating back, I picked up my purse and made my way out of the ballpark. Not sure where I'd end up, I took off walking toward the setting sun.

Depending on how you interpret those things, whether you believe in destiny or not, my timing was either right on or terribly off. I'd gone first to my room, then the library. But I was too restless to sit still, so I began walking the campus again. I was wandering aimlessly, trying to figure out where I'd go, when a car pulled up to the curb nearest me and came to a squealing halt. Out of the corner of my eye, I saw that it was Mack in his snazzy little sports car. I'd just cleared the main campus and passed the bookstore, and I had a wild impulse to duck into it, hiding behind the towering shelves of books. Instead, I walked over to Mack's car with a sense of dread. All he said was "Get in, Clare. Please."

Neither of us said a word when he did a U-turn and headed back toward campus. I was too embarrassed that he'd caught me to even glance his way, though I did notice when I'd sheepishly crawled into the car that he was still in his baseball uniform. When he returned to the practice field and parked the car by the gate, I figured he was about to call me a coward and tell me to get myself right back into the stands. Instead, Mack eyed me warily, jiggling the car keys in his hand. Finally he asked, "Can I trust you to stay here while I shower? Or should I lock you in the car?"

I managed a small smile and a nod. "I'll be here."

"You swear?"

"I swear."

Again he didn't say anything when he returned and drove the car away from the field. It was that soft pearl-gray time when the sun has retired but dusk hasn't yet pulled up the covers of the night. After we passed campus, Mack turned the car down a tree-shadowed lane that led to the Black Warrior River. I stole a glance at him, but he was remote, unreadable. When he pulled the car into an isolated spot facing the river, he glanced my way for the first time since we'd left the field. "Mind if I let the top down?" he asked.

I nodded eagerly. "I'd love it."

"As much as you love baseball?" Mack smiled wryly as he pressed a button and the taut white top folded up like an accordion, opening up the opalescent night sky above us.

I shook my head. "That's not why I left." I had no intention of telling him the real reason, but I was ashamed of myself. He'd been nothing but nice to me, and I'd repaid him with rudeness.

"I know why you left." Mack regarded me, his face flushed and his eyes stormy as rain clouds. "When I went for you after practice, the catcher's girlfriend, one of the few decent ones in the bunch, took me aside and told me the others were being their usual bitchy selves, saying crap about you being there with me, and that you'd left. I'm really sorry about that. I wouldn't have had it happen to you for anything."

I looked down at my hands, picking at a ragged cuticle. "I know you wouldn't. It's not like me to be so sensitive. I just felt—" I stopped and shrugged, not looking his way. "Guess I felt out of place. But even so, I shouldn't have run off like that. It was silly of me. Not to mention rude and thoughtless."

I could feel his eyes on me. "Shit, I don't blame you. I probably would've done the same thing in your place. If we hadn't been so late, I'd have taken you up there to meet some of the nicer ones and made sure you felt comfortable before leaving you. I can only imagine how intimidating that bunch can be."

I shrugged again. "I think they were just upset because they thought that I was . . . uh . . . there to make your girlfriend jealous, maybe."

Mack was silent so long, I dared to glance over at him. "Ah," he said finally, nodding. "So that was what it was about, huh? Might've known."

I picked at the fingernail again, and Mack added gently, "I hope that's not what *you* thought. That I only took you to make another girl jealous."

"Oh, it doesn't matter," I said lightly. "I mean, even if you did, no harm done." I tried to give a carefree laugh, Dory-like, but it came out a pathetic little mewl.

"I wouldn't do that to you," he said solemnly, and I nodded, eyes lowered. After a long silence, Mack sighed and said wearily, "Okay, I didn't want to say anything, but I've been trying to break it off with a girl I've been seeing all semester. She's not taking it very well, and a lot of her friends were at practice today. So that's what it was about."

Who could blame her for not wanting to lose you, I thought, but to him I said, "Really, it's okay! You don't owe me any kind of explanation."

"Look at me, Clare," Mack said, and I raised my eyes to meet his, reluctantly. When our eyes locked, it was impossible for me to look away.

"I thought something happened between us last night," Mack said softly. "Something that's never happened to me before. All my life I've known I was looking for something, though I had no idea what. Last night I saw you, and suddenly it was clear. Oh, so that's it, I thought, and it was so obvious to me that I wasn't even surprised. I was"—he paused to struggle for the right word—"I was almost *relieved* to have found you, if that makes sense. And I thought that you felt the same way. But if it didn't happen for you, too—if I was wrong—then you need to tell me now. Before I get my stupid heart broken," he added with a crooked smile.

I stared at him in astonishment. Before he got *his* heart broken? I couldn't be hearing him right. "Clare?" he said, tilting his head to the side. Stunned, I moved toward him blindly and instinctively, my hands reaching for him like a drowning person might reach for a life preserver. Moving quickly, Mack pulled me close against him, and all he said was "Clare . . . oh, my God." With that, I was lost. The fears, the inhibitions, the uncertainties left me. Like the car top, they folded in on themselves, disappearing from my sight and allowing the crystal beauty of the night sky to shine down on us.

From that day on, Mack pulled me into the magic circle that he, Dory, and Son had formed, and he made sure I stayed there in spite of everything, all the odds against us. When Dory recovered from the initial shock of the two of us as a couple, she got caught up in the romantic but foolish notion that I could be Mack's salvation, conveniently forgetting her own warnings. Of course! she declared. She'd been wrong, and I was *perfect* for Mack, being so different from the shallow, frivolous girls he'd always had by the droves. She was convinced I was Mack's destiny, sent by the gods to save him from himself. I doomed myself by falling into the same trap. I was not the first woman to make the mistake of thinking she could save a man from his demons, but not many others failed as spectacularly as I did.

Chapter Six

❧ ❧ ❧ ❧ ❧

After my unsettling encounter with Son, the rest of my day feels fractured, as though a thunderstorm blew up in the middle of a cloudless day, bringing with it a chill wind and dark sky. I've been jumpy and unable to concentrate since Son left. Between clients, I called Dory and asked if I could come out and talk with her after work. I thought doing so would help settle me down, but it didn't. Even during a session, my mind kept wandering back to the past and the memories that Son's visit had stirred up. I made a mistake by talking to him first thing this morning, and I've been angry and exasperated with myself since. I thought I'd learned that the way you start a day usually determines how the rest of it goes. Stupid me, I allowed Son's outburst to poison everything, even the air I breathed. Or so it felt. The minute the last client goes, I can't wait to get out, and I leave early, rare for me. Etta's so tickled that I think she's going to shove me out the door before I can change my mind.

Outside Casa Loco, I pause to inhale a deep breath of the tangy air blowing in from the bay. My first thought is to go to the waterfront park and sit on one of the benches. The feel of the breeze on my face, as well as the calming influence of the wide expanse of Mobile Bay, will surely dissipate my tension. I used to go there often. I'd watch pelicans soar over the bay before they dropped down to float on the waves like small brown dinghies. Sometimes I'd take Abbie, and we'd bring along a sack of stale bread. She'd break off chunks and toss them high, then squeal with joy when the seagulls dove for them with their high-pitched calls of "Aahh, aahh!" Zoe Catherine taught Abbie the difference between their winter and summer plumage, and she's probably the only child on the beach who can point to a mottled brown gull and pronounce that it's not fully grown yet. *Abbie* . . . It hits me what I want to do this afternoon. I want, and need, to be with Haley and the kids. Recalling what day it is, I reverse my path, heading back toward town.

As soon as I push open the door of Mateer's, a blast of cold air from the air-conditioning hits me in the face like a splash of ice water. I spot Haley and Jasmine before they see me. Their table is in the back but in full view of the front door, where they can watch everyone who comes in and out. Mateer's is the equivalent of a village pub, *the* place to be if you want to observe the people of Fairhope and hear the latest talk. Every Monday afternoon from September to June, right after the faculty meeting at the elementary school where they teach, Haley and Jasmine can be found here, drinking margaritas or one of the martinis Mateer's is known for. They call it their mental-health break, saying if their principal weren't such a prick as to schedule faculty meetings on Mondays, they wouldn't have to spend so much on booze. This is their first one since school started. They don't see me because their heads are bent together as they whisper, giggling like two teenagers instead of a couple of respectable teachers approaching thirty. I pause a moment to relish the sight that still has the power to touch me: the contrast between my daughter, fair, flaxen-haired Haley, and Etta's youngest, Jasmine, with her ebony skin. Although the schools of North Florida were fully integrated by the time I entered junior high, there was still a chasm caused by the ugly years of segregation, so I had no black friends growing up. Haley and Jasmine have been as close as sisters since their preadolescent days.

When I get to their table, Haley jumps to her feet, her face lighting up. "I'm not believing it—look who's here!" For a moment her striking resemblance to Mack takes hold of me like a cold hand around my heart, and I stumble on a loose tile.

"Hey! You get started on a dirty martini early, Aunt Clare?" Jasmine cries, and I laugh with them.

"I wish," I say, hugging and kissing both young women before pulling up a chair and dropping my briefcase to the floor. I used to stop by on Monday afternoons and have a drink with them on a fairly regular basis. Matter of fact, even though we live within a few miles of each other and we've talked often on the phone, I haven't seen Haley in weeks. Between my demanding work schedule, Dory's problems with Son, and Lex's recuperation, there's been no time for lingering over dirty martinis—or any other kind, for that matter.

Haley motions for the waiter, and I order a glass of merlot, even though she and Jasmine boo and hiss, saying I should have a margarita instead. "Maybe I'll get my favorite person another one," Haley says, and Jasmine jerks her head up.

"Whoa, girl. That'll be your third, right?" she asks, and Haley grins.

"Who's counting?"

Both young women laugh, and I smile indulgently. When you're unwinding from the tensions of being closed up in a room of kindergarten kids all day, everything brings on high hilarity, especially the longer they stay and the more drinks they have.

"Just teasing, Mom," Haley says. "I limit myself to two and make them last as long as I can. Right, Jazz?"

Jasmine pretends to consider the question, and Haley pokes her playfully with an elbow before turning her attention to me. "Mom? Some of the teachers were asking me about a letter to the editor that appeared in Friday's paper. I hadn't seen it, so the librarian gave me her copy. I was furious about it! Did it hurt your feelings?"

I shrug. "A little. But things like that go with the territory."

"Mama was mad about it, too," Jasmine tells her. "She swears she's calling that old fool who sent it and giving him a piece of her mind. I told her that Haley and I would call him, too. Dumb redneck!"

I pat her arm but say firmly, "I talked to Etta and got her calmed down. I'm touched that all of you want to defend me, but trust me. The best thing to do is ignore it."

"Mom's probably right, Jazz," Haley says. "I'd love to find that Mr. Allen and spit in his face for saying shitty things about my mother. But if we do anything, it'll stir things up. If we don't, it'll die down."

I agree with a nod, then ask Haley, in an effort to change the subject, "Did Austin pick up the kids today, or did you leave them in after-school?"

She glances at her watch. "He's picking them up in a few minutes, believe it or not. Since Mr. Big got that promotion, he doesn't have time for anything but work. He's as bad as you, Mom. Everybody I know is a workaholic. Except me." She cuts her eyes over to Jasmine. "Well, and you, Jazz."

"So, how's it going with his new job now that school's started back?" I ask, taking a sip of my wine. At the beginning of the summer quarter, my son-in-law, Austin, was promoted to head of special services at the nearby community college where he's worked since he and Haley married. With her job as a kindergarten teacher and Austin's as a counselor in the learning lab, their budget has always been tight, so both are hoping the promotion will provide them with more necessities and even a few luxuries. The downside is, Haley worries that the long hours and extra responsibilities of Austin's job will be as much of an adjustment for her as for him. She says that she's gotten spoiled, having Austin around to help so much with the kids and domestic details. Fair or not, the major responsibilities of running a household often fall on the wife and mother, as she's about to find out.

"Oh, it's going full force." Haley gives me a tight smile, pushing a silky strand of hair behind her ear. "Already I can tell that things are going to be really different at the Jordans' humble abode."

"Austin's new hours will take some adjustment, but you'll do fine, wait and see."

"If not," Jasmine offers, "your mom's a shrink. She'll straighten all of you out. Right?"

With a laugh, I pat her arm fondly. "If not, I'll send Etta over to do the job instead."

"There's a scary thought," Jasmine says with a shudder. "Mama doesn't take any crap off anyone. She's always on my case."

"A mama's prerogative, my dear. I'm the same with Haley."

Haley shakes her head. "Not true. You've been the perfect mother from day one. The best thing that's happened in my life, without a doubt."

Startled, I blush and say lightly, "Goodness, sweetheart. I thought that honor belonged to Mr. Perfect."

Jasmine winks at me. "Ranking above Mr. Perfect! Now, that's something. You'd better be flattered."

"I'm not only flattered, I'm stunned," I agree. Haley takes a lot of teasing among her girlfriends for the way she dotes on her husband, even after several years of marriage and two children. She and Austin met in her first year of college, when she fell hard and fast for him and never dated anyone else, reminding me of how it had been with me and Mack. When she called to tell us that she'd found the perfect man, my first thought was: Uh-oh. On meeting this paragon, though, I had to admit she'd come close. Bright, handsome, and witty, Austin Jordan is also an idealist dedicated to helping students with learning disabilities. Although Haley joins her female colleagues in the popular sport of male-bashing, she's mainly talk.

"I never said Austin was perfect," Haley protests. "How could he be, considering his gender?"

Jasmine snorts. "Or the way I put it, he's got one, doesn't he?"

Haley's silver-gray eyes are soft as she regards me thoughtfully. "Okay, let me amend the perfect-mother pronouncement, then."

"Watch out," Jasmine says. "You're about to take a nosedive, Aunt Clare. Told you no one could compete with Mr. Perfect."

"I can't allow you to outrank Austin until we see more of you, Mom," Haley says with a frown. "Abbie misses her grams bad, and I haven't seen you in over a month."

"I know, I know." I sigh. "That's part of the reason I'm here. To see you—and Jasmine, of course." We raise our glasses, touch them, and smile at one another. "And to arrange a time to visit the kids. When I leave here, I'm going to Dory's, but I'd like to come by your house afterward, if that's okay. I know it's a school night, but I don't think I can wait till this weekend to see the kids. I'll read them a bedtime story and be on my way."

"They'll be thrilled to see you. I can't wait to tell them." Haley studies me over the salted rim of her margarita glass. "On top of everything else, you've been hard at work getting things lined up for the new retreat site, haven't you? Gramma Zoe told me that you and your Yankee boyfriend were at the Landing Saturday, planning for the remodeling. That's so exciting!"

Jasmine's dark eyes dance playfully. "I didn't even know you had a new boyfriend until Gramma Zoe told us. About time, and he's *cute*, too. I like big men, myself. More to love."

"You like any kind of man, girlfriend," Haley says dryly.

"You both know better than to listen to Zoe Catherine," I say. "I've told her and everyone else that nothing's going on with Lex and me."

Haley smiles mischievously, nudging Jasmine with her elbow. "Rye is going to be so jealous, Mom, you with a new boyfriend. Right, Jazz?"

"Oh, you two!" I put a hand over my eyes. "Don't start on poor Rye again, please."

Haley and Austin, and now Jasmine, have picked up where Mack left off, teasing me about Rye. All during our marriage, Mack insisted his cousin was in love with me. It didn't help that Rye never got around to marrying, in spite of being one of the most eligible bachelors in the area and having an endless string of beautiful girlfriends. I tried in vain to convince Mack that it wasn't me Rye was in love with, it was Dory, but Mack didn't believe it. After Mack died, Rye fell rather naturally into the role of my escort, so everyone assumed we'd end up together eventually.

Haley turns to Jasmine, eyes gleaming wickedly. "Hey, did I tell you about the time Austin and I dropped in on Mom late one night on our way home from the movies?"

"I hope you learned to knock next time," I tell her tartly.

"Oh, goody! I can't wait to hear this," Jasmine cries.

"Because Rye's car was parked out front, we knew Mom would still be up," Haley says with a chuckle. "So Austin and I go barging in and catch my *mother* and my dad's cousin in a compromising embrace! Austin said it's a good thing we weren't a few minutes later."

I look at Jasmine and shake my head in denial. "That's absolutely ridiculous, and Haley knows it. Rye was teaching me to tango."

"Tango, smango," Jasmine hoots. "Sounds to me like he was teaching you to shag."

The two of them laugh so loud that other patrons glance our way to see what's causing such hilarity. "Not funny," I say, pointing a finger at Jasmine. "I'm telling your mother on you, young lady."

"One thing you can say about Rye," Haley says, looking around but lowering her voice so as not to be heard by all of Fairhope, "at least he believes in keeping it in the family."

"Hey, you should marry him, Aunt Clare. You wouldn't even have to change your name," Jasmine adds.

Haley leans toward me. "But best of all, you've inspired a new joke for our book. Don't you think this makes the new one more appropriate, Jazz?"

"Oh, God," I say with a groan. "Why does hearing that make my blood run cold?"

As their contribution to the first divorce-recovery retreat I held, Haley and Jasmine made a booklet that they called "The Lighter Side of Divorce," xeroxing copies to give out to the participants. I'd been hesitant; even though it was cute and funny, I wasn't sure how the participants would react to it. I'd ended up putting the booklets in a basket with a sign inviting them to take one if and when they needed a touch of humor. I was stunned when the booklets were such a hit that Haley and Jasmine couldn't turn them out fast enough. Everybody wanted copies for their friends, and Haley and Jasmine were currently in discussion with a local press about publication. The booklet contained anecdotes and lists that Haley and Jasmine made up, in addition to the divorce jokes they were always adding.

Haley goes on, oblivious to my glare. "Listen to this one, Mom: 'If you get a divorce in Alabama, are you still cousins?'"

Their laugh is more subdued this time, but my face flushes when I notice several people glance our way again. I hiss at Haley, "People can hear us, and they'll know who we're talking about."

"You sound a little paranoid to me, Doctor," she replies.

"Oh, really? How many men in Fairhope are named Rye?"

She holds her hands up in resignation. "Okay, okay—I can always tell when I've pushed you too far. Besides, since you've got a new boyfriend, the one who shall remain unnamed is out of the picture anyway. Right?"

"Wrong on both counts, Miss Priss. I don't have a new boyfriend, and I still do things with you-know-who when I can. For my last mental health break, he took me dancing."

"Dancing or shagging?" Jasmine asks.

Try as I may, I'm unable to maintain my scowl, and I end up laughing with them. "Now you girls see why I haven't been here in so long."

Haley says, "Time to move on to other gossip—bet Mom hasn't heard about you and Tommy."

"How could she?" Jasmine snaps. "There's nothing to hear."

"Uh-oh, do I detect a love interest?" I ask.

"Ask Jazz how she knows your buddy Lex Yarbrough, Mom, and where she's seen him to know that he's cute." Haley takes a sip of her margarita, licks salt off her lips, then says, "Jazz has started spending a lot of time at the marina. She's decided she wants to buy a boat."

"A boat? Really, Jasmine? What kind of boat?" I'm surprised to hear this, since she's never been particularly interested in boating that I know of. Plus, like most teachers, she has a very limited budget.

Jasmine covers her eyes with her hands. "Don't listen to her."

"Oh, she doesn't care what kind of boat it is as long as she can keep it at the marina," Haley goes on. "Then she'll have an excuse to see Tommy. Not that she could miss him."

It takes me a minute to know who she's talking about, and I stare in surprise. "You don't mean Tommy McNair, do you?"

Haley nods, grinning, and Jasmine says, "Haley's gotten it in her head that I'm interested in Tommy, but it's not true. I just think he's nice, is all."

Haley's gray eyes sparkle. "Here's how it happened, Mom. A couple of weeks ago, Jasmine was at the waterfront, bar-hopping, and her car wouldn't crank. So Tommy McNair came out, and being a big old macho guy, he tried to fix it. Of course, it's such a piece of crap that he couldn't, so he ended up giving Jazz a ride to her apartment. Since then they've been talking on the phone a lot. Plus, Jazz suddenly develops an interest in boats and has gone by the marina several times, pretending she's thinking of buying one."

"They don't sell boats at the marina," I remind her.

"True, but they have all kinds docked there, and folks go to look at them, see which kind they like best, right?"

Jasmine pokes at her margarita with the straw. "Daddy's always wanted a boat. Maybe I'll win the lottery and buy him one. I can't help it that Tommy McNair works at the marina."

Haley looks pleased. "See! Told you, didn't I? Jasmine's got the hots for Tommy! Why else would she take such an interest in boats?"

"Didn't Tommy go to high school with y'all?" I remember him from various school functions, but as Haley said, he'd be hard to miss. He worked for the previous marina owner as a dockhand, and when Lex took over, he kept Tommy on. The only thing that concerned Lex was Tommy's weight, though it didn't affect his work as Lex had feared. Although a sweet-natured and overly polite young man, Tommy is so overweight that he's the brunt of jokes around town, with folks calling him Tommy the Ton of Fun, among other uncharitable things. I pray that isn't the basis of Jasmine's attraction to him. She's always struggled with her weight and has a really poor self-image as a result. Consequently, most of her boyfriends have been what Haley refers to as losers, but only when she's being charitable. When Jasmine was younger, Etta put her on every diet imaginable, even sending her to pricey summer camps for overweight teens that Jasmine called her fat camps. She'd lose weight for a while only to put it right back on, which would plunge her into depression and cause her to eat more. She's such a lovely girl, with her rich dark skin and almond-shaped eyes, but she sees herself as too heavy to be attractive, and it has impacted her whole life.

"Besides, I couldn't go out with Tommy McNair even if I wanted to," Jasmine tells us, tilting her glass to get out the last drops of her margarita. "Daddy wouldn't let me."

Haley laughs. "That's crazy. You're almost thirty years old. Your daddy doesn't tell you who you can go out with."

"You know how he is," she retorts. "He would have a fit if I dated a white guy."

"Jasmine," I say with a sharp intake of my breath. "That's ridiculous. I've known your daddy for years, and he's not a bigot."

"Oh, yes he is when it comes to me and my sisters. He's always told us that we'd better not even *think* about going out with white men. Claims it would cause us too much heartache."

I lean back in my chair and study her. "That's not bigotry, hon. That's just a father wanting to protect his beloved girls." The truth is, there's something to what Jasmine's saying. R.J.'s overprotectiveness has been lamented for years by Jasmine, her sisters, and Etta.

"Like only white guys cause heartaches." Haley tosses her head. "Gimme a break. All men do. It's in their genes. Get it?"

"I'm through with men, myself," Jasmine says with what sounds like genuine sadness. "Come on, Aunt Clare, admit it. Most of your clients come to you because the men in their lives turn out to be shits, right?"

"Ah, no, I wouldn't say that. Actually, I have quite a few male clients as well. And—"

Haley waves her hands to stop the conversation. "Hold that thought. You're not going to believe who just came in the door." Jasmine and I turn our heads, but Haley says in a lowered voice, "Don't look. She'll see us gaping at her."

"She?" I ask. "I was expecting none other than Tommy McNair."

"Naw, that door's not wide enough for Tommy," Haley says. Jasmine's and Haley's chairs are facing the door, while mine is turned so I can't see, and Jasmine leans forward to whisper, "Ohhh, you're going to love this, Aunt Clare!"

"Now you've got my curiosity up." Casually, I pick up my wineglass and turn around to motion for the waitress to bring me a refill. As I do, I see her, Elinor Eaton-Yarbrough. Elinor stands poised just inside the door, her cool blue eyes scanning the bar area. She's her usual stunning self, in an ivory silk blouse with ropes of pearls hanging from her neck, a pencil-slim skirt, and tall suede heels. Her blond hair is upswept in a French twist, and tiny diamond studs gleam in her ears.

"Where's the party?" Jasmine mutters, and I reply, "Oh, she always dresses like she's having tea with the queen of England."

"Wonder if she's meeting a lover?" Haley pronounces it with a fake accent, emphasizing the last syllable. Her face lights up, and she leans over to whisper, "Hey, I've got it, Mom, a way you can kill two birds with one stone. Fix her up with Rye."

"I wouldn't wish her on anyone," I say with a snort.

"Probably wouldn't work unless you can convince him that they're related somehow."

"Hayden Jordan, you should be ashamed of yourself! Ever since your dad died, Rye has tried to be like an uncle to you. He'd be hurt to hear you talking like that."

"Oh, Mom, you know I adore Rye. I just can't resist teasing you." Haley follows Elinor's progress with her eyes. "Aha. Now she's prissing her fanny over to that little table for two by the window. So she can spot her lover as he approaches, I guess. Don't turn your head, Mom, or she'll see you."

"I'm not, don't worry. But I've got to go in a minute. How am I supposed to get out of here without her seeing me?"

"You can't," Haley informs me. "Besides, you don't want to leave before you see who she's meeting, do you? Oh, look, she just took out her compact and put on more lipstick. Wonder if it's that stuff she sells in her store. Thirty-seven dollars a tube!"

"For lipstick?" Jasmine screeches. "Honey, I didn't spend that much on my last dress, and you know how much material that takes."

Grimacing, Haley motions for her to lower her voice. "Shhh! She's going to hear us." She hunches over like a spy in a movie and whispers, "She's purring like a cat with a bowl of cream, so I guess she just spotted him." I watch in surprise as both Haley and Jasmine gape. They turn to look at each other, eyes wide, then turn back to me. Sotto voce, Haley says, "Whatever you do, Mom, do *not* turn around."

Of course I can't resist, and I look just in time to see Elinor greet the man she's meeting, tilting her head prettily toward him. Like Haley and Jasmine, I'm surprised to see that it's Lex. He sits down heavily, his back to our table. It's obvious that he's just come from the marina, still in his khakis, Docksiders, and a windbreaker with the marina logo on it.

"See, told you that all men are pigs," Haley hisses. "Even old farts like him. That son of a bitch."

"Haley!" I say sharply. "Don't be absurd. As I tried to tell you, Lex and I are not romantically involved, so it's not like he's two-timing me or something."

"Huh. That's exactly what he's doing, sneaking around meeting his ex like that."

I laugh lightly. "Nonsense. First of all, nobody's sneaking around; they're sitting right there for all of Fairhope to see. And Lex has been very open about his efforts to be on better terms with his ex. I think it's good that he's speaking to her again."

"Looks to me like she's wanting him to do more than just speak," Jasmine says. "Got her skinny old white hand on his arm, and she's leaning way over, almost in his face. Probably trying to give him a look-see down her blouse. Like he ain't seen what she's got a million times."

I glance down at my watch. "My dears, this has been a riot, but I absolutely have to go."

"You can't!" Haley reaches for my arm to stop me. "No way you can get out of here without walking by their table."

I stand up, even though both of them motion frantically for me to sit back down. "It will not bother me one whit to walk up to them, say hello, then walk right out the door," I say, getting my purse. "Matter of fact, I have to. I'm going to Dory's while Son's at a vestry meeting, and I sure don't want to be there when he gets home."

"Is he behaving himself now?" Haley asks, frowning. "And more importantly, is Dory okay?"

I hesitate, then say, "She's doing well, but I'll tell you about it when I come by tonight, okay? I really have to go now."

"Wow, Aunt Clare!" Jasmine's face glows with admiration. "Are you actually going to walk over to your boyfriend while he's out with another woman and say hello? Takes a lot of guts. If it were me, I'd slip out the back door."

"Oh, well, Mom," Haley says with a wink. "There's always Rye, who's looking better all the time. At least he's family. And not a Yankee."

"On that note, I'm definitely leaving." Picking up my briefcase, I hug both young women and kiss their cheeks before turning to walk out. When I pause at the table by the window, Lex starts to get to his feet, but I motion for him to stay put.

"No need to get up. I've got to run but just wanted to say hello." Forcing a smile like the hypocrite I am, I tilt my head toward Elinor. "How are you, Elinor?"

"Good, thank you, Clare. And you?" She says it nonchalantly, but a self-satisfied smile turns up the corners of her lips, shaded a deep ruby red with her thirty-seven-dollars-a-tube lipstick.

"And there's Haley and her friend." Lex waves at Haley and Jasmine but doesn't appear to notice their frosty nods in return. Looking up at me, eyes troubled, he says, "Haven't you checked your cell today? I left you a message."

"Actually, I haven't. It's been one of those days. I'm off to Dory's, so I'll give you a call later, okay?" I've taken a step toward the door when Elinor's question stops me, and I turn back to her reluctantly.

"Ohhh, that's your daughter?" She's looking at Haley and Jasmine with such avid curiosity that I wonder if she's going to ask which one is mine. "She's quite lovely, isn't she, Lex? Her hair color is so unusual."

I resist telling her that Haley's blond hair doesn't come from a bottle, unlike some I could mention. Instead, I hear myself saying in a quiet voice, "She gets her coloring from her father."

Elinor is still staring at the girls, and when I look their way, too, I'm relieved to see that their heads are bent together as they talk, so they don't see her. "I'd heard that you had a daughter, but we haven't met," Elinor says, turning her gaze to me.

No way I'll risk taking her over to meet the girls, considering what they might say to her. That's all I need today! I mutter something inane about Haley being a schoolteacher, so she probably hadn't been in Elinor's shop, but her next question catches me off guard.

"A schoolteacher? But she looks so young! Surely she's about Alexia's age?"

I glance at Lex, but if he notices anything snide about Elinor's question, his expression doesn't give him away. He's watching his ex, but rather glumly, it seems to me. "No," I say finally. "Haley's several years older than Alexia. She's almost thirty and has children of her own."

Either Elinor is innocent, and she hasn't heard Haley's and my story—which I very much doubt—or she's an accomplished actress. I suspect the latter, because she blinks up at me in what appears to be complete surprise as her hand goes to her throat. "Good heavens! You must have been, what, eighteen when she was born, Clare? A mere child yourself."

With a smile, I nod at her. "Eighteen when she was born? Yes, as a matter of fact, I was, Elinor. Now, if you'll excuse me, I really have to run." To pay her back for her probing, before leaving, I put a hand on Lex's shoulder and give it a proprietary squeeze.

Outside, I wonder if Elinor could possibly look more smug. Heading toward my house to get my car for the drive to Dory's place, I recall something that had slipped my mind after the crazy day I've had. Although I'd hoped to catch up on some paperwork yesterday, I'd been unable to resist going back to the Landing. Now that I knew the retreat site was really going to happen, I returned with paper and pen to take more notes for the remodeling. Before leaving the house, I called Lex to see if he wanted to come along, saying I'd pick him up on my way. He hem-hawed around before blurting out that he couldn't go because he'd promised to spend some time with Elinor. Surely the fool hasn't let her talk him into anything stupid—like getting back together? But if not, then why did Elinor appear so pleased with herself? And Lex looked really drawn and tired, his brow furrowed. He was just getting back on his feet after the divorce when Elinor came back into his life and threw him for a loop. It's another thing I see often in my practice, when the partner who wanted the divorce starts playing mind games with the other. It can get quite unhealthy, with both partners unable to let the other go. Shrugging, I pick up my pace. Oh well—if Lex refuses to see Elinor for the sly, devious woman she is, there's nothing I can do to help him. After all the years in my line of work, I shouldn't need more proof that love is truly blind.

❦

Pulling up and stopping the car in front of the Rodgerses' house, I'm blown away, as always, by the perfection of the location. When they married, Dory and Son settled in Fairhope, as they'd always planned, moving into the Rodgerses' summer cottage a few miles away. It was a temporary living arrangement until they found their own place, and Son located a perfect piece of waterfront property, halfway between Fairhope and Point Clear. Son opened a branch of the family real estate business, and even though he was no stranger to wealth and privilege, no one could've predicted the astonishing housing boom that hit the Gulf Coast then, or known how Son would profit as a result. Once real estate agencies began to spring up along the coast like forest mushrooms, Son's company was never as prosperous, but he's remained one of the wheelers and dealers of the Fairhope area.

The Rodgerses' house is without question the most spectacular one on the bay, yet it has an entirely different effect than Zoe Catherine's property. The Landing has a wild, sweeping grandeur, but here, the serenity is as palpable as the mist over the bay behind the house. It's odd that such a setting has brought so little peace to its occupants, a thought that strikes me as almost unbearably sad as I park the car and turn off the ignition. The house and surrounding lawns have been featured in several gardening magazines because of Dory's unusual landscaping, with the startling indigo expanse of Mobile Bay as a backdrop.

A unique feature of the house is the tower, which boaters often mistake for a lighthouse, the way it stands amid the live oaks on the shoreline. Dory originally designed the tower as a kind of playhouse for their two boys, Jackson and Shaw, with a game room upstairs for Ping-Pong and billiards. But because of its spiral staircase and rounded walls, I've always viewed the tower as Dory's magic circle manifest in cedar and glass. The bottom floor, which has an attached greenhouse, is reserved for her gardening projects and is also the location of the infamous workshop that Son trashed. Once Shaw left for college, Dory began the project of converting the tower into her own space, changing the game room into a home office and modernizing the bottom floor, turning it into a studio rather than a workshop.

I knew trouble was looming when Dory began the project and Son claimed that Jackson and Shaw would be devastated at the loss of the game room they'd had since they were little boys. Jackson, who's worked with his dad since finishing college last year, lives with his girlfriend in an apartment downtown, and Shaw's in a frat house at Georgia Tech, so it was ludicrous of Son to claim that the young men cared about the childish game room. Dory outsmarted Son—not a difficult task—by converting a large guest room into a game room and moving all of Jackson's and Shaw's stuff into it. Then she and I raised a glass of champagne in celebration while Son lurked in the hall, pouting.

Standing outside the double front doors of the main house allows me to see all the way to the glass sunroom in the back, elevated to overlook the bay. I let myself in once I see Dory there, perched on a mat and meditating, her head bowed and hands folded as though in prayer. I was hoping she'd be in the tower, but she'd said to look for her in the kitchen, since she'd be cooking dinner soon. I tiptoe down the hallway, trying not to disturb her meditation, but the cypress floor creaks under my feet. Dory opens her eyes, and her face goes soft at the sight of me standing there. The dying light from the late-afternoon sun streaming in the windows behind her gilds her silhouette, and she looks as lovely as an Aztec goddess.

"I was trying to sneak in without interrupting you," I say as she gets to her feet with the grace of a swan.

"If you're doing it right, you can't be interrupted," she informs me with her sweet smile as we hug. She then nods toward one of the white leather sofas strategically placed to get the most of the view of the bay. "Let's sit down, okay?"

I obey, but Dory kneels in front of a low, enameled table and reaches for a decanter of ruby-red liquid holding the pomegranate juice that is one of her more recent health-food kicks. She pours some into the bottom of two goblets, then fills them with soda water. Squeezing a lime wedge into each, she hands me mine and clinks hers against it as she says, "Not exactly champagne, but at least it bubbles and fizzes."

I raise my glass and say, "To your tower, the magic circle you've always talked about."

"It is, isn't it?" Dory says in surprise. We look at each other, and she asks me, "Remember when I first told you about my obsession with circles? You must've thought I was a fruitcake."

"God, that seems like a long time ago!" With the tip of my finger, I stir the juice and soda. "Our lives haven't quite turned out like we imagined, have they?"

"Does anyone's, you think?" She sips her drink in silence for a few moments, then looks at up me. "Clare? Son told me about going to your office this morning and acting like a damned cretin. I was furious when he told me, and I let him have it. He said Etta called the cops on him, but you wouldn't let them come. I wish to God they'd thrown his ass in jail until he cooled off. It would've served him right, carrying on like that."

"You know I wouldn't let that happen."

Putting her glass on the table, she lowers her head and says in an anguished voice, "I didn't know about it until Son came home for lunch and I mentioned that you'd called. I could tell by his expression that something was wrong, and finally he said that you must've told me what happened. I had no idea what he was talking about, so he spilled it out, the whole awful thing. I said that I hoped by God he was happy, because nothing could've made your point clearer. You hadn't wanted me with him because of tantrums like that, and he knows it. But you know? Son used to always have an excuse, no matter what. It was never his fault. This time was different. He took full blame and was really sorry for the way he behaved. Like I told you Saturday, he's a changed man."

I'm sure my expression reveals my thoughts because Dory says grimly, "It'll be harder than ever to make a believer of you, won't it?"

I lean over to put a hand on her arm. "I haven't seen any proof of Son's being a reformed man—definitely not after his shenanigans today—but I'll be glad to be proved wrong about him. All I want is for you to find some happiness, if there's any to be found."

She chews her lip, deep in thought. "You know, I don't think you've ever realized how much I want your approval. How I've always wanted your approval."

This shocks me, and I don't know how to respond. I've always thought I was the one who longed to be accepted by her. Could it be true that she feels the same way about me? Dory sips her drink and looks past me, out the window to the bay. The sun has disappeared, and Mobile Bay is opalescent with twilight. Her face is composed and her voice even, but her eyes still hold a faraway sadness in their depths.

"From the first day we met in that study group," she says softly, "I admired you so much. There were no gray areas for you. You knew exactly how you felt about everything, and you stood by your principles, no matter the cost." She states it with no hint of censure, but I grimace.

"Jesus, that makes me sound like such a pious little shit."

She smiles, cocking an eyebrow at me. "Well?"

I put my empty glass beside hers on the table. "Dory? Son said that you'd had another crying episode. I'm pretty sure it's just an emotional release, but I'm concerned about you. Stress is more dangerous than any of us realize, and you've had more than your share lately."

She nods solemnly. "I'm feeling much better now. My meditation is helping me to regain my balance." She glances my way, then clears her throat. "Ah, the plans are complete for the anniversary party and the ceremony beforehand. That's all I'm going to say about it, except for this: It was so very thoughtless of me to have asked you what I did, and I regret it. If I could take it back, I would." She stops and looks at me helplessly.

It hangs heavy in the air between us, like an ominous rain cloud. Eyes lowered, I jiggle the ice in my glass. I have to take several deep breaths before I can make myself say it. When I do, it comes out so quietly that Dory doesn't hear me. "I'll do it," I repeat, my voice stronger this time.

"You'll do it?"

I nod, and Dory's hands fly to her mouth, her gold-green eyes bright as jewels. "You will? Really? You'll stand up with me at the renewal ceremony?" Again I nod, unable to speak, and Dory regards me suspiciously. "You're sure about this?"

"I'm sure."

"Oh, Clare—" she begins, but I wave her off.

"I'll do it, but I'd rather not talk about it, okay? Let's give it a little time."

"I don't want you to if you don't feel right about it," she says with a frown, and I shake my head.

"You know how stubborn I am, and I wouldn't do it if I didn't feel like it was something I need to do. Something I want to do," I amend quickly.

"I do know that. It's that fierce integrity of yours that I love most about you. There's no way I can tell you what this means to me . . ." Her voice falters, and she takes a deep, trembling breath. "I can't tell you how much—"

But we're interrupted by the slamming of the back door, and both of us jump when Son appears, poking his head around the kitchen door. "Hey!" he calls out. "You two through with your girlie talk?"

"Come here, Son," Dory commands in a tight voice. "I believe you have something to say to Clare."

I get to my feet with dread, but Son is an entirely different person than he was this morning. What I see is the public persona of Andrew Jackson Rodgers, Jr., smooth, affable, and charming, the man from the coffee shop last Friday. He removes his sports jacket and loosens his tie as he approaches the sofa, the civic-minded business-man returning from a vestry meeting, doing his Christian duty by helping to run the affairs of his beloved church. When he stands in front of me, he hangs his head and tries to look sheepish. I can't help myself: I experience a mean-spirited thrill of joy when I notice for the first time the thinning spot on the crown of his head. Son is nothing if not vain, especially over his head of golden-brown curls.

"I'm too embarrassed to face you, Clare," he says meekly, then peeks up for my reaction. "I can't believe I acted like such a jerk this morning."

I have no intention of letting him off the hook easily. "Neither can I. I certainly hope you'll never do anything like that again."

"I told Clare she should've let the sheriff haul you off to jail," Dory says, her arms folded as she glares at him. "Would've served you right."

Son shakes his head mournfully. "I don't know what came over me. I was so worried about Dory that I lost my head. It was the stupidest thing I've ever done."

I gasp, but before I can say what I'm thinking, Dory beats me to it. "You showed your ass, all right," she says with a snort, "but I'd say trashing my workshop wins the Son Rodgers gold medal of stupidity."

"I know, I know," Son moans. "I told you this morning, Clare, and I told Dory at lunch, all I'm asking for is another chance to prove how much I've changed."

"*One* more last chance, huh?" I say dryly, but it's lost on Son, naturally, and he nods eagerly.

"That's all I'm asking! I know I'm gonna mess up every now and then, and I messed up big-time this morning. But from now on, I'm going to do better." He looks first at Dory, then at me. "Tell you what, Clare. In front of both of you, I'll make this promise." He raises his hand as if to say the pledge of allegiance. "If I fuck up like that again—or any way at all—Dory won't have to kick me out. I'll leave. I swear to God, I'll leave and never bother her again. She can have the house, the land, whatever, and I won't even argue. How does that sound?"

He adds the last part with a lopsided, dimpled grin and the implied assurance that I'll be unable to resist him. Give him one thing, he never gives up trying, but he's dumber than I imagined if he doesn't think I'll call his bluff. I hold out a hand to him. "You've got a deal."

"You won't regret this, wait and see." Son brushes aside my hand in order to pull me into a hug, and I pat his back halfheartedly, my eyes meeting Dory's over his shoulder. She's looking at me so hopefully that I make myself return her smile.

⤜

The soft, sweet bodies of Abbie and Zach burrow against me, one on each side. I'm propped on a stack of pillows in Abbie's antique white bed, the headboard featuring a colorful field of wildflowers painted by Dory. The two children are deliciously warm and damp, smelling like shampoo and bubble bath, dressed in animal-print PJs. I hold up the book so they can see the pictures as I read one of Abbie's favorite stories, *Are You My Mother?*, about a little bird who falls out of his nest, then goes on a search for the mama bird.

Tonight Zach's big brown eyes, so like his daddy's, are drooping sleepily, and his thumb keeps going to his mouth in spite of Abbie's attempts to shame him. "Only babies suck their thumbs," she tells him haughtily, and Zach dutifully removes it, only to forget and plop it back in when I turn the next page.

By the time we finish the book, Zach has fallen asleep, his little body limp and heavy against me. His long eyelashes sweep against his cheeks, and his thumb is firmly planted in his mouth. I kiss the top of his fuzzy head, and he stirs, his round pink mouth pumping his thumb steadily. Abbie reaches over to pull out his thumb, but I stop her. "It's okay, honey," I whisper. "He needs that thumb now, but he'll stop when he gets a little bigger, don't worry."

"But Grams, his teeth will stick out," she cries, looking up at me in horror. "Gramma Zoe said so, and she said for me *not* to let him do it."

"Your teeth don't stick out, and you sucked your thumb when you were two, like Zach. Trust me, okay? Has Grams ever lied to you?"

Abbie thinks about it for such a long time, her face screwed up in concentration, that I can't help but laugh. "I'll move Zach to his room, pumpkin, then I'll be right back to tuck you in, okay?" I ease down and put my legs over the side of the bed before gathering Zach in my arms.

As usual, Abbie grabs hold of my arm and tries to keep me with her. "One more story, Grams—pleeeze!"

"Now, Abbie, what did your daddy say? Two stories and that's it. It's already past your bedtime, and we cheated by reading the bird book twice." I lean over and whisper, "But don't tell Daddy. That's our secret, okay?"

As if on cue, the door of her room opens, and Austin sticks his head in, frowning. "I knew I'd catch you begging Grams for one more," he says, stern-faced. "Bedtime for you, young lady." He crosses the room and takes the sleeping boy from me, and Abbie stands on the bed and reaches across me, grabbing her father around the waist. "Dad-dee!" she pleads. "Can't Grams read me a short one?"

"She most certainly cannot. Give me a good-night kiss, then let Grams tuck you in and say your prayers with you," he says, leaning over to kiss her cheek. Not content with a mere peck on the cheek, Abbie grabs her daddy around his neck, hard, which almost causes him to lose his balance as she plants wet, noisy kisses on his cheek. When he straightens up, Abbie looks at me and grins, her face aglow and her eyes shining.

"I'm going to marry my daddy when I grow up," she announces, and I smile at her, ruffling her stick-straight blond hair, which always flies around her face despite her mother's endless attempts to tame it with braids, barrettes, or bows. Abbie looks so much like Haley that it's astonishing, but she has her daddy's whimsical, gap-toothed smile.

"Then what will your poor mama do?" I ask her, helping her under the covers while Austin moves across the room with the sleeping Zach, rolling his eyes at me as he goes out the door.

"Oh, she can be married to him, too," Abbie says magnani-mously, throwing her arms around my neck and pulling me down for her good-night kiss. "Or she can get her a divorce, like every-body else."

"Abbie Jordan!" Try as I may, I cannot keep from smiling rue-fully. "You know that's not true. Not everyone gets divorced, al-though it must seem like it sometimes."

"Uh-huh, they do, too. And besides, I know that's what *you* do."

"What?" I dare ask.

"Help people who don't want to be married anymore get them a divorce. That's what you do, isn't it, Grams?"

I sigh and look down at her. The door opens, and Austin sticks his head back in, eyebrows raised, but I wave him away. When he leaves, I turn back to Abbie. "No, sweetheart, that's not what Grams does, but I can see how you'd be confused about it. What I do is try to help people adjust—I mean, ah—not be so sad when things don't work out and they *have* to get a divorce. Nobody wants to get divorced, but sometimes . . . well, sometimes it just happens, and . . ." I falter, not sure how to explain such a thing to a four-year-old.

"Know what? Lindsay in my Sunday school? Her mommy and daddy got a divorce, and she has to live with her mommy, but her brother lives with her daddy. I don't want Zach to live with Daddy if Mommy and Daddy get a divorce and I have to live with Mommy! What will Zach do for a big sister?" Her wide eyes are troubled at the thought, and I kiss her cheek again before turning out the lamp by her bedside. She's afraid of the dark, but her seashell-shaped night-light provides enough illumination for me to see her clearly.

"Shhh. You're a lucky little girl, Abbie-kins. Your mommy and daddy love you and Zach more than anything, so you'll always be a family."

She's quiet for a moment, then she brightens and says, "Oh! So Lindsay's mommy and daddy didn't love her and her little brother that much, right?"

Way to go, Grams. Open mouth, insert foot. "That's not what I meant, honey. I'm sure that Lindsay's mommy and daddy love them and were very sad when they had to get a divorce. What I want you to remember is this: Your mommy and daddy love each other as much as they love you and Zach, so you don't have to worry about anything like that, okay?"

Her brow furrowed under wispy bangs, Abbie studies me. "You promise?"

"I promise, sweetheart. Now, let's say your prayers, and remember what I always say to you, okay?"

"Sleep tight, and don't let the bedbugs bite."

Haley and Austin are putting supper on the table when I leave Abbie's room and go into the kitchen. They fed the kids earlier and insisted that I stay while Austin grilled some fresh bay scallops for our supper. I protested, not wanting them going to that much trouble on a school night, but they wouldn't hear of my leaving. Austin has fixed our plates, a mound of salad greens glistening with oil and vinegar, topped with sweet bay scallops, grilled deep brown. We join hands and bow our heads for the blessing, reaching across the table awkwardly with just the three of us, then squeeze hands after the "amen." It pleases me more than I let on that Austin and Haley are devout Episcopalians, committed to bringing up the children in the church. In spite of what my detractors say, I'm an advocate of strong ties to the church and community as an important part of a family unit.

"This looks marvelous, Austin," I say, shaking out my napkin. "Now I'm grateful that you twisted my arm to stay."

"And I'm grateful that scallops were on sale today," Haley says with a twinkle in her eyes as Austin flushes. We tease him about his thriftiness, though I let up once I noticed him becoming so defensive about it. Mack, who never liked Austin as much as I did, finding his son-in-law a bit too goody-goody for his taste, was the one to start it. He was merciless with the teasing once Haley told us that Austin washed and reused aluminum foil, plastic wrap, and dental floss.

"Not funny, Haley," Austin says touchily.

Unperturbed, Haley passes a basket of French bread my way. "I'm glad you rescued them from the half-price bin, honey, because I'm starving. I had a measly peanut-butter-and-jelly sandwich for lunch, but not a thing since."

"Except a couple of margaritas and a ton of taco chips," Austin remarks, dodging when she swats at his arm. "And as you know, Clare," he continues, "if your daughter had prepared dinner tonight, we'd have been lucky to get a peanut-butter sandwich."

"Bull hockey," Haley says. "I'm getting to be a much better cook. That *Southern Living* subscription you gave me, Mom? This weekend I made two things from the September issue, and they were really good. Weren't they, Austin? I fixed Curry Coconut Shrimp and served it with Pear and Walnut Salad."

"Which one was which?" Austin asks, then winks at me.

"Very funny. The kids didn't much like the curry, but they ate every bit of their salad. And I'm going to make a leek and potato frittata Sunday morning."

"The kids won't eat that crap," Austin tells her. "They always want my pancakes on Sunday."

"Oh, I'll bet they'll eat frittata, Austin," I chime in brightly.

"It'll be somewhat like scrambled eggs, with hash browns added. Maybe you should leave the leeks out, though."

"What are leeks, anyway?" Haley asks, and Austin snorts. The main conflict I've observed in their marriage has to do with Haley's domestic skills, or lack thereof. A couple of times I've been a witness to a sure-enough shouting match when Austin complained about Haley's cooking, the house not being cleaned to his satisfaction, the laundry piled up, or the fridge full of moldy leftovers. He's a confirmed neat freak, while the happy-go-lucky Haley is oblivious to mess and clutter.

"Besides," Haley says, putting a hand on Austin's arm and smiling up at him prettily, "there's no sense in me being in the kitchen when you're such a good cook."

Usually Austin melts when she flatters him, but his face remains impassive as he says testily, "Has it ever occurred to you that I might enjoy coming home to a nice dinner occasionally? It's difficult to work as hard as I do, then come in late and have to cook."

"Oh, *pardon* me," Haley snaps. "Like I don't work hard, too."

"Yeah, right. Kindergarten kids! Spend one day struggling with surly college students, and you'd see the difference in what we do. Not only that, you're home by four o'clock. You have no idea."

Haley turns to me indignantly, seeking support. "Can you believe this? Austin has turned into a chauvinist pig since he got that new promotion! Mr. Big wants a Stepford wife or something."

"All men want a Stepford wife, honey," I say lightly. "*I* want a Stepford wife."

They both chuckle, and the tension dissipates. When the phone rings and Austin starts to get up, Haley says, "Let the machine get it." Again she turns to me for help, an occupational hazard I encounter often. "Another bad thing about the new job. They call Austin constantly. He never has a free minute anymore."

Austin gets to his feet and starts for the phone. "Unfortunately, it goes with the territory," he says over his shoulder.

When he's gone and we can hear his voice in the hallway, discussing a problem at the learning lab, Haley sighs mightily. "It's every single night and all weekend. I swear to God."

"I believe you. But . . ." I hesitate, biting my lip. It's such a difficult thing, not interfering in your kids' lives.

"But what?" She leans toward me with a frown.

"Just that it takes a while to adjust to a new job. You have to set your boundaries. Austin will learn to do that as he gets used to the job and determines his responsibilities. Maybe you should leave it alone for a while, let him work it out."

Haley's thoughtful. Then she plops a scallop in her mouth. After chewing carefully and swallowing, she tilts her head and regards me. "Is that your professional opinion?"

"My very best professional advice," I say with a smile.

"Not everybody's mom is a therapist. Guess I'd be a fool not to listen to you, huh?"

"You could never be a fool, sweetheart, even if you tried."

Haley rolls her eyes to the ceiling. "You of all people cannot say that with a straight face."

Austin comes back into the room and stands with his hands on his hips, looking from me to Haley with his eyebrows raised. "Did I miss something?"

"Just Mom giving me advice, is all."

"Thank God. Now if only you'll listen to her," he says.

Haley gets to her feet and goes to her husband, kissing him lightly on the mouth and then on each cheek. "I love you, sweetie, even when you act like a turd," she declares.

Austin puts an arm around his wife's shoulder and says casually, "Love you, too." He turns and looks down at me. "Why don't we have some of that chocolate cake Clare brought?"

It's later, on the drive home, that I recall Haley's offhand remark about her being a fool. Coupled with her unexpected comment at Mateer's this afternoon, I have to wonder what's going on with her. Even though she and I have put the heartbreak of the past behind us—as much as it's possible—every now and then it surfaces, like a log submerged beneath murky waters that is dislodged by an unexpected current. One thing I'm sure of, nothing can be gained by its reappearance. Especially now, with Mack dead. Once we'd buried him, Haley and I buried that awful period in our lives and, hopefully, our guilt with it.

Chapter Seven

≈   ≈   ≈   ≈   ≈

Several days after the hellacious one that started with Son bursting into my office, I don't get home from work until after dark, an hour later than I planned. I realize how tired I am only as I kick off my shoes in the foyer and lean against the front door, eyes closed, before getting up the energy to move again. Lex is here, his Jeep out front and the lights on in the back of the house. I didn't call him to say I was running late due to a crisis with a client—Helen Murray again—but I should have. I should've asked him to meet me at Mateer's or the Colony instead of here. I've invited Lex to dinner, but no way I can cook now; I'm way too wiped out. Part of my plan had been to go by the pier and get some fish fresh off the boat for our supper, but they were closed. Oh well. That's why the Lord invented grilled cheese sandwiches, I guess.

Walking back to the kitchen, I loosen the belt of my white slacks, pull out my silk shirt from the waistband, then unfasten the heavy gold earrings Dory gave me for my birthday, dropping them on the sideboard of the dining room. By the time I enter the kitchen, I'm half undressed, and it feels so good I decide not to even mention going to a restaurant for dinner. Grilled cheese it is. In the kitchen doorway, I stand for a moment, not taking in the sight I'm seeing. Lex, whom I've thought of as the most undomestic of men, is at the stove, where he appears to be cooking something in an iron skillet. Something, I realize, that smells so rich and buttery it makes my mouth water and my knees go weak. "What on earth?" I say.

"And hello to you, too, Clare," he says cheerily, but he doesn't look up from the skillet. "You're just in time."

"In time for what?"

Frowning in concentration, Lex glances my way. "Dinner." He does a double take when I unbutton the top button of my blouse as I walk over to the stove to see what he's cooking. "But it can wait, if you have something else in mind," he adds, grinning.

"Not very likely, since I can hardly muster up the energy to undress."

"You're doing a pretty good job of it."

"Look who's talking, you barefooted yard dog." I stand by the stove with my hands on my hips and watch as he swirls a huge pat of butter around in the sizzling skillet, filling the kitchen with a wonderful smell. Then, as precisely as a surgeon, he makes an oblong slice on the top of a couple of hoagie buns, opens them up, and plops them into the browned butter.

"Couldn't find the right kind of buns," he mutters as he flips them with a snap of his wrist, "so I had to improvise. Won't be as good, but it'll have to do."

"Lex, did I miss something? We've been friends for—what?—a few months now, and I've never seen you cook a thing. Not a fried egg, or a piece of toast, or a—a—hot dog, even. Yet here you are, not only cooking up something fabulous-smelling but acting like you know what you're doing."

He flips the buns again to brown on the other side. "I'd be a disgrace to the state of Maine if I couldn't make a decent crab roll."

"Oh, bull. No way you're making crab rolls." I laugh and move away from the stove to grab an opened bottle of Shiraz and pour myself a glass. "I was planning on making us a grilled cheese sandwich," I say over my shoulder. "That's what you're doing, isn't it? Not crab rolls but some kind of Yankee grilled cheese? Hope it goes with red wine."

Jerking up his head in surprise, Lex stops grilling long enough to stare at me. "Don't tell me you made a big deal of inviting me to dinner, then planned on serving me grilled cheese sandwiches?"

"Well, no," I admit. "I was going to do something wonderful and healthy with fish and fresh vegetables, but I didn't count on working so late. I just decided on grilled cheese when I walked in the door. And I know how to make them light, with nonfat cheese and make-believe-it's-butter, or whatever you call that stuff."

"I told you I'd take you out to dinner, but no, you insisted on cooking." He scowls and waves the spatula at me. "When I get here precisely on time, I see to my surprise that you've got nothing out for dinner, and nothing in the fridge, either. *Nada.* So I go into action. It will be your great fortune and even greater honor to partake of my crab rolls. Lobster rolls are much better, but these are quicker."

"I still don't believe you." I take a sip of wine. "Where are they, then?"

"Where are what?"

"The crab rolls!"

"You have to make them. Like most food, they don't magically appear on the table. Actually, that's not true, in your case. Sit down and I'll bring yours to you." He nods his head toward the little table with the built-in cushioned seats under the bay window.

Silent but still skeptical, I obey, then watch him go to the fridge and pull out a small bowl with a flourish. "The crab mixture," he explains, as though conducting a cooking show, with me as the audience. He takes a couple of plates and, on each one, centers a crispy browned roll oozing with what I can only hope is play-like-it's-butter. Opening them gently, he piles the crab mixture inside and brings our plates over to the table. Returning with the wine, he refills my glass, pours his, and sits down heavily. "Mud in your eye," he says, raising his glass carefully so as not to slosh a single drop.

The crab roll is incredible, tart with lemon juice and mayo, crunchy with chopped cucumbers and capers, and oh so sweet with lump crabmeat. I fall on mine, so famished that I don't say a word until I've finished every morsel and used my fingertips to collect the crumbs. "Mmm," I say, licking my fingers. "That was unbelievable!"

"Haven't eaten anything all day, have you?" Lex is halfway through his, and I look at the remaining half longingly. Rolling his eyes, he breaks off a huge piece and hands it to me. I devour it, too hungry to be ladylike. "Slow down," Lex scolds. "I made a blueberry pie, too. A true taste-of-Maine supper."

"You did not!"

Laughing, he pushes back his chair and goes to the counter, where he opens a bakery box. "Naw, I bought the pie. The blueberries you guys have down here aren't worth a damn. They're big as baseballs."

"What does that mean? The bigger the better, right?"

"Pure Southern propaganda. You'll see after you've had Maine blueberries. Tiny little turds, but man, are they sweet. We'll have to wait till next August now, but I'll order some wild ones from Bar Harbor and make you a *real* pie."

"Better be careful," I say with a smile. "You'll spoil me. I could get used to this." As soon as the words are out, I reach for my wineglass, wishing I could take them back. I've worked so hard to maintain a platonic relationship, then to make a crack like that! I dare to glance sideways at Lex, relieved that he didn't notice, so intent was he on putting two slices of pie in the microwave and punching in the time. While the pie is heating, he spoons decaf into my coffeemaker nonchalantly.

"Shall we have our little discussion here at the table while you eat your pie, or do you want to go into the den and put up your feet?" I ask when he pours our coffee.

Eyebrows raised, he glances at me as he pulls out his chair and sits down. "What discussion?" he asks, trying to appear innocent.

"You know what discussion. The one I invited you over to have."

"I knew there was a catch," he says with a shake of his head. "Always strings attached to your invitations."

"Lex! You promised. I called and asked if you wanted to talk about your evening with Elinor at Mateer's the other night. And you said no, not over the phone. So I said come to dinner, then."

"You misunderstood me. You thought my saying 'not over the phone' implied I would talk face-to-face instead."

"Well, of course I did, idiot. Anyone would."

"Doesn't count, because I had to cook my own dinner," he says with a twinkle in his eyes. "Since I had to cook, I don't have to talk."

"Oh, no, you don't. It doesn't work that way, mister. Tell it."

But Lex shakes his dark head again, then says casually, "There's nothing to tell. Just Elinor's usual crap. One day she's all lovey-dovey, and the next time I see her, she's remote and cold again. Been that way our entire relationship." He stops to glare at me defiantly. "And I'm not going to talk about it, you hear?"

"But you *need* to," I cry, leaning toward him. "Elinor's trying to get you back, isn't she?" When he shrugs, refusing to look at me as he eats his slice of pie, I smile wearily. "Must be something in the air. First Son and Dory, now you and Elinor."

"Elinor didn't say anything about us getting back together," he says gruffly. "She just wants us to be on friendlier terms, doesn't want me acting like a jerk and upsetting Alexia. You know. I've told you all that."

"And how do you feel about it?"

Lex lays down his fork to glare at me. "Do you people have that phrase engraved on the front lobe of your brain? You must say it in your sleep."

I return his glare, but he switches gears on me. "You want to hear all about Elinor," he says, "yet you never say anything about your so-called friend, pretty boy."

"I assume you mean Rye."

"I mean that cousin of yours who has the hots for you."

"Jesus, Lex! You know how to play dirty, don't you? I've told you, he's not *my* cousin, he's Mack's. You don't really think Southerners are like that, do you?" I ignore his look and say suspiciously, "And what's this about? You've known from day one that he and I are close and see a lot of each other. Why ask me about him now?"

Ignoring my question, Lex frowns at me. "How old is that guy, anyway? Too old for you, that's for sure."

"He most certainly is not. That's ridiculous."

"How old is he, Clare?"

"Ah . . . he's sixty-two," I admit, "but you'd never know it. He's in great shape."

"Must be all that dancing you guys do," he grumbles.

"You've never offered to take me dancing! And I've said many times that it's something I really enjoy, the best stress reliever in my life. But I can hardly go dancing by myself, so Rye and I have been doing it for years." Flushing, I hastily add, "Dancing, that is."

Lex looks shocked. "For *years?* What about your old man? He actually allowed you to go out with other guys? Alabama men are wimpier than I thought."

I sigh mightily and shake my head. "I'm not believing we're having this conversation. After our wedding dance at the reception, Mack never danced another step. He hated it as bad as you seem to. So he was delighted that I had Rye to dance with." I don't dare tell Lex about Mack's teasing; I've got sense enough to know that he'd be even worse. Instead, I repeat, "You still haven't told me why you're asking about Rye."

"When I first got here, he called, and I answered your phone. I talked to him."

With a sigh, I put my face in my hands. "Not again! Poor Rye."

"He was checking to see if you had a retreat this weekend, or if you wanted to go to some dance with him Saturday night."

"I'm afraid to ask what you told him."

"All I told him was that you were taking a little nap while I prepared dinner."

"A nap! Ha. Rye knows me better than that."

Eyes gleaming wickedly, Lex grins, enjoying this. "I said I could go upstairs and wake you if he'd hold on, but I'd rather not. I implied we'd worn ourselves out since you got in from work."

"Lex, that's *awful*. Surely you didn't say that. You're teasing, aren't you? Please tell me you're teasing."

"Call and ask him. I'll bring you the phone."

"I'm afraid to. I don't believe you, but you're such a crazy fool, I never know when you're kidding. Tell me the truth—you didn't really do that to Rye, did you?"

He looks at me a long moment before shaking his head ruefully. "Of course I'm having you on. You don't think I'd talk to a poor elderly cousin of yours like that, do you? Jeez! What kind of person do you think I am?"

❧

I met Lex Yarbrough the first of the summer, the magical night of his first Jubilee. In our area, Jubilees are more than a strange phenomenon of nature; they are a celebration of life on Mobile Bay. When you're new to this region, you hear so many stories and legends associated with Jubilee that it becomes a must-have experience. My first summer in Fairhope, right after Mack and I married, I thrilled just to hear the word. Mack and Son had talked about Jubilees as though the Almighty sent them as a special sign of His favor to those smart enough to live on the Eastern Shore of Mobile Bay. I questioned this by asking if Buddha felt the same way about the folks at the only other place in the world Jubilees occurred, somewhere in Japan. Naturally Dory thought the Jubilees were mystical experiences full of symbolic interpretations, but she teased Son and Mack as well, asking why, if the people here were in such good favor with the Almighty, the fish didn't wash up on the shore already cleaned. Although a lot of hard work and missed sleep is involved with Jubilees, nothing has ever dampened my enthusiasm for them. I'd worked myself into such a state of anticipation that my first one was almost a holy experience. Even today, all these years later, I can't resist the Jubilee cry that goes up and down the shore whenever one occurs.

I have my own personal bell ringer, Zoe Catherine. The first night of June brought with it a full moon, and Zoe Catherine called me right after midnight, startling me out of a deep sleep. It took me a minute to realize she was saying that Jubilee Joe had appeared to Cooter, and that she and Cooter were getting dressed to leave. If I wanted to take part, I should meet them at the beach about half a mile north of the marina.

"Now lemme speak to Rye," she demanded. Unlike Haley and Austin, Zoe doesn't tease me about Rye, but she refuses to believe that we aren't lovers. A lusty woman who has had more than her share of men, Zoe finds my avowed abstinence incomprehensible. That night I told her that as far as I knew, Rye was at home in his own bed, and she cackled before hanging up abruptly.

Rye, too, loved Jubilees, but only as an excuse to socialize. A lot of people hauled beer or snacks to the shore, but not the ever elegant Rye Ballenger. He was a popular addition to the festivities because while everyone else was gigging fish, Rye was making runs back and forth to his antique-filled waterfront house, making sure his friends didn't run out of his special mixture of Southern Comfort, crushed mint leaves, and sugar. The longer the Jubilee went on, the more smashed Rye and his high-society friends got.

I almost didn't go that night. There again, the mysterious workings of fate, if you believe in that kind of thing. Although I tried to make myself get up, I kept dozing off. It was one of the few weekends I didn't have a retreat, and I'd planned to take some much needed time off. The phone rang again, and this time it was Rye, as excited as a boy after Zoe's call. "You cannot miss a Jubilee, Clare!" he declared, horrified. The old guard and aristocrats of the town took offense at anyone not genuflecting at the mere mention of Jubilee; anything less was a sacrilege. "It might be the only one we have this summer," he added for good measure. "I'm mixing juleps as we speak." I told him I'd think about it, hung up the phone, then dozed off again. When he called back fifteen minutes later, I said all right, all right, I was on my way.

Even though the Jubilee cry hadn't gone out yet, a fairly large crowd was gathered on the shore when I left my car at the marina and walked to the place Zoe had said she'd be. Because I couldn't bear to gig fish, I carried only a net and sack with me. I'd left a cooler in the car, not wanting to tote it, and my flashlight was on a cord hanging from my wrist. Although only a light breeze blew over the bay, it was chilly, and I was glad I'd worn a hooded pullover with my jeans. Mack always waded barefoot in the waters of the bay when we had Jubilees, as most people did, but I'd learned long ago to wear sneakers. Even though I liked nothing better than going barefoot in warm salty water, Jubilees always brought tons of seaweed, and I hated the way it felt whipping around my feet and legs. I wasn't real fond of the jellyfish and stingrays that came ashore, either.

I didn't see Zoe Catherine and Cooter Poulette among those gathered on the shore, but Rye was easy to spot, with his fair hair gleaming silver in the full moon. Because he was so well known and beloved in town, Rye was usually in the center of things, and tonight he stood in front of a small fire as its flames danced in the breeze. On a Jubilee night, all up and down the shore would be little bonfires with clusters of folks huddled around them, warming themselves from the cold wind.

When Rye spotted me, he waved with enthusiasm, and I greeted those gathered around him holding their paper cups of his juleps, the friends and neighbors I'd shared similar nights with over the years. One of the main things I loved about these occasions was the carnival atmosphere, the hushed expectancy and camaraderie. We were all neighbors then, and people who didn't even know one another shared stories of past Jubilees as well as their coolers, sandwiches, and drinks.

"Clare, darling," Rye cried, eyes bright as he tossed me his car keys, "be an angel and run to my car and fetch the other container of juleps, would you?"

I stood frozen for a moment, and Rye looked at me oddly until I shook it off, grinned heartily, and replied, "You bet!" before turning to go. He had no way of knowing that for a heart-stopping moment, in the cold light of the moon, he looked enough like Mack to stop me in my tracks. It was a trick of the moonlight; as soon as he turned, the spell was broken, but it shook me to the core. Lugging the half-gallon jug of juleps, ice clanking with every step I took, I decided that if I had any sense, I'd avoid Rye when I returned. Because another unsettling incident had occurred between us recently, I was already uneasy in his presence, disturbed about some confusing feelings I'd been experiencing with him.

After delivering the juleps, I hurried off to look for Zoe Catherine and Cooter before Rye could stop me, since he was trying to insist I stay with him and his friends. Like Rye, Zoe and Cooter were easy to spot, but for different reasons. If you got within a hundred yards and weren't deaf as a post, you could hear them. As two of the old-timers, Cooter and Zoe Catherine always tried to outdo each other telling Jubilee stories. Plus, both had hearing problems, which caused them to yell louder and louder. Zoe was seventy, but Cooter had a couple of years on her, and therefore more stories, which infuriated her. Not only that, Cooter had been raised in Daphne, a town a few miles up the bay that was nicknamed "Jubilee Town." Cooter thought that gave him some leverage over Zoe as chief storyteller, but he had to talk fast to outdo her. I spotted them in front of one of the many piers dotting the shoreline, and sure enough, they were in the center of a group and talking nonstop, each ignoring the interruptions of the other.

On the outskirts of Zoe and Cooter's crowd, Austin was standing by the fire, holding Abbie. Wrapped in a long robe I'd given her that past Christmas, Abbie lolled against her daddy's shoulder, half asleep. Usually neither Zoe nor I called them at night because the phone might wake the baby, but all rules went out the window when it came to Jubilees. I slipped behind the group and put an arm around Austin's shoulder, leaning over to kiss Abbie on the cheek. She murmured and stirred but tightened her hold on Austin when I tried to take her. I knew how Abbie operated; on being awakened by the phone, she would've gotten up and begged so pitifully to come with her daddy that he would've been unable to resist her.

"I'm surprised to see you two," I whispered. Austin couldn't hear me because of Zoe and Cooter's big mouths, so I had to repeat myself, and he grinned, leaning his head toward mine.

"Looks like now it was a false alarm. Cooter is swearing that he saw the ghost of Jubilee Joe, but I'll bet what he saw was Gramma Zoe getting up to go to the bathroom. If she was in her birthday suit, that would've scared the ghost so bad he'd never show up again."

I sighed. "If Zoe dragged me out of bed for nothing, I'm going to kill her, then *her* ghost can haunt the Landing."

Austin inclined his head toward a couple standing next to him. "Let me introduce you to my replacement at the learning lab, Clare. This is John Webb and his wife, Wanda, who've just moved here from Auburn and are anxious to experience their first Jubilee. My mother-in-law, Clare Ballenger."

The Webbs were a perky, bright-eyed young couple who looked like siblings, dressed almost identically in plaid Bermudas, polo shirts, and matching windbreakers (his yellow, hers pink). They shook my hand enthusiastically and went on and on about how familiar they were with the work I was doing, and how impressed they were with the concept of the retreats, and how honored they were to meet me. Finally I was embarrassed enough by their gushing that I excused myself and left them, moving closer to the water's edge, where Zoe and Cooter held court.

Oblivious to the seaweed and possibility of stingrays, eels, and jellyfish, Cooter was standing ankle-deep in the gently lapping waves of the bay, his britches rolled up to his knees. His thick steel-gray hair, hanging from beneath a Red Man chewing tobacco cap, was caught by the wind, which was blowing much stronger now. Even in overalls, Cooter looked so much like an Old Testament prophet that you expected him to be holding a staff and dressed in flowing robes. His face was long and craggy, with sharp jutting cheekbones that hinted at his Native American ancestry, and he had deep-set black eyes that smoldered like coals. When Cooter got tanked up or on his high horse, as Zoe called it, he looked even wilder because he was slightly walleyed, one of his eyes straying a bit to the left. Unless he got excited, then it would stray even farther, which frightened Abbie but caused Zach to squeal with delight.

I realized that Austin and the Webbs had followed me when Austin, standing behind me, snickered and poked John Webb with his elbow. "That's the crazy old guy I told you about, the boyfriend of Haley's grandmother," Austin whispered. "Wait till you hear him."

Cooter has a couple of oddities of speech that greatly enhance his status as an eccentric in a town that glories in its characters and loves telling stories about them. One is his use of malapropisms. Everyone loves telling about the time he went to the ice-cream parlor to buy himself and Zoe a frozen yoga in a cone. He couldn't eat real ice cream, he told the girl at the counter, because it gave him loose vowels. Another time, at the ballpark, Cooter ordered a couple of hot dogs with mustard and sour crotch. When he wasn't able to finish both hot dogs, Cooter declared that his stomach must have been bigger than his eyes.

Cooter's also known for his colorful expletives. With cupped hands, he scooped up bay water, which he drank with a loud slurp, smacking his lips and wiping his mouth with his sleeve. "Yep," he declared in a voice that could be heard halfway to Mobile, "old Joe was right, by God. Sumbitch is always right. Water's so damn salty I can hardly swallow it."

Although Zoe snorted derisively, several people left the milling crowd to follow Cooter's lead and scoop up handfuls of water for tasting. "You couldn't pay me to do that," Austin said out of the side of his mouth, and Wanda Webb shuddered.

"Doesn't matter how salty it is, Cooter, you old fool," Zoe declared, arms akimbo. "If a Jubilee is coming, you can smell fish from here to New Orleans. I don't smell a thing, do y'all?"

She looked to the crowd for affirmation, which started everyone sniffing the air. Dressed in her fatigues and boots, Zoe was a fitting companion for Cooter, with her unpinned white hair flying around in the breeze, making her appear as wild as the night. "The seaweed's not thick enough, either," she added for good measure, kicking at the water with her booted feet.

"Aw, hell, woman," Cooter shouted, throwing his arms high. "You can't tell how much seaweed is here till you get them boots off and your big toe in the water! Y'all don't pay her no mind. She's crazy as owl shit."

"You get stung by a jellyfish like I did," Zoe yelled back, "and you'd be wearing boots, too, if you had any sense. Don't you remember me getting that jellyfish sting, you senile old fart?"

Austin raised his voice to be heard above the racket. "I'm taking Abbie home, Clare," he said, shifting her in his arms. "I don't want her waking up and hearing them using such profanity." Abbie had fallen asleep, a limp rag doll in the curve of her father's arm, and I pushed her soft sweet hair off her face for another kiss. No point in reminding Austin that Abbie had grown up with the vocabulary of her great-grandmother.

"I'll take her if you want, Austin, and let you stay with your friends. I've seen dozens of Jubilees, and this could go on for a while."

But Austin said he realized how exhausted he was, and he was going to call it a night. "If it comes after all, bring us some of your loot. You stay here and talk to the Webbs, okay? Wanda is especially interested in hearing more about the retreats, since she did her thesis on the benefits of group therapy."

When Austin left and the Webbs began chirping enthusiastically, I forced myself to feign interest, even though I felt like putting my hands over my ears and groaning. The Webbs were a nice enough young couple, but talking shop was the last thing I wanted to do. With only a flicker of guilt, I retrieved my net and sack and told them that I needed to get my cooler if I was going to get enough fish for Austin and Haley, then scurried away. When I looked over my shoulder, Cooter was holding a finger high in the air, testing the way the wind was blowing, while Zoe yelled at him that it didn't matter which damn way the wind blew, no Jubilee was coming tonight, and he'd gotten everybody out of bed for *nothing*, the dumbass.

I met Lex Yarbrough as I was trying to decide which would be worse, staying around Zoe and Cooter's crowd and talking with the overzealous Webbs, or going back to Rye's group, most of them good and soused by now. Since I'd vowed to avoid Rye, I decided

I'd go home instead and get back into my warm bed, thinking Zoe was probably right. In spite of the full moon and the extra-salty water and the ominous stillness of the bay earlier on, tonight appeared to have been a false alarm.

To return to my car, I had to pass a lone figure kneeling in front of a fire made up of a bundle of sticks not much bigger than a bird's nest. He was tossing another handful of sticks on, which I assumed he'd just gathered along the shore. Passing so close by, I would've been rude not to speak, so I paused by the fire to say, "So, what do you think? False alarm or Jubilee?"

The man got to his feet politely, brushing the sand off his knees, and removed his baseball cap before smiling down at me from what seemed an enormous height. The fire was so small it offered little illumination, but I could tell that he was dark and craggy and sort of tough-looking, in spite of a rather sweet smile. He seemed massive, with shoulders as wide as a refrigerator, until I saw that most of his bulk came from the oversize jacket he wore. My first thought was, Jesus, was he expecting *snow?*

"Does it not have the right feel, or is it just me?" I said with a shrug. "The signs are there, but still . . ."

"What signs are those?" he asked in a rich, lilting voice, and I tilted my head to look up at him. There was something odd about his voice, but I couldn't put my finger on what.

"Oh, you know. The water's plenty salty, and—"

He interrupted me with a hearty laugh. "The water is *salty?*" He said it in such obvious surprise, his eyes dancing merrily. "Isn't it always?"

"Ah! You're not from here, are you?" I felt like an idiot, realizing he was most likely a tourist and had no idea what I'd been talking about.

But he nodded. "Am, too. I live in Fairhope." He was grinning down at me like he was having me on, and I studied him, trying to read his face in the moonlight and the meager flames of the fire.

"No way." I'd realized it wasn't his voice that was odd; it was his accent, and I was having difficulty with it. "Sounds like you're—what?—Scottish?"

"Scottish?" He appeared genuinely taken back.

"Okay, not Scottish, but what?" I persisted. "Australian?"

"Me an Aussie?" He grinned again. "Not a chance. Those guys are too big and rough for me."

I laughed, enjoying our little game. "Well, you're definitely not Southern. And you're not a Yankee, either, but I can't quite place the accent. Or brogue, rather. More like a brogue. Ah—you're Irish!"

He folded his massive arms as he regarded me solemnly. "Yawp. You're right, me lassie. Irish."

"Oh, bull. Nobody in Ireland says 'me lassie.' Surely not! Where're you from, really?"

"I told you, lassie. Fairhope."

"You are not. For one thing, I know everyone here, and for another, nobody in Fairhope talks funny like you do."

"*I* talk funny!" Again he tossed back his head and laughed a great big laugh. "I can't understand half of what you guys say."

"You guys!" I cried. "I was wrong—you *are* a Yankee. Right? Or maybe Canadian?" He shook his head, and I sighed. "Okay, I give up."

"I live here now," he told me. "But I was born and raised in Bar Harbor, Maine."

"*Maine?* I never would have guessed it. Well, obviously. Bah Hah Ba, did you say?"

"That's right. Bar Harbor."

I still didn't catch the name of the town but said, surprised at the realization, "Funny, I've never met anyone from Maine."

"You have now." He stuck out a hand that appeared to be the size of a baseball glove, and we shook. "Lex Yarbrough."

"Clare Ballenger." Later, both of us would realize that we'd heard the other's name from his ex-wife, but neither of us made the connection at the time.

"Lot of Ballengers in these parts," he said, but I had to ask him to repeat himself because I thought he said "in these *pots*." Lex proved to be right; until we got to know each other well, neither of us could understand half of what the other said.

"My husband's people," I replied.

"What does he do? Maybe I've met him."

"Pardon me?"

"Your husband. What does he do?" He was looking at me like he couldn't decide which I was, retarded or deaf.

"Oh! Well, he's . . . ah . . . He died."

Lex looked taken aback but recovered enough to say, "Sorry to hear that. So you're a widow, then?"

A *weeder*? "Ah, yeah. I am. I guess I am." Realizing how that must sound, I quickly asked, "So, when did you move to Fairhope?"

"Let's see. Several months ago now. Damn, time goes by so fast, I can't recall the exact date."

"And what brought you here?"

He inclined his head in the direction of the marina. "Retired from the navy and bought the marina."

Had we kept talking at that point, it would have all clicked into place; I'd certainly have remembered the visit of Elinor to my office and known who he was. But both of us jumped at hearing the cries of "*Jubilee!*" coming from the people standing near the shoreline. It started at the pier where Zoe Catherine and Cooter were, and soon traveled the length of the beach until it was only a faint echo in the distance.

"You've never seen one, right?" I asked breathlessly, and he shook his head.

"Nope, but it's all I've heard about."

"Come on, then," I cried. "Grab your net or gig or bucket or whatever you brought, and let's go."

"You caught me. I didn't bring anything, because I didn't really believe the stories. Figured it was just tall tales," he admitted, but a note of excitement crept into his voice. It was impossible not to catch the feverish anticipation that accompanied the Jubilee cry.

I handed my net to him. "Here. You scoop and I'll hold the sack." It was an old croker sack Mack had given me for that purpose. Nowadays, most people brought buckets, but Mack never used anything else, saying croker sacks were not only easier to fill but also to drag across the sand, once filled. In addition, the crabs couldn't crawl out, like they did from buckets. The only problem with the sack was an obvious one: You had to get the captured loot into water as soon as possible once you filled the sack and left the bay.

Lex and I hurried to the pier just in time to see Cooter dancing around in the shallow water, waving his hat high, and whooping. Then he fell down on his knees and raised his arms to heaven like a praying evangelist as he cried, "Thank you, Jubilee Joe! Thank you, thank you, thank you!"

"Would you look at that," Lex muttered in astonishment. "Is that old coot nuts or what?"

"Just another of Fairhope's many characters. And that's his name, believe it or not."

Lex's eyebrows shot up. "His name is Nuts?"

"Of course not." I laughed. "It's Cooter. Cooter Poulette."

Lex shrugged. "Can't ever tell with you Southerners. Just the other day I met a fellow named Fuzzy, and he had a buddy with him called Screwy Louie."

"Look!" I grabbed his arm and pointed to the moon-bright waters of the bay, where hundreds of mullet were exploding into the air like popcorn. Zoe had been right: The salty smell of fish rode strong on the breeze blowing in from the east. Tugging on his sleeve, I dragged Lex closer to the water's edge, then turned my flashlight downward to show him the droves of blue crabs crawling out of the bay sideways, making their way past the spidery seaweed that lapped at the water's edge.

"Holy Mother of God," Lex Yarbrough said reverently, and crossed himself. All around us, people were running and shouting and laughing, splashing barefoot in the fish-filled waters. Some were gigging the flat, bug-eyed flounder and whiskered catfish, while others were scooping up nets full of gray shrimp and claw-waving crabs. Wordlessly, Lex and I worked together, pointing and bending and gathering the riches of the sea as though picking from a garden at harvesttime. In a matter of minutes, the croker sack, which I'd kept at the water's edge to submerge the fish, was full.

"We've got all we can handle," I said, straightening up and rubbing my back. "And we need to get them put away immediately."

It was getting close to dawn when we made our way through the ecstatic crowd, Lex half toting, half dragging the soggy croker sack and yipping playfully when one of the crabs tried to pinch him through the hemplike material. We spoke to folks we passed on the way, and I was surprised at how many called out to Lex in greeting. When I commented on the number of people he knew, he regarded me oddly, then said he'd met lots of folks since he'd moved here. Since he'd been alone when I encountered him, I'd concluded he must be reclusive; it wasn't long until I realized what an absurd notion that was, as friendly as he was.

Once we came up behind the marina, Lex pulled up the croker sack as though to hand it over to me. "These are yours. Gathering them was one of the great experiences of my life, and I thank you for including me."

"So your first Jubilee was good, huh?" I said, pleased.

"It wasn't just good, it was unbelievable," he said. "If I could convince Maine lobster to have a Jubilee sometime, I'd make a fortune."

Laughing, I motioned toward the sack. "Although it's not lobster, a lot of good eating there. For several days, too." But Lex shook his head in protest, still trying to hand over the sack.

"No way I'm taking all of them," I cried. "Eating your catch is part of the Jubilee experience. Unless you don't like fish?"

He looked shocked, as though I'd suggested he might prefer eating the croker sack instead. "Me not like fish? Ha. That's a good one. Not only was I raised on the sea, I was born into a family of professional fishermen."

"Yeah, but those were Yankee fish. Lobsters and clams and mussels." I racked my brain for other fish I associated with New England. "Cod and haddock and halibut, right? You haven't lived until you've had a Southern feast from a Jubilee, blue crabs and shrimp and flounder and catfish."

Lex nodded toward a door in what appeared to be a storage room under the marina and said, "Tell you what. I know a place we can get these fellows in a cooler of salt water, then we'll sort this out."

The room was a large area obviously used not only for storage of fishing and boating equipment but also for cleaning and keeping fish. Against one wall was a deep, old-fashioned sink and drainboards, two chest freezers, and several coolers. Lex dumped the contents into the sink, and we sorted through our wriggly treasures like kids after Halloween with trick-or-treat loot. Lex admitted he'd turned down the fish not because he didn't like them; it was that he had no place to cook them. Since he was a relative newcomer to town, inviting him to my house the following night for a seafood feast seemed like the only neighborly thing to do.

"I'm tired but not sleepy. What about you?" he asked as we washed up after storing the fish and deciding that he'd be the one to clean them, since I was doing the cooking. We'd walked out to my car, where he'd placed the cooler of shrimp for Austin and Haley, and we stood looking at the bay. It was still dark, the white moon hanging high above us, but the beginnings of dawn could be seen on the horizon. A tinge of gray lightened the blackness of the sky where sky and sea merged. Most of the crowd on the shore had gone, the festive atmosphere dissipated.

"I'm always too wired after a Jubilee to sleep," I said, stretching my arms wide. The exhaustion would hit later.

"Want a cup of coffee, then?"

"I'd kill for one. But nothing around here will be open this time of the morning."

Lex tilted his head to indicate the marina, looming behind us. "Marina is."

"Really? Looks closed to me. Oh! You're having me on again, right?"

"Nope. I got the keys, remember?"

I blinked, then gasped when it hit me. "Oh my God. You're the owner of the marina!"

"I told you that. It's got a coffeemaker and plenty of decaf inside."

"Y-you . . . you're . . ." I stammered and blushed, realizing that he had said it earlier, yet I hadn't heard it. Not really.

Lex was looking at me suspiciously. "I'm *what?*" he said with a scowl.

I swallowed rapidly, buying time. This had happened to me before in my profession. Not too often but occasionally. I'd meet someone at a party, and after hearing the name, I'd have to struggle to keep my face expressionless while making small talk. But I'd be thinking, So this is the woman my client's husband is having an affair with.

Whether it was the intimacy and camaraderie of sharing a Jubilee or what, I told Lex why I reacted as I did. In spite of my strict policy of being closemouthed about my clients—even former clients—I admitted, "It seems that I've met your ex-wife."

"Elinor?" he asked, his eyebrows shooting up again.

"Do you have another one?"

He shook his head ruefully. "She's more than enough."

Amen to that, I thought, but said instead, "I didn't make the connection until now. But your wife—or ex-wife, I mean—well, she told me . . . ah, that you two had moved here after you retired, and that you'd . . ."

When I faltered, Lex put his hands on his hips and rolled his eyes. "No telling what the hell Elinor told you. She's been bad-mouthing me all over town."

"That makes two of us, then," I said, and we stared at each other. I could tell the moment it clicked by the startled expression that crossed his face.

"Holy crap," he gasped, taking a step backward. "Clare Ballenger! You're that therapist."

I nodded, grimacing. But Lex surprised me by what he did next. Throwing his head back, he bellowed with laughter. He then threw his arms around me and pulled me into a bear hug.

"I've been wanting to do this ever since she told me about you. Matter of fact, I thought about looking you up, just to give you a hug. I've never met anyone else with the guts to tell Elinor Eaton-Yarbrough to piss off."

❧

When Lex came over for the Jubilee feast, I invited several others, thinking it'd be a good chance for him to meet some other Fairhope folks. Dory and Son were still together then, and I wasn't surprised to find that Son and Lex already knew each other from the marina. Etta and R.J. came, too, along with half a dozen other friends of mine. Ironically, the two closest to me who ended up being the most curious about Lex couldn't make it: Rye had another party to attend, and Zoe Catherine was too worn out after being up all night with the Jubilee. The feast was a festive evening, full of platters of seafood, mugs of beer, and much talk and laughter, telling endless

Jubilee tales. After everyone left, Lex stayed and helped me clean up. Asking if he'd like to return the next night to help me finish off the leftovers seemed the natural thing to do once he described in such pitiful detail the little galley kitchen in his quarters and how he never cooked anything but TV dinners.

Within a couple of weeks, Lex and I were spending almost every free minute together—a big change for me. The first evening I walked into the reception room of Casa Loco, long after my last client had left, and found Lex waiting for me, I gasped. He'd called earlier that afternoon, and I'd agreed to meet him for a drink after work. "Lex!" I cried, then looked at my watch. "Oh, dear. I stood you up." He scowled and took me by the arm, escorting me out the door over my protests. After it happened a few more times, I learned that if I didn't get the office closed by six o'clock at the latest, he'd be waiting with his dark scowl. Lex became Etta's hero, since she'd tried unsuccessfully for so long to keep me away after closing time.

Once he introduced me to sunset rides on one of his boats, he had me. I loved sailing, which I'd had few opportunities to do during my childhood, in spite of being raised near so many bodies of water. Mack had once given me a sailboat named after me; after it was destroyed by a hurricane, we never replaced it. Sometimes Lex and I sailed, with me as eager helper, hoisting jibs and pulling ropes; other times we took out his twenty-seven-foot Sportfisher; occasionally we cruised in a smaller sloop. Whatever the vessel, Lex succeeded in luring me from my office in the late afternoon, and we spent endless hours exploring the wide waters of Mobile Bay, or the hidden coves and channels along the shoreline.

The question that inevitably comes up between any man and woman who spend that much time together was settled early on in our relationship, and once it was settled—except for Lex's kidding—it did not intrude again. Looking back, I can still make myself laugh, remembering.

Since so many of my weekends were spent with the retreats or group meetings, I took Friday afternoons off, and Lex and I would spend Friday and Saturday afternoon and all day Sunday boating. One Sunday afternoon Lex loaded his small sailboat on a trailer and picked me up, saying he wanted to try out a channel of water around the Bon Secour area that he'd heard raves about. We both agreed that it was our most glorious afternoon yet. It was late June, before the heat wave of July hit, and it'd been balmy and almost cool, coming right after a sudden shower. Lex grumbled because there was no wind, so still that the sails hung limply, and the boat barely rocked. To me, it was sheer heaven. There wasn't another boat in sight, and we drifted aimlessly down a creek so golden it looked as though the sun had tipped over and poured it out.

Once we anchored the boat, we opened the supper we'd picked up at the deli, cold bottles of pinot grigio, goat cheese, rustic bread, and olive spread. Afterward, we propped ourselves up on the cushioned benches of the boat and watched the sunset. Because the boat was small, we were scrunched together, shoulders touching.

"I never want to leave here," I said drowsily, lulled by the food, the wine, and the gentle rocking of the boat.

"Peaceful, eh?" Lex agreed. "Pretty, too. Don't know when I've seen the water this nice. But wake me up if I fall asleep, Doctor Lady."

"Same here, Man of Maine," I said, yawning and fighting to hold my eyes open. Within a matter of minutes, both of us had dozed off.

I awoke with a start to discover that my head was nestled against his shoulder, his arm around me. I looked up, sleep-dazed, to find Lex gazing down at me speculatively. Not for the first time, I admired his very fine eyes. I stirred, trying to straighten up, and Lex tightened his arm around me. With a touch like the flutter of a moth's wings, he reached out to stroke my cheek with the back of his hand.

"I'm thinking maybe I ought to make a pass at you," he said gruffly.

I couldn't help it; I laughed, loud. "Oh, please. No reason to feel obligated."

"Yeah, there is, too. For one thing, you're practically lying on top of me."

Blushing, I tried to pull away, but he didn't loosen his grip. "Then let go so I can get off you," I said, red-faced.

"I don't think I want to. Matter of fact, I'm pretty sure I don't."

"Lex—" I began, and he sighed mightily, moving his arm so I could wiggle out from under it.

"Oh, crap. Here comes the part I've been dreading."

"And what is that?"

"You know. When I put the move on you and you tell me that, based on my ex-wife's description of me as a lover, you wouldn't have me on a silver platter."

"Surely you don't think she told me things like that. Do you?" He'd been relentless in trying to get me to tell him what Elinor had said about him. Out of the blue, he'd bring it up, eyes twinkling with mischief. At a restaurant, I'd ask him to pass the butter, and he'd refuse, saying he'd do so only if I told him what Elinor said.

"Naw," he said. "If she'd told you the truth, you would've already jumped me. I would've had to fight you off the first night we met."

I laughed again, hoping the inevitable confrontation, the mating dance, could be avoided if we kept up the bantering. "You're such a crazy man. And I mean that fondly."

"Maybe I need to see a therapist," he murmured.

"Anyone would have a field day with you, believe me."

Silent for a few minutes, he peered down at me again and said, "Well, what about it? Want to or not?"

"Want to *what?*"

"You know . . . if I'd made a pass at you and—"

"Please don't tell me that is your pathetic way of making one."

"What do you want me to do, get down on my knees and beg?"

I lowered my face into my hands, my shoulders shaking in mirth. "I ain't believing this. Be still my heart!"

"Guess I'm not very smooth, huh? Maybe I need to brush up on my technique."

"Oh, I'd say you need more than a little brushing up. I'd suggest you take a course."

"Do you offer one at those retreat things of yours? If so, sign me up."

"Yeah, right. It's our most popular course."

"No kidding?"

"Of course I'm kidding, idiot." I took a deep breath and began. "Listen, Lex . . ."

"I'm listening."

"Ah. Okay. Know what I'd really like?"

"Sounds like we're finally getting to the good part."

"I'd like for us to be friends. I think—"

"Aw, shit. I *knew* that's what you were going to say. Whenever a woman says that, here's what she really means: You're the world's biggest loser, and you've got about as much chance with me as a fart in a whirlwind."

"Shut up and listen," I said in exasperation. "Don't you think a man and a woman can be friends, like two men or two women?"

"Yawp, sure. If the two men or two women are gay."

"Come on! Have you ever had a close female friend? And just this once, please be serious."

He thought for a long moment. "Well, there was a woman in the navy who was my buddy. You know, like a guy or something. But Elinor would never let me hang out with another woman. Not a chance."

"Now be honest. You said that about making a pass because you thought you were supposed to, didn't you? Because there we were, in a compromising position. You intended it as a joke, but there was a lot of truth to the statement that you felt *obligated* to make a move."

"You said that, not me."

"But didn't you? Feel an obligation just because that's the way things are?" I persisted.

He shrugged, avoiding my eyes.

"Tell you what," I continued. "Why don't we try becoming close friends instead of lovers? I don't know about you, but I've had enough heartache to last me a lifetime. I like you, Lex, very much. You're funny and cute and sweet, and I really enjoy being with you. But frankly, I don't want to have an affair at this point in my life. I have no intention of getting involved in another relationship, not after the way my last one ended. And I bet you feel the same way. Am I right?"

"If you say so." His eyes were thoughtful. "Naw, you're probably on to something. Going through all that crap again is the last thing I want. After Elinor . . . Christ! I may never have another woman. That one about did me in."

"Well, then. Let's give it a try. If it doesn't work for either of us, though, we have to be honest and say so. Can't have any possessiveness. You go out with other women all you want. Matter of fact, I have some nice women friends I'll fix you up with."

"Oh, hell, no. You can forget that."

I laughed. "Okay, strike that. But how do you feel about the rest of it?"

He glared at me. "How come it feels like you're reading to me from some psychology article?"

"That's the last thing I want. Strike everything, and let's just see how it goes."

"Hmm. Okay, I guess."

"So you'll give it a try?"

"Yawp. Guess so," he said with a shrug.

"It'll be a good thing for both of us, wait and see."

I settled back into the seat and so did Lex, but this time neither of us was self-conscious if the boat swayed and threw us together. We lay back for a long time with our shoulders touching, watching the red sun sink into the creek, turning it from gold to fire, and listening to the song of the cicadas and crickets on the banks. Suddenly Lex nudged me and said, "Clare?"

"Hmm?" I was drowsy again, not wanting to leave.

"You awake?"

"Not really," I murmured. "Why?"

"If this plan of yours doesn't work out, do you think . . . ah, you know . . ."

I couldn't stop myself. After several tension-filled days dealing with Dory's problems with Son, I was overdue for an emotional release. It started out as a muffled snort but ended with a howl, and Lex watched in amazement as I laughed helplessly until tears rolled down my cheeks.

Chapter Eight

❧ ❧ ❧ ❧ ❧

When Etta comes into my office to say that I should call Dory back, I punch in the number with a sense of dread. I assume Dory's call has to do with details for the renewal ceremony at the church, which is coming up in a few days. To my surprise, she wants to go with me to the Landing as soon as possible. Can we? I tell her I'll pick her up ten minutes after my last client has gone.

Before leaving to get Dory, I make the other call I've been dreading, to the marina. Lex and I haven't talked since the night he came over and fixed crab rolls for dinner, an unusual length of time for us. Since we met, we've either seen each other or talked almost every day. At first I thought he was pouting because I'd gone to a dance with Rye the following weekend, and I shrugged it off. This past Saturday afternoon, we'd planned to work at the Landing; however, Lex left a message on my phone saying he wouldn't be able to after all. Elinor had called to say she needed to see him. I waited all week for him to let me know what was going on, but nothing.

He answers the phone with an irritated bark of "Marina." All of my numbers are blocked, for obvious reasons, so he doesn't know it's me.

"Sounds like I caught you at a bad time," I say, cringing.

"Oh, hi, Clare. Yeah, it's pretty crazy here. Things go to hell in a handbasket when I'm away." The irritation is gone, but he sounds harried, distracted.

"So you've been out of town?"

"Yeah. Listen, I'll tell you about it. I've been meaning to call, but . . . you know how it is when you get back and everything's piled up."

"Of course. Just give me a ring when you get caught up. Dory and I are going to the retreat site in a few minutes, but—"

"Aw, shit. I've really let you down there. Sorry, but . . . Well, like I say, I'll fill you in soon as I get a chance. And I'll still help out at the Landing, you hear?"

"No problem." But as I hang up, I wonder what he means, saying he'll *still* help out. Now it's finally hit him that Elinor wants him back? If that's the case, not a chance she'll allow it. Matter of fact, if Lex gets back with her, our relationship will be a thing of the past. It's looking less likely that I'll be able to count on his help at the Landing, but the thought of losing his friendship saddens me even more.

When I pick up Dory, she gets breezily into my car, her face flushed and eyes bright. I have to admit that she's looking happier each time I see her.

"Wow. Don't you look great," I say, pulling the car out of their driveway onto the Scenic Highway.

Dory laughs lightly. "Try not to sound so surprised."

Digging in her tote bag, she pulls out a plastic bag of candied ginger and offers me a piece. She's always been addicted to the stuff and now claims it helps with the hot flashes of midlife. A shiver of memory: Mack, turning up his nose at her proffered sack of candy and saying, "That weird shit you eat, Dory, is gonna kill you one of these days," to which Dory retorted, "If all the Jack you drink doesn't kill you, then I've got nothing to fear."

Dory and I munch sugar-coated strips of ginger and make small talk on the drive out, catching up. Neither of us mentions the upcoming ceremony, the reconciliation with Son, or the plans for her new business; we stick to the safe topic of Wayfarer's Landing instead. One day last week Etta and I were working on the calendar when Etta asked if Dory would still be heading up the White Rings for our upcoming events. I replied that I'd wondered, too, since she was not only back with Son but also going ahead with plans for her landscape design business. Etta rolled her eyes, dialed Dory's number, then pressed the speakerphone button. When Dory answered, I suppressed a laugh as Etta said bluntly, "Hey— we need to know if you gonna help us or not?" To my relief, Dory chuckled and said, "I'm too scared of you not to, Etta." Then she added, "Seriously, I made it clear to Son that I intend to have my own life now, and if he doesn't like it . . . We've been through that, and neither of us liked the way it turned out. So count me in."

I glance at Dory now and smile. "The new retreat site—it wouldn't be happening without you, you know." She pooh-poohs that, but I won't allow it. "Okay, it would happen," I concede, "but no telling how long it'd take to get off the ground without your help. I don't have time to do fund-raisers and train volunteers. Your work is such an essential part of what I do. And your generosity—I hope I've expressed my gratitude often enough so you know how much it touches me." In addition to heading up the White Rings, she also sponsors participants who can't afford to attend. Since starting the retreats a few years ago, I've held them at the only place available, the Conference Center and Inn, where the cost has been high but unavoidable. With my own retreat site, I'll be able to make better use of volunteers and keep the cost down, enabling more participants to attend.

"Anything I do is payback for what I owe you," Dory says solemnly. "Whether you believe it or not, helping with your first retreat changed my life." With a laugh, she adds, "Says who, huh? Ha. Guess I should've attended instead of just helping."

"You said it, not me."

"I sat in on all the sessions, and hearing the participants tell their stories was such an eye-opening experience for me. Until then I thought I was the only person in a codependent relationship or with a dysfunctional family."

"Precisely the point of the retreats." We turn off the highway, and I glance Dory's way in warning, paraphrasing one of our favorite lines from the movie *All About Eve*: "Fasten your safety belt, my dear. We're in for a bumpy ride."

Grabbing the door handle as we bounce along, she asks me, "So you've got everything on hold until the site is completed?" I tell her I'm doing only one more retreat until the new site's ready. I've tried to offer one every two months or so, but they've been so popular, with such long waiting lists, that I plan to have them once a month at the Landing.

"When the site's ready, it'll be full speed ahead," I add as I park the car. "I'm reworking a lot of the material, having new brochures made, and lining up some great presenters. Plus, I'm having some productive talks with a man I hope to bring in to conduct the all-male retreats. But that won't be anytime soon. I've got to convince myself they won't be more trouble than they're worth."

Dory looks at me in disbelief. "Everything associated with men is, so why would the retreats be different?" In truth, she's not one of my detractors in having all-male retreats, but I have plenty others. My colleagues scoff, saying that men won't go for that sort of thing. Stubborn as ever, I'm determined to prove them wrong, though it'll be a challenge. Men make up such a small part of my clientele, and they react to divorce differently than women do. For one thing, they're much more likely to remarry again, and sooner. I think about Lex and fear that sheer loneliness might send him back to Elinor. Although our friendship has helped me with my loneliness, it evidently hasn't been enough for him.

"You're deep in thought," Dory remarks as she unbuckles her seat belt.

"I was thinking about Lex, actually."

"Is that god-awful ex of his trying to get him back? That's the rumor going around town, you know." She throws her tote bag over her shoulder but pauses to look at me before getting out.

I shrug. "I'm sure she is, but Lex keeps swearing otherwise."

Dory's eyes on me are like lasers. "That makes me so mad with you that I could kick your butt from here to town!"

"*Me?*" I stare at her, aghast. "For what?"

"You know good and well what. You claim to be Lex's friend, yet you'll let him go back to that haughty bitch, wait and see. I cannot believe it."

"I'll *let* Lex go back to Elinor? Come on, Dory. Like I could stop him." Like I could stop you from taking Son back, a thought I keep to myself.

"Oh, for God's sake! No way you can be that blind." Dory lets out a mighty sigh, then rubs her face in exasperation. "I feel so bad for him."

"For Lex? But why? Because of Elinor, you mean?"

"No, that's not what I mean, and you know it," she mocks. "Every time I've been around you and Lex, I've felt so bad for him that I could hardly stand it."

"This is crazy. I have absolutely no idea what you're talking about."

"Yes, you do. You just won't admit it. It's obvious to everyone that the poor guy is smitten with you."

"*Lex?*"

"He's in real danger of falling in love with you, I think. Oh, he tries to cover it up, acting the fool to hide his feelings. Obviously he's got enough sense to know that you'll push him away, like you do every man who gets too close to you."

"That's ridiculous. Lex is still in love with his ex-wife, as he's told me and anyone else who'll listen. Positive proof that love is blind."

"Oh, bull. He only says that because he doesn't think he has a chance with you. You've erected this huge wall around your heart, and no one can get past it. No one! It's the same thing you did—and continue to do—with Rye. You know how close I've always been to Rye, and it's about killed me to see the way you've done him. Now I see it all over again with Lex. Believe me, I can understand it after Mack, but still. I try to keep my mouth shut because it makes you so mad, but sometimes I can't stand it any longer, and I have to speak up."

"Oh, please. You are so, so wrong. Let's just drop it, okay?"

"Fine." She sighs, shaking her head in resignation. "Just frigging fine. I knew that's what you'd say. But *I* say that you're full of shit."

"Okay, if it makes you feel better, I'm full of shit. Now that we've agreed on that, let's do what we came out here to do and see the new retreat site."

Happily, Dory forgets about me and my love life as soon as she and I walk through the old fish camp, making our way carefully through the piles of construction material, lumber and buckets of paint, stacks of flooring, and all sorts of rubble. It's the best tactic to get her off the subject of me; she exclaims in delight as I show her the way everything is coming along and the way it should look when completed in a few months. As I expected, Dory's suggestions are priceless, and I pull out my notebook to jot down her every word. In each area, she stops and stands with her hands on her hips, frowning thoughtfully. Finally she snaps her fingers and presents the perfect solution to whatever problem I've raised. Once we've completed the walk-through and arrived back on the porch, Dory plops herself on the front steps and motions for me to join her.

"Now that I've seen it," she says, "I can tell you the real reason I asked you to bring me out here."

The worn stone steps are warm from the day's sun, so I sit gingerly next to her. "Aha. Ulterior motives, huh? I should've known." Smiling at her, I realize that things have shifted between Dory and me in spite of our heated exchange in the car. Or maybe because of it. We're no longer tiptoeing around each other, holding our breath. The tension that both of us admitted to when she first returned to help with the group is beginning to dissipate. Our friendship is on its way back.

More than that, I see that the old Dory is on her way back as well. "I have the most incredible idea," she declares, and her eyes glitter like they used to before they were rendered dull by Son's demands.

"I can tell, and I cannot wait to hear it."

"I didn't want to say anything until I had you out here. Plus, I had to be able to visualize it. I had to be here to soak up the ambiance of the place before telling you about it." I nod to urge her on, but Dory holds up a hand. "Before I tell you what it is, I need to show you something, okay?"

"Of course," I say, puzzled.

"Remember you asked me to design a logo for the brochures? You wanted something to bring out the idea of wayfarers. It was right before Son and I split up, and I figured it was a sly attempt on your part to get my mind off him."

I can't resist saying, "It really worked, didn't it?" Dory pokes me with her elbow, and I say, "But it doesn't matter now anyway. I've decided to call my part of this place Wayfarer's Landing, which might affect the logo."

"You're not going to believe this. I'd designed a logo then, but I misplaced it, with everything that's happened since."

I assume that means Son threw it out with everything else in her workshop, but I don't ask. Oblivious, Dory goes on. "Now that things have settled down, I've had time to go through all my unfinished projects. When I found the logo design, I can't tell you how happy I was. Let me show it to you, then I'll explain what it means." Breathlessly, she digs in her tote bag and brings out a sketch pad. I scoot over to sit closer to her, and she holds up a page.

"What is it, a maze?" I ask, taking the pad and staring at the design she's drawn there, a circle with many pathways of concentric circles, all of which lead to a center spot.

"It's a labyrinth, not a maze, though the words are often used interchangeably."

"A labyrinth! Of course—I'd forgotten how you've always had a thing for them, and all your visits to the different kinds. You sent me a postcard of one in France, remember?"

She nods solemnly. "The famous one at Chartres. Seeing it was one of the great experiences of my life, and a labyrinth is the perfect logo for the retreats." She pulls out a pencil and points to the path of the labyrinth, tracing the stops and starts, dead ends and backtracking, until the tip of the pencil reaches the center. "See? Walking the labyrinth is a journey, a difficult and complicated one. But finally you make it to the center. And when you do, guess what you do? You question how you got there and why. Then you begin the journey again." Her face alight with excitement, she draws a circle around the center spot of the design. "Don't you see? It's what the retreats are, and our affirmations, and it's the way you close the sessions."

"You're right." I repeat my closing remarks by memory, I've done them so often: "What have we learned about loss during our time together? Hopefully we've found that loss is always a journey of self-discovery. And we now know that the journey has not ended; it has just begun."

Dory puts a hand on my arm. "Don't you see, honey? All along, my so-called magic circle has been a labyrinth. A pathway leading me round and round, with all sorts of stops and starts, but always back to the center. And I think that's true of all of us. So here's my idea. I would like to build a labyrinth out here at the retreat site."

I sit back in astonishment. "What a fabulous idea. I've never seen a real one—only your photos. What will it look like?"

"I'd like to build it of river stones. Or rather, outline the paths with them. I have some ideas sketched out, but I had to see what you thought first. I also needed to check with Zoe Catherine to see if she'd let me do it. God, she's so wonderful, isn't she? I talked with her before I called you, and she said for me to put it anywhere I wanted, even her front yard. I told her I had to sell you on it first. If you agree, I'll start on it pretty soon, as soon as it gets a little cooler. That way it'll be ready for the first retreat."

"You don't have to sell me on the idea—I love it. I couldn't be more thrilled. Come on, let's find a good spot for it. Will it take up a lot of space?"

She nods as I reach out a hand to pull her to her feet. "Oh, yeah. Sure will. Another reason I thought it'd be perfect out here, and why I needed to ask Zoe's permission. At one time I'd planned on building one in my gardens, but I couldn't make it work out, the way they're shaped. I knew there was plenty of land out here and lots of possibilities for a location. But we'll have to find a way to keep Zoe's birds off it, won't we?"

I laugh as we set off walking, arm in arm. "Oh, I don't know. A little bird shit on the pathways of life seems like the perfect touch to me."

Dory soon finds what she declares to be the ideal spot, in a grassy area beyond Zoe's bird sanctuary. It's a clearing marked off by a rough circle of five live oaks, which excites her even more. "It's a sign! Do you have any idea what the number five represents?"

"I'm afraid to ask."

"Well, five is a pentagon, so that's an endless concept. Which means five symbolizes endlessness and continuity. In addition, five is a circular number, so it carries the power of the circle. Does that make sense?"

"Not a bit, but I love the way it sounds."

Dory walks off the diameter of her labyrinth half a dozen times, or so it seems. At last, she wears herself out, and we sit leaning against one of the tree trunks, where she pants and we share the bottle of green tea she carries in her tote bag. Once she's rested, she turns her head toward me curiously. "You do know the legend of the labyrinth, don't you?"

I frown, shrugging. "Hmm . . . not really. It has something to do with the Minotaur, right? That half-bull, half-man?"

"Here's the way it goes: On the island of Crete, the king built a labyrinth to house the Minotaur, who required a blood sacrifice in order to appease the gods and spare the island. The king imprisoned a lot of local folks in order to feed them to the monster, which kept everybody safe and happy—except for the poor fools being fed to the Minotaur. One day a beautiful young man named Theseus is in the group captured by the king, and he's spotted by the king's daughter, Ariadne."

"I have a feeling I know where this is going," I say, leaning against the tree trunk with a smile.

Dory nods, her eyes half closed and her hands behind her head. "Naturally, Ariadne falls in love with Theseus and doesn't want him to end up on the monster's dinner plate. She gives him one end of a long thread so he can go to the center of the labyrinth, slay the Minotaur, then use the thread to find his way out. And he does, which makes him a mythic hero who can marry the princess and live happily ever after."

"That's why I love the old myths. They're so true to life."

Dory sits up and props her elbows on her knees. "Oh, but here's the cool part of the story. Instead of settling down with the princess and enjoying a life of riches and ease, Theseus, being a true hero, returns to the isle of Crete so that he can free the remaining hostages. Once he frees them, the whole group of prisoners, led by Theseus, dances a wild dance of freedom and celebration, following the winding paths of the labyrinth to the center."

"Wow. The classic myth of initiation, trial, and triumph. Old Jung must've wet his pants when he first heard it."

"It's classic Jungian, but better." Dory's lost in thought for a minute, then she says, "To me, it's not just the slaying of the monster, or finding a way out of the maze, or even the sacrifice of returning to the island. Initiation, trial, and triumph. Instead, it's the dance of celebration! To really walk the labyrinth, the dance has to come afterward, don't you think?"

Before I can answer, a piercing, unearthly shriek comes from the direction of Zoe Catherine's cabin. Jumping to our feet, Dory and I stare at each other wide-eyed.

"Jesus Christ," Dory gasps. "Was that a peacock?"

"She has one by that name, but if it's him, he must've been attacked by a wildcat. I've never heard any of them make that kind of racket. We'd better go see."

We scurry across the wide grassy space that will become the labyrinth and arrive at the path leading to Zoe's cabin and aviaries, hidden away in the thick trees. Several of her peacocks are wandering around the yard, dragging their long tails. If a wildcat or fox is on the loose, they're being awfully nonchalant about it. A couple of them are perched on the low-hanging boughs of a dogwood tree, their tail feathers hanging down like the cloak of an emperor, iridescent and majestic. Surely if a predator were after them, they'd all take flight. Zoe Catherine has taught me that they roost only in the tops of trees, where they can be on the lookout for enemies. When not roosting for the night, they sometimes perch on lower branches, but only sparsely leafed ones, so they can see all around. Zoe is nowhere to be seen, but Cooter's pickup is parked nearby. I assume they're in one of the boats, fishing on the creek.

Shading my eyes from the late-afternoon sun, I look toward the dock and immediately see where the racket is coming from. "Come on, Dory," I cry, and we take off for the creek. "Dear God—it looks like something has happened to Cooter."

Before we reach the creek bank, we see that both Zoe Catherine and Cooter are on the dock. Zoe is yelling, Cooter is yelling, and

Genghis Khan is running our way, crying his raucous cry. The ducks are waddling down the creek bank in terror, flapping their wings and quacking louder than I've ever heard them as they head for the water, where they plop in and paddle away.

"What on earth?" Dory says, but both of us stop in our tracks when we reach the creek.

For someone in his seventies, Cooter is moving with amazing speed. For one disconcerting moment, I think he's performing one of his wild dances, like he was doing at the Jubilee. Then I see that, rather than dancing, he's hopping from one foot to the other, trying to get away from Zoe, who's holding on to one of his flailing arms with both hands. They're both yelling, but it's hard to tell what Zoe's saying because of Cooter's cussing.

"Goddamn damn *damn,*" he yells, dancing from foot to foot. "Let go of me, woman! I'm gonna kill that sorry son of a bitch! I'm gonna kill that rat-fuck bastard!"

"You're not killing nobody, you old fool," Zoe shouts as she yanks even harder on his arm. "Be still long enough for me to see how bad you're hurt."

Dory and I stop and stare in astonishment as Cooter falls to his knees with so much force that Zoe loses her grip on his arm. "Ow!" he cries, his face contorted in agony. "I'm dying! He's killed me, the sorry piece of shit! Call an ambulance! Call the undertaker!"

"Cooter—Zoe!" I shout, running on the dock, Dory not far behind. "What is it? What's wrong?"

Cooter sees me, and his face lights up with relief, although his weak eye is wallowing around like a loose marble. "Clare! Go to the house and call 911, and hurry up before I die on this shit-covered dock."

"Stay where you are, Clare," Zoe says. Having lost her grip on Cooter's arm, she grabs the straps of his overalls instead. "The idiot's not dying, but he won't be still long enough for me to see how bad he's hurt."

Dory drops to her knees in front of Cooter, who's still yelling "*Ow! Ow! Ow!*"

"Cooter?" Dory says in her low, calm voice. "You have to tell us what's wrong before we can help you. Where are you hurting?"

"It's his ass," Zoe Catherine says solemnly.

Dory gets to her feet. "His *what?*"

"His ass," Zoe shouts, as though Dory is deaf. To our further amazement, Zoe begins to unbuckle the straps of Cooter's overalls. "Hold still and let me look at it, fool."

"What's wrong with it?" I dare ask Zoe as Dory puts a hand over her eyes.

"Quit that, Zoe Catherine," Cooter cries, hitting at Zoe's hands. "You're not about to pull down my britches in front of these women."

"Zoe, what happened?" I ask again, beginning to get exasperated. It's obvious that Cooter's not seriously injured, even though, the way he's carrying on, you'd think he was dying.

Zoe succeeds in unbuckling his overalls; but, still kneeling in front of her on the dock, Cooter grabs the straps and hangs on for dear life.

"I can tell you exactly what happened," Zoe says over her shoulder to me and Dory. "Cooter had a wad of Beechnut chewing tobacco in his back pocket, and he was kneeling on the dock with his ass way up in the air, pulling in a crab line. Genghis came up behind him and pecked at his pocket, trying to get the tobacco out. Beechnut has always been his favorite brand."

"I thought somebody had shot me, and I almost fell in the creek," Cooter yells. "Turn loose of my britches, woman."

On hearing this, I can't look Dory's way. "Maybe you should get a tetanus shot, Cooter," I suggest. "Would you like me and Dory to drive you to the clinic?"

"I would not," he replies indignantly. "Getting shot once is enough for me, thank you. Besides, I got one of them technical shots last year when I stuck a fish hook in my hand."

"Zoe Catherine, if you'll wait," Dory says, "Clare and I'll turn around so you can . . . ah . . . check and see what kind of injury Cooter has."

"I can tell you without her looking," Cooter shouts, struggling to his feet. "That pissant of a peacock pecked a hole in my arse. And I'm gonna shoot him soon as I can get my gun out of the pickup. Let go of me, Zoe!"

Before Dory and I can turn our heads away, and with Cooter struggling against her, Zoe pulls out the back of Cooter's overalls, sticks her head in, and announces, "Aw, that's not so bad. It's not even bleeding much. I've been pecked lots worse before."

"Not where he pecked me, you haven't," he says.

"Not on the ass," Zoe agrees, "but plenty of other places. It hurts like the devil, I'll give you that."

"That pea-damn-cock won't ever peck anyone again once I get my gun," Cooter roars, yanking the straps out of Zoe's hands and muttering to himself as he struggles to refasten them.

"Let me get you some Merthiolate, honey. That'll fix you up," Zoe says, pushing past Cooter and heading toward the house.

"Shit fire and save matches!" Cooter cries. "You're not putting Merthiolate on *my* arse."

"I'll get the whiskey bottle while I'm there," Zoe says over her shoulder, "and you won't feel a thing."

Dory stops Zoe as she's about to jump off the dock. "Zoe?" she whispers with a worried frown as she glances back at Cooter, who's still ranting and raving. "Don't worry—Clare and I will stay and make sure Cooter doesn't go after his gun, okay?"

Zoe laughs and waves her hand. "Oh, phooey! Y'all go on home if you need to. Cooter's not going to shoot Genghis. He loves that old bird too much to shoot him. They fight all the time. Can't anybody get along with Cooter Poulette, no matter who they are."

Dory and I start home, but we don't get far. After asking Cooter if he's okay, if he needs us to do anything for him, and getting his muttered "no thanks," that he's fine now, neither of us says a word as we return to my car. In silence, I back out the car, then head down the long driveway toward the highway. But when I reach for the air-conditioning button, Dory's eyes meet mine. "Oh, my Lord in heaven," she cries with a snort of laughter.

"Don't get me started," I sputter, but don't make it any further. Once I start, I can't stop. I pull over the car to get myself under control, then both of us wipe our eyes and look at each other. Hearing that irrepressible laugh of hers, I know that the old Dory is indeed back.

❧

I've promised Abbie that I'll take her to the beach one last time before it gets too cool, just the two of us, and when I find a time to make that happen, we take off. She wants the *real* beach with *real* waves, she says, not the boring old waters of the bay. Although I don't relish the drive to Gulf Shores, I give in and take her the following Saturday. It's been way too long since the two of us had an outing. I pack a picnic, and we head off for a day at the Gulf of Mexico. Early that evening, when we arrive back in Fairhope, we're worn out, sticky with seawater, and pink-cheeked in spite of the sunblock I slathered on both of us.

Although they started their marriage in a small apartment in Fairhope, Austin and Haley now live in a tidy little cottage on the outskirts of Daphne, which is not that far from Haley's school yet closer to the community college where Austin works. It's in a friendly, safe neighborhood where a lot of young couples with children live, and there are sidewalks and a park. It's just turned dark when I pull into their driveway behind two other cars. I wanted Abbie to stay overnight with me, something else she hasn't done for a while, but she insisted on returning home, since her parents were having a party to celebrate the start of another school year. Or that was Abbie's version. Haley scoffed at that, saying they weren't having a real party, just some folks over for a cookout, but Abbie never wants to miss out on anything. Her mother lets her help, setting the table or serving hors d'oeuvres or passing out napkins. Abbie adores dressing up and being fussed over by guests.

"We shouldn't have stopped for ice cream, Abbie-kins," I say as I park the car. "It made us run late. Now you'll have to hurry and shower and get all dressed up, because the cookout is already under way."

Abbie turns her sun-kissed face toward me, her round gray eyes shining. "Guess what, Grams? Jasmine is bringing a new boyfriend. Mommy says he's real nice, but I can't say anything about him being fat." She shakes a finger in an imitation of her mother's lecture. "It is very rude to say things like that, calling people fat."

Haley's prediction at Mateer's a few weeks ago proved to be correct, and Jasmine's interest in Tommy McNair has blossomed into a real romance. "You already know that, sweetie," I say to Abbie with an indulgent smile. "You'd never be rude and hurt anyone's feelings, would you?"

"I wouldn't, but Zach keeps saying it. I told Mommy not to worry, I'd put my hand over Zach's mouth if he said it at the party."

As soon as I unfasten her seat belt, Abbie grabs me around the neck, gives me a sticky, salty kiss, and bolts for the house. Haley has invited me to stay for the cookout, but I've begged off. Tired from the day at the beach, I'm looking forward to going straight home, taking a long shower, and hitting the sack. But I can't drive off without saying hello to everyone, at least.

I follow my nose to the backyard, where Austin is grilling hamburgers on the deck. Zach is riding his Big Wheel around in circles on the deck as he says something that sounds suspiciously like "Fat, fat, fat," which I pray is his version of a driving noise instead. After hugging Haley and Austin, I shake hands with John and Wanda Webb, who are standing next to the grill with Austin, beers in hand.

The Webbs always look as perfectly put together and wholesome as the model couples in a *Southern Living* magazine.

Jasmine is leaning against the rail, talking quietly to a young man I recognize as Tommy McNair, and I go over to greet them. Jasmine looks lovely, with her face aglow, her hair slicked back in a stylish knot at the nape of her neck, and large gold hoops in her ears. Even though he's quite heavy, Tommy McNair has a sweet face and soft brown eyes like a doe's, with long thick lashes. As we chat, he and Jasmine keep glancing at each other, moony-eyed, and I relax, relieved to see that the attraction doesn't seem to be a result of Jasmine's poor self-image after all. On the contrary, they appear to be quite taken with each other.

As I say my goodbyes and start to leave, Haley touches my arm when I pass by her on the deck, where she stands next to the grill with Austin and the Webbs. "Wait, Mom," she says. "You should take a hamburger home for your supper."

"No, no, I'm fine." I wave her off, but she protests.

"Don't be silly. You've got to eat, and we have plenty."

"Take one with you, Clare," Austin says as he flips a burger and squints through the smoke.

"Thanks, but I'm a recovering vegetarian," I say, stealing a line from Dory. I rarely eat red meat but don't want to hurt their feelings.

Austin pooh-poohs my protests and inclines his head toward Haley. "Get your mom a paper plate, hon." When she goes to the kitchen, Austin watches her leave, then rolls his eyes toward me. "You might change your mind when you see these burgers. Haley went to the store, and instead of getting ground beef, she brought back a meat-loaf mixture that's mostly ground turkey. They may not be fitting to eat."

The Webbs chuckle, and I say, "Oh, I'm sure ground turkey burgers will be just as good. Healthier, if nothing else."

Haley returns with a paper plate and a piece of foil, and as Austin is dishing up a patty, she says, "Did Austin tell you I got meat-loaf mixture instead of ground beef? Zach was pitching a fit for Cocoa Puffs, embarrassing me to death, so I just grabbed something and ran."

"Actually, Haley, meat-loaf mixture looks quite different from hamburger," Wanda Webb says with a big smile, tilting her blond head prettily.

"We could have brought the meat if you'd given us a call," her husband, John, says to Austin.

"Tell you what, Haley," Wanda says perkily. "Y'all come to our place next weekend for a cookout, and I'll show you the secret ingredient for my burgers. Everybody says they're the best they've ever eaten."

"Hey, thanks, Wanda," Austin says, grinning. "That sounds great. I'm sure Haley will appreciate any secrets you can show her in the kitchen. Truth is, she can't cook squat."

Wanda puts a hand to her throat and widens her eyes. "Who does the cooking, then?"

"Yours truly," Austin replies with a smirk.

"Cooking's never been my thing," Haley admits. "It's always been Austin's department. But I don't want the kids eating junk food, and Austin doesn't have as much time anymore, so I've made up my mind to learn."

"I'll be glad to give you lessons if you'd like," Wanda gushes, then cuts her eyes toward Austin. "John would have a *fit* if I didn't have his supper waiting for him every night."

Stopping on my way down the steps, I'm unable to resist saying with feigned innocence, "I didn't realize you were home all day, Wanda. Somehow I had the impression that you were a counselor in the learning lab, too."

She looks at me in surprise. "Oh, I am. Remember, Dr. Ballenger, we talked about it that night of the Jubilee?" It takes her a minute to understand what I'm actually saying, so she adds hastily, "But I schedule my day in order to get home before John and have a nice supper waiting for him. His job is so much more demanding than mine, it's the least I can do."

Austin grins. "Sometimes Haley has a nice frozen pizza waiting for me."

I look over at Haley, who's glaring at Wanda and Austin. Good for her—maybe Haley will remind Susie Sorority that she not only works outside the home but also has two small children to care for, then tell Mr. Perfect to cook his own damn dinner if he doesn't appreciate her efforts. Instead, I bite my tongue and wave goodbye again, hurrying down the deck steps with the foil-wrapped meatloaf burger in hand. Lately Austin and Haley have spent most of their free time with John and Wanda Webb, and I've been pleased, thinking what a nice young couple they were. Now I wonder about Wanda. Maybe she's one of those women who tries to make herself look good by putting other women down. As I go around the house to my car, their laughing voices, light and carefree, float on the air like the smoke from the grill, and I silently scold myself. Occupational hazard, overanalyzing everything. Don't look for trouble, I always tell my clients. Because if you do, you will be sure to find it.

❧

Back home, I luxuriate in the long hot shower I promised myself, washing off the salt and sand and suntan lotion. In my rattiest nightgown, I prop up on a stack of pillows in bed, a pile of reading material on the table beside me, and sigh with pleasure. Why does nothing on earth feel better than turning in early, all alone, with a whole evening to lie in bed and read? It's been way too long since I've allowed myself the luxury of doing absolutely nothing. After listening to my messages from the usual suspects, Dory, Rye, and Lex, I turn off the ringer on the phone. Any problems that arise tonight will have to wait until tomorrow. My relaxing evening of reading doesn't last nearly as long as I'd hoped, however. After an hour, I can no longer stay awake, so I turn off the light and fall into a heavy sleep.

I'm not sure what wakes me, but I jump up, heart pounding and mouth dry. Was it a dream, or did I hear a noise? I fall back on my pillow and look around the shadowy room, illuminated by the eerie whiteness of the moon. My bedroom overlooks the backyard, so I never draw the curtains. Tonight a half-moon appears to have been placed by a benevolent god on a leafy branch of the spreading magnolia outside my window. I remain still, listening. Is that scraping noise a limb brushing against a window screen? How can that be, when there is no wind? I look again at the magnolia, etched boldly against the sky, and not a leaf stirs.

There it is again, like the rustling of leaves. It's coming from downstairs, but I'm not sure where. Could it be a mouse in the kitchen? Or—what?—someone trying to break in the back door, cutting into the screen, knowing I live alone? Maybe a deranged husband of one of my clients, Helen Murray's, perhaps, seeking vengeance, intent on slitting my throat as I sleep. Had I not been forced awake by the noise, I'd never have known what hit me. Did I lock the back door? Half the time I don't, and I shouldn't be so careless. Fairhope is as safe a place as possible, but still.

Throwing off the crumpled sheet, I put my legs over the side of the bed and move to the door. Then I creep down the unlit stairs, pausing each time one of the old steps squeaks. The streetlamps in the front of the house light my way, although it's still dark and shadowy, with pieces of furniture looming large and ominous like the monsters of childhood nightmares. Peering around the kitchen door, I see that everything is in its rightful place, and no mice scurry away. I glide across the cool tile of the kitchen floor and check the back door: locked.

Back on the stairs, I hear the sound again. This time there's no question where it's coming from, and my breath catches in my throat. Mack's room. Retracing my steps down the stairs, I turn to the hallway and walk through the shadows to a small room at the back. It stays closed off, used occasionally for storage but not entered otherwise, although my cleaning woman, Carlita, keeps it in pristine condition.

From the time we moved into the house, this room belonged to Mack. He claimed it as his study the first day we planned the renovation. I push open the door and walk in, sighing in relief. The mystery is solved. The same thing happened one other time, but I'd forgotten. I'd heard the noise in the daytime then, with none of the uncertainties and fears that nightfall brings. Ghosts show themselves only in the dark of night, and if Mack were going to haunt any room in the house, it'd be this one. Smiling at my foolish fancies, I walk over and pull the chain on the ceiling fan, which whirls with a rasping sound, the noise that penetrated my sleep and woke me. Carlita was cleaning in here today and, as she did on one other occasion, forgot to turn off the fan. Once I pull the chain, the room is silent as a tomb.

But for the furniture, the room is bare, because when Mack died, I packed away all his stuff. Except for one thing—the gun rack he had specially made for his collection of hunting rifles and shotguns. The day after the accident, I asked Rye to take it away. I didn't care what he did with it as long as he got it out of my sight forever. Moving through the cold moonlight, I cross the room and sit down in the brown leather chair that belonged to Mack's father. Although Papa Mack gave him a desk when we first moved in, Mack brought the chair from his father's house many years later. Right after his father died, Aileen, Mack's stepmother, told him and his stepbrothers to come get what they wanted. Afterward, she sold the house on the bay and moved to Miami with the considerable fortune Papa Mack had left her, most of which was supposed to have been Mack's inheritance. Minus occasional visits to her sons and grandchildren who still live in this area, Aileen stays away from Fairhope. In poor health, she didn't even come to Mack's funeral.

I sit on the edge of the leather chair and look around the room, which remains vibrant with Mack's presence even though it's been swept clean of his things. God, I can still see him sitting at the desk, his back to the door. Sometimes I'd come in, tiptoe across the room, and stand behind his chair, poised to put my hands over his eyes. "Tea rose," he'd say without turning around. "If you're going to sneak up on me, baby, change your perfume." But I couldn't because tea rose was his favorite, the scent he gave me every year. I'd lean over him, my arms wrapped around his shoulders, and bury my face in the sweet skin of his neck, inhaling hungrily.

If tea rose was my signature aroma, Mack's was pine and cypress and mudflats and marsh grass and wood smoke, the smells of the outdoors that he loved so much. I appeared calm and collected throughout the whole ordeal of Mack's funeral because I was dazed with shock. But I had one bad moment. At the funeral home, the family had to be there a few minutes before the visitation; Zoe, Haley, Austin, and I held one another up as we walked into the visitation room, with its muted lighting and hymns playing solemnly in the background. Because of his head injury, Mack's casket would remain closed, a photograph of him in his baseball uniform on an easel beside it. Haley and Zoe had dissolved at the sight of the photo, but I'd sought out the funeral home director, standing discreetly to one side.

"Would you open the casket?" I said, my voice rising to a wail as I pulled frantically on his arms, and Rye came to take me away, looking apologetically at the poor guy. "All I wanted was to put my face on Mack's neck," I sobbed into Rye's shoulder. "I wanted the smell of him one last time."

Tucking my feet under, I lean back in the chair and allow myself to remember the way it was before Mack left me forever. We'd been so crazy in love, consumed by a fire that never really died out.

In spite of everything, I loved Mack Ballenger in a way I'll never love anyone again. I'm sure of that now, these long lonely years after his death. After all this time, my grief is still as raw as a fresh wound. I've survived by channeling it in other directions, as a trench dug out from a stream of water will direct the water's flow elsewhere. Dig enough trenches, and the stream will become a trickle.

My eyes fall on the small sofa in the corner. I remember when Mack brought it home, a year after we married. I'd complained long and loud about his buying it because our budget was so tight. Mack had been determined not to work in his father's bank, so he was renovating old houses, and I was working at a therapy practice in Mobile, in addition to driving back and forth to LSU for my doctorate. Even if we could've afforded it, I thought the sofa was hideously ugly, squat and plaid and cumbersome. But Mack had loved it and lugged it into his study. When I remember the way we ended up using the cushions, I lower my face into my hands.

The following year the renovation was finished, and we had a housewarming party to celebrate Mack's long hard year of fixing up our house. Exactly two weeks later, Hurricane Frederick slammed into the Gulf Coast, hitting the Fairhope area particularly hard. Mack could do nothing but watch the damage to our beloved house in horror and disbelief. We grabbed the cushions off the ugly sofa and barricaded ourselves with them as we huddled under the staircase. From there, we watched the new shingles of his roof, which had caused Mack the most difficulty and inflamed his old shoulder injury, fly by the windows like little missiles. I wept in Mack's arms and tried not to see the hurricane as symbolic of the outside forces that are always out there, waiting to sweep in and bring destruction to whatever it is we spend our lives building.

I raise my head, wishing I hadn't come down here and resurrected the ghosts of the past, yet unable to get up and go back to my lonely bed. I packed up Mack's things and closed off his study in an attempt to put my loss behind me. And most of the time, it worked. But tonight it won't let me go, release me so I can return to the life I've made without him. Start out by putting your feet on the floor, I tell myself. That's easy enough, isn't it? Just put your feet on the floor and get out of this damned chair that Mack's presence still occupies. Don't dare lean your head back and close your eyes, because it will come back to you, that awful day when Mack went into the swamps and never came back. Worst of all, you'll be forced to face what you haven't been able to all these years—what really happened that day and what it was that drove Mack to the woods in the first place.

Chapter Nine

❧   ❧   ❧   ❧   ❧

The Grand Hotel in Point Clear is exactly that—grand. Nestled in some of the most magnificent oaks on the Eastern Shore, it's a place of such elegance and splendor that it takes my breath away. As if the hotel and grounds weren't glorious enough, it has a dazzling and panoramic view of Mobile Bay. Even I have to admit that it's the perfect setting for an anniversary party, especially if you've got big bucks like Son Rodgers and can afford to rent the entire dining room, which seats over two hundred, and hire a world-class jazz band. While waiting for the happy couple to appear, I look around in amazement, trying to keep from gaping. The buffet tables border on the obscene. Heavy silver bowls as big as washtubs are piled high with boiled shrimp or lump crabmeat; there's a reddish-pink prime rib that's the size of a whale; in the center is an ice sculpture of a soaring swan with the wingspan of an albatross. Rye nudges me and mutters, "Guess the Son King is trying to recapture the good old days of his reign at Versailles."

"Shhh," I say, poking him back. There's a flurry of excitement at the door, and Son and Dory appear. I can't get tickled just as the happy couple walk in, or the tears I held back during the ceremony might come pouring out. But it's Dory who bursts into tears as she enters the expansive dining room to the cheers of the well-wishers gathered under a ceiling of silver balloons and streamers. Even Son is touched, and when he pulls out a handkerchief to dab at his eyes, I move out of reach of Rye's elbow.

Jackson and Shaw, looking handsome and sophisticated in white dinner jackets, step up to stand by their parents, and Jackson taps on the microphone to quiet the crowd. "Ladies and gentlemen," he says with a tremulous smile, "allow me to present my mom and dad." After a round of applause and waves from Son and Dory, Jackson leans in to the microphone to ask Father Gibbs to say a blessing. Afterward, the distinguished, silver-haired priest links arms with Dory and Son and poses for one of many pictures that will be taken that night. My heart sinks when Dory catches my eye and motions for me to join them. I dare not look Rye's way as Son plants himself between Dory and me with a big grin, his arms around both of us while flashbulbs go off. Dory's tears have vanished, and her bubbling laughter floats over the dining room like the streamers twirling from the ceiling. Jackson reminds everyone that the buffet is ready, and I make my way through the crowd, seeking out Rye.

It would've been a much more difficult evening to get through had not something occurred that dissipated any remaining tension between Dory and me and lightened my mood considerably. When Dory asked if I still had my bridemaid's dress, I admitted it was in the attic, but no way in hell would I wear it. She'd engaged a seamstress to update her wedding gown, and I let her have a look at the bridesmaid's dress after realizing the only other thing I had was the cocktail dress I wore to every dressy event I attended. But showing up in black at Dory's renewal ceremony, even if appropriate, would've been seen as a contradiction to my avowed support. I'd either have to find time to go shopping in Mobile, or get something from Elinor's shop, neither of which was appealing. So I stood in front of the mirror in Dory's bedroom as the seamstress struggled to squeeze my middle-aged body into a size-four bridesmaid's dress. When I met Dory's eyes in the mirror, I snickered. Bad move. The zipper popped open, and a seam split with a sickening sound. Dory tried to keep a straight face, but soon we were both howling while the poor seamstress sat back on her heels helplessly. Dory insisted I wear a dress she'd bought in France, which she tactfully described as loosely fitted. It was a lovely thing of hand-loomed champagne lace, and Dory was right, sort of. Except for a daring neckline and snug bodice, it fit me perfectly.

"I'm not wearing this," I said, red-faced. "I've never worn anything cut this low, even a swimsuit."

Dory said of course I hadn't worn anything like it, and that was my problem. The seamstress chimed in and said it was très chic; she was probably afraid she'd have to repair the bridemaid's dress if I turned it down. Dory added, "If you've got it, flaunt it. Elinor's flat as a fried egg; think how jealous she'll be when you stroll by with Lex on your arm." At my bemused expression, she asked sharply, "You *are* going with Lex, aren't you? That's what he told me when I asked him to the renewal ceremony." It was a relief when Dory had overruled Son and declared the ceremony should be limited to a small group of family and close friends. Otherwise, Son would've invited half of Fairhope.

Grimacing, I told her the truth, knowing what I was in for. "I did tell Lex I'd go with him, but Rye reminded me I'd already promised him."

Dory blinked. "You told *two* men you'd go to the party with them?"

I nodded sheepishly. "Not intentionally, of course, but it turns out I did."

She clapped her hands in glee. "La-de-da. Cinder-priss-butt-rella going to the ball with two gentlemen callers!"

"Cinderella went to the ball alone, remember? Which is what I wish I were doing."

Oblivious to the shocked face of the elderly seamstress, Dory studied me for a long moment, then said in all seriousness, "Something

I've been meaning to say to you, Clare. This abstinence thing of yours has gone on way too long. Maybe the dress will do the trick, but if not, I might have to put a bug in Rye's ear."

"So help me, Dory," I said, "if you say one word to anybody, I'll never speak to you again."

I'd barely gotten home when Haley called me. "Hot damn, Mom!" She laughed. "Dory just told me about your two dates. Not bad for an old broad, huh? I feel bad for Lex, though. Probably hurt his poor old Yankee feelings, but it serves him right for two-timing you with his ex."

"I'm hanging up now. And you, young lady, are out of my will. Disinherited. I'm never speaking to you or Dory again, and I'm leaving everything to Abbie and Zach."

"Uh-oh, I'd better behave, then. If you marry Rye, you'll be rich, and I'll be sorry. Hey, will I inherit twice, since you'll be both my mom and my cousin?"

After we leave the mile-long buffet line at the party, I try to maneuver Rye in another direction so we won't be seated with Dory and Son, but Dory's having none of it. As soon as I sit down, she puts a hand to the side of her mouth and whispers, "Told you that dress was sexy. Rye can't keep his eyes off you. Tonight's the night."

"Don't you dare start that," I hiss.

Rye, who's sitting on the other side of me, turns his head our way, and I stop midsentence. "I heard my name, Dory," he says, and I hold my breath.

She smiles at him and flutters her lashes. "I was just saying how terribly handsome you look in your tux, darling. But you always do, whatever you wear. Clare's a lucky woman."

"Hey, what about me?" Son cries indignantly.

"You're a lucky man, too, Son," she says, then turns her attention back to me. "I expect a full report in the morning," she whispers in my ear. "Salacious details for my next meditation."

Son glances around the table at the other couples, mostly his and Dory's relatives, and chuckles uneasily. "Looks like Dory's not gonna let us in on her and Clare's secret, folks."

Dory puts her hands to her cheek in mock horror. "I'm so sorry! I didn't mean to be rude, but I didn't want to embarrass you, love. I was telling Clare that you look almost as handsome as Rye tonight."

"Aw, really?" Son grins. "Thanks, sugar." Holding his glass high, he says, "Hey, y'all, I'd like to propose a toast to the best wife any man's ever had." His face aglow, he turns toward her. "Talk about lucky! I'm the luckiest man alive that Dory has put up with me for twenty-five years."

"Amen to that," I mutter. When we click our glasses, Rye smiles at me knowingly. Both of us have been reluctant to admit that so far, Dory has been right about Son's miraculous conversion. Except for the time he burst into my office, he's behaved admirably. Rye said if Son keeps it up, we'd better be careful, or hell will be freezing over.

I turn my attention to my dinner plate, even though it's difficult with Rye watching me so closely. I'm not sure if it's the daring neckline or what, but Dory's right—he's been staring at me all night. After the plates are cleared away, I join in the light chatter around the dinner table, and he continues to regard me. My cheeks burn when the others at our table glance from me to him curiously. Dory keeps smirking and nudging me under the table until, pretending to straighten my chair, I shift out of her reach. Finally the endless dinner is over, and the toasts begin. With a sigh of relief, I turn my chair to face the podium where Jackson and Son stand, trying to get the attention of the noisy crowd. Thankfully, I don't have to make a toast. Dory had been so thrilled that I'd agreed to stand up with her at the ceremony, she'd granted me a major concession by saying casually, "Let the guys handle the toasts, okay?"

The toasts go on and on, and after each one, a beaming Son

bends over to kiss his bride. Just when I think I can't stomach it a minute longer, Father Gibbs takes the floor and launches into a long-winded tribute to the happy couple, the perfect opportunity for me to study the guests. Directly in my line of vision is the table where Lex sits with Elinor. When I'd called him to explain how I unintentionally accepted two rides to the party, he'd pretended to misunderstand me and said, "Since there's not room for the three of us in my Jeep, guess we're taking his Mercedes." When I admitted that Rye had asked me first, Lex said with a snort, "Well, hell. I'll take Elinor, then," and hung up.

The table where I tried to steer Rye before we were intercepted by Dory is positioned by the door, where Zoe Catherine sits with Cooter. Zoe hadn't wanted to come, though Dory had begged her so piteously that she'd given in but said she was leaving after dinner. She'd confessed later that she was nervous about bringing Cooter to such an elegant function with all of Fairhope society in attendance, especially with the free-flowing booze. In the buffet line, I did a double take when I spotted the two of them entering. Zoe was in a getup I'd never seen before, something she and Cooter must have found at one of the flea markets they frequent, searching for material for her nature sanctuary. Flung dramatically around her shoulders was a black-and-turquoise shawl embroidered with a huge sequined peacock, and her white hair was piled high into a bun and secured with chopsticks. Or they looked like chopsticks. Knowing Zoe, they could be anything. And I wouldn't have recognized Cooter. I'd never seen him in a suit before, though Zoe has assured me that he keeps one on hand for funerals. With his long gray hair slicked back in a ponytail, cowboy boots, and a string tie, he looks like a desperado who hitched his mount outside and meandered in to see where the noise was coming from.

Another table I keep eyeing is Haley and Austin's. A hopeless romantic, Haley was aghast that I'd dreaded the renewal ceremony, saying even though I didn't like Son, I had to agree it was a sweet idea, didn't I? I most certainly did not, I informed her shortly, but it didn't dampen her enthusiasm. On the contrary, she hoped to convince Austin that they should do the same for their tenth anniversary next year, and she couldn't wait for the service. At the church, I'd entered from the side door with Dory and Son, Jackson, Shaw, and Father Gibbs, so I hadn't been able to see the folks in the candlelit chapel until afterward. As Rye and I were leaving, I'd been surprised not to see Haley there. I feared their sitter hadn't shown up, and regretted that she missed it. At the Grand Hotel, Rye was gallantly helping me out of the car when I spotted Haley and Austin at the front door. I was about to call out to her when I realized they were hissing at each other furiously. "Uh-oh. Trouble in paradise," Rye murmured. He's far from the fatherly type, but to give him credit, since Mack died, he's made a clumsy effort when it comes to Haley and the kids. Inside, I'd sought Haley out, but she'd been sullen and noncommittal, glaring at Austin out of the corner of her eye. I beat a hasty retreat, reminding myself that I was off duty tonight.

After the buffet dinner is cleared away and the toasts completed, the jazz band plays "Tenderly," and Dory and Son lead off the dancing. With her hair in an elegant chignon, Dory looks stunning, as only she could in an altered wedding dress, and the soft lights overhead catch the sparkle of the diamond anniversary ring Son gave her, with a rock the size of an ice cube. When the band starts up a bluesy version of "Sitting on the Dock of the Bay," Rye grabs my hand and leads me to the dance floor.

I'll always be grateful to Rye for bringing dancing into my life. Mack hated to dance, and I'd always been labeled uptight and studious, so I didn't consider myself much of a dancer. A year after Mack died, Rye called to say by damn I'd grieved long enough; he was coming over to take me out. I'd been too downhearted to protest. We ended up at Mobile's ritzy country club, and Rye, who'd been my dance partner in the past when Mack wouldn't, pulled me onto the floor. Listlessly I'd let him drag me through a couple of waltzes but had frozen when the music changed to a fast song. The only fast dance I knew how to do was the dirty bop, since no one raised in Panama City could escape learning to bop at the Hangout, a dive on the Miracle Strip. With a shrug, I began dirty-bopping all around the highly polished ballroom floor, much to the horror of some of the staider members of the country club. Once he recovered from the shock, Rye followed my lead, and soon a crowd of onlookers encircled us, applauding. Since that night, Rye and I dance regularly, and I love it so much that I've recently incorporated a session of folk dancing into the retreats.

I barely have time to catch my breath before the band moves into "On the Sunny Side of the Street," and Rye grabs my hand again. He and I have danced together so often we've perfected our movements, but I'm still flustered when the other dancers on the floor stop and watch us do our showy fox-trot. Afterward Rye, a shameless show-off, asks the band to play a Latin song so we can demonstrate the tango he's taught me. Tango has become such a hot dance that I'm given a much needed rest when everyone lines up for Rye to teach them as well.

Sinking into my chair, I gulp down half a glass of water before saying to Dory, "So Son's learning to tango." Having been an agile athlete on Bama's tennis team, Son is a good dancer, and I see him among the crowd waiting for Rye's demonstration. "You should try the tango, Dory. It's hard but really fun," I say.

She shakes her head. "I'm a spazz when it comes to fast dancing. I'd rather watch."

"As graceful as you are, you'd be great at the tango. Watch them—it's like a ballet." When she turns her attention to the dance floor, I study her over the top of the water glass, and she catches me.

"What?"

"You look so happy, honey," I say softly. I've known Son too long to concede, but it's impossible to deny her new contentment.

She's been hard at work designing a website for her garden design business, which Son is helping her with. So far, so good.

"Things are going so well that it scares me," she admits. "I figure the gods are lying in wait, thunderbolt in hand." Something on the dance floor catches her eye, and she turns her head quickly. "Look who Son's dancing with."

After her teasing about Rye, I can't resist turning the tables on her. "Well, well. Whose prayers did the gods answer, mine or yours?"

Son is locked in a sexy tango embrace with Elinor Eaton-Yarbrough, who is dressed for the part in a sultry dress of shimmering black with a slit designed to reveal a long shapely leg with her every move. A part of me—the worse part—notes that the ever elegant Elinor is an awkward dancer, and I have the unkind thought that she's gotten on the dance floor only to show off how great she looks in the dress and mile-high heels. Every man on the dance floor watches her bug-eyed, tongues hanging out.

Dory whispers, "After landing a dance with the goddess, Son will be so full of himself, he'll be unbearable." When I suggest "More unbearable?" she and I laugh together as we'd always done before the disturbing events of last summer. Raising a hand, Dory motions to Lex, who is sitting alone at a nearby table. He joins us, pulling up a chair.

"You're not going to give the tango a try, Lex?" I say, my eyes on the dance floor. Rye is dancing with Elinor now, sweeping her so far backward that he appears to be mopping the floor with her long blond hair. When she comes upright, her eyes are wide and her face is flushed, and I hide a knowing smile. As I've discovered, dancing with Rye requires letting go of one's inhibitions.

"Me do that?" Lex rolls his eyes. "When's the last time you've seen a moose doing the tango?"

"Stop it," Dory cries, punching him on the shoulder. "You're always putting yourself down that way."

"Oh, I wouldn't say moose," I say, deadpan. "Bull, maybe, but moose, no. Lots of bull, actually."

"Ha ha," Dory drawls. "Pay her no mind, Lex. She's miffed because your ex just took her boyfriend."

I give Dory a look, but Lex laughs it off. Then, with a nod of his head, he indicates Jasmine dancing with Tommy McNair. Haley told me that Tommy and Jasmine are taking a couples' exercise class at the Y, and it appears to be having some results. Jasmine's smiling up at Tommy, and his doe eyes are tender as he gazes down at her.

"Speaking of dancing moose, get a load of my dock boy," Lex says. "Big as he is, if he can tango, there's hope for me."

"That's enough," I say sternly. "The three of us sound awful. No more politically incorrect comments, okay?"

Lex eyes me. "Better not get around Jasmine's brothers-in-law, then. I was jawing with them a little while ago, and they're sure cracking on poor Tommy."

"Oh, dear," I groan. "Etta was afraid of that."

Leaning forward, I search the room until I spot R.J. and Etta watching the couples on the dance floor. Etta had told Dory with real regret that she and R.J. wouldn't be able to attend the party because their two older daughters would be visiting, celebrating R.J.'s sixty-fifth birthday on Sunday. Dory had insisted Etta bring everyone, saying we'd have a birthday toast to R.J. when the champagne arrived, which we had. Now my heart sinks when I see the expression on R.J.'s face. He's watching Jasmine dance with Tommy, his jaw rigid and his dark eyes cold. Neither Jasmine's sisters nor the two brothers-in-law look much happier.

"Nothing but trouble there," Lex says. "I tried to talk to Tommy some the other day, but I don't know if I got anywhere."

I turn to stare at him. "The music must be too loud. I could've sworn you said *you* talked to Tommy about his love life. I'd give anything to have been a fly on the wall."

Lex pulls back indignantly, thumping his chest. "What'd you

think, I can't discuss matters of the heart? An older, experienced man like me is the perfect one to talk to a lovesick pup like Tommy. Jeez! Give me some credit."

Applause breaks out on the dance floor, the dance lessons over. When the band starts playing "Moon River," Dory shoves Lex my way. "Don't let Rye Ballenger show you up, Lex. Come on, ask Clare to dance."

"Hell, no," he snorts. "She stood me up and hurt my fragile male ego. Let her dance with pretty boy, see if I care."

"You're just saying that because you can't dance," I retort.

"I dance as good as that prissy boyfriend of yours."

Dory stands and takes Lex by both hands, pulling him to his feet. "Well, godalmightydamn! If you two are going to fight about it, we'll dance instead. C'mon, Lex, show these Rebs that a Man of Maine can cut a rug."

To my utter astonishment, Lex waltzes her away with as much grace and skill as Rye. I stare at them openmouthed until his eyes meet mine over Dory's shoulder. With a sly grin, he winks at me.

After Rye and I slow-dance to one of my favorite songs, "My Funny Valentine," the band announces a fifteen-minute break, and I pull away, somewhat flustered. It was our first slow dance of the evening, and Rye was at it again, making me uncomfortable by staring at me the whole time, his eyes aglow. Surely Dory hasn't said anything to him. My hand in his, we are heading back to our table when a commotion breaks out on the other side of the dance floor. I know instantly where it's coming from, and I release Rye's hand.

"Oh, dear. Looks like Haley and Austin are having some kind of row," I say, glancing in their direction. "I'll go see what's going on, okay?"

"I'm coming with you." His hand on my waist, Rye steers me across the room to where Haley and Austin are seated with several of the younger couples. Earlier, all of them were on the dance floor, Haley bebopping away, so I assumed everything was fine.

When Rye and I reach their table, it takes me a minute to figure out what's happened, since the young couples are standing around the table, everyone looking awkward and embarrassed. Haley is sprawled on the floor in front of her chair; the commotion we heard was her cry as she fell. One of her high heels has come off, and her skirt is hiked up around her thighs. Red-faced, Austin is helping her to her feet, saying, "You okay? Not hurt, are you?"

Evidently Haley started to sit down after they returned from the dance floor, and somehow missed the chair. I rush to help, taking one of her arms while Austin pulls on the other. Rye holds on to the back of her chair as we get her seated, and Austin reaches down to pick up the shoe Haley lost, then kneels beside the chair to put it on her foot. "Sure you're okay?" he asks her again.

Haley covers her face with trembling hands, and I lean over her, pushing her disheveled hair from her hot, flushed face. Her hair is baby-fine and difficult to pin up; I noticed earlier that she'd managed an elaborate twist for the occasion, held in place by a festive rhinestone clip. But it's halfway to her shoulders now, the clip dislodged and dangling. Rye pats her shoulder awkwardly as I ask, "Did you hurt yourself, sweetheart?"

She shakes her head miserably. "Just embarrassed," she mutters. She removes her hands from her face but keeps her head lowered as she adds, "Well, maybe my ankle. It hurts a little."

Austin takes her ankle in his hands, turning it to see if it's sprained. While he's examining it, Jasmine and Tommy arrive. "Haley!" Jasmine cries. "What happened?" Jasmine kneels on the other side of Haley, pushing Austin out of her way, and he gets to his feet.

"I—I fell," Haley says. "But I'm fine. Really, I'm fine." It's obvious that she's more humiliated than hurt.

Jasmine takes Haley's hands and tilts her head sideways to study her friend's face. "You had too much to drink, girlfriend?" she whispers.

Haley nods glumly. "A little bit, I guess. And these new shoes are slippery. Guess I lost my balance when I started to sit down," she adds, then glances up at Austin sheepishly.

"I tried to tell Haley to go easy on the champagne, but she wouldn't listen to me," Austin says smugly. "At least she didn't fall flat on her face on the dance floor."

Jasmine glares at him, and Haley tugs on her arm. "He's right, Jazz, so let's just forget it."

With a self-satisfied nod, Austin adds, "She has no one but herself to blame. I tried to tell her—"

"What did you say?" Jasmine's voice is like a whiplash, and I cringe.

Taken aback, Austin repeats himself. "I tried to tell her not to drink so much, but—"

"Yeah, I heard that," Jasmine interrupts sarcastically. "But I also heard your shitty comment about blaming her."

I look at her in surprise, wondering where the animosity is coming from. As far as I know, Austin and Jasmine have always gotten along well. Folks at the nearby tables are watching us curiously, and when I spot Etta heading our way, I step in to put an end to this before it accelerates into a scene.

"Jasmine," I say, "why don't you take Haley to the ladies' room to freshen up? She needs to wash her hands, and you can help her get her hair up again."

Turning to Austin, Rye says casually, "Ask the bartender to give you a little club soda on a towel, son. It'll get the dirt off your knees. Dance floors are always dirtier than you think."

Mumbling his thanks, Austin brushes off his trousers, then turns to follow Jasmine and Haley. When I make a move to do the same, Rye stops me. "Let them handle this, sweetheart. You and I better head Etta off before she comes charging over here like a drill sergeant."

Seeing Etta stop Jasmine to question her, I slip my hand under

Rye's arm. "I've got a better idea. Let's go to the terrace and get some fresh air."

With a night wind blowing off the bay, it's cold on the lantern-lit terrace, and I hug myself while taking great gulps of the stinging salt air. Rye turns his back to me and lights a cigarette. "Christ! What was that all about?" he mutters as he inhales, closing his eyes blissfully.

"I'm not sure, but I have a bad feeling about it. And listen, I've been meaning to tell you how much it means to me, your interest in Haley—"

He interrupts me indignantly. "Haley and the kids—they're all the family I have now. All that's left of Mack, who was more like a younger brother than a cousin to me, as you well know. I may not be able to show her, or tell her, but I adore Haley."

"I know. She loves you, too, and needs you even more. I hope you know how much."

Mollified, he looks pleased as he reaches up to push a silver-blond lock of hair off his forehead, the cigarette between his long fingers. Being with Rye in any kind of muted light is always disconcerting because he's so like Mack yet so unlike him: Mack reflected in an opaque gilded mirror. Because of Mack's strapping build and sensuality, and his cousin's engaging charm, Dory once commented that Mack and Rye together made up the perfect man— one for the bedroom and the other, the ballroom.

Startling me out of my thoughts, Rye says, "Is it just me, or was Austin being a shit?"

I nod. "He was, wasn't he, about her drinking champagne? There's been a lot of tension between them lately."

"You'd be the one to notice it before anyone else did," Rye says with a casual wave of his cigarette.

"You'd think so, wouldn't you? But you know the old saying about the cobbler's children going without shoes. Austin's new job is causing most of the problems. Haley keeps telling me it's stressing him out, but I've kind of blown her off. Maybe I'd better pay more attention from now on."

Rye looks relieved. "The new job! Of course. If that's what it is, they'll be fine after he gets used to it, don't you think?" I nod hopefully, and he says, "Austin's always been a good kid. Or so he seemed to me. Mack liked him, didn't he?"

"Oh, we liked Austin from day one. Me more so than Mack, though."

"Ah! I didn't realize that."

I shrug. "Mack liked Austin, but he always found him a bit . . ." I pause, searching for the right word. "*Pious,* I guess. Austin was too much of a goody two-shoes for someone like Mack."

Rye smiles, looking out over the bay. "Yeah, Mack would be the last person impressed by piety, wouldn't he? But you know, Mack was a good person, wasn't he? A really good, decent person. If it weren't for the drinking, he'd still be with us." He stops to fan away a cloud of smoke.

I turn my head sharply. Neither of us has dared bring up that forbidden subject for such a long time. "You think he was drunk? That day when he went to the woods—you think that's why—" But I stop myself, biting my lip.

Keeping his eyes straight ahead, Rye sighs wearily. "Clare, honey, Mack was one of the best hunters in these parts. Any of us can trip over a log, or get tangled up in vines, or whatever. But only the most inexperienced hunter would hold a rifle in such a way that if something happened, it would go off."

Hugging my arms tighter, I turn my head to the bay, too. A cold white mist is forming over it, like a lost cloud. I hear myself saying, "I thought at first that if I loved Mack enough, I could save him from the dark part of his nature. When I realized how wrong I was, it almost killed me." Shaking my head, I smile bitterly. "Oh, great choice of words!"

Rye puts out his cigarette and motions for me. "Come here."

When I obey, he wraps his arms around me, putting my head on his shoulder. "You're shivering! Want to go back inside?"

I shake my head and lean in to him. Rye's not as tall as Mack was; with my heels adding a couple of inches, I can easily rest my cheek against his. When Mack held me, he'd put his chin on top of my head. Encircled in Rye's arms, I feel warm and safe. He holds me comfortably, while Mack's embrace was always erotically charged. He'd never simply hold me, as Rye is doing. What began as a hug would end with our feverish, urgent undressing of each other, and many times we'd sink to the floor on top of our discarded clothing, his mouth fastened on mine and my legs wrapped around his.

"Surely you don't blame yourself for what happened to Mack," Rye murmurs, his cheek pressed to mine, and his breath warm on my ear. "I've never worried about your thinking that because . . . well, hell, you're a therapist, so I figured you had better sense."

"I couldn't give him what he needed. You know how much I loved him, but it was never enough."

"Mack could be quite needy." He lifts his head to look over my shoulder, deep in thought. "You didn't see that about him for a long time, did you? I'm afraid he's where Haley gets her neediness. That's why he was drawn to you in the first place. And Haley, too. I mean, why both of them depended on you so much. You're the kind of person others depend on, you know."

"Good thing, in my profession."

Catching me off guard, Rye puts his hands into my hair and tilts my face toward his. Looking down at me, he murmurs, "But what about you? What about your needs?"

Our eyes lock, and I feel an unexpected but not unwelcome surge of desire at the feel of his hands on the back of my neck, his body against mine. Instinctively I move in closer and tighten my arms around his waist. I'm surprised by my response, a longing I haven't experienced in such a long time.

"Clare?" he says, his eyes searching my face.

"Ummm?"

"We need to talk."

"About what?"

"Oh, I think you know. Surely you know."

His lips move toward mine at the same moment the double doors leading to the terrace are flung open and bang back together. Rye and I jump apart, startled by the sound. Dory stands there, grinning. I step out of Rye's embrace, and Dory sashays toward us, my shawl in her hands.

"Here!" She tosses me the shawl, and I reach to grab it, dazed. "I've been looking all over for you, Clare. Then someone told me you were out here. I was afraid you'd be cold, but I had no idea you had Rye to keep you warm."

"Great timing, darling," he mutters, reaching in his pocket for another cigarette as Dory laughs, throwing her head back. An exquisite white cashmere shawl is draped around her shoulders, and she pulls it close against the cool breeze as she regards us slyly, crossing her arms.

"Oh, were you about to make a move, Rye?" she mocks, eyes dancing. "Don't let me stop you. I'm on your side, remember?"

"Has she said anything about me?" I ask him suspiciously.

Rye reaches out and pushes an errant strand of hair behind my ear, smiling. "It's the other way around, my dear. Dory knows how I feel about you."

"Dory needs to mind her own business," I say testily.

"It's too cold out here for you two to be making out, anyway," she goes on, unperturbed. "Wait till after the party. But for now let's go back inside. The band's starting up again, and Haley's fine. Austin went home, saying he was tired. That's the other reason I was looking for you. Is something going on with him?"

I sigh as the three of us walk across the terrace, Rye between Dory and me with an arm around each of us. The moment of passion has passed between me and Rye, and his arm on my shoulder is companionable again.

"I don't know," I say, "but I intend to find out."

Son meets us at the door, his face alight with excitement. I recognize the telltale signs of his having had too much to drink, the lurching walk, the glazed eyes. "I was coming to get you all," he says, slurry-voiced. "Boy howdy, Jasmine's on a tear tonight. First she jumps Austin, and now she's telling off one of her brothers-in-law. I can't tell if it's Derrick or Shawn, but she's giving him an earful."

"Yeah, Son, they all look alike, don't they?" I mutter wearily.

Dory pushes past Son to see what's going on, and we follow her into the warmth of the dining room. "Oh, Lord," she says. "It's Derrick, and Jasmine's giving him a piece of her mind. Wonder what *that's* about?"

"You know," I say. "Remember Etta told us how the family feels about Jasmine and Tommy?"

"The Ton of Fun?" Son says. "Jasmine's folks are not too hot on the idea of her bringing a big fat white guy into the family tree. Ha! R.J.'s about to shit a brick. Can't say as I blame him. Me, I wouldn't want my daughter with somebody like Tubby Tommy."

"You don't have a daughter," Dory reminds him dryly.

He turns his bleary eyes to Rye. "Be glad you never had kids, man. When they're little, they step on your toes; when they grow up, they step on your heart."

"I never knew you were such a philosopher, Son," I say. "Looks like Jasmine and Tommy are leaving. Poor Etta. She was so excited about everybody being here for R.J.'s birthday."

"The joys of family life," Dory says.

"Etta's planning a big lunch for R.J. tomorrow," I say with a sigh. "Sure hope this doesn't spoil it for her."

Hands on hips, Son surveys the scene. "Naw. If Etta's survived almost fifty years of marriage and three kids, she can live through anything."

I surprise myself as much as the three of them by clapping Son on the back with a grin. "For once in your life, Son Rodgers, you may actually have said something profound."

Rye is unusually quiet on the ride home after the party, and I steal a couple of glances at him, puzzled by his introspection. His behavior has been out of character all night. Unlike Mack, Rye has never been given to brooding or dark moods. One of the reasons I like being with him is his flippant banter, which keeps everything easygoing and uncomplicated between us. After Dory interrupted the almost-kiss on the terrace, he and I rejoined the party with ease, lapsing back into the comfortable companionship we've always had. When the band returned from their break, we danced until midnight without awkwardness or uneasiness. He held me close during the slow dances, whispered his usual outrageous flattery in my ear, and chuckled when I blushed. From time to time, both of us danced freely with others. Or rather, Rye did. Once I fast-danced with Son after he grabbed my hand and pulled me to the floor when the band struck up a jazzy version of "The Twist." I was surprised that he remembered: At Bama, Mack and I went with him and Dory to a party at Son's frat house, where Chubby Checker entertained. Since Mack and Dory wouldn't fast-dance, Son and I entered the twist contest and came away with a first-place trophy.

After doing the twist with Son, I was surprised when Lex led me to the floor—until I saw Elinor dancing with Rye. Even so, she kept her eyes fastened on Lex and me. After the song was over, she came after him with her purse and wrap in hand, saying he'd been out too late. Lex protested that his doctors had released him from the recovery regime, but he allowed her to lead him away. When they stopped to say goodbye to Son and Dory, Elinor slipped her arm around Lex's waist and snuggled close, with her gleaming blond head on his shoulder. As they walked to the door hand in hand, I rolled my eyes Dory's way, and she smirked.

When Rye pulls to a stop in front of my house, he turns to me and says, "Sorry I kept you out past your bedtime. You're exhausted, aren't you?"

"I am." He looks tired, too, even somewhat sad, and I squeeze his hand. "Stay put, Sir Galahad. I can walk myself to the door." When he protests, as I knew he would, I lean over and kiss him lightly on the cheek, then reach for the car door. "Good night, sweet prince. I had a lovely time."

"I was proud of you," he says. "You did really well at the ceremony, and you couldn't have been nicer to the Son King. No one there knew that you'd gone under such duress."

"We both did good, didn't we?" We look at each other and smile wearily. "But what choice did we have? We had to do it for Dory."

"Maybe Son's conversion was the real thing," he says in wonder. "He was sure on his best behavior."

"I'll give him a month." When Rye chuckles, I repeat my good nights and turn to open the door.

He takes my arm to stop me. "You don't want me walking you to the door, do you? You're afraid I might ask to stay." Aghast, I open my mouth to protest, but he puts a finger over my lips. "Shhh. It's okay. I saw that Dory embarrassed you on the terrace tonight."

"I can't believe the stuff she's saying. She knows how things are with you and me, and that we're close friends because it's the way we want it."

He regards me steadily, then says, "This summer I told you I was ready for that to change. More than ready. But I wasn't sure if you understood what I was saying."

In spite of my discomfort, I can't help but smile. "Come on, Rye. What part of 'Sweetheart, I'd like for you to consider marrying me' do you think I failed to understand?"

"Since you cruelly dismissed me with a laugh, I wasn't sure."

I lower my eyes, abashed. It's true; earlier this summer, when Rye walked me to the door after one of our nights of dinner and dancing, he kissed me lightly on the lips, like he always did, and made his startling suggestion that I marry him. I replied that there was no way I'd have the broken heart of every woman in Fairhope on my conscience, then went into the house, leaving him standing on the porch alone. I felt badly about it, but I'd been so flustered, I wasn't thinking straight. Until now, neither of us has mentioned it.

"You've been such a dear since the first time we met, Rye," I say finally. "If it hadn't been for you that first night I came to Fairhope, I probably would have run all the way back to Panama City."

"Ha. I'll never forget that night—Mack bringing his fiancée to Papa Mack's to meet the whole family. What a nightmare for you."

I smile in remembrance. "I was terrified. They were so grand and so snooty. I assumed Mack had exaggerated his bitchy step-monster, Aileen, but no. And his dad! I'd never seen a father and son with such a bad relationship. Since my big, boisterous family was so different, the Ballengers were like something out of one of my abnormal-psychology books. And that was before I met Zoe Catherine."

Rye chuckles. "That was your reaction, understandably, but mine was the opposite. I was thrilled. I thought a poised, confident young therapist-to-be was exactly what Mack needed, and was bound to help the whole crazy bunch of us."

"If I appeared poised and confident, it was an illusion, believe me."

His eyes grow dreamy, and he says, "God, how I envied Mack, having found you. But I also felt bad for you, knowing what you were marrying into."

I squeeze his hand and say softly, "You and I hit it off instantly, didn't we? Like we'd known each other all our lives. You could've been the big brother I always wanted to have. Every time I worried about marrying into such a family and moving to Fairhope,

I thought about you and knew I could do it. I never told you that, but there it is."

Our eyes lock, and he says, "You know the problem with you thinking of me as a big brother?" Before I can answer, he murmurs, "This." He reaches over to take my face in his hands. This time his kiss is far from a brotherly one, and I'm shaken and breathless when he releases me. Without looking at me, he leans over, opens the door, and says, "Good night, my dear." Flustered, I swallow hard, then stumble out of the car and hurry to the safety of my house, like Cinderella running from the ball.

☙

Early the next morning, Dory is at my back door. I've slept later than usual, and I stand with my robe clutched around me and blink sleepily at the sight of her silhouetted in the sunlight. She appears to be as surprised to see me as I am her, and she cries, "What are you doing here?"

"In case you've forgotten, I live here."

"But I thought you'd be at Rye's!"

"Oh? And thinking me not home, you came over here to snoop around, maybe?"

At least she looks somewhat embarrassed. "Well, no—I saw Rye's car at his house and figured you were there. But I had to come by your house on my way to church, so I thought I'd stick my head in the door and see for sure."

I stare at her, aghast. "I'm telling Father Gibbs on you. What will he think of you? The very day after you renew your wedding vows, you're out spying on your friends, hoping to catch them in bed together."

She leans against the door frame, since it's apparent that I'm not going to ask her in. "So you were in your own bed last night, and

Rye in his. Damn! He'd asked me to put in a good word for him, but I guess I was too subtle."

"Dory, you're a lot of things, but subtle ain't one of them. And what's this about putting in a good word for Rye—were you trying to be Miles Standish to his John Smith? Or whoever the hell that was. That's so crazy. Rye can speak for himself."

"Best I recall, he did last summer. And you turned him down. Which proves you're the one that's crazy, not me. The only men I know who are that good-looking, funny, sensitive, and sweet are gay."

"Unlike you, I do not need a man to make my life complete."

"Maybe not to make your *life* complete, but . . ." Her voice trails off, and she shakes her head sadly. "I can't believe you've got two men on the string, yet you aren't sleeping with either of them."

My laugh is a mixture of exhaustion and exasperation. "Between you and Zoe Catherine, who needs Dr. Ruth? Do either of you ever think about your own sex life?"

"I don't know about Zoe, but when I do my meditations, what do you think I'm meditating about?"

I roll my eyes to the ceiling. "Jesus Christ!"

"Speaking of which, I'm on my way to the early church service, so guess I'd better go." She's dressed sedately in heels and pearls, her hair still twisted into the prim little chignon at the nape of her neck. She gives me a hug, then starts down the front steps, where I stop her.

"If you like Rye so much, why don't you leave Son and marry him yourself?" I can't resist asking her.

She shakes her head. "I adore Rye, but if I were to leave Son, I'd have a go at your Yankee boyfriend. Although he appears to be a big old teddy bear, I think he's hot."

"If I thought you'd leave Son, I'd fix you two up in a New York minute."

Instead of laughing, as I expected, her expression is serious as she studies me. "I'm only halfway teasing you about this, Clare.

The truth is, it breaks my heart to see what's happened to you since Mack died. He made you afraid to love again, didn't he?"

"And you call me Madame Freud?" I say with a dismissive wave.

"The problem is, you won't allow anyone to love you, either. And that's what I'm worried about." But she turns and hurries down the steps before I can come up with a good response.

Chapter Ten

❧ ❧ ❧ ❧ ❧

Almost a week after the anniversary party, I find sheer chaos at Haley's house, and I stand in the door for a moment before taking a deep breath and entering. Welcome to the house of horrors, I think with a wry smile.

Since Halloween is coming up, Haley is making decorations and costumes for the kids, and every available space—floor, table, desktop, counters—is cluttered with black and orange construction paper, crepe paper, black or white material, masks, wigs, fangs, paint, scissors, tape, and glue. Every holiday on the calendar is a high-feast day for Haley and her kindergarten students, but especially Halloween, Thanksgiving, Christmas, and Easter. "Hey!" I call out. "Anybody here?"

Somewhere under a pile of black satin—I figure the makings of a witch's costume—come squeals of delight, and after a lot of rustling, two masked faces appear. "Oh, no," I cry in mock horror. "Monsters live in this house! I thought I'd come to the Jordans'."

Abbie, a ghoulish rubber mask over her head, gets so tickled that she tangles herself up in the black satin and falls down, which causes her to squeal even louder. Pulling herself to her feet, she cries, "I'm a mean monster. You'd better run!"

Zach has managed to get his mask so twisted that he's peering out of one eye socket, and his mouth is where the other eye socket is cut out. "Me a mean monster, too," he says, holding his chubby arms over his head.

"No, Zach," says Abbie. "*I'm* the mean monster, not you. You're a baby monster. Baby monsters don't know they're supposed to be mean."

"I see two mean monsters," I say, ever the appeaser. "And I'm so scared that I'm running away before they catch me." Pretending to run, I kick off my clogs and scamper around the room, staying just out of reach of Abbie as she chases me, making weird noises I can only assume are her version of monster growls. Zach toddles after her, but when I allow Abbie to catch me and I pretend to scream in terror, he throws off his mask and grabs me around the legs.

"It's not really monsters, Grams." His face is troubled when he looks up at me. "It's just me, Zach."

I pick him up and kiss his reddened cheeks noisily, causing him to giggle and kick his feet high. The back door opens with a bang, and Austin comes in. It's still strange to see him in a suit and tie, and I manage a little wave, hard to do with Zach's arms so tight around my neck that I'm about to choke. As usual, Abbie leaves me to run into her daddy's arms. Austin hugs her briefly but is scowling so darkly, I figure he's had a difficult day.

I haven't seen Austin since the night of Dory and Son's anniversary party, and when I called Haley the next day, she explained their fight. The sitter couldn't come until time for the party, so Austin, who'd been speaking at a meeting in Orange Beach, assured Haley that he'd be home in time to stay with the kids so she could go to the renewal ceremony. When he was late and she couldn't reach him on his cell, she'd gotten worried. Then he strolled in, nonchalant and unrepentant that she missed the ceremony, and they'd had a big row. She admitted that he'd refused to dance with her, saying she'd had too much to drink. They'd made up the next day, and all was well. Austin had just been tired and grumpy that night, Haley insisted.

"Hi, Clare," Austin says, an edge to his voice. "Where's Haley?"

"Don't know," I reply with a shrug. "I just got here and was playing with the kids."

"Mommy's in the attic, getting down the Halloween stuff," Abbie says, tugging on her daddy's arm. "I'm gonna be a monster on Halloween, Daddy. But I won't scare you, I promise."

When I release Zach, he runs to his daddy, but Austin barely hugs his son. Instead, he looks around the room in disgust. Their cottage, though cozy and charming, is small, with an open floor plan sectioned off into living areas: the kitchen in the back, a sitting area in the front, and the dining area to the side, centered under a bay window. "Oh, great!" he says. "Mommy's in the attic pulling down more of this mess, like we don't have enough already."

"Mommy's making Halloween stuff for us and her class, too," Abbie tells him solemnly.

As if on cue, Haley comes into the room, arms laden with sacks and baskets overflowing with even more Halloween material. Spotting me first, she cries, "Mom! I didn't hear you come in." Reaching around the sacks and baskets, I give her a hug and kiss, and then she spots Austin. "Oh, good, Austin—glad you're home early. You can help me get down the rest of the stuff from the attic."

Austin rolls his eyes. "Bullshit. I'm not bringing down anything else. You've got enough for every kindergartener in Baldwin County already."

"Mommy!" Abbie cries, gray eyes wide with shock. "Daddy said a bad word. Does he have to pay a quarter, too?"

"Bu-shit, bu-shit, bu-shit," Zach babbles as he claps his hands.

"Rough day at work, sweetie?" Haley says sarcastically, eyeing Austin balefully as she sets down the sacks and baskets, kicking aside a place for them.

"Tell you what, Haley." Austin's voice is still stretched tight as a drum. "I'll go to the attic and look for the tablecloth, but I'm not bringing down any more Halloween junk."

"Oh, God," Haley moans. "Not *that* again. I told you, the table-cloth's disappeared."

"And I told you, that better not be true," he relies coolly.

She turns to me. "We're having Austin's staff over Saturday night for dinner, and he wants to use the tablecloth his grandmother gave us for a wedding gift." Glancing at Abbie, she lowers her voice and adds, "I can't find the g-d thing, and he's having a fit."

"Oh, no, it's better than that, Clare," Austin says. "First of all, my grandmother made it. It's hand-embroidered. And second, we've never used it. The reason? Haley doesn't want to iron it."

"Oh, bull. I tried to iron it," Haley protests. "It's covered with embroidered flowers—I mean, it's beautiful; don't get me wrong—but the flowers puckered, and it looked worse ironed than it did wrinkled. That's why I haven't used it. So I packed it away, but I can't remember where."

"Oh, sweetie, I have a tablecloth you can use," the appeaser says with a bright smile. "If I can find it. I never use tablecloths any-more."

"See?" Haley points a finger at Austin triumphantly. "Told you nobody expects us to use a tablecloth. Everyone uses place mats nowadays, even the Martha Stewart clone Wanda Webb."

"And I told you that we're having an elegant dinner for my staff if I have to do it myself. We're using our china, our silver, and my grandmother's tablecloth. Do . . . you . . . understand . . . me?" Austin enunciates each word in a loud, exaggerated manner, as though talking to a deaf child.

Out of the corner of my eye, I see that Zach and Abbie are watch-ing their parents arguing as though at a tennis match, their heads turning from one to the other. My heart sinks, and I'm at a loss as to what to do. A cardinal rule of mothers of adult children: Avoid inter-fering in your kids' lives if at all possible. I'm itching to pick up something and clobber Austin with it, and I eye a papier-mâché witch's broom wistfully.

"And I told you," Haley says, her voice shaking with anger, "that I can't find the tablecloth, Austin! And even if I could, I couldn't iron it to suit you."

His jaw tightens as he spits out, "You can't find it, and you can't iron it. You can't do anything, can you, Haley? Not a goddamn thing."

"Dod-damn," Zach chirps, dancing. "Dod-damn 'tupid Mommy."

"Now see what you've done," Haley yells, grabbing for Zach. Her sudden motion causes Zach to cry out in surprise, and Austin throws his hands high.

"What *I've* done? *Me?* You scared him to death, yelling like that."

Interfering parent or no, I can't let this go on, and I step between them, holding up my hands like a referee with a whistle. "Whoa, both of you. Stop this and listen to me, okay?"

But Austin shakes his head, his eyes cold. "No, Clare. I'm tired and I'm hungry and I don't want to hear any more. I'm taking the kids to Mickey D's for supper." He throws Haley a look, then jerks his head to Abbie. "Get your jacket and your brother's, and let's go get a Happy Meal."

"Goody—a Happy Meal!" Zach echoes as he bounces up and down, and I can't help but wonder if his parents appreciate the irony.

Abbie and Zach run to the back door, where their backpacks and windbreakers were tossed as they came in from school. As they struggle to get their jackets on, Haley turns to Austin, pleading. "I don't want you taking them out for junk food again tonight. I'm going to fix dinner if you'll just give me time."

"Yeah, right," he says, looking around. "It'll take you an hour just to put all this crap away. I'm hungry now." Eyes narrowed, he gestures toward the kitchen. "Besides, what are you cooking? I don't see anything."

Haley crosses to the fridge and flings open the freezer. "I have chicken strips in here," she says, pulling out a package, "which can be thawed in the microwave in no time. I was planning on doing that dish the kids like so much, the one with the cheese and broccoli."

With a smirk, Austin says, "I assume you have broccoli? And cheese?"

"I have cheese . . ." Haley mutters, then her face brightens. "Instead of going to McDonald's, run to the grocery and get—"

"No!" Austin shouts, and Haley cringes. "You know how crowded it is at this time of day and how I hate to go. Can't you *ever* plan anything ahead of time?"

"Don't yell, Daddy," Abbie says from the back door, hands on her hips. "That's very rude."

"Dod-damn Daddy," Zach chimes in helpfully.

Austin rubs his face, then looks at his kids. "Hey, guys, I'm sorry for yelling. Daddy's just tired and hungry, okay? And Zach, don't say that, buddy. It's not a nice word, and Daddy didn't mean to say it."

I can't stand it anymore, interference be damned, so I say with false cheerfulness, "Look, why don't *I* run to the store? Won't take but a second." Throwing Haley a look, I add, "It'll give you time to put away this stuff, then I'll help you fix supper. How does that sound?"

"Would you, Mom?" Haley says, her relief obvious. "That'd be great."

≫

The following day, I leave a message on Haley's cell phone and insist that she stop by my office right after school. Abbie is in preschool this year, and Zach is at St. John's day care. When Haley has faculty meetings or one of her mental-health breaks with Jasmine, she drops off Abbie at day care for an extra hour, so I tell her to call the day care center and make the arrangements as soon as she hangs up. Reluctantly, she gives in. She knows what I want to talk about, and she doesn't want to hear it.

"I know you'll take Austin's side, Mom," Haley says glumly as she sits next to me on the sofa in my office.

"It's not a matter of taking sides," I protest, "but if it were, I'll always be on yours, honey. Drink your tea. You'll hurt Etta's feelings if you don't. And tell me this: How long were you going to let things go before telling me how bad things have gotten with you and Austin? I was appalled yesterday."

She shrugs. "I've tried to tell you, but you wouldn't believe me."

"That's not fair, nor is it true. All you'd said was that Austin's feeling pressured by his job, and he's tired and cranky a lot. It's gone way beyond that. And you hadn't told me he was taking it out on you, either."

Looking up, Haley's eyes brighten. "You saw it, too! I hope you'll tell him not to do that. You need to tell him—"

I stop her. "Whoa. *You* need to tell him, honey, not his mother-in-law. You must be very clear that you will not tolerate his belittling you, especially in front of the children."

"He'll listen to you, but he never listens to me. Besides, I'm afraid to tell him."

"Afraid?" I lean toward her in alarm. "Hayden Jordan, you'd better tell me the truth. Has Austin ever done anything—"

She shakes her head before I can finish. "God, no, Mom. Jesus! Austin's not one of those guys."

I study her, narrow-eyed. "No pushing, shoving, things like that? Sometimes it starts out that way, and the next thing you know, it's a slap or a punch."

"Not Austin. You know him well enough to know that."

"So I thought, but I've been surprised before. What I'm really concerned about, and what I'm beginning to see, is verbal abuse. Is that what you're afraid of, what he'll say to you if you stand up for yourself?"

She shrugs, but I can tell she's uncomfortable. "Not exactly. Guess I'm afraid that he won't love me anymore."

"Oh, honey." I take her hand and give it a shake. "We talked about that before you married him, remember?" At the time Haley told me she thought she loved Austin more than he loved her. Even though I figured it was premarital jitters, I talked to her about neediness and what an unattractive quality it was, with the potential to damage any relationship. Her response disturbed me then and still does. "I see what you're saying," she said, "but you were the opposite with Daddy. If you needed him, he never knew it because you were so independent, and that hurt your relationship just as bad. So who can say which is worse?"

"Listen to me," I say now, squeezing her hand until she relents and meets my eye. "You can't *make* anyone love you, Haley. Just like you can't command respect. Respect and love both have to be freely given. Or maybe I should say, respect you must earn, but love comes with no strings attached. But you have to think enough of yourself to demand equal footing in a relationship. Promise me you'll talk to Austin about the way he treats you when he's stressed out, okay? And if things don't get better, I will push for marriage counseling, so be warned." When she groans, I laugh lightly. "Sorry, honey. Occupational hazard."

Haley lets out a long, weary sigh, then glances at me. "Austin's right, you know. I'm a terrible wife." She lowers her eyes and picks at a fingernail, a childhood habit that reappears whenever she's upset.

I throw my hands up in the air. "See? That's what verbal abuse does. Of course you're not a bad wife. You're a wonderful, loving person. Granted, I'd like to see you make more of an effort in some areas of your marriage, which we've talked about. Martha Stewart you ain't, and having an orderly, well-organized household is more important to Austin than to you. But marriage is made up of compromises."

"Oh, that's an original, Dr. Ballenger."

"I know you've heard it all before. But that doesn't make it any less true. If you know Austin likes to come home to a hot meal, the two of you work out something both of you can live with, like taking turns cooking, or whatever. Big surprise: Life goes much more smoothly when things are well planned and orderly."

"I threw away that damn tablecloth," she blurts out.

"Haley, you didn't!"

"I did, too. I scorched it so bad, I knew Austin would go apeshit if he saw it. I feel terrible about throwing it away, but I panicked. His poor grandmother would die, if she weren't already dead."

"Oh, dear. Not good."

"Don't I know it. I felt so bad I got my friend Beth, you know, who sews, to teach me how to embroider so I could make another one. But I was such a klutz, I quit. Beth said she'd do it, but it'd take months. So I said forget it. If I had another one, I'd have to iron it, too."

"If Austin's dead set on using a tablecloth for entertaining, take my advice and buy perma-press."

"Oh, don't worry, I'm heading to Target this weekend. But Mom, I hate the way Austin tries to play the big shot at work, throwing fancy dinner parties and stuff like that. Other folks at the college don't do it. Sometimes I think he's just trying to impress John and Wanda Webb."

"What *is* it with Austin and those two?"

She shrugs. "You've got me. I've gotten so I can't stand Wanda, but I can't say anything because Austin says I'm jealous of her. Puh-leeze! Austin thinks both she and John are perfect, and they act like he's Jesus Christ reincarnated. It's funny to me that Austin has so little time for his family now, but he always finds time for them. I used to think Wanda had the hots for Austin, but now I think John is gay and *he's* the one who does. Not that I blame him—marrying Wanda would turn any man gay. I'm sick of both of them."

"Okay, that does it," I say briskly. "I've heard enough. Here's what you're going to do, young lady, and what I'll do in return. Leave here, fix a nice dinner, get the kids down, then have a talk with Austin. Tell him that the two of you *must* see a marriage counselor, and right away. That's your part. Meantime, here's what I'll do. I'll get on the phone and start calling until I locate the best person for the two of you to see. Can't be someone who knows me well, or Austin will think—"

"He won't do it," Haley interrupts. "He'll say we can't afford it, wait and see. You know what a tightwad he is."

"Let's cross that bridge when we get there. I'll work out a barter or a professional discount or something. Promise me you'll do this. Promise?"

She nods glumly, and I go soft inside, just looking at her. With a sigh, she leans in to me, and I put my arm around her shoulder. "Oh, sweetheart, this seems bad right now, I know. But we'll get through it together, like we have everything else. Okay? Just like it's always been, me and you together."

≈

Although Haley wasn't a child of my body, she became a child of my heart in a most unexpected way. My decision to adopt her became a landmark case in the state of Alabama: Stepfathers often adopted stepchildren, but it was unprecedented for a stepmother to do so. My lawyers tried to talk me out of it, saying it was unnecessary. In fact, it was the most necessary decision I'd ever made, in many ways more crucial than deciding to marry Mack or starting a career as a therapist.

Five years after we married and moved to Fairhope, Mack and I sat in my doctor's office and received the devastating news: There would be no more babies for us. Our first child, a son we named

Daniel, was born prematurely while I was working on my therapy license, driving back and forth to work at a family practice in Mobile. As tiny and fragile-looking as a bird emerging from the eggshell, Daniel lived six weeks, hooked to so many tubes and wires it was hard to tell a baby was underneath. Although Mack and I could caress and talk to our perfectly formed son in his incubator, neither of us ever held him. On the night we lost him, the staff sent us home from our endless vigil because he'd seemed so much stronger that we should be able to hold him soon, and they insisted we rest up for the big event. We collapsed into an exhausted sleep until I sat straight up with my heart pounding, awakened by the sound of a baby's cry. A dream, I knew, but I made Mack get up and drive me to the hospital. Arriving at the neonatal unit, we tried to push past the team of doctors and nurses who rushed forward to stop us. By their stricken faces, we knew Daniel was gone, even before seeing the tubes and wires hanging uselessly over the sides of the horribly silent incubator.

Because Mack and I were young and inexperienced in the ways that life can break even the strongest of us, our grief seemed inconsolable. We had yet to learn that consolation can be found in a seemingly small gesture of love. Dory kept our house filled with flowers, and Zoe Catherine, the most gregarious and outspoken of women, came and went without a word to anyone. We didn't even see her, just the evidence that she'd been by: food prepared, laundry folded, the house cleaned. She was as unable to accept my gratitude to her as I was to adequately express it. I prayed that if nothing else, her ministrations might be the catalyst to bring Mack and his mother together, but it didn't happen. Mack had grown up feeling like an abandoned child, a pain that never left him.

When I got pregnant a year later, we celebrated too soon and too readily; I miscarried the day after. I carried the next baby a month longer, making the miscarriage more of a blow. After a battery of tests and a painful correctional procedure, I was soon pregnant again. That baby, too, I lost during the first trimester. After more extensive tests, a gut-wrenching verdict. Along with the news that it was useless for us to keep trying, Mack and I were given a list of adoption agencies, both domestic and foreign. "Some lucky child is out there waiting for parents like you two," the doctor told us, seeing us to the door.

For a long time afterward, both Mack and I dealt with the blow in unhealthy ways. I went back to school for a doctorate in addition to working full-time, and I stayed away for days at a time. I picked divorce recovery for my dissertation topic because the research was scanty and challenging; I had no way of knowing that decision would start my career in a whole new direction. Mack had quit his hated banking job and started to work restoring old houses, and I convinced myself that his work filled the void for him in the same way mine did for me. I even told myself it was a good thing, and we were lucky not to need a family to make our lives complete. I didn't know that, alone and aimless, Mack had found another way to deal with his pain. Although I was trained to spot the signs of alcohol abuse, I failed to notice them in my own husband.

Then came the day that turned our lives upside down. Mack received a registered letter from a law firm in Orange County, Florida, demanding he contact them regarding an urgent matter. When he blew it off, a sheriff's deputy served him papers a few weeks later, just as we were sitting down to one of our rare dinners together. Mack collapsed onto the sofa, white-faced and trembling, and I grabbed the papers from him. A paternity suit had been filed against Macomber Hayden Ballenger III, of Fairhope, Alabama, by the surviving kin of Shirley Marie Scott, of Naples, Florida. When I was able to speak, I asked the question any wife would: "Mack? Who is Shirley Marie Scott?"

I thought Mack wasn't going to answer me, and when he did, his response told me the letter wasn't a mistake, as I'd hoped. "This means that . . . she's dead?" Mack said blankly. "Shirley's *dead?*"

When I replied that normally you didn't have surviving kin otherwise, he blinked in bewilderment.

"Paternity," he said. "She had the child, then."

My legs no longer held me up, and I sank down beside him. Finally I was able to say, "You'd better tell me about it."

It turned out to have been a deliberate omission, Mack never telling me, or even Dory and Son, about Shirley Scott. Dropping his head, he admitted that he'd been ashamed of her, and even more ashamed of his treatment of her. He'd picked her up in Gulf Shores while they were both still in high school, a tough girl from the wrong side of the tracks who'd dropped out of school to move there with a girlfriend. Shirley initiated him into another world, fast and furiously. Mack confessed that he was as enamored of her as he was of the pot they smoked during sex, and the thrilling way it heightened the experience for both of them. Only because of his training as an athlete did he give it up, albeit reluctantly. And not altogether, either; each time he went home to Fairhope from Bama, he found himself going to Gulf Shores, toward Shirley's inviting bed. The last time he'd been with her was the weekend before he met and fell in love with me. After the team had played a game in Mobile, he'd gone to Gulf Shores to see Shirley, then sneaked back into the hotel where the team was sleeping, without the coach ever knowing he'd been gone.

That summer, however, Shirley presented him with the news: She was pregnant. He was in despair, knowing that his father would disown him, and he'd lose me as well. Desperate, he got rid of her in a way that was easy for him at the time: He paid her off. With money for an abortion and a new start, nineteen-year-old Shirley returned to her hometown of Naples. "That was ten, eleven years ago," he said in despair. "There's no way the child could be mine."

I met his look, unflinching, and said tightly, "It's a paternity suit, Mack. I guess you'll find out in court, won't you?"

With Rye representing him, Mack ended up settling the case out of court for a staggering sum in back child support, paid out to Shirley's relatives, since he had no proof of the large amount of money he'd given her previously. After she'd blown the money Mack gave her to start over, her life spiraled out of control. With a baby and no education, no way of supporting herself, Shirley got by the way she always had, by latching on to any man she could. After being involved in several abusive relationships, she ended up doing hard drugs, and her child was passed from relative to relative. A week before her thirtieth birthday, Shirley overdosed on cocaine, leaving behind an eleven-year-old girl and a piece of paper with Mack's name and address on it.

I wasn't home when Mack and Rye returned from Naples after settling the paternity case. Instead, I was in Baton Rouge, completing the final edits of my dissertation. By the time I returned to Fairhope, Mack had gone back to work on the houses he was restoring. This time it was with a different purpose: He'd gone heavily into debt to settle the case, paying off past years of child support and court costs, and he worked such long hours that I rarely saw him. Not only was he working off his debt, he was also avoiding me, going to bars after work rather than face me. It was the worst time of our marriage. He adamantly refused to discuss the case, or what he'd found in Naples, and would walk out of the room when I questioned him. At last, I could stand it no more, and I went to Rye.

"Of course we saw the little girl, Clare," Rye said, sitting behind the big mahogany desk in his office and looking at me with pity. "Poor thing's not a very appealing child. Scrawny and in bad need of braces, not very healthy-looking. The kid's had a rough life, I'm sure." As I was leaving, however, he said with a wistfulness I hadn't yet heard from the carefree, fun-loving Rye, "But you know? Beneath that mess of hair, I got a glimpse of Mack's gray eyes."

To this day, I'm not sure what made me head straight to the Landing after I left Rye's office. All I knew was, for some reason I wanted desperately to be with Zoe Catherine. I found her at the bird sanctuary, working on a cage for a red-tailed hawk whose legs were taped up. Seeing me, her face lit up. "C'mon," she said. "I need to show you something."

Zoe led me to the dock, jumped into a battered old canoe, and motioned for me to pick up an oar. Seemingly without a care in the world, she chattered about the injured hawk as we paddled down the creek, me following her lead and dipping my oar in synchronicity with hers. My gloom lifted, and I found myself reveling in the smooth glide of the canoe over the mottled green waters of the creek, the salt-sweet air on my face, the soft splash of the oars. For the first time in weeks, I heard my laughter as Zoe brandished her oar to scare away a couple of ducks that followed us, their webbed feet moving under them like little eggbeaters. Shaking her head, she told me, "See that big-billed one paying me no mind a'tall? That's Jimmy Carter. Rosalynn will set him straight, wait and see." Sure enough, after much quacking and flapping of wings, the two ducks gave up their pursuit and returned home, twitching their tails and leaving a gentle wake behind them.

At a bend in the creek, an inlet of land formed a natural beach, white-sanded and reedy. Zoe motioned for me to hold my oar still. "Shhh," she warned, a finger held high. "They're making so much racket they won't hear us, but I don't want our movement to scare them."

I almost dropped the oar into the water. On the beach were hundreds of pure-white birds with a startling streak of black on their heads. The sheer numbers and stark black-and-white colors were magnificent, but I knew it was their tiny chicks Zoe had brought me to see. In the turmoil of the last weeks, I'd forgotten other times when a new batch of ducklings or baby birds or fledglings appeared and Zoe had called me to come see them.

"They're not seagulls, are they?" I raised my voice to be heard over their clamor, and Zoe shook her head.

"Naw, they're terns. Gulls sound different." It was true; even I could tell the chirplike call of the tern was different from the strident cry of a seagull. Because of their numbers, the noise was astonishing. "But here's what I wanted you to see," Zoe added. "Watch!"

She pointed at the hordes of terns that circled and flew in and around their colony, landing with bites of insects in their black bills to place in the gaping mouths of their downy offspring. "Both the mama and papa fly off in search of food," she told me. "Going for miles sometimes. And they make several trips every day. But here's what you can't believe! When they come back, no matter how long they've been gone, or how many hundreds of little ones there are in the colony, they always fly straight to their own babies."

I eyed her skeptically. "Come on. How's that possible?"

Zoe shrugged. "Damned if I know. I mean, the little boogers look just alike, don't they? But it's not appearance the parents go by. Bird experts claim that the parent and chick recognize the sound of each other's call. How do they even hear them, much less recognize their call, I wonder."

We sat motionless and watched the colony of birds until the sun began to sink over the top of the trees, and Zoe picked up her oar. "Them spoiled ducks will pitch a hissy fit if I'm late with their supper," she said, and I reached for my oar reluctantly. In spite of the deafening clamor of the terns, the creek was so peaceful, I wanted to float down it forever. At that moment I longed more than anything to disappear around the bend and never come back.

I looked over my shoulder one last time as we rowed away. "Thanks for bringing me out here," I said to her. I was in the front of the canoe with her in the rear. Once we'd left the tern colony behind, the quietness of the creek floated over us like downy feathers.

We paddled in silence for a few minutes until Zoe said in an even tone, "Birds are strange creatures. Sometimes when the parents are gone, things happen to their little ones. Parents fly off foraging for food, and when they return, a predator's made off with their chick. What folks don't know is how they grieve, same as humans. Oh, the scientists, they'll swear it don't happen, but I've seen it too many times. Had a pigeon who pure grieved herself to death after a raccoon made off with her babies. But something even odder. That same bird will be the one to take care of the fledglings left behind when a mama or papa bird doesn't come back. Guess it's something nature has worked out to help them both. Beats all, don't it?"

I froze, the oar trailing in creek water turned copper by the sun. When the canoe landed on the sandy bank, Zoe crawled past me and pulled it far enough ashore that she could tie it to a dock post while I sat motionless. Finally I raised my eyes to find her waiting for me, standing in the scarlet water as it lapped gently around her booted feet. "You know, don't you?" I said. Mack had made me swear not to tell anyone about the paternity suit, and against my better judgment, I'd agreed, too heartsick to argue.

Zoe held out a large strong hand and pulled me to my feet. I climbed out of the canoe, and she regarded me with her keen dark eyes. "Mack came out here yesterday," she said mildly. "Needed to be on the water and fish for a while, he said. I could tell something was bad wrong, and I figured he needed the creek to help him work some things out in his mind. The creek's good at that." She paused and sighed. "You know that Mack don't talk to me, Clare. Never has. But I was waiting when he got back, and he was so tormented that it all came pouring out of him."

"And he told you about the little girl? Haley?" Zoe nodded, and I asked breathlessly, "W-what did he say?"

She shook her head. "All he said was he felt bad for her, being passed around to the relatives. He's paying good support for her, but they're such a sorry bunch, he's afraid they'll blow it and not half take care of her. He said he wishes he could take her in, but he can't ask that of you."

"Oh, God, Zoe! What am I going to do?" I cried, wiping away traitorous tears.

Zoe looked at me steadily. "I know what you'll do, because I know who you are. I've known it from the first time I saw you."

"But what if I can't? You don't know how bad this has hurt me."

Her gaze was gentle. "Yeah, I do, honey. Yeah, I do."

"I don't know how I can—"

"Here's how. You're not gonna do it alone," she said, and reached out to give my hand a squeeze. "Neither one of us could live with ourselves if we let that little girl turn out like her mama. And Mack—he's not as strong as you are, and you know it. He won't do the right thing unless you do." Turning abruptly, she motioned for me to follow her. "Come help me feed these ducks before they start raising hell."

Half blinded by tears, I stumbled after her as she retrieved a bucket of feed. She'd always made it herself, filling it with every possible ingredient her birds needed in their diet. When I knelt to hold the metal bucket for her, she pried it open and said, "Seems to me like we always have a choice, Clare. We can take the crap life hands us and turn it into something else. Or we can let it take us. Problem with that is, by the time it turns us loose, we might not like what it's turned us into." And raising her fingers to her mouth, she whistled her birds to supper.

❧

It turned out I was wrong that day, thinking I couldn't love Mack's child. I hadn't counted on the way my heart flip-flopped when I dropped her off at school and watched her walk bravely up the steps, blond ponytail bobbing against her thin neck. I hadn't been prepared for the lump that formed in my throat when a woman stopped us to say how much my daughter and I looked alike, the

day Haley got her braces and we went out for a milk shake to celebrate. I couldn't have imagined my shout of joy when Mack announced that the judge had awarded him full custody, opening the
way for me to begin adoption proceedings. When I told Haley,
having rehearsed my best professional talk about biological and
adoptive mothers, she'd surprised me by asking if the papers meant
she could start calling me Mom. I'd been so taken aback, I couldn't
speak; misinterpreting my hesitation, she kept calling me Clare
even after the adoption went through.

That summer after Haley came to live with us, I took her and
Jasmine to the beach, where they swam and dove into the Gulf as
Etta and I sat on the shore in the shade of a rented umbrella. Haley
turned her blond head, waved at me, and called out as easily as if
she'd been saying it all her life, "Hey, Mom, watch me swim!" With
those words, the ice that had formed around my heart when I first
heard about her shattered into thousands of tiny pieces and simply
melted away.

Chapter Eleven

❧   ❧   ❧   ❧   ❧

W hen I leave the old fish camp—or what I keep reminding
myself to call by the new name of Wayfarer's Landing Retreat Center—I take a short cut to the labyrinth site, going behind
Zoe Catherine's cabin. Genghis Khan sees me and struts along behind me. I'm on a covert mission, so I shoo him back to Zoe's yard,
since I can't trust him to remain quiet. He jerks back his head
huffily but leaves with his dignity intact by chasing Catherine the
Great and pretending he wasn't following me after all.

My presence disturbs the birds in their aviaries, the pheasants
and pigeons and doves, which squawk and screech and flap and
rustle their wings in protest. The construction going on across
from their lodgings has had all of Zoe's birds in a dither for the past
two-plus months, which I feel bad about. She pooh-poohs my concerns by saying they're just spoiled rotten, is all. When I wonder
how they're going to react to so many folks being at the Landing
for the retreats, she says they'll pout at first, but they'll get over it. I
need to stop pampering them, she insists. Makes them too hard to
get along with. Genghis is the most arrogant, stuck-up peacock
she's ever seen, she says, and it won't hurt him to be taken down a
notch. It'll be good for the peacocks to share their territory with other
people like them. Cooter told me it was Zoe's fault for pampering her

birds. She's always thought Genghis hung the man in the moon, he added in disgust.

The path comes up behind one of the five oaks that encircle the labyrinth, and I pause next to the closest one and peer around its massive trunk. Dory made me promise I wouldn't come out here until the labyrinth was finished, because she wanted to surprise me, but I was unable to resist. When I saw the dump truck rumbling away after emptying its contents, I knew I'd never be able to continue my inspection of the new building while the labyrinth was being put together. No way. As I take in the scene unfolding before my eyes, I raise a hand to my mouth to keep from gasping and giving myself away. What I see is almost impossible to take in.

Dory told me that she had summoned the dozen or so members of her White Ring Society for the big day, putting out the word for them to bring along anyone they could. I expected to see them and maybe a half-dozen others. Instead, more than fifty people are gathered at the site, standing in little groups around the mounds of river stones that the dump truck left. There are children and teenagers and white-haired men and women, people of all ages, sizes, colors, and shapes. But the one that surprises me the most is Son Rodgers, brow furrowed as he stands next to Dory with his hands on his hips, studying the pile of rocks and contemplating the task of edging the paths with them. On a glorious bronze Saturday morning in early November, when Alabama, Auburn, Florida, and FSU are playing big football games, the size of the crowd almost brings me to my knees.

My conscience gets the best of me, and I slip away from the tree trunk and return down the pathway, hoping the squawking of the birds won't give me away. The least I can do is not spoil the surprise for Dory.

For the last couple of weeks, I've watched her lay out the groundwork for the labyrinth in preparation for the rock edgings, using methods I wouldn't have thought of in a million years. Once

she had the dimensions calculated, she brought in a couple of surprising resources, both former teachers of her boys. One was the
high school physics teacher, who constructed what looked like a
giant drawing compass to mark off the circles from a center point.
How he calculated the center, I have no idea, but he and Dory ham-
mered a huge stake in it, then took a rope with a pointed stick tied
to the end to measure the circles. Following behind them, the football coach walked off the circling paths of the labyrinth as he
pushed a little wheelbarrow-looking contraption and left a white-
chalk outline behind, the way yard lines are marked off for football
games. The next day Dory brought in the crew of gardeners who
help keep her gardens immaculate, tillers in hand. After they de-
parted, the paths were laid, and the white-chalk pathways were
edged by shallow trenches necessary for holding the rocks in place.

On the day after the trenches were dug, Dory grabbed a low
branch of an oak on the outskirts of the labyrinth and hoisted herself up on it, laughing at my openmouthed astonishment. Then she
held down a hand for me. "Get your butt up here, Clare," she said
as I stood beneath the tree and stared at her in disbelief. "Only way
to see a labyrinth when it's being laid out is from above."

"No way in hell," I protested. "Heights make me dizzy."

Dory rolled her eyes and continued her climb up the tree. "If
you don't see it from up here, you might as well not see it," she
called down.

Like a fool, I hoisted myself up and crawled after her, then clung
to the trunk in terror as Dory laughed at me for not going any
higher. I dared look down when I heard a noise beneath us and saw
Zoe Catherine bending over to unlace her boots. Freed of her shoes
and using her long toes as leverage, Zoe grabbed the same branch
Dory had used and pulled herself onto it, as agile as a monkey.

"What do you think you're *doing*?" I screeched as Zoe passed
me while I held on to the trunk for dear life. Zoe kept climbing until she reached the place where Dory had settled into the fork of

two fat branches at least six feet above my safe perch, which was only a few feet from the ground.

"Getting a good look at this pretty thing Dory's made, is all," Zoe yelled down to me. "Come up here where I am. You can't see pea-turkey squat from there."

"You don't have to climb much farther, Clare," Dory called. "A few more feet and you'll see the whole pattern."

When I hesitated, Zoe scoffed, "When's the last time you climbed a tree, girl?"

"Probably forty years ago," I muttered, anchoring my sneak-ered foot on a small limb before gripping a higher one with both hands as I inched upward.

Zoe snorted. "No wonder you're so uptight, then. Everybody needs to climb a tree every once in a while. I do. Lot of times you'll find me perching right beside my birds."

"I wouldn't go around telling people that if I were you, Zoe," I said, huffing and puffing as I made my way up. "Folks around here already think you're crazy."

Unperturbed, Zoe said, "The world looks different from up here."

And it did. Not daring to look down, I held my breath as I pulled myself up, ignoring Zoe and Dory's laughter at my leg-trembling fear. When I got to a place where their feet were swinging above me, I grabbed a sturdy-looking branch in a death grip and lowered myself onto it. Straddling it like a horse, I gripped a small limb sprouting from it, my saddle horn. Eyes closed, I took several deep breaths as I got up my courage to look down, and when I did, I let out a whoop of delight.

"Hey, this is amazing!" I cried, and Dory laughed.

"Told you," she said smugly, and Zoe, who was squatting even higher up the tree than Dory, let out a raunchy rebel yell.

What had appeared from the ground to be nothing but trenches dug in concentric circles took on a remarkable shape from the advantage of the tree. "Dory," I gasped, "it's the logo you designed!" The promotional material was almost ready, with the logo on everything: handouts and brochures and website and name tags. To see a forty-foot-wide version of a two-inch design was even more dizzying than climbing a tree. It seemed unimaginable that Dory could have envisioned such a thing, and I called up to her, "Isadora Shaw Rodgers, you're a genius."

"Guess that means you like it." Dory's voice floated down like the yellow leaves of the oak, which flitted and twirled past me like sunbeams. "But this is nothing compared to how it's going to look with the rocks in place. Just wait till you see it then."

"Hey, when it's finished, let's bring a bottle of champagne up here to celebrate," Zoe Catherine suggested.

"Only way I'll be here is to stay on this branch till then," I said with a shaky laugh. "Once I get down, I won't ever get the nerve to climb back."

But I do. After the crowd of volunteers departs and the rock-edged pathways are completed, Zoe Catherine takes a bottle of champagne and climbs one-handed to her perch in the oak tree. Dory sits where she was last time, beneath Zoe in a place where two branches form a Y, and I'm a few feet farther down, hanging on to my saddle horn.

"I'll take a swig, then pass it down to y'all," Zoe tells us as she pops the cork. Holding the bottle high, she shouts, "To Wayfarer's Landing!" then turns up the bottle and chugs it. After wiping her mouth on the back of her hand and burping lustily, she scoots on her belly like a cat stalking a bird and hands the bottle to Dory.

Dory holds up the bottle in a salute before drinking from it. Like Zoe, she lies low on the branch as she leans down to pass the bottle to me. "Watch out, it's slippery," she warns.

My hands shake like the leaves fluttering in the breeze when I have to let go of the branch. After grabbing the bottle by its wet, cold neck, I straighten up and press it against my chest, my heart hammering and my legs tightening on the branch I'm straddling. Once I've settled back into my perch, I ask Dory, "Think anyone ever had communion in a tree before?"

"Only if they were really, really lucky," Dory says with a grin as I hold up the bottle in a salute to her, then to Zoe.

"To the two people who made it all possible," I offer as my toast, and unexpectedly, my eyes fill with tears. Blinking them away, I chug the champagne, then wipe my mouth with the back of my hand like Zoe did.

"Hand it to me now," Dory commands.

I shake my head. "If you want it, you'll have to come get it. No way I can climb up there carrying a bottle."

Dory sighs in exasperation, but before either of us moves, Zoe calls down, her voice lowered to a hush. "Look who's coming. Shhh! Don't tell him we're here. Let's watch and see what he does."

"Oh, no, that's an awful thing to do to him," I cry in protest, but both Zoe and Dory tell me to shut my mouth. I watch guiltily as poor Lex enters the clearing, striding purposefully toward the labyrinth. He promised to come out this afternoon to see it; he's probably been looking for me. One thing for sure, he'll never expect to find me where I am. If I were a true friend, I'd warn him he's being watched; I'd kill him if he did this to me. Zoe Catherine smothers a giggle when Lex takes off his Red Sox cap and scratches his head. "Thought for a minute he was fixing to pray," she says under her breath.

"That does it—I'm telling him we're here," I say indignantly, but again, both Zoe and Dory shush me.

"Wait, please," Dory begs. "It's too good an opportunity to see the effect the labyrinth has on somebody. We're like angels on high, watching a pilgrim."

"Angels, my ass," I hiss. "That's more ludicrous than Lex being a pilgrim. God, he's going to murder me for this!"

"Then you'd better shut up so he doesn't find out." Dory smirks when I throw her a dirty look, but like a fool, I keep my silence. By that time Lex has walked over to the labyrinth and is studying it curiously.

Watching Lex pick up one of the river rocks and test the weight of it, I realize that he's surprised me in a way I hadn't thought I could still be in my business. When Elinor decided she wanted him back, I figured it was a done deal; I'd seen it happen so often. Women who are the ones to initiate a divorce have no idea how readily the men they leave will take them back. Can't recall the statistics, though I have them filed away somewhere. Lex, however, hesitated. On his own, without the usual advice I'd give to a client in the same situation, he's been playing it cool with her. Even after Elinor enlisted the help of Alexia, he held back. He's paid for his reticence because his daughter barely speaks to him now, claiming he's hurting and humiliating her mother. Although he and Elinor are seeing a lot of each other, Lex is still at the marina and she at her house. No doubt Elinor blames me, but I haven't influenced him in his decision. Unusual for a man who claims to still love his ex, he is proceeding with commendable caution.

"Is he going to walk the thing or just look at it?" Dory leans down and whispers to me when Lex replaces his cap, pulls his glasses out of his pocket, then squats to read the sign she made at the entrance to explain the mythic story behind the labyrinth and how it relates to the retreat participants.

"Not a chance in hell he'll walk it," I whisper back. "If he does, I'll bring you the champagne bottle."

"You're on," she says, and Zoe squawks, "Hush up, you two—he'll hear us and spoil our fun."

Yet again Lex surprises me. When he removes his cap this time, he holds it over his heart in what appears to be reverence, and he walks the labyrinth paths slowly and deliberately, taking his time. As Dory's sign explains, there are traditionally seven circles around the center, since seven has always been considered a sacred and magical number. Once you've walked the seven paths and entered the center, the return path becomes the eighth one. According to Dory, the number eight, made up of two circles, is a symbol of new beginnings: Complete seven days, and the eighth one is a new start.

Dory also swears that the way people approach labyrinths says a lot about their attitude toward life. On their trip to Europe this summer, she visited the famous labyrinth laid out on the floor of the cathedral in Chartres. After walking it herself, Dory stood aside and watched the various ways others walked it, which fascinated her. Some people took to the path with great joy, and some ponderously. Many walked it as though on a holy pilgrimage, while others cavorted through playfully. She watched a young man in punk attire arguing on his cell phone as he walked, gesturing wildly; and a frail, elderly couple who had to hold each other up as they inched their way to the center. One of her favorites was the businessman who entered the cathedral purposefully, walked directly to the center of the labyrinth without bothering to wind through the paths, stood there a moment, then walked out the same way, a satisfied smile on his face. She was also intrigued by what people did in the center. Some danced or whirled; others bowed their heads or prayed or lifted their arms high to the cathedral ceiling, and many laughed. What interested her most was that everyone did *something*. As bad as I feel for spying on Lex, I'm so curious to see what he does that, against my better judgment, I keep my silence.

I'm so surprised by what he does when he reaches the center that I look up at Dory, who appears to be as taken aback as I am. When her eyes meet mine, she grimaces and mouths, "I'm sorry, hon." Tilting my head to glare at Zoe, I am gratified when she too looks shamefaced. Nothing can be done now but stay put, and make the two of them swear they will never tell Lex we witnessed this.

In the center of the labyrinth, Lex gets down on one knee, his head bowed low. Then he buries his face in his hands as his shoulders shake mightily with huge, racking sobs. I feel so bad for him that I want to jump down from my perch and comfort him, but there's no way without revealing my shameful spying. I'm caught in a trap of my own making, like the Minotaur of legend. Except the poor Minotaur didn't do anything except have the misfortune to be born a monster. I feel like a monster and want to place my hands over my ears when Lex crosses himself and begins praying. I don't want to hear his prayer, but if I let go of the branch to cover my ears, I'm bound to lose my balance and fall. The only thing I can do is turn my head away and try to shut out the sound of his anguished voice. "Oh, Lord," he prays, "I come to you with a heavy heart, full of guilt and shame, and I ask for your forgiveness." Because Lex is always acting the fool to cover his pain, I should've realized the torment he's been going through with Elinor and Alexia. He's been a much better friend to me than I have to him.

"I have committed a mortal sin," Lex continues. "I've broken one of your sacred commandments by looking at a woman with lust in my heart. Actually, it was more than one woman. It was those three sitting in that oak tree." Jumping to his feet, he grins and points to us, yelling, "Gotcha!"

Zoe Catherine lets out a squawk; Dory howls with laughter, and I come close to falling out of the tree. The bottle slips from my hand as I lose my balance and lurch sideways dizzily, but I manage to grab the branch with both hands before what could be a disastrous plunge ten feet down. Leaping over the rock-edged pathways with surprising agility, Lex runs to the foot of the tree, crying, "Hang on, m'lady—your knight in shining armor to the rescue!" Before he arrives, though, I jump down and land fairly gracefully instead of sprawled out on all fours. Fortunately the champagne bottle didn't break when it landed with a thud on the mossy floor beneath the oak, or my landing could've been different. I'm too embarrassed to face Lex, so I keep my eyes lowered while I nonchalantly brush dirt and leaves off my jeans.

"Hey, Yankee man," Zoe Catherine calls down, "get yourself up this tree! You've got to see the labyrinth from here."

"Yeah, right," Lex hoots. "I can see me climbing my fat ass up there."

"Aw, come on, Lex," Dory says from her perch, her face high with color and her eyes bright. "It'll be your penance for pulling our legs like that. You had me in tears, I was so moved."

"Serves you right for spying on me." Hands on his hips, Lex glares at me as I struggle to keep a straight face while muttering, "Sorry."

I link my hands together, forming a stirrup, and hold them out. "Put your foot here and hoist yourself up, Lex, then Dory can pull you the rest of the way."

Dory scoots down to the branch where I was and leans forward, extending her hand. With his hands on his hips, Lex looks first at me, then up to Dory in disbelief. "Have you two lost what little minds you have? You'd have better luck getting a moose up that tree than me."

"Bull hockey," Zoe snorts. "Cooter climbs trees with me all the time. C'mon, Man of Maine—if Cooter can climb a tree, as bad as his arthritis is, I guaran-damn-tee that you can."

Lex's eyes twinkle with mischief as he looks up at Zoe. "Speaking of that most fortunate of men, allow me to offer my congratulations to the future Mrs. Poulette."

"*What!*" Dory and I shriek at the same time, and Dory leaves her perch to climb down. When she gets close enough, she holds out her arms to Lex before jumping down. To my amazement, he catches her as easily as if she were Abbie or Zach, and they laugh together.

Zoe begins her descent, and I tilt my head to call up to her, "Zoe

Catherine Gaillard, I'm going to kill you if you've accepted Cooter's proposal without telling me first."

Landing on the ground next to us as easily as one of her doves, Zoe lets out a mighty sigh. Although Zoe and Cooter have been companions and lovers for years, with both of them seemingly content with their relationship, recently Cooter put in for Zoe to marry him. Zoe pooh-poohed the idea, telling Cooter she had no intentions of marrying him or anyone.

Instead of responding to me, Zoe pounces on Lex. "What did that fool Cooter tell you?" she cries.

Lex grins, enjoying this. "Not just me, Swamp Woman. He's telling everybody in town that you're going to marry him."

"Really? Did he actually say Zoe had accepted his proposal?" Dory questions.

Lex shrugs. "I assumed he wouldn't be telling it if she hadn't." He winks at me, but I reach out my hand for Zoe's. All joking aside, I know her well enough to know she's furious.

"Don't worry, Zoe. It's just Cooter running his mouth," I say, squeezing her hand. "Everybody knows how he is."

But Zoe is having none of it. Jerking away, she whirls around and stomps off, heading toward her house. "That lying son of a bitch!" she shouts over her shoulder. "I told him I wasn't studying getting married, but did he listen? No! Betcha he'll listen to my twelve-gauge, though. He just thinks Genghis injured him. Ha! Little old peck from a peacock won't be anything compared to an ass full of buckshot!"

Dory stands next to me, laughing, as she shades her eyes with her hand to watch Zoe disappear through the woods. "Remember the day Genghis pecked Cooter in the butt, Clare?"

Lex glances from Dory to me in alarm. "You guys don't think she'll shoot him, do you?"

"Maybe they'll have a shotgun wedding," I say with a smile.

Dory links one arm through mine and the other through Lex's. "Come on, y'all. Let's go calm her down, or Cooter's wrinkled old behiney might pay the price. Here's a Zoe story I bet you don't know, Lex. Ever hear about the robbers?"

"I don't believe I've told him that one," I say as we leave the tree for Zoe's house, arm in arm. "It made her even more notorious in these parts."

"Tell it, sister," Lex says.

"After Zoe's crazy old daddy died," Dory relates, "Mack and Clare were worried about Zoe staying out here all by herself. Remember, Clare? Since people knew the Gaillards once had money, they might think she was rich. Which was ridiculous; her daddy had lost both his mind and every penny he ever had a long time ago."

"It was before Zoe took up with Cooter," I add, "and she was completely alone out here."

"Sure enough," Dory continues, "one night a couple of thugs come up Folly Creek by boat and sneak into Zoe's cabin. Zoe's asleep in her bed when they come bursting in and tell her they've come for her money. 'You can have it all,' Zoe says real pitifully. 'It's in a money box under my bed. Just please don't hurt a helpless old woman.' Shaking and playing like she's scared to death, she reaches under the bed and pulls out a twelve-gauge shotgun with one hand and a twenty-two rifle with the other. Before they know what's hit them, Zoe starts blasting away with the shotgun."

"She *killed* them?" Lex gasps.

"No, but they probably wished they were dead, she filled them so full of buckshot."

"It's what she did next that's even better," I say with a laugh. "There was no 911 then, but while the thugs were jumping around and yelling from the buckshot, Zoe dialed the sheriff and told him to get out to the Landing right away, that she'd just killed two guys who broke in her house. She then aimed the rifle at them."

Eyes dancing, Dory grins. "They hauled ass so fast, Zoe said all she saw of them were heels and elbows. How they managed to get back in the boat and get themselves away, as full of buckshot as they were, no one knows. It made all the papers, and nobody's bothered Zoe since."

"It was soon afterward that Cooter came courting. Remember, Dory? As a neighbor of Zoe's, he was interviewed by the paper for the story. He swept Zoe off her feet by saying in print how he'd like to know her better."

"That's not the half of it," Dory says. "He also said he never knew that Zoe was such a spitfire—but after all, looks can be conceiving."

Lex throws back his head and laughs. "After that story, I wouldn't want to be in Cooter's shoes when Zoe finds him. Only good thing is, he'll probably withdraw his proposal."

≥≥

Dory leans over my chair, snaps her fingers in my face, and I jump, startled out of my reverie. "Hey," she says softly, laying a hand on my shoulder. "You okay, honey?"

I reach up to pat her hand, smiling. "Yeah. Just thinking, is all."

"Uh-oh. That can be dangerous." Dory plops down on the chair next to mine and sits with her elbows on her knees, regarding me with a frown.

"Thanks for coming tonight and working your usual magic," I say to her, picking up my pen and sticking it behind my ear.

"I hope we'll have enough refreshments," she remarks. "Bigger group than I expected tonight."

"It's too big, but I have trouble turning anyone down, as you know."

"That's not what you're worried about, is it?"

I lay my head on the back of the chair, looking past her. "No. I wish that's all it was. It's Haley and Austin."

Dory furrows her brow. "I figured it. What's going on?"

"Oh, things have really been tense with Austin's new job, and they've been fighting a lot. I talked them into seeing a marriage counselor in Mobile. I even insisted they see a man, so Austin wouldn't think all the women in his life were ganging up on him."

"Do you think he's helping them?" When I shrug, palms up, she tells me, "Son and I went to the steak house Saturday night, and Haley and Austin were there."

"Really? They didn't tell me they saw y'all. I was doing my part by keeping the kids. Their counselor advised them to go out alone once a week or so, if possible. It should relieve some of their tension."

"If that's the plan, maybe they can get a refund." She shakes her head sadly. "Oh, honey, I wasn't going to tell you, but . . . it was pretty bad. They argued the whole time. Haley went to the bathroom crying, and I followed her. She begged me not to tell you, but she said Austin has really changed since he got his promotion. And some friends of his? Something about this couple he works with being a bad influence on him, which didn't sound good."

She and I stare at each other. "It never ends, does it? It's like the poster you gave me, the one I put in the john."

She found a great poster a few years ago that she gave to me for my birthday, and I hung it next to the mirror in the bathroom at Casa Loco. My clients love it and are always asking where they can get one like it. Under a picture of tall, scary waves pounding a rocky shore, the caption reads, LIFE JUST KEEPS COMING AT YOU.

꙳

Anxious to show everyone how hard she's working to make things better on the home front, Haley insists on hosting our traditional family dinner on Thanksgiving. I try to discourage her; failing that, I make a pitch for having it at my house, with a kitchen twice the size of hers. "You and Zoe and I can prepare it together," I say enthusiastically, "wouldn't that be *fun*?" Haley won't hear of it. If it kills her, she declares, she's cooking turkey and dressing, giblet gravy and cranberry sauce, candied yams, green beans, and pumpkin pie. Zoe Catherine can bring her toasted pecans and killer sweet tea; Rye his fine wines; and I can buy rolls from the bakery. But by God, she's doing everything else by herself.

Thanksgiving morning, I listen to a panicky message from Haley. She'd gotten up early to start cooking, the kids excited about helping her. Beaming with pride, she'd shown me the timetable she'd drawn up for the dinner preparations, and I'd congratulated her. She was smart, I'd told her, to do a lot of the prep work the day before. At the time I just didn't know how smart.

"Mom, call me as soon as you get in, *please*! It's an emergency. I've been cooking the damn turkey for four hours, and it still has ice in the middle. Then I burned the corn bread for the dressing, and Zach put Play-Doh in the green beans. Abbie wanted to help, but she dropped the cranberries all over the floor, and she's running around chasing them. Oh—and how long are you supposed to cook a stupid pumpkin pie before it sets? I've had this one in the oven for two hours—oh, shit, here comes Austin!" In a whisper, she added, "Call me on my cell, and we'll talk in code, okay?"

My cooking skills are decent, but this is way out of my expertise. Although I hate to bother her in the midst of her own preparations, it's Dory I need. I play Haley's message for her but can't jot down Dory's suggestions until she stops laughing. Then I put my head on the kitchen table for several long minutes before getting up the courage to make the call to Haley.

I know Austin is within earshot when Haley answers her cell with false cheeriness. "Mom! Hi. No, I'm still cooking. Been cooking all morning." She pauses, but before I can say anything, she sings out, "Oh, it's going great! No, really, everything is turning out beautifully."

"I called nine-one-one-Dory," I tell her, not sure why I'm whispering. "She thought your oven was faulty until I told her you burned the corn bread. You forgot to thaw the turkey, she said, and you put too much milk in the pumpkin pie. Cover the edges with foil and keep baking it until it doesn't jiggle when you shake it. Make a little tent for the turkey with foil, and bake that sucker two more hours, then take off the tent till it browns. Last, she says to wash the Play-Doh off the beans and the dirt off the cranberries, and bribe the kids not to tell."

She hears me, but you'd never know it by her reply. "But Mom, I didn't want you to bring anything!" Haley pretends to listen, then says, "Well, if you insist. I'm cooking a pumpkin pie, but yours will be eaten, too."

"Ah . . . I have a Mrs. Smith apple pie in the freezer," I whisper.

"One of your apple pies! The kids will love that. Gramma Zoe called to say she's bringing her corn-bread dressing and giblet gravy, no arguments. She always fixes a washtub full, so I've decided not to even bother. And Rye's housekeeper made a ton of candied yams, so he's bringing those, along with some of her cranberry sauce."

"What are *you* cooking?" I can't resist asking.

"I came up with the idea of putting the turkey in the oven for a few hours to thaw, and it worked like a charm. Let me run now, Mom, and check on it. It's nice and brown, but I don't want to overcook it. See you this afternoon!"

In spite of such a rocky start, the Thanksgiving feast turns out beautifully. The kids decorated the table using miniature pumpkins as candleholders, surrounded by fall leaves. The centerpiece looks especially spectacular sitting atop the infamous tablecloth that Austin's grandmother hand-embroidered and Haley recently "found" in the attic. I dare not meet Haley's eyes when Austin proudly shows the intricate pattern to Zoe Catherine, who exclaims over it enthusiastically. Since Rye's waterfront home is one of the most elegant in Fairhope and he knows quite a bit about fine linens, he struggles to keep a straight face as Austin reminisces about his boyhood when he sat by his granny's rocker and watched her embroider the pink and yellow flowers around the border. Rye raises an eyebrow at me quizzically, and I remark that you can't find handiwork like that anymore, especially with so many places like Target selling cheap imitations.

After the feast is over, the kitchen cleaned, and Zoe and I have wrapped up enough leftovers for Haley to feed the family for a month, Rye and Zoe Catherine take their leave. Zoe doesn't like to drive after dark, and Rye has promised friends he'll stop by for coffee and dessert. He missed an annual Thanksgiving dinner with some of his closest friends to attend Haley's gathering, and I attempt to express my gratitude when I walk him to his car.

"Come with me, Clare," he says, and I shake my head, telling him I'm all partied out. The truth is, the kids have gone to bed, worn out with the festivities, and I'm anxious to spend some time alone with Haley and Austin. Haley has sworn to me that things are better, but I'm skeptical. On and off today, I picked up on the tension, even though I tried not to notice every little thing they said to each other, overanalyzing, looking for trouble. When I first arrived, Abbie showed her father the surprise I'd brought her and Zach, a copy of the book *The Giving Tree*.

"That's me," Austin said.

Abbie laughed. "No, Daddy, silly—it's a tree!"

Glancing sideways at Haley, Austin said, "Daddy's like that Giving Tree, Abbie. Give, give, give, that's all he ever does." I smiled politely, and Haley stood behind him and made a gagging noise while pantomiming poking a finger down her throat.

When I return to the house after waving Zoe and Rye off, Austin meets me at the door carrying the dishes Haley borrowed from me, a basket in each hand. "Got you all packed up and ready to go," he says briskly. "Turns out Zach wasn't asleep after all, so Haley's checking on him."

I open my mouth to protest but think better of it. Instead, I smile and say I can manage the baskets by myself. I can tell it's a tempting offer, but Austin's manners get the best of him, and he carries out the heavy baskets awkwardly. "Whew!" he says after he places them in the trunk and straightens up, rubbing his back. "Those are heavier than they look." Winking at me, he adds, "Maybe you can get one of your boyfriends to carry them in for you."

"Maybe so," I say breezily. His mocking tones irritates me, so I quickly open the door of my car before I say something I might regret.

Again the ingrained manners come through, and Austin holds the door for me. Before I get in, however, he clears his throat and says, "Ah, Clare? Haley told me you'd worked out a deal with the marriage counselor we're seeing, Dr. Wade. As much as I appreciate it, I don't feel comfortable with your doing that. So I told him we wouldn't be back after the Thanksgiving holidays. I hope you understand."

I stare at him, shocked. "If it's the money—"

He kicks at the gravel of their driveway, hands in his pockets and head lowered. "Well, it's that, too. But mainly he's not really helping us."

"I wish you'd said something sooner. I assumed—" I stop myself, annoyed that he'd waited to complain until they'd had six sessions with Dr. Wade. "I mean, I can certainly find someone else."

"No, no. I don't want you doing that. To tell you the truth, I don't know if anyone can help us."

I shiver in the chill wind and pull my sweater tighter. "On the contrary, I feel good about the way things are going now. The two of you are doing so much better."

He shakes his head and refuses to meet my eyes. "I don't know. It appears to be hopeless."

"Austin! My God—*please* don't say that. Of course it's not. Believe me, I've seen a lot of marriages in trouble, and yours is nowhere near that point."

"It's not me. It's Haley. I don't think she loves me anymore."

"How can you say that? She absolutely adores you. To the point where her friends tease her about Mr. Perfect. She fell for you the first day you two met. Mack and I—" My voice catches, and I take a breath before going on. "We were so happy for her, finding someone like you. Someone who loved her as much as we did. And we knew she'd be safe with you. Just wait; you'll find out with Abbie and Zach. That's what you want for your kids, more than anything. You want them to find the right person to love, who will love them in return. Someone they will be *safe* with. You understand what I'm saying, don't you?"

He shrugs. "That's the way you want to see me and Haley, but that's not the way it is. All of Haley's attention and affection go to Abbie and Zach and her kindergarten kids, not to me. And Jasmine, of course. Yak, yak, yak—that's all Haley and Jasmine do, get on the phone and run their mouths. To tell you the truth, I've felt neglected and unimportant for a long time. I've given everything to Haley, and I've about given out. In more ways than one."

"The Giving Tree," I repeat, and he nods glumly. "Listen, Austin, have you told Haley any of this? Because she has no idea you feel that way, I can promise you. She'd be astonished to hear you think like this. It would kill her, as much as she loves you."

He rolls his eyes. "Yeah, right."

I grab his arm, hard. "Promise me you'll tell Haley exactly what you just told me. Then forget your pride and go back to Dr. Wade. Or to someone else. Anyone! But you owe it to your kids to do everything you can to save your marriage. Promise me that you will, please."

He promises halfheartedly, then closes my car door before I can argue any further. That night I can't get to sleep, playing our conversation over in my head like the proverbial broken record, but this one is stuck on a blues song of heartache and despair. In spite of the festive family dinner and the joking and laughter and conviviality around the table, things seem to be spiraling out of control. It's like the hurricane Mack and I watched from our barricade under the stairs so many years ago: All I can do is stand helplessly by and watch as everything flies past me. Unless the winds shift drastically, the Jordan household appears to be directly in its path.

Chapter Twelve

❧　❧　❧　❧　❧

To my utter astonishment, Austin moves out five days after Christmas Day, which fell on a Sunday this year. The Friday after, Haley calls me at my office, where I'm finishing up the treatment notes from an unscheduled session with a suicidal client. Therapists often say that neuroses, dysfunction, and crises do not take holidays. I've had emergency appointments almost every day of the holidays, which have been as hectic as Christmas always is. Come hell or high water this weekend, I'm turning off all my phones, I promise myself.

Haley is crying so hard that I think something has happened to one of the children, and my heart thuds violently. "Mom . . . oh, Mom," she gasps between sobs.

I force myself to remain calm even though I'm suddenly faint and nauseated. "What's happened?"

Her tear-choked voice sounds as though it's coming from an underwater cave. "A-Austin! Austin . . ."

"Something's happened to Austin?" I cry. I feel a shameful, guilt-filled relief that at least it's not one of the children. That I'd never be able to bear.

"He's . . . he's . . . Oh, God, Mom. He's moved out of the house. He's gone."

"*What?* When?"

"Now. Just now. He . . . he came in and got his suitcase. And he left. He just left."

"Wait a minute! This is crazy. What do you mean, he just left?"

But her sobs turn to wails, and as slowly and distinctly as I can while fighting my rising panic, I say to her, "I'm coming right over. Hang up the phone; don't do anything or go anywhere, and I'm on my way."

My admonition to Haley was unnecessary; she couldn't have gone anywhere had she wanted to. Limp as a dishrag, she's sprawled on the sofa staring into space when I walk in the door. As soon as she sees me, though, she collapses into tears again, burying her face in her hands. As I hold her in my arms and murmur useless words of reassurance, I'm glad Austin isn't here. If I could get my hands around his neck, I'd wring it. As I was driving over, the timing behind his surprise move hit me: The kids are in Huntsville. When Austin and Haley married, she was dismayed that he insisted on their spending Christmas with his parents. Mack and I weren't happy about it, either, but Austin was unbending, saying we could have Thanksgiving, but his parents got Christmas. Once the kids came along, he'd relented somewhat, and now they wait until Santa has come on Christmas Day to pack up their gifts and travel to Huntsville.

I barely know Austin's parents, I realize: Colonel Jordan is retired from the military and works at Redstone Arsenal; his mom is a teller at the credit union there. When Haley and Austin returned last night, I'd been surprised to hear that they'd left the kids in Huntsville. In a whispered conference, Haley confided that Austin had insisted, claiming his parents wanted to spend more time with their grandchildren. She suspected it had more to do with the New Year's bash they were attending; now they wouldn't have to pay a sitter.

Pushing back her damp hair from her face, I ask Haley if she could've misunderstood. Austin had planned on returning to Huntsville after New Year's weekend to get the kids, right? Maybe he missed them so much that he went after them. He'd taken his suitcase, but that didn't mean he was leaving.

Haley shakes her head and grabs another tissue from the box on the floor. "Nice try, Mom. Go look in his closet."

Everything is gone. I open Austin's chest of drawers to find it empty. All of his toiletries are gone from the bathroom. With a sick feeling, I come back and sink down beside Haley on the sofa. "Tell me what happened," I say in a weak voice.

She's either calmed down since I arrived, or cried herself out. "I thought everything was fine when we were at his parents' house," she tells me. "We had a fairly decent time, even though it's more exciting to watch paint dry than go to the Jordans'. Austin and his dad watched football; the kids played with their toys from Santa; and Austin's mama and I cleaned up." In spite of her distress, we can't help but smile at each other. We've always joked about Mrs. Jordan's fanatical housekeeping being Austin's gold standard, one Haley didn't have a prayer of reaching. She shrugs slightly. "Before we went, we'd had the usual whirlwind exhausting December, but you know how I love Christmas. Hectic as it was, it was still fun to me."

I say, swallowing hard, "If not, you did a good job of faking it."

After my disturbing conversation with Austin on Thanksgiving, I waited a week before calling him at work. He was far from happy to hear from his interfering mother-in-law. I was following up on our talk on Thanksgiving, I told him firmly. With an exasperated sigh, he insisted he'd just been tired that day, that he and Haley were fine. I hung up unconvinced. In the days that followed, each time I checked with them, it was the same: No, we're fine now, and no, we don't need to see a marriage counselor, and yes, we're too busy to talk. Now I could kick myself. In a troubled marriage, it isn't uncommon for things to hold together during a period of distraction, such as holidays, only to fall apart afterward.

"Wait, Mom—I just realized something," Haley says with

a start. "Looking back over the holidays, I see that Austin went out of his way to avoid being alone with me. You know how it is from the first of December on: Between church and work, we went out almost every night. It was always rush-rush, coming in and getting the kids ready, then hurrying out again. At the Jordans', his parents and a dozen other relatives were there. I'd actually looked forward to the long drive from Huntsville, thinking we'd have plenty of time to talk."

"How did that go?"

"It didn't. On the drive home, Austin played a book on tape that Father Gibbs had loaned him for the Sunday school class Austin teaches. Oh, get this. It was one of those books about leading a Christlike life." She stops to stare at me, wide-eyed. "Austin kept pointing out things to me. He'd rewind it and say, 'Listen to this.' "

"What kind of things?" I ask with a sick kind of dread.

"His favorite was something about living at the foot of the cross. He said that was him, living at the foot of the cross."

It's hard to keep the scorn out of my voice. "You know, Austin has developed quite an elevated opinion of himself lately."

"No, the problem is, he has an unelevated opinion of me," she mutters.

"Oh, honey, that's the way some people elevate themselves, by putting others down. That's another reason I've warned you that you have to stand up for yourself and establish an equal footing in your marriage. It never works when the balance is off kilter and one partner puts his or her needs above the other. It's a recipe for failure. So you didn't get to talk, and you got in really late last night. What happened today when he left?"

Haley shudders as though a chill has gone through her. "It was surreal. He got up early and left—even though the college is closed for the holidays, he still goes to his damn office all the time. The middle of the afternoon, he came home. Without a word, he went to our room and got out his suitcase. Then he told me he was leaving. Cool as could be the whole time. Like you, I thought he meant going to Huntsville to pick up the kids. That was crazy, I said, he wouldn't get there till midnight, and his folks wouldn't like him coming in so late. But Austin said he wasn't going to Huntsville until Monday, as he'd arranged with his parents. He said that he'd decided that we needed some time apart, that it had been coming on for a long time—" Her voice breaks, and she puts a hand over her mouth.

I put an arm around her shoulder, and she cries out, "When I asked how he could leave me *now*, at Christmastime, he looked me straight in the eyes and said he didn't have a choice. He couldn't live like this anymore, he said. Then he swore that I wouldn't even miss him. All I did was talk on the phone to Jasmine and play with the kids, and he'd felt neglected for ages, he claimed. According to him, he might as well not live here."

I narrow my eyes and ask, "Was that the first time he's said anything like that?"

"No, he's said things like that before, and so have I. I mean, I've said all he does is work and neglect me and the kids, so he might as well not be here. You know, the kind of stuff that folks say when they're fighting."

"It does sound pretty typical."

"Here's what gets me—he's been planning this for a while. That's why he left the kids at his folks' house. He admitted it, and I was so stunned, I couldn't even respond."

"That's a first," I say in an attempt to lighten her gloomy expression, but she doesn't seem to hear me.

"It gets worse," she goes on. "When I asked him if he still loved me, he said he didn't know. He didn't *know*!" she wails. "Oh, God, what am I going to do?"

I rub her back as she leans in to me, her face buried in my shoulder. "Listen to me, honey. My guess is, he's gone on to Huntsville, and that might be a good thing. Let him cool his heels for a few days, start to miss you—"

She stops me with a snort. "A few *days*? His car was piled up like the Beverly Hillbillies'."

"Well, we wouldn't expect Scrooge to rent a mover, would we?" I say dryly. "Where is he going? Wait, let me guess—the Webbs', right?"

Haley shakes her head. "He knows some professor who's going on sabbatical over the winter quarter, and Austin arranged to stay in his apartment, which is right next to the college. He says he would've waited until summer to ask me for a 'trial separation,' but this place was too perfect to turn down. I guess that means he got it free."

I rub my eyes wearily. Not a good sign, making arrangements to stay elsewhere for an extended length of time. Not quite the same as spending a few days at his parents' or with friends while he thinks things over. Although Haley is in bad shape, I have to ask the question I dread. After a long silence, I clear my throat and say, "You say Austin's getting the kids on Monday?"

She nods despondently. "Yeah. He'll do that; don't worry. I had a panicky moment of thinking he and his parents would try and take my kids, that the whole thing had been a trick. Then I thought, Get real, Haley. His folks love them, but they're both too uptight to have little kids around all the time. You should see Austin's mom following Zach and wiping up after him. Ha! No way they'd keep them more than a few days."

"I wasn't thinking of them keeping the kids," I admit. "I wondered what you'll tell Zach and Abbie when they get home and their daddy's not here."

Haley closes her eyes and rests her head against the back of the sofa. "Austin said he'd tell Abbie before bringing them home. Zach is too little to understand. But get this—here's what Austin told me that he planned on telling Abbie: He's going to be away for a few days because he's helping a friend out, staying at his place and taking care of it while the friend is out of town. When I called him a chickenshit, he said if I didn't like it, I could tell Abbie myself."

A rage sweeps over me that frightens me with its intensity, and I fight for control. I cannot lose it. One of us has to stay together. After several deep breaths, I say, "Regardless of what he tells her, Abbie's not going to handle it well, her daddy not being here."

Haley is quiet for a long time, then she says, "You know, Mom, because of the way I was raised—before you and Daddy found me—all I wanted was for my kids to have a good, safe home. I thought by marrying someone like Austin, I was making sure of that, and they'd never be from a broken home. I wouldn't have done this to them for all the money in the world."

"Of course you wouldn't. None of us would."

"But I did, don't you see? *I'm* the one to blame, not Austin. You have trouble admitting it, but he's right. I should have done more to hold on to him, to be the kind of wife he wanted me to be. If only I'd paid him more attention, or showed him how much I love him, or whatever. Anything but this."

"I don't want to hear you say anything like that again, you hear me? It's utter nonsense. All of this started when Austin got promoted to a big job with a lot more responsibility than he'd ever had, and it was too much pressure. He dealt with his stress in an unhealthy manner. Sweetheart, I've seen hundreds of couples in trouble, and my guess is, Austin will be back home. Wait until he doesn't see his kids for a week or two. One thing about him, he's devoted to the children. He thinks he can get by with telling Abbie that lie, but she's not stupid. He'll have to tell her the truth. And when he does, let me tell you something. Abbie and Zach? He might tell them he's leaving you, but he'll be leaving them, too. Once he has to face that reality, he'll most likely come to his senses."

Haley grips my hands in both of hers, and her face brightens. "Do you really think so?"

"I think there's a real good possibility. Now I want you to get some things and come home with me. No way I'm leaving you alone tonight. Best thing you can do is stay with me this weekend. We'll watch videos and eat popcorn and chocolate ice cream, then on New Year's Eve, we'll buy a bottle of champagne and drink the whole thing by ourselves."

"But you're going to a party with Rye. I'm not messing up your weekend."

"You're not, believe me. Rye has a hundred women he can take instead."

She shakes her head. "No. I should stay here in case Austin comes back."

I stand up and take her hands, pulling her to her feet. "Don't be ridiculous. He'll call you if he has a change of heart. No argument. You're coming home with me, and I'll bring you back Monday."

Haley is listless as I help get her things together. As bad as she's been today, one thing I know in spite of the optimism I'm showing for her benefit: It's only going to get worse. If Austin has truly left for good, it will get much worse before it gets better.

❧

In spite of my years of experience in such matters, I'm taken by surprise when Austin executes the separation from his family with a precision that makes my blood run cold. Haley told me that when he brought the children home from Huntsville the first Monday of the new year, he was like a robot, with jerky movements and blank, unblinking eyes. He told Abbie he'd be gone for a few days, then he waited until she and Zach were asleep before leaving the house. That had been bad enough; although Haley was spared the ghastly scene of the kids watching their father walk out the door, Austin had broken down and reached out for her as he started to leave. But when she'd moved toward him, he'd fled, weeping as he slammed the door in her face. Haley had decided to be waiting alone when he returned with the kids, although it appeared I'd have to hog-tie Jasmine to keep her away. I convinced her that after Austin left, she should show up with a pizza and a half-gallon of chocolate-marshmallow ice cream. I wonder if Austin realizes he's a marked man. If he survives Jasmine's fury, it will be all the proof I need that miracles still occur.

Jasmine's not the only one out to get Austin. When I called Zoe Catherine to tell her, she reacted pretty much as I expected. I had to hold the phone away from my ear as she yelled into the receiver, describing which of Austin's privates she'd cut off once she found out where he's hiding—or, as she put it, which rock he's crawled under. But after she's vented her rage, she starts showing up unexpectedly at Haley's house, and I'm reminded of those grief-shrouded days after Mack and I lost our baby, when Zoe ministered to us in her own unique way. When I took Haley home on Monday, we found that her grandmother had come into the house, straightened up and done the laundry, and left a bowl of boiled shrimp in the fridge and a platter of cookies for the kids. The next day Zoe asked Haley and the kids to spend the night at the Landing because she had some baby birds she needed Abbie and Zach's help with. In many ways, Zoe Catherine is better with Haley than I am during these first awful days after Austin's departure. I go by the book, advising and trying to apply the best methods of coping I can find. Zoe's actions, on the other hand, are spontaneous and from the heart. All the psychology books in the world don't measure up to her comforting presence.

Once school starts back, I honor Haley's wishes by leaving her alone for a few days until she can get the kids back into a routine, always hard after the holidays but especially now, with their daddy gone. As I'd predicted, Abbie didn't buy Austin's story, and Haley couldn't lie to her. Instead, she told her that they would be separated for a while so they could think about how much they'd been fighting and how to stop it. I worried more about Abbie's reaction than I let on to Haley. When I asked if Abbie had cried, Haley said no, she'd done nothing. She'd gone so quiet that Haley called Austin and made him reassure her. Evidently he had, Haley told me; Abbie hadn't asked about her daddy since. Haley saw that as a good sign, but I knew better.

Although staying away right now is one of the most difficult things I've ever done, I agree with and respect what Haley's doing. Rather than having someone there as a buffer for the kids each day when they return from school, she's determined for the three of them to establish a daily routine, stating firmly that children feel more secure with a schedule. Although an indifferent housekeeper, Haley is a well-grounded mother, with her degree in early-childhood education as a foundation. I worry more about her than I do the children. That worry will come, though, I know; one thing for sure, it will come.

When I visit the kids for the first time since Austin left, Abbie is sitting on the floor, cutting out snowmen from white construction paper, and Zach is lying beside her on a giant panda-bear pillow that Rye gave him for Christmas, his thumb in his mouth. Haley sits at the kitchen table, putting smiley or frowny faces on a stack of kindergarten papers she's grading. The cluttered room is as chaotic with toys and school supplies as ever, and my first thought is, At least they can enjoy the mess without Austin's disapproval. After their squeals of greeting and wet, sloppy kisses, I sit cross-legged on the floor beside Abbie, exclaiming over the snowmen with their yarn caps and mufflers and black button eyes.

"Look, Grams," Abbie cries, digging through the stack until she finds one and pulls it out. "Mommy said for me to make snowmen to decorate her classroom, but I made snowwomen instead."

"Let's hear it for sisterhood," Haley murmurs without looking up from her papers.

I smile when Abbie holds up a skinny one with yellow yarn hair. "Snow Mommy!" she announces, then giggles when she shows me a tall one with cotton balls pasted on top of its head. "And this one is Gramma Zoe. Snow Zoe—hey, that rhymes." A large round one with black loops for hair is Snow Jasmine.

I put my hands over my eyes. "Uh-oh. Is Snow Grams pretty or ugly?"

"Pretty!" Zach cries, almost knocking me over when he jumps up and grabs me around the neck. "I love my grams the bestest."

"Not better than Mommy! You'll hurt Mommy's feelings." Abbie wags her finger at him sternly, and Haley hoots.

"Your granddaughter sure has a strong inner parent," she remarks to me.

"Hmm . . . I have noticed that tendency." I reach out to tousle Abbie's white-blond hair once Zach releases his death grip on my neck and settles in my lap instead. "That means she'll be a good mother one of these days. Right, Abbie-kins?"

"Right. But when I get to be a mommy, *my* husband is not gonna leave me and make me cry," Abbie states solemnly.

I cut my eyes to Haley. "I walked right into that one, didn't I?"

"I'll be so nice to my husband that he won't leave me," Abbie continues, oblivious. "Daddy said sometimes big people can't get along, so they live in different houses. But that doesn't mean he doesn't love Mommy anymore. Is that true, Grams?"

Before I can come up with my best therapy-based reply, Zach socks the panda-bear pillow with a chubby fist and cries, "Daddy made Mommy cry. I'm gonna hit Daddy." He pounds the poor panda bear until Abbie jerks it away from him.

"No, Zach! That's *bad*. Only bad kids hit things. Right, Mommy?"

"Bad Daddy! I hate Daddy," Zach yells, socking the poor panda in spite of Abbie's efforts to push him away, and Abbie screeches, "Mommeee! Zach's talking ugly about Daddy, and you said you weren't going to allow that."

"Welcome to the wonderful world of Disney." Haley sighs, putting aside the stack of papers and rubbing her face wearily.

$\rightsquigarrow$

The following Saturday morning, I blink in surprise when I open the front door and find Zoe Catherine. It's a dazzling cold day in early January, the air tart and crisp as a winesap apple, and I've dressed warmly in old sweatpants and a sweatshirt the White Rings gave me for Christmas that says THE NUMBER ONE CAUSE OF DIVORCE IS MARRIAGE. Zoe is bundled up in her army fatigues and a chamois-colored hunting jacket, with a brown knit cap pulled low over her ears and her white braid flopped over her shoulder. Her face is high with color, and her black eyes are snapping. "C'mon," she says, with no other greeting. "You gotta see this."

Over her shoulder, I see she's left her pickup running, the door flung open. "Can it wait? I just put a pot of lentil chili on the stove." I don't add that I'm inviting Lex for supper because we haven't gotten together since long before the holidays, both of us being so busy.

"Turn it off and get your jacket."

I know Zoe well enough to know there's no use arguing with her, so I do as she commands. Without another word, she turns the truck around and heads back toward the Landing. Even though I glance her way curiously, she doesn't tell me where we're going. It makes no sense; if it's a new bird at the Landing, why didn't she just call me to come out? It's hard to read her mood, exactly: She appears to be seething with anger. Which makes no sense. There's never any mistaking Zoe's anger; she rants and raves and squawks and yells with total abandon but never seethes quietly. Something is bundled at my feet: another of her care packages for the kids. This one appears to be brownies in plastic wrap on a sack of pecans. It looks as though she was heading toward Haley's but stopped to get me instead.

"Some of those pee-cans are yours, if you want them," she says, noticing me eyeing the sack. "Left over from that old tree behind my cabin. Ha—everything out there is old, even my damn trees."

"Of course I want them. I must've been a squirrel in another life, much as I love pecans."

"Speaking of nuts, look at this, would you?"

With a squeal of tires, Zoe turns off the road and slams to a stop. I stare in surprise, uncomprehending. We're at Cooter's roadside produce stand, a place that could only belong to Cooter Poulette. Matter of fact, it looks just like him. It's a rambling, unpainted shack with dirt floors and crudely constructed bins for the produce. In the summer, the bins overflow with local tomatoes, corn, string beans, peas, cantaloupes, and watermelon, but in the winter months, usually the only thing in them are oranges, tangerines, and grapefruit. Any season, Cooter sells boiled peanuts, which he cooks and sacks himself. For a while he carried duck eggs from the Landing, which were quite popular, but he and Zoe had a falling-out over them, so they're no longer available. All Zoe told me was that Cooter hurt the mama duck's feelings and she refused to lay eggs for him anymore. "I tried to tell the old fool not to mess with Hillary Clinton," Zoe snorted.

Although the produce stand is open to the elements in the front and screened on the sides, the back is solid, and Cooter keeps a small heater there, next to the peanut boiler and a couple of rocking chairs. He is a lackadaisical businessman, as might be expected, and you never know if he'll be running the stand or on the creek fishing. We see his grandson in the back, propped up by the heater, but Cooter's nowhere to be seen.

I look at Zoe quizzically. "Don't tell me you dragged me all the way out here to see Cooter Poulette."

"Of course not," she snaps. "Far as I can tell, the dumbass is not even here. But look what he's done! I've never been so humiliated in all my born days."

She points to the front of the produce stand, and I laugh and put a hand over my mouth. I've forgotten about Cooter's infamous sign. At one time Cooter's sign was the talk of Fairhope. A few years ago, Zoe and Cooter found a treasure at a flea market, a discarded church sign with boxes of letters, which Cooter hung in front of his business. One night Cooter got drunk and changed the letters on the sign to read BETTER OVER THE HILL THAN UNDER IT! His cronies got such a kick out of it that Cooter got inspired and began putting up more outrageous sayings. Eventually he tired of it, and the sign said simply GONE CRAZY - BE BACK SOON.

Today, though, Cooter has outdone himself. In bold letters, he's put WIFE WANTED. APPLY WITHIN. Underneath, he added details: *Good-looking older man desires woman with better sense than the one who turned him down.*

"Would you look at that!" Zoe Catherine cries. "If Cooter Poulette is good-looking, I'll kiss your behiney in the middle of downtown Fairhope."

"You going to fill out an application?" I say with a grin.

"You think he's joking? When I drove by this morning, three women were lined up, filling 'em out. Cooter was here, and he was looking them over, I tell you. They were nothing but floozies, either. *Old* floozies!"

"Guess you've blown your chance with Cooter. Christmas Eve, he got down on his knees and begged you to marry him, did he not?"

"Yeah, and his arthritis is so bad, he couldn't straighten up afterward. I tried to call his boy to come help me but couldn't get ahold of him. So I had to put Cooter to bed bent over like a pretzel."

"Why do you think he's gotten it in his head that he wants you two to get married after all these years?"

Zoe Catherine shakes her head. "Aw, I do feel kind of sorry for him. But not sorry enough to marry him," she adds quickly.

"Sorry for him? He's not well?"

"It's not that." She stares out the window of the pickup, her brow furrowed. "Poor Cooter can't stand to be by himself any-more. Says he gets so lonesome, it drives him crazy. I get lone-some, too, but that's no reason to get *married*. Lonesomest folks I know are the married ones. And what makes him think I want to spend the rest of my life taking care of an old man?"

"Why don't y'all just live in sin?"

"Suits me fine, but no, Cooter's never been married. Did you know that? In spite of a couple of common-law wives and a few kids scattered around, he's never made it to the altar. He says he wants to get married just once before he dies, to see if it's as bad as everybody says."

I study her, choosing my words carefully. "You've had lots of men, but you only married once. Did you love Papa Mack?"

She eyes me suspiciously. In spite of my probing, she never dis-cusses her relationship with Papa Mack. All I know is, she met him fishing at the Landing. Evidently Papa Mack, a staid young busi-nessman, was enchanted with the wild, dark-haired beauty, and they had a brief but passionate romance. As was customary in those days, the parents of the young couple quickly married them off when Zoe got pregnant at age eighteen. The marriage soon soured, and Zoe was so miserable living in town at Papa Mack's big old mausoleum of a house that she took her baby and disap-peared. As innocent as one of her doves, Zoe knew nothing about power and political influence, but she was soon to find out. Re-straining order in hand, the sheriff found her and took Mack back to his father. Both of them told Zoe they'd be forced to charge her with kidnapping and lock her up if she came around her son again. Mack was poisoned against her, told that she'd deserted him. He grew up resenting Zoe and thinking she'd abandoned him to a stepmother he hated, who hated him in turn. I've always known that Zoe was much more destroyed by the whole thing than she's ever let on.

Scowling, Zoe shrugs. "*Love?* I don't have no idea what love is.

You've got all those degrees, yet I'll bet you don't know any more about it than the rest of us."

"That's for sure," I agree. "All I know is, since the beginning of time, it's been the basis of more songs, stories, and poems than anything, for something so little understood."

"I reckon that's why—folks trying to make sense of it."

"Think you'll give in and marry Cooter?"

Zoe looks at me as though I've lost my mind. "You tell me, girl, why I'd want to do something again that I messed up so bad the first time." She turns her head to glare at the sign. "And I sure wouldn't, after Cooter pulling something like this."

"Dare you to go inside and get an application."

"The day hell freezes over."

I open the door of the truck. "If you won't, then I will."

"*You're* going to marry Cooter?"

"Yeah, right. Be still my heart! My guess is, he just put up that sign to get your goat. And it worked, didn't it?"

"Huh! Cooter's got the big head so bad that he got his grandson to make a hundred applications on his computer. A hundred! If I wanted to make a fortune, I'd buy Cooter Poulette for what he's worth and sell him for what he thinks he's worth."

Before Zoe can stop me, I run inside and tell Cooter's grandson I want several of the applications. He looks at me curiously, peering over my shoulder to the pickup, but Zoe has ducked down. As though everyone doesn't know her green truck with the Landing Nature Preserve printed on the side.

I've barely closed the door of the truck when Zoe Catherine pulls away so fast that the wheels spin in the dirt, spraying sand and rocks behind us. Cooter's grandson stands up to see what is going on. "Oh, Lord, this is a scream," I tell her. "Look, he even has a place for the applicant's photograph. He wrote the whole thing to aggravate you. Aw, that's kinda sweet! Anybody who'd go to so much trouble must really love you. Listen to this. 'Circle the ones that apply. A) likes to cut bait; B) likes to fish; C) likes to clean fish; D) likes to eat fish; E) none of the above. Note: If you circled E, might as well throw the damn application away.' "

When I look at Zoe for her reaction, I see that her lips are turning up at the corners, but she catches herself and frowns. "What you gonna do with those applications?" she snaps at me.

"Have fun with them. I can't wait to show Dory and Rye and Lex. Oh, and Haley. It'll do her good to have a laugh now."

"Take a few and leave the rest for me. I'll fix him up, teach the idiot a lesson he won't forget."

"What are you up to?"

She smiles her mischievous smile. "What you think? I'm gonna fill out every one of them. Make up names. Paste on pictures of the ugliest hags I can find. Matter of fact, I'll get Haley to help me. I'm heading to her place after I take you back home."

I laugh, shaking my head. "That's a great idea——" I stop, turning my head to watch the car that just whizzed past us in the other lane. "Zoe! Turn around." I realize I should've known better when Zoe squeals the truck into a wide U-turn. I grab the door handle, yelling, "Jesus Christ!"

"If Jesus is in that car, I can catch him," Zoe says, throwing me a wicked look.

"Actually, it's Austin. But he'd probably think I was right the first time."

Throwing me forward as far as the seat belt will allow, Zoe slams on the brakes, and the driver of the car behind us sits on his horn before screeching past us, giving Zoe the finger. Not surprisingly, Zoe rolls down her window and sticks out her hand, middle finger erect. "Hope I never get too old to do that," she says, chortling. "It's more fun than it ought to be. Now, you follow Austin Jordan all you want to, but not me. I don't care what the little shit does or where he goes."

"Indulge me, okay? I've got my reasons. But hurry. We've already lost him."

Zoe glances at me in disgust. "You want me to catch him, you better hang on. He can't outrun me, I guaran-damn-tee you."

"Don't let him see us, or he won't turn off. That's all I want to see, if he turns in to the driveway where the Webbs live. If I can remember which one it is."

"The Webbs? That prissy little thing who works for Austin, the one with the husband who's always grinning like a possum?"

"John and Wanda Webb. See, I'm wondering about their role in all this. I have a feeling that's where Austin's staying. Every afternoon when I've left my office and started walking home, I've seen Austin's car heading their way. I didn't think anything of it at first, but now I wonder." Zoe turns her head to look at me, puzzled, and I gesture toward the road, shrieking, "God Almighty—watch where you're going!"

"I don't get it. Haley told me that Austin was staying at some professor's house who's gone overseas."

I shake my head in disgust. "I don't believe that anymore. I got suspicious when he wouldn't tell her where the guy's apartment is, and the only way she can reach him is at work or on his cell phone. I think he's at the Webbs', and he told Haley that story about the professor so she wouldn't show up there. Though I doubt it's her he's worried about. More likely it's you or Jasmine he's afraid of."

Zoe snorts. "That boy got any sense, he'd better be. I ever see him again, I'll cut off his tallywacker and feed it to the fish in Folly Creek."

I roll my eyes. "Gosh, I can't imagine why he'd think he has to hide from you. Look! He's turning in now. What's the name on the mailbox?"

"Webb." Zoe turns her head to grin at me. "Hot damn! We got him."

❧

Back home, I'm so surprised to answer the phone and hear Austin's voice on the other end that I sink into a kitchen chair. Ever since he moved out, I've left him dozens of messages, begging him to call me. In an effort to get him to return my call, I said I was terribly concerned about him, that I loved him, and if he'd talk to me, I'd just listen and not condemn him. All I wanted was to help him and Haley and the kids through this difficult time. I didn't expect a response, and I didn't get one.

"Clare?" Austin's voice is tentative, shaky. "I saw you and Gramma Zoe today when you turned around to follow me."

"Austin, I beg you—please, let's talk! Can you come over now? Or to my office? Would you feel more comfortable in my office?"

His sigh is ragged and full of pain. "This isn't easy for me."

"I know. I can only imagine what you're going through. It's bad for everyone. None of us is immune. It's an awful thing."

"I'm sick about it," he says, his voice breaking. "Just sick. I'd never hurt Haley and the kids, you know that." His laugh is tired and bitter. "Yeah, right, huh? My head's all screwed up. I don't know what's wrong. I'm so confused and . . . I don't know . . . screwed up now."

"Austin, you're trained as a counselor. You *know* you need to get some help. I won't offer to find you someone, because I don't think that's what you need. Find someone yourself, someone you trust to help you get your head on straight."

"John's a counselor, you know. John Webb?"

"No. It can't be a friend, you know that."

There's a long pause before he says, "How's Haley doing?"

Weighing my words, I reply, "Well, she's holding up for the kids. That's how she's making it now. But she's not good. She's having a difficult time." My voice catches, and I put a hand over my mouth to stifle a sob.

"Next Friday night, I'm getting the kids," he says in a weary voice. "Only time I've seen them since I left. But Haley agreed to let me have them for one night. Clare? You think the kids will be okay?"

"No, I don't. I'm sorry; I know that's not what you want to hear. But they don't understand what's going on. Zach is angry. He got in trouble at day care the other day for hitting a kid. That's not like Zach, and you know it. He doesn't know how to deal with any of this."

"Oh, God, I'm sorry. I'm so sorry . . ." His voice trails off, then I hear a click and the phone goes dead.

Chapter Thirteen

❧   ❧   ❧   ❧   ❧

Lex isn't buying it. He narrows his eyes and stares at me suspiciously before saying, "You don't like to take the boat out in the winter. Last time we went—the week after Thanksgiving, right?—it wasn't nearly this cold, and you bitched and moaned the whole time. Drove me so batty, I ended up taking you back to shore, remember? I'm not taking you boating until spring, so you can forget it."

I shrug nonchalantly as I tighten the cap on a thermos of coffee I brought along. "What if I put a slug of bourbon in our coffee?"

"You're on," he says with a grin.

He's right; it's brittle cold on Mobile Bay, the air sharp as crushed glass, but it is a glorious blue day, with winter sunbeams dancing on the rippling water like ballerinas draped in diamonds. I had to beg Lex to take the Catboat rather than a motorboat; he argued that the wind was too still to sail. I couldn't tell him I wanted the smaller sloop so we could explore the shore slowly and silently. Once we get the boat out and it's too late for him to turn back, I'll fess up.

Lex has taught me a lot about boating. I've gotten pretty good at helping him with the synchronized dance of sailing, especially on the Catboat, because it has only one sail in the peak. We motor out from the marina, then cut the engine and hoist the jib. "Hope you're going to be happy rocking around a bit," he says, shading his eyes to study the mainsail as it flutters listlessly in the slight breeze. "Doesn't look like we're going to have much of a wind."

"Good." I give him what I hope is an innocent smile. "Just what I want, a quiet and peaceful day on the bay."

He continues to eye me skeptically, and I tighten my jaw to keep my teeth from chattering. I'm barely able to move, since I've got on so many layers of clothes, including a knit cap that covers my head completely, and the leather gloves I borrowed from Lex for our outing. Because of the tight-hugging cap and the curved sunglasses I wear to block the breeze from my watery eyes, Lex tells me I look like a grasshopper. A fat one, he adds, laughing every time I move awkwardly in my thick green jacket. When he hopped on board wearing only chinos with a cabled sweater, a nylon windbreaker, and his Red Sox cap, I demanded that he go back for a heavier jacket. "Aw, hell." He laughed. "Believe me, honey, this ain't nothing."

"Remind me never to go to Maine," I mutter now.

"Oh, no, you don't. You said you'd let me show you Bar Harbor, remember? Hey, maybe we can go next summer."

I steal a glance at him as he adjusts the tiller. When a gust of wind slaps his hair against his forehead, he takes off his cap impatiently and runs his fingers through his thick hair to tuck it under. I'm at a loss to determine where Lex is coming from these days. He's clammed up about Elinor, despite what I consider skillful probing on my part. True to his word, he's continued to help out at the retreat site, but we haven't been seeing each other as we were this summer. The only time I saw him during the Christmas holidays was the night he came over to bring me what he claimed was a small gift. It turned out to be a tasteful and expensive sterling silver fountain pen, which made me glad he liked the nautical clock I'd presented him. We had a really lovely evening drinking eggnog and singing along with carols on the stereo.

Lex and Elinor spent most of the holidays with Alexia, who arrived in Fairhope to stay with her mother. Lex told me both of them were pissed at him because he wouldn't go to Boston with them to celebrate the New Year and take Alexia back to college. He'd gotten angry in return, saying they didn't understand that the marina couldn't be closed down for the holidays like Elinor's shop. They went without him, and he gave his staff the holidays off and ran the marina alone. I'd called to tell him everything that was going on with Haley but hadn't seen him. So why this sudden talk of our going to Maine together, I wonder.

"You know what I'd like, Lex? Let's have our picnic at that little inlet we went to last June." It's Sunday afternoon; I've talked him into the outing by telling him I put the lentil chili I made yesterday in a thermos and said we'd have a picnic. I also brought along wedges of corn bread, the bourbon-laced coffee, and some of Zoe's brownies.

Again his look is suspicious. "You know how long it'll take us to get there?"

I shrug. "So? Tommy's running the marina all afternoon, you said." The dockmaster at the marina is on the verge of retirement, part of the reason Lex has been so busy lately. He's planning to promote Tommy to dockmaster, and Jasmine is thrilled, convinced her family will come around if Tommy gets a better job. Things are still iffy; Haley told me Tommy had confided to her that he'd wanted to give Jasmine a ring for Christmas but was waiting until things got better with her family.

"I'm not worried about the marina," Lex says. "I'm worrying about you becoming an ice sculpture of a grasshopper by the time we get there."

"I'm not that cold," I lie. "Really. Come on, Lex! We haven't had an adventure in such a long time."

"Why do I have a feeling that something is going on besides a Sunday picnic?"

From his perch behind the wheel, he studies me as I lean back on the cushions, my jaw clamped shut. If my teeth chatter or I shiver when the freezing air stings my face, he'll turn the boat around and take me back. "Oh, I get it!" he says all of a sudden. "That cove is the place where I put the make on you when we first started seeing each other. Or rather, where I tried to. You've come to your senses and realized what you've been missing all this time."

"Believe me, if it were seduction I had in mind, I'd pick a better spot than the cockpit of a Catboat. It'd be on a bearskin rug in front of a roaring fire and under a pile of blankets."

Lex turns the wheel, and we heel left sharply. I grab the rail behind the cushions to keep from falling on my face, and I yell at him, "What are you *doing*?"

"I know just the place," he says with a grin.

"Okay, okay, I'll tell you everything if you'll straighten the boat up. You know it scares me when we heel over."

"And I've told you a dozen times I won't let you fall overboard. Maybe I should, though, getting my hopes up like that." He throws me such a dark look that I laugh.

"Then you'll be sorry, because you won't get to hear why I brought you out here today."

"Since it wasn't to seduce me, tell it to somebody who might give a shit."

Rising, I move to sit by him and put my head on his shoulder and arms around his waist. "I've missed you these last few weeks, Man of Maine. I haven't had so much fun since the last time we were together."

"Missed you, too, Doctor Lady. I'm glad you didn't fall overboard." He places an arm around me comfortably, and I relax against him, allowing his sturdy bulk to block off the sea spray. Somehow, in the mysterious way of relationships, things have shifted, and we've moved back into our comfort zone. Ever since the night of the anniversary party, things have been off kilter between us, tilting one way or the other like the leeway-leaning sailboat. Evidently he was more aggravated with me about Rye than I realized. Laughing, Dory told me that the next day Lex had called to ask what was wrong with me that I preferred a fop like Rye over a hunk like him. She replied it was obvious that I didn't know how to appreciate a *real* man. It's more than his dislike of Rye, though. Elinor has become bolder in her efforts for a reconciliation, which he doesn't bother to deny anymore. The time we once spent together now belongs to her.

"Could we get a little closer to the shore once we pass Point Clear?" I ask, my voice muffled against his shoulder.

"You say when."

Lex doesn't question me again as we glide steadily over the blue-gray bay, and I pray the cold wind won't pick up. Along the shoreline are beautiful waterfront houses, invisible from the inland highway but spectacular from this vantage point. We passed Dory and Son's house a few miles back, and I watched Son get in his car, going to play golf. It still amazes me that things are going so well with them, which I don't even pretend to understand. As though reading my mind, Lex asks in an offhand manner, "Did you and pretty boy make it to the Rodgerses' New Year's party?"

I shake my head. "Haley was with me then, and in bad shape, so I didn't go to anything that weekend. Thank God. After Christmas I was partied out."

"You're not still pissed at Dory for getting back with Son, are you? Seems like he learned his lesson and straightened up after she left his ass this summer. He's not near as big a jerk as he was when I first met him. Or maybe it's just me."

I poke him with my elbow. "That's not true—you're still a big jerk."

"Ha ha. Well, are you? Still pissed at Dory?"

I look up at him indignantly. "I was never angry with her, exactly. I was just disappointed."

"Aw, bull. You were so mad, you could've bitten a ten-penny

nail in two, but you'll never admit it. And what's this 'angry' shit? Nobody but one of your people would say that. Guess you guys don't get pissed. You get *angry* instead," he mocks.

"Oh, hush. I've been mad, seething, peeved, furious, *and* pissed with you plenty of times, buster."

"Not as mad as I've gotten with you, I bet."

I shrug. "How would I know? You're so full of it, I can't tell when you're serious and when you're not."

He holds the wheel lazily with two fingers as he glances down at me. "You may not be able to tell whether I'm having you on or not, but I can promise you one thing: You'll know when I'm serious."

"I'll remember that," I say dryly.

When we get farther down the shore, I reach inside the storage bin and pull out the binoculars. Lex watches me, then sighs, loud and long. "I was waiting for you to tell me, like you promised, but since it appears you aren't going to, what the hell are you up to? Not spying, surely?"

"Actually, that's pretty much it," I say lightly, putting the binocular cord around my neck.

"*Spying?*"

"Spying," I repeat.

He stares at me, aghast. "Couldn't you lose your license or something?"

"Yeah, but I'd have to get caught first. Okay, we're almost there now, so get the boat as close to the shoreline as you can. But not close enough that anyone on the shore will recognize us."

"Disguised as a grasshopper, you should be fine. And I have a brown hooded jacket in the bin that I can put on, and I'll look like a walrus. Guess that's why you're wearing those ridiculous sunglasses, so you won't be recognized."

"I'll have you know I paid a whole dollar for them at the Dollar Store."

"They ripped you off."

"Wait," I cry, pointing to a neat little blue house on the shoreline. "There's the place I'm looking for. Drop anchor here."

Adjusting the bill of his cap to shade his eyes, Lex follows my gaze to the blue house. Although it's encircled in towering oak and pine trees, the back part of the house, which is several feet from the shore, is cleared away for a water view. I can see it plainly, even without the binoculars. An open deck edged in white lattice runs the length of the house, with massive baskets of ferns hanging on either side. To the right of the house is a garage, blue-painted and white-trimmed as smartly as the house, and the presence of an outside staircase confirms what I've suspected: There's a room, perhaps an apartment, over the garage.

"You'd better tell it, sister," Lex says without turning his gaze from the house.

"A young couple live there, John and Wanda Webb," I explain. "They're colleagues of Austin's. I believe they work for him in the learning lab."

"So that's where my state tax dollars are going," he says. "Learning labs must pay damn good."

"Obviously someone's family has money. Austin told Haley he was staying at the house of a professor who's on sabbatical, but I began to suspect that he was staying with the Webbs instead. Now that I see the room over the garage, I'm even more convinced."

Lex frowns. "Why wouldn't Austin tell Haley where he's staying?"

"I have a feeling it has something to do with Jasmine and Zoe Catherine threatening to dismember him. How would you like those two showing up on your doorstep if you were Austin?"

"I wouldn't like them showing up on my doorstep, and I'm not him. But let me get this straight—you brought me all the way down the coast just to see if this couple has an extra room?"

"It's more complicated than that. At church this morning, Haley told me that she had a surprise visitor. Wanda Webb came to see her and the kids, claiming to be all broken up over Austin leaving them. Haley hadn't liked her much before, but Wanda was so sweet and sympathetic today that Haley changed her mind. Still, the more Haley told me, the more I wondered. Wanda kept asking if she'd seen a lawyer, stuff like that. Haley's so naive, it never occurred to her, but I suspect Wanda was there to get information. If I find out that Austin's staying here, it proves a couple of things. One, Austin flat-out lied about the professor's house, and two, Haley needs to be on guard with Wanda."

"You always so suspicious of people?"

I smile. "In my profession, I'd better be."

"You're in luck. Looks like the lady in question just walked out on her deck. See her? In the orange and blue sweatshirt?" Lex leans over and points to the shore, and I clutch his arm.

"Auburn colors! The Webbs are big Auburn fans." Lifting the sunglasses to my forehead for a clearer view, I see a woman on the deck and groan. "Oh, crap. That's not her. Guess I've gotten the wrong house."

I scoot down in the seat and raise the binoculars for a closer look. When Lex snorts, I hiss, "Hush! You know how sound travels on the bay." I adjust the lenses. "Definitely not her. This woman's about the same age as Wanda, but she's a brunette and a whole lot chunkier. Wait! A man's coming out to join her. Well, well. A pair of lovebirds."

In spite of his derision, Lex gets into it, lowering himself beside me and taking the binoculars away from me to peer through them, almost choking me when the cord around my neck goes taut. "Pay dirt," he says, passing the binoculars back. Seeing his expression, I raise the binoculars with a sick feeling in the pit of my stomach.

The man on the deck is Austin. Smiling, he comes up behind the woman in the Auburn sweatshirt, then lowers his head to her neck as she leans in to him sensuously, her chestnut-brown hair falling in a tumble over her face. I watch him turn her around to kiss her, pulling her close. I close my eyes and fumble with the binoculars, yanking them off and letting them fall with a clunk. When I'm able to speak, I say in a choked voice, "Get me out of here."

Without a word, Lex raises the anchor, and a breeze fills the sails, lunging the boat forward. Once we are well out of sight of the blue house and Lex begins to lower the jib in order to motor in, I help him with jerky, awkward movements, blinded by the tears rolling down my frozen cheeks. I don't bother to wipe them away, and I don't look for the sunglasses I've discarded. When I start shaking uncontrollably in the stinging wind, Lex barks at me to take the wheel. Reaching into the storage bin, he pulls out the hooded sweatshirt, which he tries to drape over my shoulders. "You've got on so damn many clothes, even an XXL won't go around you," he says. "Hang on, though, and I'll get you home faster than you can say 'rotten cheating bastard.'"

☙

In all our years in the house, I can count on one hand the number of times either Mack or I built a fire in the old fireplace in the living room. Lex has one going by the time I come downstairs. I numbly changed out of my salt-damp outdoor clothing and pulled on the warmest thing I could find, thick cotton socks and a fleece sweatsuit as spongy-soft as a worn blanket. Wondering if I'll ever be warm again, I sink in front of the roaring fire as though its flames can penetrate all the way to my heart, which sits in my chest like a heavy lump of ice.

Lex comes in from the kitchen carrying two coffee cups and hands me one before he settles himself beside me. "Latte," he says. We've spoken two words since we left the boat: When we entered the house, he asked, "Firewood?," and I answered, "Basement."

"The bay must have frozen my ears off," I say. "Sounded like you said latte."

"Taste it."

I raise my head after a tentative sip of the best latte I've ever had. "You couldn't have made this."

He ducks his dark head, pleased. "A trick I learned from a cook at the officer's club in the Philippines. Mix some brown sugar and cream together, whisk it around, then heat it up good. Pour strong coffee over it, and you've got a fake latte."

"Full of surprises, aren't you?"

He watches me over the rim of his cup. "Guess you could say it's been a day of surprises."

Placing the cup on the floor in front of me, I lower my face into my hands and rub my eyes. "God, I have to be the biggest fool on the planet." I raise my head to stare at him wearily. "Matter of fact, I should turn in my license. How I could have been so stupid is beyond me. It's more than stupid, actually. It's irresponsible."

Reaching over, he picks up my cup. "Drink it while it's hot. You need it." Watching me until I raise the coffee to my lips, he tilts his head curiously. "It never occurred to you that Austin's sudden departure might have been brought about by a cheating heart, huh?"

I shake my head. "Not once. Jesus Christ. If Haley had been a client of mine, it would've been the first thing I'd thought of. It explains everything: his picking fights with Haley, becoming dissatisfied with everything she did, the sudden departure, everything. How could I have been so blind? All the classic signs were there, but I failed to see them. I mean it: After a blunder like this, I should turn in my credentials."

"Position coming open at the marina if you're interested. Big shoes to fill, though."

"I wouldn't hire me if I were you."

We fall silent, and I turn my face toward the warmth of the fireplace. Greedy little fingers of fire grasp at the stack of logs, and I smile a bitter smile. "Get this. Just last night I called Haley to say I felt hopeful for the first time since Austin left, that I'd talked with him and he'd said he was having a difficult time. He told me that he was mixed up and confused, and I actually felt sorry for him. He said his head was all screwed up."

Lex hoots. "He's confused, all right. But based on what we saw today, I'd say it was the other end."

"Haley told me Austin had called her and said much the same, about being mixed up and not wanting to hurt her. She was so full of hope that I allowed myself to get hopeful, too. Matter of fact, that's the main reason I wanted to see the Webbs' place today, hoping I was wrong."

We sit lost in our own thoughts, the fire crackling in front of us. Finally I say, "Tell me the truth, Lex. When I told you about Austin moving out, did you suspect another woman was involved?"

He blinks at me. "You're serious, right?" When I nod, he rolls his eyes to the ceiling. "Maybe you're right, Doctor Lady. Maybe you should turn in your badge. It was the first thing I thought of. No man I know would move out of his house and leave his kids because his wife's not much of a housekeeper. No way. That boy's got him a little tart somewhere, I thought. But you never mentioned it, so I figured you knew him better than me. Not only that, it's what you do for a living, right?"

"Thanks. I feel much better now."

"Well, hell, don't ask me if you don't want to know. Here's what I think you should do." Reaching beyond me, he selects a slender log from the stack he's piled beside the white marble fireplace. When he places it in my hands, I look at it blankly. "Use this to beat yourself up," he says.

Before I can come up with a retort, the phone rings. I don't answer it, even after I hear Haley's voice on the machine. Or perhaps I let it go because of the sound of her voice, which is more upbeat than it's been lately.

"Hi, Mom, guess what? Wanda just left, and we had a really good visit. She brought us a casserole for supper and stayed almost all afternoon. Next time she sees Austin, she's promised to talk to him and see if she can find out what's going on, then let me know. She thinks he's just overworked and he'll come to his senses. I know you've been worried about me, but I just wanted to let you know that I feel a lot better now. I love you, Mom, and we'll talk later."

I stare at Lex, and he scratches his head quizzically before saying, "Maybe this woman Wanda doesn't know what's going on." I start to protest, and he holds up a hand. "Wait, now—think about it. She wasn't at her house this afternoon because she was at Haley's, right? Austin knew she'd be away, so he sneaked his sweetums in. That's possible, isn't it? Maybe loverboy has her fooled, too."

It makes sense. "I hope you're right, but I'm pretty skeptical at this point." I stretch out my hands to the fire and sigh. "Wonder if I'll ever get warm!"

With silent and efficient moves, Lex builds up the fire, and I smile at him gratefully when he finishes and dusts off his hands. "God, that feels wonderful. I never realized a fire could be so comforting. From now on I'll use the fireplace more."

He nods, pleased. "A fire can make everything seem better."

"Maybe I'm still cold because I'm in a state of shock. Guess I need some time to think about what we saw this afternoon and how it changes things."

"Want me to leave so you can have some time alone?" When I hesitate, he adds, "Even though you promised me chili and corn bread if I'd freeze my ass off taking you out in the boat?"

"You liar! You told me you weren't cold."

"Never told you I wasn't starving, though."

"Tell you what—I'll get us a bowl of chili if we can eat it sitting on the floor in front of the fire."

"Is there another way to eat chili?"

After supper and Zoe's brownies with more cups of latte—these heavily spiked with bourbon—Lex and I sit shoulder to shoulder on the rug in front of the fire, propped against the sofa with our legs stretched out in front of us. With a soft throw draped around me and my feet toasty, I've finally thawed out and am feeling full and drowsy. When I tell Lex, he grunts and says, "Before you go to sleep on me, tell me this. What you saw this afternoon, you plan on telling Haley?"

"I can't stand the thought, but I'll have to. The picture has changed considerably, and she has to know." I rub my face. "It's going to kill her. It will absolutely kill her."

"She's a fragile little thing, isn't she?"

I nod. "Always has been, but it's no wonder. She had such a hard start in life, and now this."

"How do you think Mack would've handled it?"

I glance at him, surprised at the question. Leaning my head against the sofa, I consider it. "Well, first he would've gotten drunk, the way he dealt with everything. Then he would've wanted to kill Austin."

"Just as I thought. Think that's primarily a male reaction?"

"Heavens, no. I've been fighting an uncontrollable desire to strangle Austin myself."

"What do you think are that boy's chances of keeping his pecker attached to his body once Swamp Woman finds out about the girl-friend?"

"Somewhere between zero and zilch?" I answer with a smile.

"I don't know what I'd do if this happened to Alexia, tell you the truth. It scares me to think about it. Somebody hurt her like that, I'd probably murder him with my bare hands." He holds out his large callused hands and studies them, frowning, as though considering the likelihood of such a thing.

"Here's where the rage comes from. It's not the cheating as much as it is the lies and the denial of responsibility. Austin has made Haley feel so bad about herself, and she's full of guilt over having failed him. Why didn't he have the guts to tell her the truth? To tell her that he's gotten involved with someone else? Instead, the little shit tries to justify his dalliance by shifting the blame to her. Which isn't uncommon, by the way. Far from it, I'm afraid. It would make a big difference if he were strong enough to confront his own short-comings instead of blaming her for them. Haley would still suffer, of course. But pain is one thing and guilt another. Pain can be a clean wound unless it's infected with the poison of guilt."

After a long silence, Lex says, "I know what you mean about guilt. I feel so damn guilty about Alexia, it's driving me batty. Lot of times I can't even think about her, it hurts so bad. Gets so I don't return her calls, which makes me feel even worse."

I hold my breath, sensing I'm about to hear what's been going on with him after this long period of silence. Staring into the fire, he continues, "She's pissed off with me now, you know."

"Because you didn't go with them to take her back to school?"

"Yawp. But it's more than that. It's because I haven't moved back to Elinor's place. When Alexia calls and I answer the phone at my place, it makes her mad as hell. 'Thought you'd be living at Mom's house by now,' she'll say."

"So Elinor's asked you to move back?"

He shrugs it off. "Not really. When Alexia was here during the holidays and I was over at Elinor's, it'd piss Alexia off when I'd go back to the marina. 'Why're you going to that cramped little place of yours when we've got so much room here?' she'd ask me. Elinor would chime in then, the two of them ganging up on me." He picks up the fire iron and pokes at the fire absently. "Damn if I know what to do. You know it about killed me when Elinor filed for di-vorce. But now it's like she doesn't want me, not really, she just doesn't want anybody else to have me. Crazy, huh?"

"It's not crazy at all. I see it all the time."

"Here's what happens. Elinor and I get together, like over the holidays, and everything will be great. We'll be getting along like we did when we first met, you know? But first time things don't go her way, she'll start that crap again, about how I'm not her type and she doesn't know why she puts up with me. So I blow my stack and stomp out, tell her to go to hell. Next thing I know, she's coming over to say she's sorry, that she didn't mean it. I don't know how much longer I can keep playing her mind games."

"It's more complicated than it sounds. My guess is, Elinor loves you in spite of herself. She has a certain image of herself, and with that goes the image of the kind of man she always thought she'd marry. But fortunately or unfortunately, depending on how you look at it, she fell in love with you." When he snorts, I hold up my hand and continue. "But what you've got to ask yourself at some point is, what are *you* getting out of this?"

"I do, and that's when I get all confused. I still love her, I guess, but . . . Oh, another thing. Elinor's jealous of you, something else that causes us problems. She's even jealous of Dory. She keeps demanding that I end my friendship with you guys. Says if I were more 'sensitive' to her feelings, I wouldn't have women friends. You know me—I say I'll be friends with whoever I damn well please, and before I know it, we're fighting again."

"Sounds like both of you have a lot of unresolved issues to sort out before considering a reconciliation. You're right not to rush into anything. Make sure it's what you want and that those issues are addressed first. You don't want to get back together and have it fall apart again. I've had clients who've divorced the same person twice because they didn't resolve what tore them apart originally."

"Ha! No way in hell I'll go through that again."

"Of course not, and it can be prevented by proceeding with caution. Keep trying to help Alexia understand what you're doing and why, though. I don't think things should be sugarcoated for kids, just presented in an age-appropriate way. Alexia's old enough and mature enough to understand your confusion about her mom. Tell her the truth. Tell her what you just told me."

He shakes his head. "Naw, she won't believe me. Last night she yelled at me, saying that I'd humiliated her mom and broken her heart. When I told her she didn't know shit from shoe polish, she hung up on me. Scared the crap out of me, thinking Elinor'd turn her against me. Jeez! I'm beginning to understand why you've stayed single since your old man died. Who the hell invented marriage, anyway?"

I laugh until tears come to my eyes. Fearing that I might start crying after such an upsetting day, I get to my feet. "Okay, that's it for me. When I get this punchy, my exhaustion's caught up with me. I'm calling it a night."

When I reach out a hand to pull Lex up, he waves me off with a yawn. "I'm not quite finished with my coffee. You go on to bed. I'll tamp down the fire and let myself out."

The next morning, however, I arise at sunrise and come downstairs to find Lex asleep on the sofa, wrapped in the fuzzy throw I discarded. Pulling my robe close against the chill of early morning, I kneel beside him with an indulgent smile. With the lightest of touches, I place the back of my hand against the side of his face, trying not to wake him. I hate to see him going through such a difficult time, but I'm not sure what I can do to help. Life just keeps coming at you, I think, sighing. My sigh must have been louder than I intended, and Lex's eyes fly open, startled. "Clare?" he says, blinking at me in surprise.

"Good morning." I stroke the side of his face with the back of my hand. To be so weathered, his skin is softer than it appears. In the rosy light of sunrise, I notice a lot more silver strands threading through his hair than when we first met. He's earned every one of them this past year. "It appears we finally spent the night together," I say with a smile.

"Was it good for you?"

When I laugh and start to get to my feet, Lex surprises me by gripping my hand and pressing it against his face. I freeze when his lips move to my palm, and my fingers curl in a half-fist.

"Don't go, Clare." His eyes move over my face, questioning.

"Quit looking at me that way."

"What way?"

"You know."

"First time I've seen you this early in the morning," he murmurs. "I could get used to it."

I yank my hand away and stumble to my feet. "You can have the shower first if you want."

"We could share it."

"Lex . . ."

Tossing off the throw, he sits up with a frown. Rubbing his head until his hair sticks up every which way, he yawns, stretching out his arms. "Naw, you go ahead. I'll go home and shower. Gotta get back to the marina, anyhow."

"You don't have to run off. I'll fix you some coffee first. Or breakfast, if you'd like. I owe you, after yesterday."

He shakes his head as he gets heavily to his feet and pulls on his windbreaker. "You don't owe me anything, Clare." His jaw is set, and he avoids my eyes as he zips up his jacket, picks up his cap, and heads toward the door.

With a gasp, I go after him and grab his arm. "Jesus, Lex! I'm sorry. I didn't mean to offend you. Come on. Don't do this."

His eyes dark and troubled, he stares down at me for a long moment. Then he softens and pulls me to him in a quick, hard hug. "Everything's going to be okay," I say, leaning in to him and patting his back. "And we'll be okay, too, you and I."

Lex pulls away from me and reaches for the door. The handle tight in his hand, he pauses to say, "I know you will be. You always are, aren't you? But I'm not so sure about me." Without another word, he goes out the door, closing it behind him, hard. I stand stunned, watching him leave. Now, what was *that* all about?

❧

As it turns out, I'm not the one to tell Haley about Austin's girl-friend. I'm so heartsick, I decide to wait a day or so while working out the best way to approach her. I can't delay too long, because she *has* to see a lawyer now. When Austin first moved out, I tried to get her to talk with Lana Martin, the divorce lawyer I recommend for my clients, but Haley refused. She was terrified that seeing a lawyer would be the first step in the dissolution of her marriage, and none of my speeches about protecting her interests or the chil-dren or anything else mattered to her. Her reaction was not unex-pected; the partner who doesn't want the divorce is almost always reluctant to see a lawyer, often going only under duress.

Because I have no intention of telling anyone what I saw on the deck of the Webbs' house until I have a chance to process it, I'm horrified to hear myself relating the whole story to Rye that very night. We planned on going to an Epiphany service at St. John's, but when I get in from work, I call him to beg off, claiming a headache. Suspicious, he says I sound strange, but I convince my-self I've appeased him. Not so. I'm pattering around the kitchen in my gown, robe, and slippers when Rye shows up at the back door.

"Headache, my foot," he declares. "It's been a long time since I've heard you sound so down, love. You'd better tell me what's going on."

Although he's known me too long for me to pull it off, I try denying it. I'm just tired and have a headache, I insist. But Rye plants his feet firmly, crosses his arms, and refuses to leave until I come clean. Motioning for him to have a seat, I blurt out the whole story of Austin and the brown-haired woman on the deck of the Webbs' house. With a coldness in his pale eyes that reminds me of Mack's deadly glare of anger, Rye makes me swear I won't do any-thing until I hear from him.

"No way," I protest. "Haley *has* to know, and it's better she hears it from me. If I wait, someone else might tell her. I should've done it yesterday."

"Trust me on this, Clare," he pleads. "Please."

Reluctantly, I agree. At the end of the week, Etta interrupts me while I'm reading over my notes in preparation for a waiting client—something she never does—to tell me that I have an urgent call from Rye. After asking her to tell my client I'll be right with her, I answer the phone with trembling hands.

With no preamble, Rye says, "Her name is Muffie Chisholm."

"*Muffie?* What is she, a stripper or something?"

"Far from it, sweetheart. Our Little Miss Muffet is quite accomplished. Real name Margaret, but she's been called Muffie all her life. She's Austin's age, thirty-two, and heads up the learning lab at the Emerald Coast Junior College in Orange Beach."

With a sick feeling in the pit of my stomach, I realize I'd hoped she'd turn out to be one of those women men have flings with but don't leave their families for. "Sounds like she and Austin have a lot in common," I say weakly.

"She has a master's degree in developmental studies and nine hours toward a doctorate at the University of South Alabama. Originally from a little town outside of Anniston, Alabama, she lives in a high-rise at Perdido Bay."

"Good Lord. How did you find this stuff out?"

"I have my ways. Get this. Miss Muffet met Austin three years ago at a workshop he led at her junior college, when she was a mere tutor. Give her a few years, though, and she takes over the place."

"Three years! Don't tell me—"

"No, no," he says quickly. "But my sources tell me she set her cap for him then."

"You're scaring me. What did you do, hire the Mafia?"

He chuckles. "Oh—bet this piece of information won't surprise you. Guess who roomed with Muffie Chisholm at Auburn and has been one of her closest friends ever since?"

"Wanda Webb."

"Bingo. Your instincts were right about that one. She's played a big role in this from day one. Hang on, it gets better. Seems like old Muffie has been around the block a few times. Twice to the altar."

"Twice at her age? Jesus! No grass growing under her feet."

"Once as a teenager, then again in college. This won't come as a surprise, I guess, but man number two was one of her professors and happily married at the time. Can't say our girl doesn't believe in the holy state of matrimony."

"Yeah, right. Everything you've told me so far makes my blood run cold."

"As well it should. What we've got is a hard-driving, ambitious, single-minded woman who's always gone after what she wanted and gotten it, whatever the cost. The only thing that stood in the way of her and man number three was a pretty little blonde named Haley."

"And two children," I add, my voice catching.

"Seems that she's convinced Austin her greatest regret is not having children of her own, so she's anxious to be a loving step-mother. But make sure you understand this, my dear. We're not talking about temporary insanity on Austin's part, or an innocent boy duped by a scheming woman. Their little affair has been going on for well over a year. All this time, while Mr. Perfect's been play-ing the role of devoted husband and father, he's led a double life." After a long silence, Rye says, "Clare?"

"Listen, Rye, I'm hanging up. I think I'm about to be sick."

❧

Both Jasmine and I are at Haley's house on Saturday morning. Austin has taken the children for the weekend, and I go over as soon as he leaves, determined not to let another day go by without having the overdue talk with Haley. Once I get there, however, I'm para-lyzed with trepidation. Sitting on the sofa waiting for her to prepare a pot of tea, I pick up a flop-eared stuffed bunny of Abbie's, and my throat tightens. What is it she calls him—Mr. Bunny? As a toddler, she was never without Mr. Something-or-other, dragging the poor thing around by its long ears. I didn't know Haley at Abbie's age; she was eleven when she came to live with Mack and me. But that first night she clutched a cheap, worn-out stuffed bunny as if it were a lifeline, and her solemn owl's eyes followed Mack's and my every move. There are times when the sight of Abbie holding her stuffed animal causes me such pain I can hardly stand it, thinking of Haley at that age. I can't even imagine the kind of life she must've had, with a drug addict for a mother who dumped her with any relative who'd take her in.

Haley is smiling and proud of herself when she comes from the kitchen area carrying a tray with a teapot and china cups. Usually her tea is a microwaved cup of water with a tea bag floating in it. She told me that the ironic thing about Austin's leaving is how she's discovered the joys of domesticity, freed of his critical eye. When she added, "Funny, isn't it, now that Austin isn't here to benefit," I told her to do it for herself and herself only.

Just as I clear my throat so I can begin the dreaded talk, the door flies open, and Jasmine comes in. I feel both relief and exasperation, because now it'll have to wait until she leaves, and sometimes her visits go on for hours. Grinning, Jasmine hands a stack of mail to Haley. "I ran into the mailman as I was coming in. Hey, Auntie Clare! I brought Haley some of Mama's shortbread. Be great with your tea."

"Nothing but bills," Haley says. Waving a manila envelope, she adds, "Except this one. No return address, but postmarked Orange Beach." Jasmine opens a cabinet door to get a plate for the shortbread, then stops in her tracks to stare at Haley, wide-eyed.

"Haley?" I say, getting to my feet.

She's standing as though struck dumb, blinking down at a piece of paper held in her hands. Her face has gone ghost-white and her lips colorless. My first thought is, Austin has filed for divorce. But it can't be—the papers don't come in the mail; they have to be served. "Haley?" I repeat, taking a step toward her.

Jasmine is quicker. Yanking the paper from Haley's grip, she cries out and puts a hand over her mouth. With jerky movements, Haley turns stricken eyes my way and whimpers. My heart in my throat, I move to Jasmine's side, and she holds out the paper for me to see.

It's a photograph of Austin and the woman with the chestnut-brown hair. They're in bed together, nude, and it appears to have been taken in a hotel room. Straddling the woman, Austin is grinning as he gazes down at her, propped on his elbows, and the woman's long, red-tipped fingers grip his back. A shapely bare leg arches around his waist, but the sheets are tangled and bunched around them in such a way that we are spared further detail.

Chapter Fourteen

❧   ❧   ❧   ❧   ❧

I can't tell if anyone is on the line or not. "Yes, hello? Is anyone
there?" I snap. I'm as irritated with myself as the caller; jarred
out of a deep sleep, I answered the phone automatically. Even with
every protection possible on my phone, I still get the occasional
crank call, so I'm reaching to put the receiver back on the hook
when I hear the faint voice of a child. "Mommy . . ." Only one
word, but I'd know that voice anywhere, and I gasp. "Zach? Is that
you, baby?" He says something I don't understand except for "Abbie and Mommy." My eyes go to the clock; it's well past midnight.

"Zach? What are you doing, sweetheart?" Disoriented, I turn
on the lamp and squint in the light. Abbie knows how to dial my
number, but not Zach. Haley had called me earlier; had Zach hit
redial, playing with the phone? But why is he up at midnight?
"Listen to Grams, pumpkin—" I begin, but he jabbers into the
phone breathlessly. This time I understand enough to cause my
heart to thud painfully.

"Mommy fro up and fro up. Abbie says Zach be a big boy and—"

I hear Abbie's voice then. Zach squeals in protest when she takes
the phone from him, and I hear Abbie say, "No, Zach! Gimme the
phone so I can talk to Grams. I told you to hold it until I got back.
Now give it here." I force myself not to yell into the phone as I
hear them struggle over the receiver, praying the connection won't

be lost as Abbie wrestles the phone from her little brother. "Grams?" Abbie says, then "Ow, Zach! Stop that."

"Abbie!" I take a deep breath to quell a mounting panic. "What's happened?"

"Mommy's sick, Grams. I heard her crying and went to her room, and she said she was sick. She threw up a hundred million times. But she won't open the bathroom door when I bang on it."

Somehow I manage to dress with the receiver pressed against my ear, and I say as calmly as I can, "Honey, listen to me. Hang up now, okay? I'm coming right over, but I'm going to call you on my cell phone when I get in my car. You answer, and I'll talk to you on the way to your house." Then I add, "Don't let Zach answer it, okay?" Poor Zach; even without that command, I doubt he has a prayer of getting the receiver away from his bossy big sister. But one thing for sure, it won't be from lack of trying.

If I hadn't been at the hospital with her, Haley wouldn't have avoided the psych ward. I can appreciate the irony of that, since a few days ago I'd gotten so angry with her that I'd threatened to put her in there myself. The day after the divorce papers were served in her classroom in front of her wide-eyed kindergarten students, Haley had been so upset that one of her teacher friends had given her a supply of sleeping pills and told her to go home and take a nap. Austin took the kids for the weekend, and Haley was so despondent that she stayed in bed the whole time, popping pills. When I checked on her Sunday afternoon, she was out of it, groggy and disoriented. I plied her with coffee and a cold washcloth, telling her that if she didn't wake up, I'd be forced to take her to the hospital. I didn't believe it was intentional—she swore she'd never do anything like that, because of the kids—but I was still furious at her, even more so when Austin brought the kids home. I told him curtly that she wasn't feeling well, but Haley grabbed his hand and begged him not to leave. Red-faced, he muttered platitudes, then dashed out the door.

When Austin filed for divorce, I thought Haley would see at last that they'd gone beyond a so-called trial separation to a permanent dissolution of their ten-year marriage. Instead, she turned a deaf ear to me when it came to Austin. Although I urged her not to call him, to let him call her if he needed to discuss anything about the kids or their situation, she wasn't able to stop herself. One evening I came into her house and overheard her crying and pleading with him to return to his family, saying she'd forgive him anything if only he'd stop the divorce proceedings and come back. Without a word, I walked across the room, took the receiver out of her hand, and clicked it off. "Leave him alone, Haley," I said sternly. "He's made his bed. For God's sake, let him lie in it."

"But this woman he's with, Mom—this *Muffie!*" she sobbed, wild-eyed. "She's been married twice, and she broke up another man's family. She sent me that picture so I'd file for divorce, but I fooled her, didn't I? She's nothing but a scheming, conniving homewrecker! Why can't Austin see that?" She'd gone on to swear that Muffie had stolen her husband, and I'd hooted, saying Austin was a person with a free will, not a Rolex watch. Rather than being destroyed by the discovery of Austin's mistress, as I'd feared, Haley had been vindicated. She'd gone from feeling rejected when Austin moved out to feeling sorry for him instead. "Poor Austin," she said sadly, shaking her head. "If it hadn't been for that awful woman, he'd still be with his family. One day he'll see her for what she is and come back to us, wait and see."

After much persuasion, I'd gotten her to see a therapist twice a week after school, a woman I didn't know but who came highly recommended. After Mack's death, I'd persuaded Haley to attend a support group for adult children of alcoholics, and it had really helped her. But this time I haven't seen much progress. Although the therapist urged Haley to attend one of my first-stage group meetings in addition to her therapy, Haley refused, insisting she couldn't stand to be around so many depressed women. I'd tried in vain to convince her that was the point: They ministered to one another.

Sitting by Haley's hospital bed the morning after the call from Abbie and Zach, I push her damp, tangled hair from her forehead and watch her sleep a drugged sleep, her chest moving up and down like that of a puppy sprawled out in sunlight. At least it wasn't the sleeping pills this time. Petite and slender, Haley barely weighs a hundred pounds, and she's one of those women who can't eat when upset. During that awful time after Mack's death, I'd made Ovaltine milk shakes to keep her going. Since Austin moved out of the house in December, she's lost twelve pounds. When Abbie called me last night, Haley hadn't eaten anything for two days. Too weak to put the kids to bed, she forced herself to eat some of the pizza she'd ordered for them, only to be unable to keep it down. It terrified me to think what might have happened if Abbie hadn't awakened on hearing her mother. When we arrived at the emergency room, Haley's electrolytes were so out of kilter that her heart was beating erratically. "Anorexia," the doctor on duty proclaimed at the conclusion of his examination, and I called him out of the room to explain what was going on. The only way I kept her out of the psych ward was by showing him my credentials and swearing she was under a therapist's care.

Slumped in a hard, vinyl-covered chair next to Haley's hospital bed, I jump when a hand is placed on my shoulder, and raise my head to see Dory. Rising, I go into her outstretched arms but resist when she tries to drag me out of the room. "Then you might as well crawl in the bed with her," Dory whispers, eyes flashing. "You look like shit. And from the looks of her, Haley's so out of it, she's not going to wake up and miss you. Come on—we won't go any farther than the waiting room."

In a tote bag, Dory has a thermos of coffee and miniature date-nut muffins wrapped in foil, still warm from her oven. I haven't thought of being hungry until I eat one, then I devour three. "Jasmine called you, I guess," I say, looking at Dory gratefully when she pours coffee into the cup-shaped lid of the thermos and hands it to me. Last night I had no choice but to ask Jasmine to stay with the children while I took Haley to the emergency room. When I called Jasmine early this morning to check on them, she thought it best that they go on to school and day care, in spite of being up half the night. Playing with other kids would be the perfect distraction at this time, she said, and I agreed.

"Umm . . . no, it was Zoe Catherine," Dory replies, popping a whole muffin in her mouth. "Jasmine called her before school. Zoe said for me to tell you this: She's bringing Cooter to his doctor for a checkup this morning, and they'll stop by afterward to see Haley."

"Oh, Lord," I say with a weak smile. "What do you think the hospital staff will say when they see Cooter again?"

A couple of weeks before, Cooter had a mild heart attack, and Fairhope was still talking about the uproar he'd caused at the hospital. Once he got to the emergency room, he'd insisted it was just his "hiney hernia" acting up again. When he was hooked up to the EKG, however, the medical staff suspected a heart attack. Cooter said no wonder—his heart was broken because the love of his life had turned down his marriage proposals. When the cardiologist on duty told him there was no such thing as a broken heart, Cooter mocked the doctor, saying he was so young that he was still wet behind the nose. The staff hadn't been able to tell what was causing his erratic heartbeat, so they probed into his activities to determine the problem. The poor cardiologist asked if he'd taken Viagra, which insulted Cooter so badly that he'd yanked off the EKG probes and tried to leave wearing nothing but a hospital gown. "I don't *need* to take no damn dick medicine, by God!" Cooter bellowed, much to the delight of the people sitting in the lobby, who cheered him on.

The only way they got Cooter back to the examining room was

to give in to his insistence that they call Zoe Catherine. When Zoe arrived, Cooter clutched his heart and howled so piteously that it set off a code blue, and the whole staff came running into the examination room. Cooter swore he was going to die right then and there because of the way Zoe had broken his heart. Zoe said she'd break more than his heart if he didn't shut the hell up. A nurse on duty was a friend of Etta's; relating the story to me, Etta and I laughed so hard, both of us bent double. "My friend said Cooter was using cuss words none of them had ever heard before," Etta whooped, wiping her eyes, "and one of the younger doctors thought he was speaking in tongues!"

Dory asks me, "What's going to happen to Haley?"

I shake my head wearily. "I'm sick with worry about her." I absently blow on the hot coffee before taking a sip. "And I feel so helpless. Seems like I'm able to help everybody but her."

Dory frowns as she chews another muffin. "I tell you, this thing with Haley and Austin has gotten me thinking. If Son dies before I do, or if we split the sheets, I won't ever marry again. Once in a lifetime is more than enough for me. Why do any of us do it?"

I smile and take a sip of my coffee. "Funny, last time I saw Lex, he said the same thing. If this keeps up, the species will die out in no time."

"Hey, what's going on with you and Lex? The other day I called him to invite the two of you to the Mardi Gras dinner I'm having, and he said he hadn't seen you in weeks. No matter how hard I tried, he wouldn't say anything except I should ask you about it, not him. Oh—and thanks for confiding in your best friend. I was embarrassed to admit you hadn't told me a damned thing."

"There's nothing to tell," I protest. "I've been too busy to see anyone lately, as you well know. Rye's mad at me, too, for not going to all the Mardi Gras stuff. Not only is Wayfarer's Landing finished and demanding my every spare minute, it seems every client is going through a crisis. Not to mention my own daughter."

"Yeah, I know how crazy your life's been lately, but I also know something is going on with you and Lex. You can't fool me. Did you hurt his feelings?"

"Evidently," I say with a shrug. "Though I have no idea what I did." Actually I do, but I'm not about to tell Dory, have her jump me.

Her eyes are soft and thoughtful as she chews. Swallowing, she says, "You know what Haley needs, don't you?"

"Please don't say another man."

"Yeah, right. That would do her in for sure. No, she's got to attend a retreat."

"I can't even get her to the group meetings. I'd love more than anything for her to sign up for a retreat, but she's so deep in denial, she won't even discuss it. I've tried, and her therapist has tried—"

"Let me talk to her," she says, her face lighting up. "And I didn't mean just any of the retreats. I meant the first one ever held at Wayfarer's Landing, on the day of the spring equinox. It's going to be awesome."

I stare at her in surprise. "She's not going to be ready that soon. Even the mention of it will scare her off."

"Not if I don't tell her what goes on."

"Dory! You know how I feel about the participants being fully aware of what goes on at the retreats."

"Okay, okay, don't get your panties in a wad. I'll just talk to her about it, okay? No pressure, and no hiding the truth."

"Let me think about it. If she'll come to the group meetings first, then—"

With a sharp intake of breath, Dory interrupts me. "Uh-oh. Lord Vader approaches."

She and I had chuckled to hear Jasmine's latest nickname for Austin, Darth Vader, saying he'd gone over to the Dark Side. If that were true, then Jasmine was hell-bent on wiping out the forces of evil. As I feared, once Jasmine and Zoe Catherine heard about Muffie Chisholm, Austin was a marked man. Zoe had taken an old bird's nest, cut out a picture of a cuckoo bird and placed it inside, then mailed it to Muffie's address in Perdido Bay. She'd made an official-looking card for it that read: "The common cuckoo, *Muf-ferius Chisohelis*, is a parasitic, opportunistic bird that shamelessly lays its eggs in other birds' nests." Jasmine was even bolder. She'd gotten Tommy to take Lex's boat out on the bay and patrol the Webbs' house until they spotted Austin on the deck. The difference was, Jasmine yelled at Austin to look their way. When he did, both Jasmine and Tommy dropped their drawers and mooned him. Jasmine said if the sight of their great big black and white asses hadn't scared Austin into repentance, nothing would.

I raise my head to see that Lord Vader has entered the waiting room and is heading straight for the two plastic chairs Dory and I have pulled into a corner. My heart sinks; although Austin has given no indication that he'll fight Haley for custody of the kids, I live in fear of it. If he were to, Haley's hospitalization for anorexia would most likely work in his favor. I've seen dozens of cases where mental instability and other such disorders were more of a deciding factor with a judge than adultery. Not only that, I've never known of a custody battle that wasn't nasty; Haley is too fragile for such a thing.

"Hello, Austin," I say, keeping my voice as even as possible. Dory gives him a withering stare without bothering to speak.

"The Webbs have a friend who works in the emergency room," Austin says, his eyes flinty and his jaw tight. "So I heard about Haley."

"The Webbs are aptly named, aren't they?" I can't resist saying. "You've probably heard that Haley's fine, then. She was undernourished, dehydrated, and her electrolytes were off. But it looks like she'll go home as soon as the doctor comes in this morning to sign the release papers."

Austin and I stare at each other until he becomes uncomfortable and looks down at his feet. "When I spotted the two of you in here, I was on my way to see her," he says, glancing up at me.

"Are you sure that's a good idea?" I ask coolly.

"You can't stop me, Clare." His voice is as even and pleasant as though we're discussing the weather. "Legally I'm still her husband, and I have every right to see her. More rights where she's concerned than *you* have, actually."

With a lunge toward him, Dory snarls, "Now, see here, you shitass——" but I put out my arm to block her.

"It's okay, Dory. I was just making sure that Austin has thought this through."

At the retreats, I suggest that the participants try to bring out the best in their exes during negotiation: Tell them you know they want to do the right thing. It's a variation of the old you-can-catch-more-flies-with-honey adage. I've heard myself say it a hundred times, but actually applying it makes me want to gag, and I understand for the first time the groans and grimaces of the participants. Seeing where I'm going, Dory settles back into her chair.

"I won't try to stop you, Austin," I add in a neutral tone, "now that I see how worried you are about Haley."

He blinks at me in surprise, then nods curtly. As he turns on his heel and leaves the waiting room, Dory and I watch as he enters Haley's room, after first pausing to straighten his tie and pat his hair into place. As soon as the door closes, Dory turns to me. "God Almighty, I see why you're so good at what you do. You're one cool customer. Aren't you afraid he'll smother her with a pillow? No alimony payments then."

"Be kind of hard to do in front of a witness," I say, getting to my feet. "Unfortunately, he's right. Until the divorce goes through, legally he's the one to make her decisions if she's not able; it's one of those laws I've worked to get changed, to no avail. So I can't keep him out of her room. But he sure as hell can't keep *me* out." Dory holds up her hand for a high five as I turn to follow Austin.

Austin scurries out as soon as a nurse comes in with Haley's breakfast, and I take the chair he's vacated. I elevate the head of the bed so Haley can eat, if I can persuade her to. She's pale and list-less, with purplish smudges under eyes that appear too large for her small oval of a face. When I ask if she's hungry, she surprises me with a shrug rather than her usual insistence that she can't even look at food. I remove a metal cover to reveal a bowl of oatmeal. "You used to love oatmeal," I say with a smile. "Remember?"

Her rain-colored eyes fill with tears and spill over, rolling down her cheeks. She swipes them away with the back of her hands. "Oh, Mom. I'm *so* ashamed of myself."

"I know you are, sweetheart. But we're all going to help you get well, if you'll let us."

"I heard you tell Austin that Jasmine took the kids to school. They must have been terrified last night, waking up to find me so sick. I can't stand to think about what I've done to them."

I pour milk and brown sugar into the oatmeal. At first she shakes her head, but I place the spoon in her hand as I reach for a tissue to wipe her tears. "You know what they told you last night. If you don't eat, you're going to get really, really sick. Last night was nothing compared to how you could be."

"Did you see the way Austin looked at me?" she says with something akin to wonder in her voice. He stayed all of five minutes, shuffling his feet and muttering platitudes, his visit obviously moti-vated by guilt rather than concern. "His eyes were totally blank," she adds. "There was no feeling left in them. Nothing at all."

Absently she dips the spoon in the hot oatmeal and lifts it to her mouth. I hold my breath as she dips it again and again. When she finishes the oatmeal, I casually unwrap a slice of toast and butter it, then smear it with apple jelly. Haley shakes her head when I hand her half a slice, but she takes it. "I don't understand!" she says sadly. "Austin might not love me anymore, but I'm the mother of his children. Not to love me is one thing, but to feel absolutely nothing for his children's mother? What is *wrong* with him?"

Careful to keep my head lowered, I busy myself spreading butter on the other slice of toast as she eats the one I've just handed her. I don't want her to see my elation at her words. Unknowingly, she's taken the first step. Since the day Austin left her, it's the first time she has said "What is wrong with him?" rather than "What is wrong with me?"

⅋

Lana Martin is a striking woman, rail-thin, tall, and elegant, with a surprising slash of white coursing through the black hair that keeps falling on her forehead. When she lowers her head to read Haley's list of marital assets, I lean back in my chair with a sigh of satisfaction. Because of her air of calm, no-nonsense competence, I've sent her so much business that it's become a running joke between us. She lives in fear that I'll change my specialty to marriage counseling, she teases me, and she'll be out of work. In spite of our joking, both of us know that my clients who're separated from their spouses and end up in her office don't want to be there. It astonishes me that Haley's here today. Following her hospitalization, she began to eat again, thanks in part to the incredible fare toted in daily by Dory, Zoe Catherine, and Etta. As she regained her strength, Haley began the move from grief and denial to anger. A couple of weeks after the hospitalization, Dory stopped to see me after taking Haley an enormous bucket of white hyacinths. "She's finally gotten pissed off," Dory declared gleefully, but I reminded her that Haley would feel sad again, too. Even so, her anger has propelled her out of a dark pool of grief into the sunlit chair across the desk from Lana Martin, divorce lawyer extraordinaire.

As is often the case when another woman is involved, the dissolution of Haley and Austin's marriage is moving at lightning speed. A married man receives a lot of pressure from the other woman to file the divorce papers, since the man who keeps promising and doesn't come through has become such a cliché. I remind myself wryly that Austin's paramour is experienced in these matters. Having successfully broken up another home, she can provide Austin with step-by-step instructions. I dare not say anything to Haley, but I believe that Austin got cold feet a few weeks after moving out. When he vacillated, Little Miss Muffet sent the photo to Haley. To think that Abbie and Zach will have a woman like that for a stepmother—assuming Austin marries her, as he seems so hell-bent on doing—makes my blood run cold. The photograph of Austin and Miss Muffet (Austin being the one sitting on her tuffet, Jasmine pointed out) became a source of depression and disillusionment to Haley, and not just for revealing Austin's cheating. Once over the shock of seeing the graphic proof of her husband's affair, she assumed it would be a prized document, leverage in what is turning out to be her inevitable divorce from Austin. Rather than burst her bubble, I took the coward's way out and let Lana Martin do it. I simply couldn't bear to.

Sitting next to Haley in the lawyer's office, I turn my head from the sight of Haley's apoplectic rage on hearing that Austin's adultery will be a fairly insignificant factor in the divorce case. It's the final insult for the wronged party, Lana tells her gently when Haley bursts into helpless tears. Lana's sympathetic eyes meet mine over Haley's bent head, and I'm grateful she didn't tell Haley the really infuriating part. Had Haley been the one caught in adultery, especially with an incriminating photograph, it would've been much more of a factor. When Haley and Austin attended a preliminary meeting with their lawyers, Haley's bitterness increased. Stopping by afterward to give me a report, she cried in outrage, "I didn't want this. None of it! Why did I have to sit there and listen to every sickening detail of Austin's affair only to have the lawyers say it doesn't really matter in the divorce?" Why, indeed, I thought, unable to offer any consolation.

The reality of divorce is an extremely bitter pill to swallow, as Haley will discover. The turmoil of the breakup tends to mask that fact. I find that the adrenaline-fueled drama is a necessary jump start for the process, however. In many ways, it's pure reflex. Prod an amoeba with a sharp instrument, and you'll get a reaction; why not an even more intense response to pain from a million-celled organism? The problem is, getting addicted to the emotional high of this phase is a surefire way of delaying recovery. I've heard every imaginable story from my clients, some tragic, others undeniably comic. One woman got her ex's new weed-eater and chased him all over the yard with it, much to the neighbors' delight; another took a baseball bat and gleefully bashed in the car her husband had spent a fortune and many months lovingly restoring. I've heard numerous stories of shocking scenes enacted during this period, one of the most memorable being a client who crashed her ex's wedding so she could scream obscenities during the church service. When escorted out by the ushers, she promptly found a ladder, stuck her head through a window above the altar, and continued her harangue.

Haley's initial phase had been self-destructive, so I'd kept my silence when she became almost murderously angry with Austin and spent hours with Jasmine, plotting revenge. The good thing about anger is, it's a fiery emotion that usually burns itself out. When Haley finally started attending my weekly group meetings and forming friendships with some of the women who are in the same stage of the process, I allowed myself a small—very small—sigh of relief. She's by no means there yet, and she will go through the usual ups and downs of a breakup. Every time she gets better, something will happen to set her back, like the night Abbie woke up crying for her daddy and pushed her mother away, inconsolable. I know that all of them—Haley, Zach, and Abbie—will have plenty of those bad days. Eventually there will be more good ones than bad, but that time is still a long way off.

The first of March, Wayfarer's Landing Retreat Center is complete, ready for final touches in preparation for the first retreat, scheduled for later in the month. Because of the trauma of Haley and Austin's breakup, my excitement has been tamped down. But the day I take Zach and Abbie to see the new building that's sprung up next to their gramma Zoe's, I feel lighthearted and carefree, full of anticipation, for the first time in months.

Abbie has changed since her daddy left, becoming quieter and more subdued, and I watch her carefully as she takes Zach's hand and runs across the driveway to the new building. She looks impossibly adorable: Jasmine French-braided her flaxen hair into two stubby pigtails, and Haley dressed her in a short pleated skirt with a white turtleneck and tights. Haley tried to tell her that the preppy look is spoiled by the silver-studded red cowboy boots I gave her for Christmas, but Abbie won't part with them. Zach's wearing his, too, but hasn't quite gotten the hang of them, and I hide a smile at his stumbling gait as Abbie drags him along behind her. I wasn't sure what I'd tell the children about the new building, but Abbie solved it. "Gramma Zoe has a new house," Zach announced, but Abbie shushed him. "No, Zach—you know the ladies who come to see Grams in her office? She's building them a place to dance."

There's a lot of activity at the retreat site on this bright, briskly cold day. The winter sun hangs high and lemon-yellow, and the air, sweet as cider, is sharp with the scent of pine needles, wood smoke, and freshly turned earth. Dory and some of the White Rings are laying the groundwork for the landscaping today. Hearing Zach and Abbie's squeals, Dory gets to her feet and turns toward them. In spite of the dirt coating her gardening gloves, she sweeps up both Zach and Abbie, one in each arm, and kisses their rosy cheeks noisily. Hearing their chirps of excitement, Etta appears on the porch, hands on her hips. With a big grin, she calls out, "Look who's here—my babies!" We joke about the children being communal property, passed around among us when we crave the feel of soft cuddly bodies and chubby arms and sloppy kisses, all given freely, with pure unadulterated affection. Zach wiggles out of Dory's grasp to run to Etta, knowing she'll let him dig through her purse until he finds a piece of Juicy Fruit gum.

"How's it coming, flower child?" I ask Dory after greeting the White Rings, who are kneeling and digging at different intervals around the ground in front of the porch, which Dory is transforming into flower beds. Or will be, once spring arrives. Everything in Dory's calendar is lunar. She has mysterious ways of determining when to plant, based on the moon cycles and the tide and the number of days after the last frost, none of which make a lick of sense to me. The Landing has been one of Dory's biggest challenges, she told me, not only because of the sandy soil and brackish water but also due to the abundance of critters. She's determined to preserve the wild beauty of the place, so in addition to planting hundreds of azalea bushes, she's adding indigenous native plants such as tea olive and oleander and sawgrass, which will survive anything, even hungry deer, raccoons, and rabbits.

After she adjusts the Bama cap she wears to shade her eyes from the sun, Dory motions widely and says, "Let me show you what we're doing." Last time we were out here, she showed me the diagrams for the placement of the plants, which amazed me. Until I met Dory, I always assumed you stuck plants in the ground and hoped they looked good in bloom, but her flower beds are as carefully laid out as a mosaic.

After a brief tour of the future flower beds, we start toward the steps of the building, lured by the fragrance of the apple cider Etta is heating up. A genius at organization, Etta insisted on coming out and making sure everything was put in its proper spot. I protested only halfheartedly, since it was a dreaded duty I'd assigned to myself. Etta earns extra pay by helping out at the retreats, so she knows everything about how they run and what's needed. But this is all new for us, and the details have been mind-boggling. All I'd needed at the conference center were my and the participants' materials; here we need cooking equipment, dishes, a stocked pantry, and linens. In spite of all the White Rings do, I'm having to hire extra help. Without knowing how everything will work out until we have the first one, I've scheduled a retreat for every month except the summer, in deference to our unbearable heat. As Etta has so aptly put it, we will start out by running on faith.

Before Dory and I reach the stone steps leading to the front porch, I stop her, glancing up to make sure the kids are still inside with Etta and out of earshot. "Are things any better now?" I ask her, lowering my voice.

Dory hesitates, then shrugs. "Oh, Clare. I can only imagine what you're thinking . . ."

I give her arm a shake, frowning. "Come on, honey. This isn't about me. You know how pleased I was with the way things were going with you and Son. I'm terribly upset."

As both Rye and I had predicted and feared, Son's good behavior finally took a nosedive. Hearing about it distressed me, but Rye swore he was relieved, saying now we didn't have to worry about the four horsemen of the apocalypse riding into Fairhope. Following the passage of our only winter months, January and February, gardeners began to look ahead, and by the end of February, Dory's seasonal business of garden design was much in demand. The reality of her work hit Son hard. To give the devil his due, he restrained himself at first, then lost it when Dory told him that of course she would continue to help with the retreats, too. When Dory related the scene to me, it hit me for the first time why Son had stayed so saintly. Dory had always given a huge chunk of her time to volunteer work; evidently Son assumed her business would replace that time, with the added bonus of bringing in extra cash. Once he saw otherwise, he did a backflip and landed with a hard and heavy thud.

"Son's still pouting," Dory tells me in a whisper. "He's gone on without me." It was a proposed trip that triggered the fallout; Bama is playing LSU in some kind of basketball tournament, and Son surprised her with hard-to-come-by tickets. She surprised him even more by saying there was no way she could go this weekend, for him to take some of his buddies or the boys instead.

"Good," I say firmly. "You and Son have always been joined at the hip, which is far from healthy. The best thing that can come of this would be his seeing he can go places and do things without always having to drag you along with him."

Dory nods and scratches her face, leaving a smudge of dirt on her cheek. Her eyes are vague and troubled. "I think so, too. But the thought of going through what we did last year tears me apart. I can't do it again, and I've told Son that. If he starts all that crap again, I don't want to think about what might happen."

"As I recall, Son swore to us that he'd leave if he did it again. I'd pack his suitcase and have it ready if I were you."

She says with a sigh, "Sometimes I don't know which is worse—splitting up and going through the kind of pain Haley's endured these last months, or putting up with Son's tantrums."

"Dammit, Dory, I'll tell you what's worse. Have you missed every single thing that goes on at the retreats?" I cry in exasperation. "It's about *recovery*. Haley will recover. The others who are coming to the retreat, they'll recover. They went through hell to get where they are, but they can put it behind them and move on. You, on the other hand, will have Son causing you misery for the rest of your life if you allow it."

Dory smiles gently and puts her hands on my shoulders. "Calm down, honey. I'm not going to allow that. I can't go back to that kind of life again. When Son returns, I'm sitting him down and telling him that, too. I intend to make myself perfectly clear."

I study her, somewhat abashed. "Well, good. Good! It's a relief to hear you say it."

Above our heads comes a small voice, and we look up to see Abbie hanging over the log rail of the porch, the red cowboy boots dangling close to our heads. "Hey, Grams! Miss Etta said for y'all to come get some cider. What are you and Miss Dory fussing about, anyway?"

With a laugh, I put an arm around Dory's waist. "We're not fussing, honey. We're just talking."

Abbie wrinkles her brow, unconvinced. "Huh! Sounds like fussing to me. Miss Etta put cim-ma-non sticks in the cider, and Zach tried to eat his. They real good."

"I can't wait," Dory says. "Cim-ma-non's my favorite."

The White Rings finish digging up the flower beds and take a cider break, then Etta gives a tour of the facilities. Again I feel excitement welling up when I follow Etta as obediently as the others, hoping I can remember where she's stored everything. The main gathering room and the kitchen underwent the most extensive remodeling and expansion. In spite of the newness of the wide-planked flooring and the freshly painted walls in the great room, and the addition of sleek cabinetry and work surfaces and a gleaming tiled floor in the kitchen, the rustic ambiance has been preserved, as I'd hoped. I'd envisioned a lodgelike setting, stylishly furnished to be attractive and appealing, with comfort as the main consideration. A soft place to fall, Dory had said, summing it up perfectly.

Giggling, the kids tumble on the new mattresses, still wrapped in plastic and atop the bunks, but I put on my sternest frown when Zach starts bouncing like a rubber ball. He has to get in one last jump, and he bangs his head on the top bunk. When his lower lip trembles, he looks around for sympathy and is instantly engulfed by his surrogate mamas, clucking and cooing and rubbing the top of his head. I motion for Abbie to follow me. "This is Gram's secret room," I tell her, opening a door to the new addition in the back. It's a small but quite doable office; I'm moving over a sleeper sofa from my house so I can stay during the retreats.

I'm unprepared for the pang I experience when Abbie curiously explores all the little nooks and crannies of the built-in desk. Lex built everything himself. When it neared completion, he wouldn't allow me to see it until he added the finishing touches. It's as compact and precise as a ship's quarters, which I expected from him. What I didn't expect was the way he'd disguised the hand-me-down wood donated by a local lumber company by sanding it so smoothly, then painting it a shade of midnight blue so dark it is almost black. The contrast of the deep blue and the white-painted walls is not only smart and chic, it also makes a great work space. Since adding the office was an expense I bemoaned, I wasn't going to decorate it, or even paint it, really, just stick an old desk and sleeper sofa in it. Now I fear I haven't adequately expressed my gratitude to Lex, and I make a mental note to give him a call. We've both played it cool since the unsettling incident between us when he slept on my couch. I've seen him at work on the retreat site, but that's it. Our once warm and cherished friendship has become cool and businesslike.

When Etta and the White Rings depart, Dory enlists the help of the kids in watering the new plants, knowing they'd like nothing better than dipping a couple of Zoe's gourds in buckets of water and carrying them to the plants. But when she goes behind the building to look for the gourds, she calls out to them to come see what she's found—hurry! In her excitement, Abbie runs off and leaves Zach behind, so I take his hand, and we follow. I groan when I see what she's called them for, afraid Dory will be transported into a religious trance. To the side of the building, in the brittle winter grass, is a huge and perfect ring of mushrooms.

"Look," she exclaims. "A fairy ring!" She turns her awestruck eyes my way. "It's a sign. A blessing for Wayfarer's Landing."

"Where are the fairies?" Zach demands, and the three of them squat reverently by the circle. I back away and leave them, glancing over my shoulder to see Dory speaking in a low voice and pointing to the ring, following the circle with her finger. By the expressions of wonder on Zach and Abbie's faces as they gaze up at her, I know Dory's passing on the stories of the magic circle that she received at their age. I start up the front steps, thinking I'll get some things put in place in my office while the kids are occupied. Then something hits me: It's the first time since Austin left that I've been with Abbie and she hasn't mentioned her daddy.

The watering is almost done when Zoe Catherine and Cooter drive up and park by the dock. I intentionally haven't told Zoe I was bringing the kids. Saturday mornings are reserved for her and Cooter's flea market junkets, which they both enjoy, and which get them out. Waving, she and Cooter get out of the truck, bundled up like Eskimos. Just as they cross the oyster-shell driveway to what is now a wide grassy lawn stretching out in front of the retreat site, Genghis Khan spots them. It's as though he was watching for them to drive up, and he heads after them, mincing along with his haughty little steps.

"Hey! Find anything at the flea market?" I call out, coming down the steps to give them a hug.

"You won't believe what Cooter's got," Zoe says, and he reaches in the pocket of his coat to bring out a small vial of white powder.

I study it, then look up at him quizzically. "You bought *coke* at a flea market?"

"Ha. Look at the label! I got it at the farm-and-market store when we stopped to get some vitamins for the guinea hens." He holds it up for me to see, and I read it, squinting.

"Since I can't read Latin, I don't know what it is," I tell him.

Cooter grunts derisively. "Damn, woman! It's that stuff you put in rooters' mash to make them more manly. So your roosters will have the get-up-and-go to chase the hens. You know."

"Oh!" Blushing, I dare ask him, "What's it called?"

Cooter shrugs and puts it back in his pocket. "Don't know. But it tastes like peppermint."

Zoe lets out a hoot, and my eyes widen. Fortunately I'm spared further details by the appearance of Zach and Abbie, who've spotted Cooter and Gramma Zoe and run around the building toward them. A grin splits Cooter's face, and he lets out a cry that could raise the dead.

"Little Owl and Princess Yellow Hair!" he shouts, then begins a war dance, bobbing up and down and patting his hand against his mouth, still yelling.

Zach takes a tumble running to Cooter, but he scrambles to his feet and beats Abbie in the race. Cooter plays with them as though he were a child himself. They've made up a whole tribe of imaginary Cherokees who roam the Landing and spy on Zoe Catherine, the mean old white woman who took their land and forced them to live in the swamp.

"Oh, no, Chief Big Cooter, it's the palace guard," Abbie yells, pointing to Genghis. "Let's get him!" They can spy on the cruel white woman only if they can get past her flock of bodyguards, who are uniformed in emerald and turquoise and gold and defend her by spreading tall shields with dozens of evil eyes. Whenever Cherokees encounter the evil eye, it scares them off, and they have to retreat to the swamp.

When Abbie and Zach take out after Genghis, who squawks in terror, Zoe puts an end to the war games. "Hey!" she calls out. "You young'uns leave Genghis alone. He's getting too old to play like that."

Cooter stops his pursuit to frown at her. "Aw, crap, woman. He loves playing with us. It's you who's gotten too old."

"Hush your mouth," Zoe snaps. "Don't start talking ugly around those babies." Seeing Zach and Abbie's downcast looks, she relents and says to them, "You can play with Genghis if you don't make him run. Like Cooter, he's got a weak heart."

Abbie looks stricken. "Chief Big Cooter's gonna *die?*"

"Sure is," Zoe tells her solemnly. "Just as soon as I get my hands around his scrawny neck."

Dory went inside to wash up, and she appears on the porch just as Cooter explodes indignantly, with Zach and Abbie staring up at him. Dory smothers a laugh when Cooter thumps his chest and shouts, "Weak! Nothing weak about *me*, you crazy old woman."

"Oh, kiss my behind, Cooter Poulette," Zoe says.

Folding his arms, Cooter glares at her. "Hell, no. I'm mad now."

With a schoolmarmish clap of my hands, I call out to Zach and Abbie, raising my voice to be heard over Cooter's big mouth. "Okay! It's getting colder out here, and we need to get back to Mommy's before dark."

Zoe leans down to them and says, "Guess we'd better go look for some cookies before you have to leave, huh?"

Zach nods agreement, but Abbie looks worried. "Can Chief Big Cooter have a cookie if he promises not to say ugly words?" she asks Zoe.

Abashed, Cooter hangs his head. "Hey, I didn't mean to, Princess Yellow Hair. Your gramma Zoe hurt my male egret, is all, calling me weak. I'm in better shape than young braves half my age."

Although Zoe throws him a look, she tells Abbie that Cooter can have a cookie if he'll behave. When they start toward Zoe's house with the palace guard trailing behind, Cooter picks Zach up and rides him on his shoulders, even though he's grimacing and hobbling slowly. With Abbie's hand in hers, Zoe stops in the driveway to wait for them.

"Aw, look at that." Dory grins mischievously, coming to stand beside me at the foot of the steps. "Makes you believe in the power of love, doesn't it?"

"Either that, or an intense terror of being alone in your old age," I say.

"Don't turn cynical on me, honey. I don't think I could stand it."

With a laugh, I put an arm around her shoulder. "Surely you jest. What on earth could I see on a daily basis that could turn me into a cynic?"

"I know," she says softly. "But still . . ." She raises her eyes and looks toward Zoe's cabin. "We find ways to make it work for us, don't we? Rather than spend our nights alone, we find a way."

Chapter Fifteen

❧ ❧ ❧ ❧ ❧

I'm a creature of habit. Regardless of what time I go to bed at
night, I get up at the same time each day without having to set
an alarm clock. After my exercise routine, I take a quick shower,
slip on a robe, then head downstairs to dish up the breakfast I've
fixed myself for years: yogurt topped with two spoonfuls of gra-
nola, which is made by Zoe Catherine and so full of sunflower,
pumpkin, and flaxseed that Mack swore it was the same stuff she
fed her birds. Since most Fairhope mornings are pleasant and
sunny, even winter ones, I take my yogurt and coffee to the arbor
outside. Half an hour later, it's time to dress and head to the office.

Monday morning, however, my routine is disturbed. With the
tray holding my breakfast in one hand, I stop in surprise when I
reach for the back door. A note has been pushed under it, and I
recognize Lex's bold scrawl: "Clare, didn't want to scare you, but
I'm outside—I need to talk to you."

Sure enough, when I go outside, Lex is sitting at the table under
the arbor, hunched over a Styrofoam cup of coffee, his face dark
and troubled. For an early March morning, it's still fairly chilly,
but not really cold. Yet Lex is wearing his marina jacket with the
collar turned up as though an arctic wind is blowing. He's so lost in
thought, he doesn't notice my approach, but when I put down the

tray, he raises his head. His eyes are red and bleary, and his mouth is a tight line, white-rimmed and taut.

"Jesus, Lex," I say in alarm, sinking into my chair. "What is it?"

He looks at me for a long moment before saying, "I fucked up last night."

"Evidently. Have you had any sleep? You look dreadful."

"Couple of hours, maybe." I wait for him to go on, but he looks away, his eyes traveling to the garden. It's been so peaceful out here these late winter mornings, with the singsong chatter of the cardinals clustered around the bird feeder, and the tartness of the salt-scented air. Finally Lex turns back to face me and rubs his face wearily. "I got drunk last night. Falling-down, stumbling, commode-hugging drunk."

I sigh and lean back in the chair. "Oh, dear."

"'Oh, shit' is more like it," he says wryly. "I won't even tell you what my blood pressure was this morning. My doctor's gonna chew my ass out good. I've put off my checkup for ages now, and I finally got it scheduled for later this afternoon. But I'm thinking of canceling it so I won't have to face him."

I take my coffee cup in both hands, cradling the warmth, trying to decide on the best plan of action. He's so resistant to talking about his emotions that I have to proceed cautiously. Usually humor works best with him, so I say lightly, "Well, it could've been worse. I was afraid you'd come to tell me that you'd gone back to Elinor."

"That, too," he says.

"Oh, shit," I say, and both of us smile.

"It was your damn fault," he says peevishly, and I stare at him openmouthed.

"What do you mean, *my* fault?"

"You left me a message Saturday, remember?"

"Of course I remember. I'm not senile yet. I was at Wayfarer's

Landing, and I called to tell you how much I appreciated all the work you did on my office. It looks great, and I really love it."

"As soon as I got your message, I sent you an SOS, knowing how anal you are about returning your messages. I asked you to call me back because I needed to talk. Good thing about having a therapist as a friend, I figured. Ha! Didn't occur to me you wouldn't even bother to return my call." He finishes off his coffee, then wipes his mouth with the back of his hand, glaring at me.

He's right; I always return my messages, and I did so yesterday. Or at least one of them. It was pretty late when I got in. Since I'd taken the kids with me on Saturday, I hadn't gotten as much work done as I'd hoped, so Sunday I returned to Wayfarer's Landing alone. I spent the day fixing up my office, stopping a couple of times to drive to Wal-Mart for supplies. Last night I had dinner at Rye's, and afterward we turned on the stereo, pushed back the rug in his living room, and worked on our tango moves for an upcoming dance. When I got home about eleven, the first thing I did was check my messages. In addition to the one from Lex, I had three frantic calls from a client. After being on the phone with her an hour, I went to bed thinking I'd call Lex first thing this morning. I had no idea he was having a crisis.

"Dammit, Lex, you did *not* say that you needed to talk. Here's what you said." In an imitation of his Maine brogue, I growl gruffly, "Hey, Clare, Lex here. Gimme a call, would ya?"

"So? Why would I be calling if I didn't need your help?"

"I can think of a dozen reasons." I put my cup down so hard that the coffee sloshes on my hand. "First of all, let me remind you that you've only called me a few times in the last couple of months. You've—"

"That's your damn fault. What you get for hurting my feelings, throwing me out in the cold."

Thinking it best not to go there, I continue, "And furthermore, you did not call me yesterday. Not technically, anyway. You simply pressed a button to return *my* call, so that doesn't count. For all I knew, it could've been something about my office, in response to what I'd said to you."

"You would've called me back if it'd been about your precious office," he grumbles. "But I need you, and what happens? You don't even bother to see what's going on. What kind of therapist are you?"

"What do you mean by that crack? I'll tell you what I'm not—I am not your therapist, thank God. Are we in agreement on that, at least?"

"That's for sure. If you were, I'd fire you for dereliction of duty."

"This is crazy. I planned to call you this morning. Since you told me nothing about what was going on with you—as usual—I assumed it could wait. Why didn't you say anything? You could've said, 'Clare, something's happened, and I need to talk to you.' "

"Any more coffee in the house?"

"No!" I slam my hand on the table, and he jumps back, startled. "I mean, yes, of course there's more coffee, but *no*, you are not going into the house until you tell me what's going on." We glare at each other until Lex sighs heavily and lowers his head. After a long moment, he looks up sheepishly.

"Then can I have some fucking coffee?"

"Oh, for God's sake." I have to bite my lip to keep from smiling, but I'm determined not to let him do this again. "Go get your bloody coffee, because it looks like you need it bad. But you're telling me everything when you get back, you hear?"

A look of panic crosses his face as he gets to his feet, banging his knees against the table. "Everything?"

"Every disgusting detail. Tell it, brother." I hand him my cup. "And warm mine up while you're at it."

I expect to have to drag it out of him, but when Lex returns and sits across from me, it comes pouring out. I sit quietly, sipping the coffee and struggling to remain silent, to keep from scaring him off with my prodding. Although he had filled me in on the basic details of his marriage to Elinor when we first told each other our war stories—as single folks are prone to do—he'd talked very little about his feelings. As usual, he'd treated them lightly and humorously.

"I went to Elinor's last night," he begins, and I nod helpfully. Then, with a note of defiance, he blurts out, "And ended up spending the night with her."

Ah. So that's it. Again I nod and sip my coffee, putting on my best professional face. When they first moved to Fairhope, Elinor and Lex bought an old bungalow on Magnolia Avenue, a couple of blocks from downtown, and restored it. After their divorce, she kept the house, and Lex moved into the little efficiency above the marina. It was supposed to be a temporary move for him until he found a bigger place, but he found it so convenient, he'd stayed. After all, he told me, like the quarters of a ship, it had a fridge and microwave, a bunk, a TV, and a john—what else could he possibly need?

"Did you decide to spend the night with her before or after you got drunk?" I say, unable to resist.

If he notices my sarcasm, he doesn't react. "I got drunk at her place before deciding to stay over."

"You got drunk, and you stayed all night." A common therapist's trick, echoing back a client's response until I come up with one of my own.

Lex seems to be waiting for me to say more, but when I watch him in silence, he shrugs. "Yeah. And quit looking at me like that."

"How am I looking at you?"

"You know." He puts his cup on the table but continues to fiddle with it, rocking it back and forth absently. "I didn't intend to spend the night at Elinor's, but sometimes it gets so damn *lonely* at my place." He shakes his head in bewilderment. "I always thought I was the kind of person who never got lonesome."

"Such a person doesn't exist." He cups a hand to his ear, and I have to repeat myself, I said it so quietly. As I do, a memory flashes through my mind. Rye said almost the same thing this past summer when he took me by surprise with his proposal. "By choice, I've been alone my whole life, Clare," Rye said. "But for the first time, I've been feeling lonesome lately. Just downright lonesome."

"So, do you think it was mainly loneliness that sent you to Elinor's?" I ask as I watch Lex over the rim of my cup.

He thinks about it. "Yawp, that's part of it. That's when I called you, by the way, before I went over there. Guess I was hoping you'd talk me out of going. Yesterday was the one-year anniversary of Elinor's and my divorce."

I stare at him in surprise. "No kidding? How time flies when you're having fun, huh?"

"I'd blocked the date out—didn't even realize it until Elinor called to ask me over. She said it was all she'd thought about all day. We had dinner together, then we started talking about when we first met, and when we got married . . . when Alexia came along . . ."

"She called you over to reminisce about your marriage, then."

He shrugs. "Maybe. But some of those memories weren't so great for me. Matter of fact, they kind of cut through me like a knife blade, and that's when I started pouring the booze." I nod, and Lex falls quiet, deep in thought as he stares into his coffee cup. Finally he says, "What got me most of all was reliving the time she left me last year. It's not easy for a proud man like me to admit this; matter of fact, it's pretty humiliating. But I begged Elinor not to leave me. I pleaded with her, even though I didn't think she'd loved me for a long time. Maybe years. You can tell these things, you know? But like a fool, I still didn't expect her to end it like that."

"Nothing foolish about it. Especially now, when she obviously thinks she made a mistake by doing so." When he looks puzzled, I say in exasperation, "You spent the night with her last night. That means you two are back together, doesn't it?"

He lets out a ragged sigh and runs his fingers through his hair. "Aw, hell, I don't know. Last night Elinor said our divorce was the biggest mistake of her life. Said she wished to God she hadn't gone through with it, but that's what it took to make her realize how much she loved me." He glances over at me and adds, "And yeah, she did ask me to move back to our house."

"What was your response?"

"I told her I'd have to think about it, because I couldn't go through all that crap again. I mean it. All that about killed me."

" 'All that' meaning?" I know what he means, but he needs to articulate it.

"All that back-and-forth before she filed. Her saying one day she wanted us to stay together, then the next that she wanted me out of her life for good. No way I'll go through that again. If I move back in, I'm not by God moving out the first time things don't go her way and she gets pissed with me."

I study him, his bleary eyes and drawn face, then lean forward to say, "What do *you* want?"

He looks at me in surprise. "I just told you. Not to go through all that crap again."

"That's what you don't want. Tell me what you want."

"I just did," he insists, frowning, and I let it drop. I ask him, "Does Elinor know that you're here?"

Instead of meeting my eyes, he watches a hummingbird dancing around the red-globed feeder that hangs from the branch of the dogwood tree, bare of its leafy foliage. "Naw. I left a note saying I was going to the marina."

I can't help but wonder if they made love, or if he was too drunk. I force myself to put the thought out of my mind and say, "Lex? You've told me the basic stuff, but I'm not sure I understand exactly what happened to cause your marriage to end. When did things start to go wrong?"

Lex's eyes take on a faraway look, as though scanning a distant sea. "From the first minute I met her, I was crazy in love with Elinor. So much so, I kind of lost my mind."

"That's as good a definition of love as any I've heard," I say with a smile. "In the early stages, it feels a little like going crazy, doesn't it?"

"Sure does. All I could think about was Elinor. I caught myself just sitting and staring sometimes, thinking about her. Damn, was she beautiful. I'd never imagined a woman could be so beautiful. Everything she did, every move she made, blew me away. I felt like I could be happy the rest of my life, just looking at her." He stops to glance my way. "But it was more than just her beauty. I'm not sure I can describe it." He sips his coffee as he struggles with the effort.

"It's okay. Just tell me how you felt," I suggest.

"I knew you'd say that."

"Lex!"

"You know I can't talk about how I *feel*. It comes out sounding hokey as hell. I felt like a fool, was how I felt. That a woman like her could even look at somebody like me . . ." He glances my way. "Bet you don't know this, but guys talk about their fantasy woman, or whatever you want to call it. Especially in the barracks or at sea. Mostly bullshit, a way of passing the time. Except with me, it was more than that. Probably had to do with me growing up in the long dark winters of Maine with nothing to do but fantasize, but I had it all worked out. How I was going to meet the perfect woman and fall in love and all that touchy-feely stuff. Sounds like a bunch of corn, doesn't it?"

"Not at all. We all have our fantasies and daydreams."

He looks embarrassed, his shoulders hunched and his head hanging down. "After I married Elinor, I found myself living my fantasy, crazy as it sounds. All I wanted was to take care of her and . . . Aw, you know, all that stuff. That never changed. All our years of marriage, it didn't change. You believe me?"

"Why wouldn't I?"

He shrugs. "Most guys I palled around with, naval guys, you know, had women on the side. Even career officers with model kids and perfect wives, they'd have their girlfriends, too. You'll think I'm shitting you or trying to adjust my halo, but I swear I wasn't like that. Just wasn't interested. I had Elinor, and I felt like the luckiest man in the world."

I struggle to keep my face from revealing my thoughts. When he said he'd gone crazy earlier, obviously he had. "So, when did things start to go wrong?"

He leans forward, elbows on his knees. "Lately I've been looking back, trying to figure it out. I think Elinor took up with me in the first place mainly to piss off her mother, one of those snooty Boston bitches. Jesus, did they have a bad relationship. Elinor's old lady was always telling her she wasn't skinny enough, or pretty enough, or smart enough. The old biddy hated my guts the minute she laid eyes on me. I was her worst nightmare."

Now I know where Elinor gets her charm genes, I think, but I keep my face expressionless as Lex continues. "Elinor's old lady tried to convince all the other high-society biddies that I was from one of Maine's prominent families, and since none of them knew jack about Maine, I guess they bought it. They sure had lots of parties and stuff for us."

"Did you like that kind of thing?" The image of Lex in Boston society is beyond my imagination.

"Hell, no. But I was a young stud and pretty full of myself back then. And I'll admit it: I wanted to impress her folks, thinking I'd make them like me. My career was going better than I ever imagined; I'd been promoted to captain; and to top it off, I'd landed a classy beauty like Elinor. Guess I was a cocky bastard."

"*Was?*" I say, hoping for a smile from him, but he furrows his brow, remembering.

"I got the big head, thought I was on top of the world. When we first married, we were stationed in the Philippines for a few years, which was right up Elinor's alley. Everything went great for us, you know? We had maids and gardeners and a fancy house and lots of friends, and Elinor seemed happy as a clam. She spent her days at the officers' club and her nights with me. She couldn't have been more loving or attentive, and I was in heaven. When we got back to the States, we were sent to Pensacola, then to Baltimore. We finally had a kid, and hell, I hoped we'd have a houseful. Not Elinor, who said one was more than enough for her, that it took her forever to get her figure back. When Alexia started school, Elinor opened up her dress shop, and stupid me, I thought everything was going great. The first time she claimed to be miserable and said she was gonna leave me, I was floored. It came out of the blue."

"I'm sure it felt that way, but it never does. Even when it's a surprise, usually we can look back and see the signs."

He shakes his head. "I was too damn busy to look for signs." He crooks his fingers to indicate quotation marks over the last word. "I was brought up piss-poor, when times were always hard. Elinor never really believed that as a kid, I went to bed hungry half the time." He pats his belly and looks up with a half-smile. "No chance of that now, huh? If I didn't work so hard, I wouldn't be able to see my shoes. Anyhow, when we had a kid, I didn't want her to ever want for anything, so I started working my ass off to provide nice stuff for Elinor and Alexia. Once Elinor's store took off, things got better. Until then I was always doing overtime, working weekends so they could have expensive things, like everybody else." He shrugs. "Maybe I was still trying to impress her folks, convince them she hadn't married a loser after all."

"The first time it came up, did Elinor say why she wanted to leave you?"

"Just that she was sick of me being such a loudmouth and a lout and not having fancy manners. Said she was ashamed to go anywhere with me. I told her she knew what I was when she married me."

"So that was her reason? She was 'sick' of you?"

He nods glumly. "Yawp. She said she'd been able to overlook things until we had a kid, but Alexia needed a dad she could look up to. Turns out I'd embarrassed Alexia at her school play." He grins sheepishly. "When Alexia came onstage, I stood up and clapped and whistled. Guess it *was* pretty embarrassing for a young girl."

"So Elinor left after that?"

"Went home to her mom and stayed half the summer, but she and her old lady fought the whole time, and the shop didn't do well without her, so she came back. It was tough while they were gone, though, not seeing my little girl. Elinor told me I could see her anytime, but first time I showed up, she'd sent Alexia to camp. I said I'd be back for my daughter's tenth birthday regardless, and Elinor claimed she'd never keep me from my child. I got there, no one was home, and none of the maids would tell me where the fuck they were. I acted the fool and yelled and kicked in the front door. When Elinor and Alexia got there, I started yelling at Elinor, and Alexia cried and ran off, scared to death of me. What a god-awful scene that was. Ended up, Elinor agreed to come home if I'd go to a marriage counselor."

"So the two of you have had counseling?"

"Couple of times after she came back. Not that it did us much good. Mainly because every time she threatened to leave, it'd scare me so bad that I'd go out and get drunk. We'd fight, then I'd sober up and promise to do better. Jeez, it was miserable. The bottom line was Elinor had stopped loving me. I filled her with disgust, I think. I had a hard time admitting it, but there it was."

Leaning over, I place a hand on his arm. "She must love you in spite of everything. She came here with you—"

"Then she promptly left my ass," he reminds me.

"Yes, but she's decided now that was a mistake. Let me assure you that you're doing the right thing to get a commitment from her before rushing back into a reconciliation, however."

He grins. "A commitment, huh? You folks have your little buzz-words, don't you?" Before I can respond, Lex slaps his knees and gets to his feet. He's said all he's going to. "Jeez, I've been yapping for an hour. You're gonna be late to work, and I've got a marina to run."

I look down at my watch. "Yeah, I have someone coming in at nine." I'll be rushed, but it was worth it. Lex has talked more this morning than he has since we've known each other. I get to my feet, too. "Maybe your blood pressure has gone down a few points, if nothing else."

"The coffee helped get rid of my hangover."

"I hope you'll have better sense than to overindulge like that again," I say, but I'm thinking I'd get drunk, too, if I were him and faced with getting back with Elinor. But it's what he wants, so I put an encouraging hand on his shoulder as we start walking toward the kitchen, Lex carrying the tray with my untouched bowl of yogurt and our coffee cups on it. "If you promise you'll keep me posted on how things are going, I swear I'll return your calls," I tell him.

But it turns out to be a promise I don't have to keep. Friday after work, Lex and I, back on good terms, plan another trip to the Landing. When he runs several minutes late, I check my messages. It's him, apologizing that he won't be able to go with me after all. Elinor just showed up at the marina, ready to discuss that commitment he's asked for.

≶

Rye's historic old house is located on a high bluff overlooking the bay, which is spectacular at night. He and I often sit on the upstairs balcony off the master bedroom suite because it offers the best view, perched among the tops of the spreading oaks like a tree house. It's such a glorious and star-stunned night that we can't resist taking our brandy to the balcony, in spite of a biting wind blowing in. We pull our chairs together for warmth and raise our glasses in a salute to Mobile Bay, a vast, shimmering piece of black silk spread out under stars close enough to reach up and touch. The lights of downtown Mobile sparkle on the dark horizon like a city of diamonds. "Wish we had a fuller moon," Rye murmurs, but I reply that it couldn't be more perfect.

We started the night with champagne, one of Rye's prized bottles of Dom Perignon he'd been saving for years, topped off with a feast of pickled shrimp and chocolate-pecan cake his housekeeper had left us, which she knows to be my favorite. "What are we celebrating?" I asked in surprise when I arrived. "Us," Rye replied mysteriously, putting his hand over mine to steady the glass as he poured my champagne.

After having two pieces of chocolate cake and licking the thick dark icing off my fingers, I'm so stuffed I don't want to move. I pull my legs under me on the cushioned rattan chair, grateful that I wore a long full skirt, which now serves as cover against the chill wind. I usually wear a swirly skirt when I go to Rye's, since our evenings almost always end with a run-through of our latest dance steps. I look over at him with a smile and raise my glass. "What a lovely evening this has been!"

He tries not to look too pleased with himself as he clinks his glass against mine. "I thought you needed a treat after all you've been through with Haley lately. And I had an ulterior motive, I'll admit."

I take a tentative sip of cognac in the fat-globed glass I hold. I've never cared for brandy, but Rye insisted I give this kind a try. The taste isn't too bad, and it feels really good going down. "That sounds ominous."

"I just wanted to gossip," he says with a chuckle. When he leans over to light a candle in a hurricane lamp, it occurs to me that he hasn't mentioned having a smoke. I wonder if he's quit, but I'm not about to bring it up. "You've been occupied with your new retreat site, and Dory's taken off with Son, so I haven't had anyone to gossip with."

"Oh, boo-hoo. Half of Fairhope would line up in a hurricane to hear one of your juicy morsels, and you know it."

Rye has the same quicksilver eyes that Mack had, but his are livelier, dancing as he says, "The well has run dry."

"You mean you've attended every Mardi Gras party in a five-hundred-mile radius and haven't picked up enough gossip to keep you happy?" I say with a laugh.

He wrinkles his nose in distaste. "Are you suggesting that *I'd* go to that debauchery in New Orleans? Please. At least our celebrations have retained an element of tastefulness."

"A tasteful Mardi Gras parade is an oxymoron, Rye." I eye him suspiciously, then say, "Wait a minute. Why are you asking me about gossip, my good man? Surely this isn't another sly attempt to get me to betray a professional confidence. I thought we'd settled that."

He swirls the cognac in the brandy snifter, closing his eyes to savor the smell. "Oh, you mean the time you told me if I ever asked you to do so again, you'd drop me in a New York minute? No, it's not a professional confidence I'm asking you to betray, but I'll get to that. First, what's going on with Dory and Son?"

"Better put your ear to the ground for the thundering of hooves, because your four horsemen might still ride in," I tell him. "Dory stood up to Son; she told him it was her way or the highway. He pouted and acted the fool, of course, since it comes so naturally to him, then damn if he didn't straighten up. His halo is back in place, so Dory rewarded him by taking off a couple days to go to a Bama game. Son's so pleased with himself, you'd think he just treed Jesus."

Rye groans. "If I'd been a betting man, I'd have lost a fortune by now, wagering my last penny that he'd never make it this far."

We sit in a comfortable silence, sipping our drinks and looking out over the bay until I say, more wistfully than I'd intended, "I'll tell you something if you swear never to tell Dory. When she and Son split up last year, I had hopes that maybe you and Dory could get together one day. Pick up where you left off that summer all those years ago."

Bemused, he tilts his head and eyes me sideways. "I had no idea you were such a romantic. I wouldn't think it possible in your profession."

I pull my shawl closer, then turn my head to look out over the bay. "I've had to watch myself to keep from becoming bitter and cynical. At times I've teetered, and it's those times when the world has looked too gloomy for me. I've felt comfortless and utterly desolate. I've concluded that life is easier when we have someone to share it with. So I have to believe some relationships are good and solid. And lasting, most of all." With a swing of my arm, I motion at the bay. "If I didn't think so, I'd row a boat to the middle of the bay and jump in, I swear I would."

He's pensive, nursing his drink, his eyes distant. "It's a romantic notion, but I'm not sure I was really in love with Dory," he says finally, surprising me. "She served an important purpose in my solitary life. I held her up as my ideal, the only woman I would've given up my treasured freedom for. It worked because she was unavailable. Ah, but that was in my youth, which is long gone now."

"Hear, hear," I say with another lift of my glass. "To our lost youth!"

"Things look quite different when you get to be my age, my dear," he says softly.

"We look at things differently in each decade of our lives, don't you think? Our needs change, but so do our desires. Or maybe they just become blurred."

"As a younger man, I prized freedom above all things," Rye says thoughtfully, but there's no mistaking the regret in his voice. "I didn't want to share my life with anyone, and I think that's why I've had so many women yet never settled down with one."

I widen my eyes in mock surprise. "Uh-oh. True confessions. If I pour you another brandy or two, maybe I'll leave here with the hottest gossip in Fairhope."

"I have many regrets, Clare."

"Who doesn't? Do you really think any of us can make it this far and not have them?"

He looks at me strangely. "Do you regret loving Mack?"

"No. Never."

"I can never tell you how much I envied the kind of love that you and Mack had. It seems to me it only comes once in a lifetime, and some of us never find it." Putting down his brandy glass on a small table in front of our chairs, Rye leans toward me, his eyes opalescent in the flickering light of the candle. "If I thought you'd love me like that . . ."

I take his hand in mine and smile at him. "I've loved you for years, and you know it."

"And I treasure the special closeness we've always shared." With a graceful move, he raises my hand to his lips. "As I tried to tell you last summer, though, I don't want to be your brother anymore. Your friendship is dear to me, but I want more. I've played it cool until I thought you were ready, but now . . . since things have changed . . ."

With a puzzled frown, I ask, "What things?"

"That's the other thing I wanted to talk to you about, the gossip going around. Everyone is saying that your Yankee sea captain is back on Magnolia Street."

I stare at him in shock. "Lex has left the marina and moved to Elinor's?"

Rye shrugs nonchalantly, releasing my hand as he reaches for his glass. "So I hear. You mean you didn't know?"

I swallow hard, too stunned to speak. "I—I didn't. I mean, I knew she'd asked him to, but the last time he and I talked, they were still discussing a reconciliation. Nothing had been decided." The shock and dismay I feel that Lex didn't even bother to tell me catches me off-guard. Then it hits me what Rye said, and I turn my head to look at him, aghast. "You think this changes things between *us*? You and me? But . . . how?"

Again he shrugs. "When you blew off my proposal last summer, I thought it might be because of Lex."

"That's ridiculous!" I say sharply, and Rye studies me with a knowing smile.

"Methinks the lady protests too much," he says.

"Nonsense. I've told you all along that Lex and I were just good friends, but you chose not to believe me. I thought you were just pretending to be jealous of him. I had no idea you thought I cared for him in that way."

He stares at me in wonder. "Then we've been at cross purposes. Guess I should've had this conversation with you long before now, but I was afraid to. I had to hold on to hope, and I couldn't bear not to have at least a slender thread."

"And what hope was that?" I ask, even though I know the answer.

"Well, I hoped you'd see that you and I were meant to be to-gether. And one day you might feel the same way about me that I feel about you. You've spent your life taking care of everybody else. I'd like to spend the rest of mine taking care of you."

"Oh, Rye." I scoot my chair closer to his and put my arms around him, my head on his shoulder. "You're such a fine man, and you're so good to me. But you have to know—what you're asking of me? I'm not sure I can love anyone like that again."

"I know that, sweetheart," he says into my hair. "I was there the day we found Mack, and I'll never forget your face, never. As long as I live, it will haunt me. But even on that awful day, I wanted to take care of you, more than anything. Now that Mack's gone, I've come to the conclusion that you and I were meant to be."

"You deserve someone who'll love you the way you want and need to be loved. Anything less wouldn't be fair to you—"

He puts a finger over my lips to silence me. "Shhh." When I raise my head to his, he kisses me, then whispers, "Stay with me tonight, Clare."

Even though the combination of his kiss and the brandy has left me feeling more responsive than I've been in a long time, I force myself to pull away, pressing my face into his neck until I can catch my breath. When I raise my head, I say in a hoarse voice, "I can't tonight. I need to sort some things out first. When—or if—I stay with you, I'd want it to be for good."

"Mmm. I like that you said 'when' before 'if.'"

"You've been my buddy for so long that it's difficult to put you in another context. I guess I need some time to readjust my thinking. After having so much of your champagne and cognac, I'm feeling so woozy that I don't trust myself."

He chuckles and gets to his feet, pulling me up with him. "Then let me get you home right now. The sooner you get your thoughts readjusted to thinking of me as a lover instead of a brother, the sooner you'll be back here, where you belong."

At home in my bed, I'm restless, unable to fall asleep. The warm, lazy feeling the brandy brought on has dissipated and been replaced by a yearning I don't quite understand. I've been alone for so long, by choice, but I'm suddenly feeling lost and bewildered, like an exile in a strange land. I sit on the side of the bed, my hands clasped in front of me, and listen to the familiar night sounds of my house. But it's cold, and I slide back into the comforting cocoon of blankets I pushed aside. Closing my eyes, I try to will myself to sleep, to stop the jumbled thoughts that won't let me be. Maybe I should've stayed with Rye, snuggled next to him on the big antique bed that dominates his bedroom. Falling asleep in his arms would've brought me the solace I seek, surely. Our lovemaking would be gentle and loving and ever so sweet. We would sleep afterward, a deep and dreamless and peaceful sleep.

His number is programmed into my phone; without turning on the bedside lamp, I press the number and hold the receiver close, on my pillow. He answers on the first ring. "Clare?" I hear the rustle of sheets but not the click of the lamp. Like me, he's in the darkness of his bedroom, except he'll have the double doors of the balcony flung wide, bringing in the stars and the quarter moon and the salt-sweet smell of the bay. "What is it, honey?"

"I can't sleep." I don't say that I'm cold and lonely and loss-haunted, and that some nights I miss Mack so badly it leaves me stunned, like a fish pulled out of the water and left gaping for air.

"Me, either," he murmurs. "Want me to come over?"

"Could you just talk to me for a minute?"

"Of course. All night if you need me to. But the sound of your voice alarms me. You sound . . . sorrowful. Not your usual sassy self, like you were earlier this evening." After a long silence, he asks, "I didn't upset you tonight, did I?"

"It's not you. It's me. Or rather, it's Mack."

"Oh, sweetheart." He lets out a long, weary sigh. I picture him rubbing his face with his long slender fingers, a gold signet ring on his left hand. Mack wouldn't even wear a wedding ring. Rye sleeps in fine cotton pajamas that I've seen his housekeeper set out for him. I know that he has a cashmere robe because it hangs behind his bedroom door, and his butter-soft leather slippers await on the antique Persian rug next to his bed. Mack slept in the buff and never owned a robe or a pair of slippers in his life.

"Listen to me," Rye says firmly. "We both loved Mack. But he's gone, and he's not coming back. One day he left us. He went into the woods, and he never came out. I don't know if he was drunk or in one of his dark funks. Maybe the coroner was right and he tripped over a tangle of vines. When he reached out to stop his fall, the gun went off. None of us will ever know. But you've *got* to let go of him."

"Oh, God, don't I know that! I'll go for days without thinking of him, and my life will be full and satisfying and meaningful. Then, when I least expect it, Mack will show up again. I'll walk into the kitchen, and he's at the table, waiting for his breakfast. In his study, he sits with his back to me, expecting me to cross the room and put my hands over his eyes. In our bed, I wake up through the night with his arms around me." I take a deep breath and release it with a sob. "It's not that I can't let go of Mack. He won't let go of me! I don't think he'll ever let go of me."

He's quiet for so long that I wonder if he's still there. "Rye?"

"I'm here," he says finally. "I'm here."

"You are, aren't you? You've been with me all along, and I want you to know how grateful I am. How truly grateful."

"I can't be Mack, though," he says, surprising me with the abruptness of his tone. "I can love you, and cherish you, but I can't ever be Mack. I can't be a substitute for him."

"Do you think . . ." I pause to take in his words, stricken. "Oh, my God. Is that what I'm doing, calling you like this? Is that what this is about?"

"I don't know," he says with a sigh. "It's been my worst fear, but it's something only you can answer." He hesitates and seems to be choosing his words carefully. "Clare? I've gone over and over the day that Mack died, trying to figure out how it happened like it did, and why. But I don't think you have. You've blocked it out, haven't you?"

"I've had to. I know I need to go back, but I can't make myself do it. It hurts too bad. And I'm afraid of what I might find."

Rye is silent a long time, before he says, "After all these years, it seems to be screaming to get out. You're going to have to go back, whether you want to or not."

≫

Haley was eleven when she came to live with Mack and me, and bringing her into our house turned our lives upside down. As Zoe Catherine had predicted the afternoon she took me to see the terns, Mack made no move to reclaim the child he thought he'd rid himself of. Although he'd taken full responsibility for her support, working long, hard hours at the backbreaking labor his job demanded, he still couldn't face up to his daughter's existence. In the beginning, he shut me out and absolutely refused to discuss her sudden appearance in our lives. He was in such obvious anguish, however, that I hounded him until he told me the terrible truth.

Breaking down and burying his face in his hands, Mack admitted that he'd heard several years ago, from one of Shirley's friends in Gulf Shores, that she'd blown the money he gave her and not had the abortion. She'd had his child instead. He swore that's all Shirley's friend told him; whether or not she'd kept the baby, no one knew. The only thing known for sure was that Shirley's drug habit had gotten dangerous. Mack was horrified by the story and the part he'd played in it. He'd abandoned a girl who was young and pregnant with no skills to support herself. He'd paid her off with a large sum that she had no idea how to manage, and she'd ended up on the streets. At that point, hearing about the baby, he could have taken steps to redeem himself and possibly saved Shirley and the child. Instead, he'd done nothing. As with his other demons, Mack dealt with it by not dealing with it, even when it tore him to pieces. When he and I lost Daniel and the other babies, he saw it as a fitting punishment, and his guilt drove him to the closest bar night after night.

I had my own demons to deal with. Zoe's words haunted me: "And Mack—he's as not strong as you are, and you know it." I took Mack's child into my house and heart, not only because it was the right thing to do but also because Mack lacked the strength to. I didn't expect to come to love her, and I doubted I'd be able to love Mack again. I knew only one thing for sure: Raising Mack's child was something I was supposed to do. I'd lost my babies, but for reasons yet unknown to me, I'd been given another chance.

I was wrong the night I told Mack I didn't know if I could accept his child or love him again, as it turned out. I not only came to love Haley with a fierce and protective love that amazed and humbled me, I could no more stop myself from loving Mack than I could stop breathing. During the remainder of our years together, I came to see love as an ever evolving thing rather than the static, unbendable sentiment I'd always thought it to be. Love changes form and motion and shape like the red substance in the Lava Lamp Haley picked out and proudly gave me for my first Mother's Day while Mack struggled to keep a straight face. I met his laughing gray eyes over Haley's blond head, so like her father's, and knew that at some point in our years together, he'd become an essential part of me, like an arm or leg. If I lost him, I would always be incomplete.

When I look back, it still astonishes me how effortlessly Haley became a part of me as well. The night Mack and I brought her into our home, neither of us could've imagined that I'd be the one to embrace her so fully, or that Mack would always be on his guard with her. It took me a while to come to the shocking realization that in spite of my initial reluctance to do so, I'd taken her in much more easily than her own father had. It wasn't that Mack didn't love his daughter; it was his inability to express that love, ironically mirroring the way he'd never allowed himself to love and accept his own mother. As I feared, Mack's horror and guilt at rejecting his child ate at him like poison, and their relationship was destined to be mired in remorse and shame. Mack couldn't look at his daughter without being reminded of the way she was conceived, of how he'd tried to rid himself of her, and of the horrendous relief he'd felt when he put Shirley on a bus for Naples, her purse bulging with what he came to think of as blood money. Most of all, he couldn't face the fact that he'd heard about Haley yet failed to act, and the first years of her life had been terrible ones.

As Haley and I grew closer, Mack pulled further away from us. Falling into old patterns of behavior, he tried to deaden his feelings with drink. On the surface, our life together appeared to have everything. I was in the process of opening my practice, and Mack's restoration skills were so much in demand, he couldn't keep up with all the business that came his way. In our care, Haley blossomed, turning into a sweet-natured and lovely young woman who made us proud. Because Mack was a binge drinker, he was able to go for weeks, sometimes months, without a drink, and during that time our life was good, wonderful and fulfilling for all of us.

Only those closest to us knew what was going on. On a binge, Mack would often go away, hiding out and drinking himself into oblivion at the fish camp, or at a hunting cabin owned by Son's family, deep in the woods near Bon Secour. At home, he'd close himself in the den with the television tuned to a ball game and the blinds pulled. Haley stayed away during that time, at Etta's house with Jasmine. Etta was very much aware what was going on in our household; she knew more than Rye or Dory or anyone else. When Mack sobered up, I'd bring Haley home. Whenever I told her that something *had* to be done about her dad's drinking, she'd panic. She'd finally found the father she'd always known was out there, and she couldn't bear the thought of losing him. Eventually Haley and I became united in our efforts to shelter and protect Mack, another bond between us. The difference was, she was a child, and I was a trained therapist. I knew better.

It wasn't that I didn't try to help Mack; instead, I let my feelings for him override everything else. When he'd go on a binge, I'd give him an ultimatum: If he continued to destroy the secure and loving home that we'd brought his daughter into, then he'd do so without having Haley and me to witness it. Both of us loved him too much, I'd tell him, to stand by and watch him self-destruct. Repentant, Mack would beg forgiveness. He'd put up a flawless front for whatever momentous occasion presented itself: Papa Mack's funeral; the grand opening of Casa Loco; all the sporting events we attended for Dory and Son's boys; Haley's graduations from high school and college; her engagement and marriage to Austin. But Mack's destructive pattern was like a runaway train. He'd sober up, get his act together, and life would be good again. Once I even got him into a long, torturous detox program, and while he was away, I told everyone he was on a restoration job in Mississippi. Long, happy months of sobriety followed, and Mack was himself again, content and carefree, loving me and bent on making things right with Haley.

Two years later, the blinds were pulled in the den once more, and I found a stash of empty bottles in the back of his closet. I collapsed to the floor in tears. Had one of my clients been where I was, I'd have advised her to face the futility of trying to save anyone else, and to concentrate on saving herself and her family instead. But I was unable to take my own directives. It seemed I could help everyone but myself.

Ten years after Haley came into our home, she left us to marry Austin and start her own life. Although it shamed me to admit it, I harbored the hope that once Haley was gone, Mack would straighten himself out. Without her presence to remind him of his failure as a father, maybe he'd stay sober at last. And it seemed as though he would, for the longest period of time yet. Then came the night in the late fall when Mack didn't come home, and I knew his period of sobriety had come to an end. The next day Haley called, breathless with excitement. She and Austin had just had it confirmed: She was pregnant. But not a word to her dad, she pleaded—she wanted to tell him herself. Could she come over?

Because I couldn't bear to spoil her happiness, I stalled her. Oh, hadn't I told her that Mack was away working? I asked innocently. The minute he returned, I'd call her, I promised. After hanging up, I swore I'd track him down if I had to, but by God, he'd be home and sober to share in his daughter's happiness.

As it turned out, I didn't have to go out looking for Mack. I came downstairs early Saturday morning, the day after Haley's call, to find him sitting in the kitchen. I had no idea when he'd come home; nor had I heard him come in. It frightened me, having someone come into the house so silently while I slept unsuspecting in my lonely bed. But when Mack raised his head, he looked so awful that I forgot my fear and everything else, and I rushed over to kneel in front of him. "Mack? My God, what's wrong?" When I took his hands in mine, I was shocked to feel how cold they were.

"I don't know," he said faintly. "I'm scared this time." His eyes, those dreamy gray eyes I'd loved since the first time I saw him, were as dark as a tomb. In their depths I saw a despair I'd never seen before. If he was drunk, I couldn't tell it. He appeared to be dead sober.

"You're freezing," I cried. "Where's your coat?" Without waiting for an answer, I ran to the den and grabbed a throw from the back of his chair, the one where he'd sit to drink until he passed out. I came back and wrapped the throw around Mack's shoulders, then knelt in front of him again. "Are you sick?" I pushed his hair back from his forehead, concerned not only by his pallor but also by the clamminess of his skin.

Rather than answer me, he stared his dazed stare, and something in his look made me think of a cornered animal. "I'm so fucked up," he said finally.

I pulled a chair next to him, keeping his cold hands in mine. "We've had this discussion plenty of times before. Yes, you are fucked up. You are *bad* fucked up, and you have been for years. But I can't help you. I've tried. I've done all I can do. You're the only one who can save yourself. You've got to let me take you to the hospital." He shook his head vigorously, and I tightened my grip on his hands. "Okay, not here. It doesn't matter where—just someplace where you can get help."

"I'm not going to one of those places," he said tonelessly. "I'll never go back. It's like being in a straitjacket. I'll go to the woods and never come out before I go there again."

Letting go of his hands, I leaned back in my chair. I couldn't do this anymore. My voice rising, I said, "You'll let me take you somewhere to get help, or so help me God, I'm through with you. I'm washing my hands of you."

Moving quickly, he grabbed my arms in a death grip. For the first time that morning, a spark of the old Mack flared in his eyes. "Please, Clare! Don't send me away to be locked up again. If you'll help me, I swear I'll sober up this time. I swear it!"

Prying his hands from my arms, I pushed back the chair and got to my feet. "*No*, Mack. You've had too many chances. I—" But I stopped myself, squeezing my eyes closed and sighing in resignation. We'd had that argument before. Next thing, he'd accuse me of not loving him, of forsaking him when he needed me most, and I'd go over all the chances I'd given him. I wouldn't do it again.

"This time is different!" he cried, getting to his feet and grabbing my arms again. "I'm going to get sober, but I can't do it without your help. You know that. I'll never be able to without your help." The throw I'd placed around his shoulders fell to the floor, and Mack kicked it out of the way. Stepping away from him, I leaned over to pick it up and held it close to me, needing its warmth.

"Please leave." I stood before him, clutching the blanket against me like a shield. If I didn't get him out of my sight, I'd weaken, and I couldn't do that. Whatever it cost me, I had to yank away the crutch of my support and make him stand on his own. "And when you go, I'm having the locks changed so you can't come here again."

What little color he had drained from his face. "You'd do that? You'd lock me out of our house? *Our* house, the one we made together?"

"I'm going upstairs to get dressed. I have a lot of work to do to-day. When I come down, I don't want to see you here. I mean it, Mack. I want you gone." Although my legs were weak and my heart thudded painfully, I turned to go, walking past him toward the stairs.

To this day, I don't know what made me turn around. When I did, the sight of him standing there, his arms hanging at his sides, tore me apart. With a stifled cry, I went back into the kitchen and threw my arms around his waist, burying my face in his chest. "I love you, Mack," I said. "And I always will. Wherever you go, take that with you."

His arms tightened around me, and we clung to each other for what would be the last time. "Clare, please help me . . ." he said hoarsely, but I pulled away from him and ran upstairs, this time without stopping to look back. Hardly realizing what I was doing, I locked the door of the bathroom and stepped into the shower, where I stood shaking and sobbing while the steaming-hot water poured over me and washed my tears down the drain.

It was later that afternoon when I went to Mack's study. He'd been gone when I got out of the shower and went downstairs, but I felt no relief, only a resigned and profound despair. Because I needed something to occupy my mind, I spent the morning doing what I'd promised myself I'd do for ages, converting Haley's lilac-sprigged bedroom into an all-purpose guest room. She'd taken what she wanted to her and Austin's apartment a few years before, but I had yet to change the room. I'd asked Mack to, but even during his times of sobriety, he hadn't. Finally he admitted that although he'd gone into the room dozens of times planning to, he hadn't been able to do it. It was as though he believed if he didn't change it, Haley might return, and they might find what had eluded them during their years together.

Haley had missed seeing the scrapbook of Mack's baseball career when she'd cleared out her room because it had fallen behind her dresser, unseen and gathering dust. My throat constricted when I found it, and I hurried downstairs with it tucked under my arm so I could put it out of my sight. Dory and I had made it and presented it to Mack as his graduation present, clippings from the newspaper and old programs and team photos, and he'd treasured it more than any gift he'd ever gotten. Entering Mack's dark and dismal little study in the back of the house, I went to his desk quickly, wanting only to put away the scrapbook and get out. Just going into the room had almost caused me to fall apart.

It was after I'd put the scrapbook in Mack's desk that something caught my eye. Turning fearfully, I saw that the door to the gun rack was ajar. In all of our years together, Mack had never left it open. A good hunter wouldn't do that, he'd told me once. Keeping the door of the gun cabinet locked at all times was one of the first things a hunter learned.

How my legs held me up to cross the room and look inside the cabinet, I'll never know. Once I saw that Mack had taken his high-powered rifle rather than the twelve-gauge shotgun he always took dove hunting, I managed somehow to hold the phone steady enough to dial Dory's number. She could find Son because he was never without his cell phone, but she wasn't in. Mack often went hunting with Son, and I hoped and prayed that he'd done so today.

I tried to convince myself that was all he'd done, grabbed the wrong gun in his haste to get out and clear his mind in the woods, as he'd done so many times in the past.

I checked a message I'd ignored earlier. Haley's voice was up-beat, with no way of knowing how her message sent chills down my spine. "I didn't know Daddy was back! You must've told him that I had a surprise for him, because he came by the apartment earlier this morning. By the time I got to the door, though, he'd gone. First time he's ever been to see us, and he didn't even wait for me; can you believe it? I'll check back later to see when we can come over to tell him our news, okay, Mom?"

It was then that I realized I hadn't mentioned Haley and her news to Mack, I'd been so distraught. Oh, God—if only I'd told him! Now I *had* to find him, to tell him to come back, and that I'd do anything to help him. I would tell him that together, we'd beat this. He had a reason now, and he could do it, I knew he could. He'd been right this morning: This time it would be different. He'd been given another chance to make things right.

I had to find Mack, but I didn't know the woods. With a sense of urgency, I tore through his desk looking for Son's cell number, throwing papers everywhere. If only Son and I hadn't had this animosity between us, I'd have had his number and wouldn't have to waste valuable time looking for it. But I'd never written it down, being too stubborn to admit there might come a time when I'd need either Son or his private number. Unable to find it, I almost collapsed to the chair in frustration until it hit me—of course! Rye could find him. Rye probably had Son's number, but if he didn't, he knew the woods. He wasn't a hunter, but unlike me, he knew the lay of the land.

I hadn't even realized I was praying silently until Rye answered and I let out a cry of relief. "Mack left early this morning to go hunting, Rye," I said breathlessly, "and he's not back. I was wondering if you might find him."

Unlike Son, who'd never acknowledged Mack's alcoholism, Rye knew everything. The first thing he said was, "Was he sober?"

I hesitated, and in that moment I knew that I would never tell Rye or anyone else. We'd find Mack, and he'd come home to Haley's wonderful news, and the two of us would make things work. I'd help him, and he'd get well, and no one would ever need to know about the terrible scene this morning. There was no reason for Rye or anyone to know that Mack had begged me to help him and I'd sent him away instead.

"Oh, no, he was fine," I heard myself telling Rye. "It's just that Haley's coming over to share some good news with her dad, and he promised to be here for her visit. He must've lost track of time."

With a chuckle, Rye said, "Oh, you mean she hasn't told Mack she's pregnant yet? He's probably the only person in Fairhope who doesn't know." He added that Mack hadn't gone hunting with Son, because he'd seen Son in town just a little while ago. But he had Son's phone number and would call him. The two of them would go looking for Mack, and they'd make sure he got home before Haley got there.

After I hung up the phone, I paced from one room to another, unable to stay still. The afternoon dragged on, and the sun set, but no word from Mack, Son, or Rye. I let two cups of tea go cold before forcing myself to stay in the kitchen long enough to prepare a fresh pot, and then my hands were shaking so badly, I sloshed the scalding tea on the front of my sweatshirt. It was after I'd gone upstairs to change out of the wet shirt that I looked out the window and saw Son's red pickup stopping in front of the house. Running and stumbling down the stairs, I flung open the door to see Son and Rye getting out of the truck as a patrol car, blue light flashing, pulled into the space behind them.

Son made it around the truck, but on seeing me in the doorway, he staggered and collapsed against the hood, his arms closing over his head. Rye's face was ashen, terrible, frozen in shock, and he moved toward me on unsteady legs. But I held up my hands to stop him, as though stopping him meant I wouldn't have to hear what he had come to tell me. I covered my ears with my hands as though shutting out the sound of my sobs would keep me from hearing them in my dreams, night after lonely night to come.

Chapter Sixteen

❧　❧　❧　❧　❧

As I knew they would, the preparations for the first retreat at Wayfarer's Landing begin to take up my every spare moment. It's on us before I realize it. It seems like one day it was the first of March, and I was at the Landing with Zach and Abbie. The next, we're nearing the end of the month, and the spring equinox is only a few days away. The White Rings are in a flurry of activity; Dory and Etta are putting in extra hours, and it's full steam ahead. To say that I'm working to keep my excitement under control is an understatement. I feel like tap-dancing down the main boulevard of Fairhope.

In spite of my schedule and the excitement of the first retreat, there's one thing I must find time to do. I keep putting it off, making excuses to myself. I pick up the phone half a dozen times, but before I can dial the number, I hang up, bemused, wondering why I faltered. Who would have ever thought that making a phone call would be such a hard thing to do? It should be simple; all I have to do is take the receiver in hand, punch in a number, then say, "I'm calling to see what's going on with you. Could we talk?" I'm determined to make the call this very evening when I get home from the group meeting, regardless. Once I make up my mind, I'm surprised at how lighthearted I feel, my dread dissipating like a heavy cloud blown away by a wispy spring breeze.

This group meeting is the last one before the retreat, and most of the early-evening group, as well as my Saturday attendees, will be at the retreat. A few of them who have signed up aren't ready, however, and those I ask to speak with in private. In the past I dreaded doing so, taking them aside and suggesting they wait for the next scheduled retreat. My request is almost always met with resistance, in the form of either pleas, tears, or arguments, and I can understand their disappointment. Most of them have worked so hard at getting over the trauma of their breakup, and to be told they aren't ready for the next step can be a blow. But for the first time since I've been doing the retreats, my dreaded task is made easier. Because of Wayfarer's Landing, now they don't have to wait so long for the next one to come around.

Since it's the last meeting of the group, we wrap up earlier than usual. Before they leave, the women stand in the doorway and moan and groan before darting out one at a time. A storm is raging outside, and a torrent of rain comes down like a gauzy silver-white scrim against the dramatic backdrop of lightning flashes. After everyone leaves, I stand in the doorway, trying to decide if I should make a run for it or wait it out. I brought my car this morning after hearing the stormy weather report, even though I felt like a fool driving the few blocks. It doesn't take me but a minute to decide, and I raise my umbrella, even though it offers precious little shelter from such a downpour. What's an obstacle course when I need the comfort of my home so desperately? It's a purely physical thing, this yearning for hearth and home, I realize with a jolt of understanding as I splash my way to the car. Nothing else is quite as satisfying as a welcoming place after a long day of work. For me, it fills a need as elemental as hunger or thirst.

But when I park in front of my house, I don't go inside. Instead, I sit in the car and watch the wipers make half-moons on the windshield. The movement is mesmerizing, as is the muted swoosh of the raindrops being swept away, only to fill the half-circle again before the wiper can make its way back. It fascinates me the way my house disappears through a gray wash of rain, then reappears in the cleared space the wipers make. Through the blur, I picture the house as it was when I first saw it, run-down and neglected and empty. The gardens were an overgrown mess choked with weeds, and the windows of the house were dark and cold, years of grime blocking out the warmth of the sun. All it needed was someone to see it for what it could be, to see how it could be turned into a source of beauty and comfort. With the enthusiasm and optimism of youth, Mack and I had thrown ourselves into transforming it. Now it's such a proud old house, and I fill with love to see it standing tall and unassailable against the pounding rain and gusting wind. How many storms has it weathered, both inside and out?

I wonder—not for the first time—what happened, why every-thing we brought to the house was not enough. Many make it on much less than we had when we started out. Materially we were fortunate, but we also had an abundance of the other things that are the most important in starting a life together. We had a deep love for each other, and that never changed. In spite of his weakness, his fatal flaw, Mack was loyal and hardworking and loving and gener-ous. Then why wasn't all that enough to save him? Why did he and I fail so miserably at the one thing that mattered most to us? It has tormented me since his death; it kept me awake all night last week; yet I'm no closer to understanding it now than I've ever been. All of us who loved Mack have our theory. Although Haley has never voiced it, she's hinted at hers, with no idea how deeply it stung me. Coming into our lives the way she did, she formed immediate and initial impressions that stayed with her. Her father was good-looking and funny and sweet-natured but weak-willed and inert, dependent on me. I was the strong, independent, take-charge one, according to Haley, and he never felt that I needed him. She can't know how wrong her assessment was. Maybe I wasn't able to show Mack, but my need for him was strong. In some ways, I was like the house. Mack had seen beneath the awkward, serious, unformed girl I'd been, just as he'd seen the potential of the house. What he saw in me was a young woman with big dreams and a determination to make them happen. Inexperienced and unseasoned, I needed someone like Mack to believe in me before I could believe in myself.

It hits me that I came to love Mack because he'd not only seen the person I could be; he made me see her, too. At that time in my life, I needed an advocate to help me realize I had as much right to dream as anyone else, and I found that champion in Mack. No wonder I loved him so passionately. If my need of him was what attracted him to me in the first place, it's not surprising that he felt empty and abandoned when he no longer felt needed. But are love and need really one, as the poet said? Or is that notion not only starry-eyed and romantic but dangerous as well?

A sob tears at my throat, and I put a hand over my mouth. Mack's faith in me was the turning point in my life, yet I turned my back on him when he needed me most. No wonder I never allowed myself to go back to that day he died; my guilt would paralyze me if I dwelled on it. I've been able to go on with my life, and it appears I'm even on the verge of loving a man again, but one thing I know for sure: I'll never be able to forgive myself for what I did.

I'm startled out of my reverie by a sharp rap on the window of the car, and I hastily brush away my tears. As soon as I roll down the window a couple of inches, the rain-heavy wind rushes in with a howl of glee. In a hooded windbreaker, Lex stands outside my car, hunched against the downpour, as wet as if he had just climbed out of the sea. "What the hell are you doing?" he shouts over the sound of the pounding rain.

"*Me?* What about you, standing in the rain like a fool?"

"I was coming to see you."

"That's pretty funny, because I was planning on calling you as soon as I got inside." We blink at each other quizzically until I cry out, "Well, for heaven's sake, don't just stand there. Let's get out of this storm."

Once we step inside the house, I make a dash to the downstairs bathroom to grab an armful of towels, leaving a trail of rainwater behind me. "Don't move until I get back," I call over my shoulder, and Lex waits obediently on the slate floor of the entranceway, trying to shake off the water like a wet dog as he stamps his soggy-booted feet. Even though he's removed his dripping windbreaker and hung it on a peg behind the door, I come out of the bathroom to find him standing in a puddle. Laughing, I throw him a towel, and he catches it in midair. "In like a lion, out like a lamb," I say.

"Who, me?" His teeth are a flash of white against the weathered darkness of his skin, and he grins before burying his face in the towel.

I take one of the towels draped over my arm and pat my face with it. "Hmm. Not totally inappropriate for you. Except for the lamb part."

"Come here," he says, motioning. Taking the towel from me, he dries my hair, one hand gripping the back of my neck. As he makes an awkward attempt to finger-comb my hair into place, I watch him, searching his scowling face. "Stop looking at me like that, goddammit," he snaps, avoiding my eyes.

"Like what?" I say with a smile.

Dropping the wet towel on the floor, he halfheartedly mops at the puddle with a booted foot. "Like you accused me of last time I was here," he mutters finally.

When I laugh lightly, Lex says, "Why were you going to call me?"

"Ah . . . why were you coming to see me?" I counter.

"I asked first."

"Yeah, but in the South a gentleman always concedes to a lady, Yankee man."

"I was coming to tell you something." His green eyes, opaque and unreadable, still are reluctant to meet mine.

"Then tell it, brother."

"I told Elinor to get the hell out of my life," he blurts out, and I gasp, raising a hand to my mouth.

"You *didn't*! When?"

"Right before I came over here. I told her I was sick of playing her stupid mind games, and I'd finally come to the conclusion that our getting back together wasn't the best thing for either of us."

"Are you serious, Lex? What did she say?"

"Aw, she flung a fit. Pretty much what I expected. She said Alexia wouldn't speak to me anymore, crap like that. All the stuff she's been pulling on me for months. But I said that Alexia is a college junior and plenty old enough to think for herself if Elinor would leave her alone and quit trying to use her against me."

"Wow. You did good," I say with a nod. "I'm proud of you. What was Elinor's reaction? Did she cry or get mad?"

"Both. By the way, you were crying, weren't you, out there in your car?"

I shrug. "A little."

"You didn't see me park the Jeep behind you, so I thought maybe you were talking on your cell phone. I waited patiently for you to finish until I realized you were sitting there like an idiot, staring at your house and boo-hooing. Figured you'd gone batty at last."

"That might be true. But I was also trying to figure out some stuff about me and Mack and how we went wrong. I haven't quite worked it out yet, but a few things are getting clearer."

He nods and rubs his hair, which glistens with raindrops like finely polished ebony. "Yawp, guess that's what happened with Elinor. It's been coming on awhile, but suddenly things started getting clearer." Tilting his head sideways, he squints at me. "Now it's your turn, Doctor Lady. Why were you going to call me?"

"Well . . . I wanted to see if you'd come over and build a fire in the fireplace. You know, like you did last time? I've been meaning to ask you for a while, but I just . . . haven't. I've wanted to, but . . ." I let my voice fall off.

Lex eyes me warily. "You were calling me to build a *fire?*" When I nod eagerly, he rolls his eyes. He rubs his chin and says, as though to himself, "A fire would feel mighty good tonight, wouldn't it? Nothing better during a storm."

I incline my head toward the living room. "The wood you brought in last time is still there."

Before entering the living room, Lex takes off his wet boots and puts them next to the soggy flats I kicked off in the hallway. Following him, I stand aside as he kneels in front of the fireplace to build the fire. Leaning back with his elbows propped on his knees, he watches until the flames reach up to grab the tidy stack of logs with long yellow fingers. With a great whooshing sound, the logs burst into flames, and I close my eyes in gratitude, savoring the warmth on my face.

Lex gets heavily to his feet with a grunt of satisfaction. "Should have us dry and warm in no time," he says as he wipes off his hands on the seat of his pants.

"It feels wonderful." Staring into the fire, I absently unwind a long cashmere scarf from around my neck, having forgotten to remove it with my raincoat. I'm glad it didn't get wet; luxurious, butter-soft, and a lovely gold-bronze color, the scarf was a Christmas gift from Rye that I love the feel of. I smile to see that Lex is watching me caress it against my cheek before I take it off.

"Let me see that thing," he says, gruffly, and I hand the scarf over. "Pretty, isn't it?" he says as he studies it. "Same color as your hair and eyes. Cashmere, eh?" When I nod, he says, "Where'd you get it?"

"Rye gave it to me for Christmas." I don't add that he said the same thing about it matching my coloring.

Lex lets out a snort of derision. "Guess that's what I get for asking. I wish I'd found it before he did, though. It's perfect for you." His expression is gloomy as he shakes his head. "All I gave you was a plain old fountain pen. No wonder you like him better."

"Lex! That's not true."

"Which part?" he asks so quickly that I laugh.

"The lovely pen you gave me is far from ordinary, and ever since Christmas, I've kept it in my briefcase. It's one of my most prized possessions, and I use it every day."

Rather than being appeased, he eyes me balefully. "Last week word was going around that you and pretty boy were hot and heavy now. Somebody saw you guys making out on a dance floor or something."

"Oh, Lord! Our small-town gossips never let us down, do they?"

"Then it's not true?"

With a laugh, I can't resist saying, "Which part?"

"Very funny. You know what I mean."

I'm silent for a moment, trying to decide what I should do. Finally I say, "I'll tell you about it, if you'd like. But don't listen to the gossips. Evidently it's been a busy time for them, because another thing going around was that you moved back to Elinor's house."

"I was over there a lot, but I sure didn't move in. I'm still at the marina." He blinks at me. "Don't tell me that's why I haven't heard from you lately?"

I shrug and say, "You heard that Rye and I were having an affair, didn't you?" At first he won't meet my eyes, then he shrugs elaborately. I'm not surprised that rumor was circulating; a couple of times I caught Rye's neighbors peering out their windows at me when I left his house late at night. "I figured folks were saying that," I tell him, "since I've been at his place a lot lately, too, like you being at Elinor's."

"The rumors went a little further than that," he says, then adds, "Folks were saying that you'd stayed over a few times, too."

"Not true. I won't be coy and pretend that I didn't consider it. But I've decided that Rye has always been one of my dearest friends, and it's best for both of us if we remain that way. I just told him last night. You sure you want to hear this, Lex?"

He thinks about it a minute, then shakes his head. "I thought I did, but I've changed my mind. You're telling me there's no affair, and that's good enough for me." With a grin, he looks down at the scarf he's holding. "Still wish I'd found this thing first, though," he says as he steps forward to loop it back around my neck. Since his hands clutch both ends of the scarf, I'm imprisoned by it, and I study him curiously as we stand facing each other.

"Lex? All along I've tried not to say anything, because it was something you had to work out for yourself, but you did the right thing about Elinor. From the first time I met you and realized she was your ex, I've wanted to say that I didn't think she was good for you." Or good *enough* for you, I think.

He sighs. "Ever since I left her place, it feels like a load's been lifted off my shoulders. I've never been a gloomy, down-in-the-mouth kind of guy, you know? Yet I've been miserable as hell lately." Deep in thought, he absently twists and loops the ends of the scarf around his hands. I could easily free myself, ducking under the scarf and stepping away from him, but I don't.

"I'm not sure Elinor's entirely to blame for all my misery, though," he continues. For the first time tonight, his eyes linger when they meet mine.

I lower my head, blushing. "Oh, Lex . . . there was another reason I was going to call you."

"Besides the fire?"

"Besides the fire." My smile is tentative, nervous. "You see—well—I've felt bad that we didn't part on the best of terms the last time you were here. The night you built the fire and fell asleep on the sofa, remember? So . . . ah . . . I wanted to say that I regret if I said or did anything to upset you. I've missed you these last couple of months." I manage another weak smile and glance up at him hesitantly before blurting out, "Actually, I missed you a lot. So much that it made me understand some things I hadn't seen before."

He's quiet for so long that I dare steal a glance at him. He gives his head a shake and says in a tight voice, "The problem is, I'm not sure you and I can be friends anymore, Clare."

Taken aback, I blink at him as my face burns hotly. Putting a hand to my throat, I say, much too loudly, "Oh! I . . . *see*. If that's the way you feel, then of course I understand. I—Well, I do understand. Really." I'm taken aback by the sense of loss I feel, and I swallow hard, too stunned to move. The rain has picked up; a gust of wind roaring down the chimney causes the fire to dance and spin wildly, casting a yellow glow on us. So eager was I to warm myself by the fire that I neglected to turn any lamps on, and we're standing in darkness, with only the fire for illumination.

Lex twists the ends of the scarf around his hands again, pulling me a step closer. He says, "It was actually Elinor who made me see that you and I couldn't be friends."

"Elinor!" I cry. "But you said you were through with her. Why should you listen to anything she has to say?"

"Because she said something that surprised me, but at the same time, it made a lot of sense. I can't get it out of my mind. It's the thing I was coming over here to tell you."

"You were coming here to tell me something that Elinor said?"

Nodding, he stares down at me. "She thinks that you and I can't be friends because of the way I feel about you. She seems to think that the way I feel about you . . . well . . . that it goes way beyond friendship."

Startled, I stare up at him before saying with a laugh, "Elinor said that! How did you respond to such an outrageous thing?"

His eyes reflect the glow of the fire, and he smiles down at me. "How do you think? I told her I've never heard of anything so ridiculous."

I'm lightheaded with relief, and my laugh sounds foolish and giddy. "Where do you think she got such a foolish idea?"

When Lex loops the ends of my scarf around his hands again, I realize it hasn't been an absentminded gesture on his part after all, fiddling with the scarf. Each turn of his hands has pulled us closer. "Damned if I know," he murmurs. "As I tried to tell Elinor, I've never even kissed you." Smiling, he adds, "One more twist of this scarf, though, and that might have to change."

I look down at the cashmere scarf wrapped around his hands. Large, rough hands, callused, but I've found them to be both gentle and trustworthy. Returning his smile as I place my hands over his, I say, "Too bad you've gotten the scarf as close as it will go. You can't twist it again."

"Want to bet?" His eyes never leaving mine, he loops the ends once more.

❧

It's two days before the first retreat, and everything moves into high gear. I have moments of sheer, unadulterated panic. Many times I wish I'd left well enough alone and continued to have the retreats at the conference center in Fairhope—it would have been so much easier. So what if the cost was so high it kept many women from attending? At least I'd be sane enough to conduct the next one. At Fairhope's conference center, the attendees were responsible for booking their own rooms at nearby hotels, but now we provide lodging, which means linens. There are four bunk rooms, with five bunks in each, beds enough to accommodate the participants in addition to volunteers staying overnight. In my office in the back, I have the daybed, so I won't have to drive back and forth. At the outlet in Foley, Dory and I had purchased dozens of towels and washcloths, sheets, pillows, and light blankets that double as spreads. What we hadn't considered was laundry. Dory blew it off, saying that she'd take the used linens home and wash them, but I wouldn't allow it, as busy as she is with her business now. Although Fairhope boasts a laundry service, they won't travel as far out as the Landing, so we compromise. I'll consent to the White Rings taking the laundry to the service, but that's it. One problem covered, a million or so to go.

At the conference center, there had been a costly meal plan, but I hadn't had to worry about food. I've hired a cook and two kitchen workers for Wayfarer's Landing, and one of the White Rings who previously ran a restaurant has volunteered to take charge of planning the meals and running the kitchen. Two days before the retreat, she calls to say she has the flu. The same morning both of the kitchen workers quit before ever getting started.

So that the participants won't have to listen to me every session, I've always brought in as many resource speakers as possible: anyone I can beg, bribe, or coerce. The lineup for the first retreat is dazzling. Because of the publicity last year about the retreats, resource speakers from all over the country have offered their services. I've lined up a child-custody specialist from Miami, a financial planner from Cleveland, and the Native American founder of an ecumenical spiritual community in New Mexico. Not ten minutes after I've hired a replacement for one of the kitchen workers, the financial planner cancels on me.

As if that isn't enough, I have a nagging concern that overrides the endless details, cancellations, headaches, and frustrations, and it's all Dory's fault. Dory, in all of her whimsical, charming, but maddening weirdness, has drawn me into her circle, and I'm in a panic.

After the work started on Wayfarer's Landing the past fall, I held several meetings with Etta, Dory, and the White Rings to plan the upcoming calendar year, discussing how many retreats to hold, how often, who would do what and when. Once I agreed to schedule the first retreat for the weekend of the spring equinox in March, Dory started pestering me with another of her fanciful notions. Catching me off guard, she begged me to hold the Asunder Ceremony in the labyrinth at dusk, incorporating the pathways. Before she could finish her breathless speech, I shook my head, saying we'd have enough to do without trying to figure out a way to light up the labyrinth. It'd be great to have the ceremony there once we've had a few retreats and ironed out the kinks, but *not* at the first one.

Dory has never given up easily, so I should've been suspicious when she conceded so graciously. At our next meeting, the White Rings and Etta took up the cause, asking me to reconsider. They had worked out the logistical problems, so there was no need for me to worry. It wouldn't be that difficult to pull off, they said. I agreed, and when Dory, Etta, and the White Rings high-fived one another in triumph, I couldn't help but smile with them.

It wasn't just the logistics that made me so hesitant, as Dory and the others knew. The truth is, the Asunder Ceremony is the aspect of the retreats I've been determined to downplay. The ceremony has been a significant part from the beginning, but I never intended for it to be the main focus. When the articles came out about the retreats, and I was on talk shows and gave interviews, it was the ceremony that got them tagged as both innovative and controversial. I was appalled when a Birmingham newspaper began their coverage with the headline DIVORCE THERAPIST CASTS MARRIAGE ASUNDER WITH REVERSE WEDDING CEREMONY. I knew what would happen. Following the article, Etta was swamped with phone calls, and we had as many cancellations as inquiries from those intrigued by the idea. The editorial pages of the Birmingham paper quoted religious fanatics, predecessors of the letter that would make its appearance in *The Fairhoper* several months later. Even less-fanatical religious groups expressed distaste at the idea, because in most denominations, marriage and baptism were the only two sacred sacraments. Who did I think I was, outraged clergy demanded, to perform such a thing, mocking a holy ritual of the church? After the flurry died down, I determined to put the ceremony back into proper perspective.

I came up with the idea for the Asunder Ceremony while doing research on wedding customs for the first retreat. I found countless ceremonies having to do with getting married, from jumping the broom to stomping a glass, but none for getting *un*married. Rituals are a crucial part of all aspects of our lives, from momentous occasions such as religious observations, graduations, and holidays, to more everyday affairs such as birthdays and sporting events. One of the most ritualized parts of our lives is in the way a death is observed, with funerals or wakes or memorial services being so necessary for closure. Ritual is not merely important, I concluded, it's essential. No wonder we have so much trouble when a marriage ends. Marriage is one of the most important steps in everyone's lives, a celebration unlike any other. Kingdoms have been built; countries split; wars started; heads rolled; religions formed; dynasties established, all as a result of the rite of marriage. But where are the rituals that mark the end of a marriage? Signing papers in a lawyer's office hardly qualifies; neither does the whack of a judge's gavel. Many of my clients told me they made up their own ceremonies—usually unsavory things such as getting drunk, stoned, or laid. In response to what I saw as a real need in the process of recovery, I created a brief ritual for acknowledging the end of a marriage, called it the Asunder Ceremony, and added it to the first retreat.

Although the retreat participants are strongly urged to participate, the Asunder Ceremony isn't a requirement, despite the insinuations of the newspaper articles. Instead, it's the grand finale of the Saturday talks, workshops, and presentations. The ceremony is on the schedule right before folk dancing, which is the way we end Saturday evenings. At first I was surprised to see the participants who wept so profusely at the ceremony go on to dance with such great abandonment afterward. Then it hit me—but of course! How many weddings have I attended where everyone was dragged onto the dance floor, from toddlers to the very elderly? Nowadays a wedding is one of the few occasions where dancing is encouraged as a means of emotional release. Over time, the dancing after the ceremony became as much a part of it as the ritual itself.

⊱

Two days before the retreat finds me and Dory in my office at Wayfarer's Landing, finishing up some of the details before Friday afternoon, when the first participants arrive. The tension has caught up with me. "Shit, shit, shit!" I cry as I slam the receiver down after yet another kitchen worker quits. "Why did I *ever* think having my own retreat site was a good idea?"

Dory gives her throaty laugh. "Here's why it was a good idea," she says, straightening up a stack of handouts. "I'm no longer in danger of going bankrupt from sponsoring so many of the participants. Out here, the retreats will be more affordable."

I stare at her, guilt-stricken. "Oh, honey, I'm sorry. What a thoughtless remark! I never want to appear ungrateful for your generosity. Any time it gets to be too much, don't hesitate to say so."

She shakes her head. "Hell, it's mostly Son's money, since my business isn't breaking even yet. With more affordable retreats, though, I can help more folks. Oh! I have the perfect person to replace your financial planner."

"Who? I've called everyone I know, but at this late date——"

"Rye Ballenger," she replies, opening up another box of handouts.

"*Rye?* You're kidding."

"Not at all. It's what he used to do, remember? Before he went to law school. His undergraduate degree from Tulane was in finance. He'll be perfect."

"Oh, yeah, like he'd do it."

Dory looks at me slyly. "He'd do it for you, even though you broke his poor old heart."

"Christ, don't start that again. I most certainly didn't break his heart. Since you demanded all the juicy details about the night I told Rye that we should remain friends, then you know he was very gracious about it."

"Of course he was, because that's the way Rye is," Dory says, and her eyes go soft. "He was still being gracious when he came over to cry on my shoulder, too, but I could tell how hurt he was."

"That's not true!" I insist. "I explained to Rye how I loved him too much to make him a substitute for Mack, which was what I'd been doing. I wouldn't be surprised if he wasn't secretly relieved that we've decided to stay friends instead of becoming lovers. Rye's been single for so long, he didn't really want things to change, is what I think."

"Yeah, right," Dory says with a hoot. "You may be a hotshot therapist, honey, but you're as bad as the rest of us about believing what you want to."

I'm not about to go there. "A session on financial planning is such an essential part of the retreats that I'm desperate. If you think Rye will do it, I'll ask him."

She shrugs lightly. "You don't have to. I already have."

"Dory!" Putting my forehead on the table, I sigh. "God, I'm so exhausted. But what would I do without you? In a matter of seconds, you took care of one of my main concerns. I never would've come up with Rye, not in a million years."

Her look is unbearably smug. "What would you do without me? I'll tell you: You'd have the most serious and down-in-the-mouth retreats imaginable, that's what. Oh, sure, the poor participants would come away with tons of new information—the ones who stayed awake long enough to get it, that is. Without my magic touch, the retreats would be duller than dishwater."

"You know, one thing I've never worried about was your lack of self-esteem."

She asks, "Who talked you into adding the folk dancing, pray tell? The first time Rye took you dancing after Mack died, you came home raving about how it made you forget your grief and all that stuff. Then why don't you add dancing to the retreats, says I? How did Clare respond? She said it couldn't be done. Now, I ask you—what's the favorite part of the retreats for everyone?"

"Folk dancing," I mutter reluctantly. "I know where you're going with this, by the way."

"Of course you do," she cries gleefully. "I thought talking you into having the first retreat on the weekend of the spring equinox was difficult. Ha! I had to *force* you to agree to holding the ceremony at the labyrinth, and you're still worried about it, aren't you?"

"No, I'm not. It just seems like more trouble than it's worth."

"When it turns out to be the most memorable part of the whole weekend, I'm going to gloat and rub it in."

"So unlike the Dory I know and love," I say dryly.

"You're being your usual uptight, obsessive self, but I'm thrilled. The women lucky enough to attend this retreat will have a unique way of acknowledging the end of an old life and the rebirth of a new one." Her face lights up as she prattles on and on about the symbolism of the spring equinox as a traditional time of passage from darkness and cold to warmth and light. When she says she cannot wait to share the legend with the women before the ceremony, I stop what I'm doing.

"That story is limited to your orientation talk on Friday afternoon,

Dory," I say sternly. "The ceremony's intended as a serious ritual, and I don't want to hear all that crap about the goddess and frozen birds and stuff, you hear me?"

While reading up on the equinox, Dory found a legend about Eostre and the equinox, and asked me if she could share it with the retreat participants in her welcoming remarks as head of the White Rings. Of course, I told her; I wasn't about to dictate what she could or couldn't say in her remarks. Eostre was an ancient Saxon goddess whose life was saved by a bird, of all things. The bird's wings had been frozen in winter only to thaw on the vernal equinox, one of the two days of the year when the length of night and day are equal. The wings thawed just in the nick of time for the bird to swoop down and rescue the goddess, naturally. The problem was, Dory was fuzzy about details, and I wasn't sure what Eostre was rescued *from*. I wouldn't put it past her to embellish the story so it would end up being an evil tyrant of a husband. Now Dory has gotten Zoe Catherine fascinated with the legend, and Zoe's been going through her books trying to find out what kind of bird it was. I'd harbored a hope that Zoe might help out with the retreats, thinking it'd be good for her, but she pooh-poohed the idea, insisting she'll be hiding in her cabin until the last participant leaves. Hand it to Dory; her equinox story has been the first time Zoe has shown much interest in what will be going on right across from her.

The way Dory keeps watching me, I can tell something's up, so I put down my pen to eye her warily. "Okay, Isadora. You can't fool your oldest and dearest. Whatever it is you're trying to get up the nerve to ask me, the answer is no."

"I *knew* that was what you'd say, so I've waited until two days before the retreat to ask. I've had dozens of e-mails from former participants who weren't ready for the Asunder Ceremony last time we had a retreat. Now they're begging to come to the ceremony. They *need* to. On behalf of the White Rings, I'd like to respectfully ask that you allow them to attend."

I argue; Dory pleads; then we compromise. It's unmanageable, I tell her: We aren't prepared for a large turnout should we have one. At last I agree to include a select few from previous retreats. Spurred on, Dory keeps at it until I hear myself agreeing to an even bolder proposal. A couple of times a year, we'll have an expanded ceremony at the labyrinth and allow the return of former participants who hadn't been ready before. But not necessarily, I warn her, on a day of the equinox or solstice.

Breathless with victory, Dory jumps to her feet, leans over my desk, and throws both arms around my neck, kissing my cheek. "See how much more agreeable you are now that you're getting some?"

My face flames as I sputter, "*Dory!* Where did you get such a ridiculous idea?"

"Oh, bull. I can tell by looking at you. Abstinence made you tense and uptight and grumpy. For the past couple of days, you've been loose and congenial and agreeable. Not to mention how great you look, with your face all aglow."

"If getting laid was all it took to make your face glow, you'd put Alabama Power out of business," I retort.

Oblivious, Dory tilts her head to the side, her cat eyes dreamy. "I wasn't sure who'd get into your bed first, Lex or Rye. But I was putting my money on Lex, he's so take-charge and masterful. I figured if Rye was such a wimp that he'd let you put him off all these years, then he didn't deserve any. For a while it looked like Lex was going to lose out, though, letting that ex of his jerk him around. About a week ago, I thought for sure Rye would make it to the finish line first. I was buying some garden supplies, and I happened to see Rye coming out of the Ralph Lauren store with a big package. I pulled over to ask him what he'd bought, and he had a two-hundred-dollar set of sheets! On the way home, I stopped by the marina to warn Lex that he'd better get off his ass before Rye got home with those sheets."

"Dory, you didn't!" Horrified, I raise my hands to my burning cheeks.

"Did, too. I've known all along how Lex felt about you. At my anniversary party last fall? I watched his face while you and Rye were dancing, looking like you were about to do it right there on the dance floor."

"Oh, pooh. Rye and I have always danced like that."

"No doubt the passion of the dance could've carried over elsewhere, if you'd let it," she continues with the same dreamy look. "Rye's loss is Lex's gain, though I do feel really bad for Rye. That night I felt worse for Lex, who was claiming to be mad at you yet unable to stop looking at you. Elinor saw it, too. Got so pissed that she grabbed him and left, remember?"

"I didn't miss her," I say. "Now, if you don't mind, I have work to do."

"When I went by the marina last week, I told Lex that he *had* to decide between you and Elinor, or Rye would be putting those fancy sheets of his to use. Probably that very night, the way things were going with the two of you at the time. It's good that something led me to talk to Lex. At first he was scowling like a thundercloud, but finally he asked me if the rumors were true about you and Rye having an affair. I told him that you never confided in me, but if they weren't true, it was only a matter of time. A few days later, he told Elinor to go to hell, then he came over to your house on a dark and stormy night, didn't he? Jesus, that's so romantic!"

"Who told you about that night?" I certainly didn't, for obvious reasons.

Dory smiles mysteriously. "I have my sources. Plus, the next morning I rode by your house to make sure his Jeep was still in the same spot."

I stare at her, aghast. "You're not only a matchmaker, you're a voyeur. Get out of here and leave me alone. Can't you see I'm busy?"

Laughing, Dory prisses out the door, giving me a little wave before leaving. With a sigh, I've gone back to my paperwork when she opens the door again and sticks her head in. "Hey—maybe you and Lex can have a double wedding with Zoe and Cooter."

"Zoe has told Cooter a million times she's not getting married, and I have no intention of doing so, either."

"Of marrying Cooter? God, I hope not. Doubt Zoe would appreciate it."

"Very funny. You know what I mean."

Leaning against the door, Dory studies me for a long moment, her eyes soft. "Oh, honey. You've taken the first step, and I couldn't be more pleased. But you still have a long way to go, don't you?"

"Oh, God, what now?" I groan.

"How long will it be before you let go of Mack?"

Flustered, I drop my pen and, grabbing for it, scatter the stack of papers I'm working on. Once I've rearranged everything, I look at Dory in exasperation. "That's insane! I let go of Mack years ago. Not that I had a choice, since he let go of me first, wouldn't you say?"

She shakes her head with a sad smile. "No, I wouldn't. Because the way I see it, you still belong to Mack. You're as married to him now as you ever were. And that suits you fine, doesn't it?"

"Would you like to sit behind this desk, Madame Freud?" I snap peevishly.

"Mack did quite a number on you, didn't he, Clare? Like he always said he'd do, he saw to it that you couldn't love again. Leaving you the way he did, he made sure you'd never be able to tell him goodbye."

I close my eyes wearily, but Dory slams the door and is gone before I can come up with a good retort.

≫

The day of the retreat dawns gray and ominously dreary, and I moan when I open my eyes. Rolling over to look out the window next to my bed, I send up a whispered prayer: "Please, Lord. If you could hold off the rain for a few days, I'll owe you one, though I don't have any business asking you anything."

Since I don't expect an answer, I jump to hear a deep voice, "You can say that again." Turning my head, I say, "You scared me to death. I thought the Lord God Almighty was speaking."

Lex grunts lazily and opens one eye to peer at me. "Sounds right to me."

His arm lays heavily on my waist, and I snuggle under his shoulder. "I'm not used to having anyone answer me when I talk to myself."

With a chuckle, he says, "Thought you were talking to the Lord."

"I was, but since I've been living alone, I've taken to talking to myself, too. Don't tell anybody, though," I add, putting a finger over his lips.

Eyes closed, he nibbles my fingers. "Let's sleep all morning."

"Can't. You've already disrupted my routine. Ordinarily I'd have been up for several minutes by now." But I close my eyes, too, unwilling to move. It's easy to leap from a cold and lonely bed you occupy alone, and much harder to leave a warm, cozy shared one.

"You don't have to go to the Landing till later," Lex reminds me, his voice muffled by his pillow. "And my dockmaster's running the marina. Another hour, then I'll make you a Yankee breakfast."

"You promise not to let me sleep longer than an hour?"

"Promise."

"You're on."

True to his word, an hour later, I awake to feel Lex nuzzling the back of my neck, his leg thrown over mine. In sleep we ended up spoon-style, with me curved snugly against him. Opening an eye, I say, "Cheater. That's not keeping your promise."

"You've obviously never had a Yankee breakfast," he murmurs, and I laugh.

"Get off me. I knew when I let you stay last night, I was asking for trouble."

"Can't believe you haven't kicked me out yet. You had my ass out of here before dawn yesterday." With his hands gripping my shoulders, he presses his mouth up and down my spine, and I shiver deliciously, hugging my pillow.

"Not soon enough. Dory saw your Jeep here," I tell him.

"I owe Dory. She came by the marina and made me see I was about to lose you if I didn't let go of my pride and tell you how I felt about you. Even worse, I was going to end up with Elinor."

"Mmm. Oh, God, that feels *so* good. Shut up so you can keep doing what you're doing. Elinor's loss, is all I can say. Dory's, too. My theory is, she wishes she could be where I am right now."

Lex lays his forehead against my back to laugh his marvelous laugh. "Honey, I may be a stud muffin, but don't think I could handle you and Dory both."

I laugh, too, then say, "If I survive the retreat, which is not looking good, we've got to talk, okay? Next week, maybe. I'll find a time."

Lex falls back on his pillow, releasing me, and I sigh in disappointment. I'm still clutching my pillow tight, eyes closed and gluey with sleep. "You'll never find that spot again," I complain.

"If I don't, it won't be for a lack of trying."

"Is that a promise?"

"Let's resume the search on Sunday, as soon as the retreat's over," he says lazily. "But first, I'll make us some crab cakes like I did that time last fall. Have them waiting when you get home. Sound good?"

"You're well on your way to spoiling me. I need to get up and get going but can't seem to wake up. It's your fault. If you could patent whatever you were doing to my back, you'd retire an extremely wealthy man."

"I'll do anything if we don't have to have that damned talk of yours."

"Lex!" That wakes me up. With an exasperated sigh, I turn over and raise up on my elbow to look over at him. "What is it with you men and talking?"

"It's because of the stuff women want to talk about. Regular women are bad enough, but a woman therapist is a double whammy."

It's impossible to maintain a stern frown, no matter how hard I try. "I have a feeling you're going to drive me crazy before this is over."

He looks at me in alarm. "I don't like that kind of talk."

"Jesus!" I laugh, giving his arm a playful shake. "You don't like *any* kind of talk."

"Let's never say a word to each other again, okay?"

I study him curiously, drawing circles with my fingertips on his bare chest. "Just what is it that you're so afraid to talk about?"

He thinks about it, then says, "Everything."

"Besides that?"

With a heavy sigh, he looks up at the ceiling, then puts his hands behind his head. "Last time we had one of your little talks, you threw me over, gave me all that bullshit about just wanting to be friends."

Laying a hand on his chest, I wait until his eyes meet mine to say, "Come on, Lex. We've been in bed together for the last two nights. Seems to me we've gone way beyond friendship. That's what I wanted to talk about, actually. I'd love it if you'd move in here." When he opens his mouth, I put my fingers to his lips. "Don't say anything now, but think about it, okay?"

When he averts his eyes from mine, staring at the ceiling again, I pull my hand away. After a long silence, Lex says, "I don't have to think about it. I don't like being here."

Indignant, I say, "Oh, really? Sure had me fooled."

"We need to get a place of our own. Here, I'm in Mack's bed, with Mack's wife. It feels like you're cheating on him with me."

I stare at him in astonishment. "That's the most ridiculous thing I've ever heard." Even as I say it, though, I hear an echo of Rye's words, the night I felt so lost and lonely that I called him late, in the dark.

When Lex won't look at me, I realize that he's perfectly serious. As he told me once, I'd know when he was. "Okay, I know what you're saying," I say with a sigh. "But I'm not trying to make you into a replacement for him, I swear. Mack's gone, and he's not coming back. He's not out of town on a business trip, and he's not my ex who's liable to show up one day. It's true, this is the room, and the bed, that I shared with him. But I've put away all his stuff, so it's not as if there are pictures of him everywhere, staring at us together. I'm not Mack's wife, and I haven't been for a long time. You're just being paranoid."

"Then why do I feel like he's in the house with us?"

"I don't know. But that's something you have to work out. It's your imagination, not mine. It's taken me a while, I'll admit, but I've finally let go of Mack."

"You may be able to figure everybody else out, Doctor Lady, but you sure don't know much about yourself, do you?" Lex says with a laugh.

With an abrupt movement, I sling my legs over the side of the bed and throw on my robe. "I've got to get going," I say curtly, my face burning. "We can discuss this another time."

I glance his way, and he searches my face before saying in a quiet voice, "I'm not looking for a brief fling, Clare. Or a fling of any kind. They're not hard to come by these days, if that's all I wanted. I'm a damn dope, I know, but I've fallen in love with you. Wish I hadn't, but there it is. If I'm wasting my time, you need to tell me, and I'm out of here."

Turning my back to him, I rub my face wearily. "Oh God, don't do this. It's taken me so long to get this far. Please don't ask more of me than I can give you at this point."

He pushes out of the bed and heads to the bathroom without looking back. In exasperation, I flop back on my pillows, flinging my arms out. When Lex comes out of the bathroom, he's dressed and buttoning his shirt, glowering at me.

"So this is the way it's going to be," I say, my voice cold and hard as a stone. "Because I'm not ready to give you what you're demanding, you're going to throw it all away. Well, fine, then. Fine! But don't you dare blame it on me. It's your choice, not mine."

"You strung Rye along for years," he says harshly. "But I'm not him. Yeah, I teased you about him, but the truth is, I felt sorry for the poor bastard. Know why? I let Elinor do the same to me. It kills something in you, and I'm not about to do it again."

"No one's asking you to!" I shout. "But you're demanding that I give you something that I'm not ready to—"

Lex stops me in midsentence by crossing the room, grabbing my shoulders roughly, and pulling me up from the bed, then kissing me, hard. When I can get my breath, I stare at him, wide-eyed. "Damn, Rhett Butler. Sweep a girl off her feet, why don't you?"

"Surprised you, didn't I? And I sure as hell shut your mouth. Bet pretty boy never did anything like that."

My arms around his neck, I say into his ear, "I take it back. You're already driving me crazy."

He pulls away from me, runs his hand through his hair, and snaps his Red Sox cap on. "I may not have all your degrees, Clare, but here's one thing I know. You're clinging to Mack, and this house he fixed up for you, because you're scared to let go of him. You'd never admit it, but you're scared shitless to fall in love again."

"Oh, bull. You don't know what you're talking about, Mr. Know-it-all," I retort.

"Is that right? Well, you have a chance to find out. You're about to go to a hotshot recovery retreat, so why don't you practice what you preach? You can tell everybody else how to heal their broken hearts, but you haven't done much for your own, have you?" Standing with his hands on his hips, Lex stares down at me before turning to go. He pauses when he opens the door, and looks over his shoulder. "Call me when the retreat's over. If you pay any attention to what's going on around you, maybe you can figure out what you want. When you do, let me know."

He leaves me aghast, and closes the door to the bedroom with such a bang that I jump. I long to yell after him, to tell him that he'd better not sit by the phone waiting for my call. Who the hell does he think he is, coming here and loving me like he's done these last nights, then walking out like that? My eyes fill with tears, and I fling off my robe as I head for the shower. How dare Lex say I haven't let go of Mack! I haven't thought of Mack a single time these last two nights Lex and I have been together, which have been satisfying in a way I never experienced with Mack. With him, there was such an intensity that I was consumed by it, lost in it. The passion I felt for Mack was like a tidal wave that swept me helplessly into a dark and bottomless ocean. With Lex, the passion is there, but it's different. It's fiery but also sweet, and it warms me utterly and completely, like the fire he built for me after the storm. Why can't that be enough for him?

I step into the shower, but it's not my usual brisk, invigorating one. Instead, I try to make it hot and strong enough to ease the tightness of my throat and a weary sadness that has taken hold of me.

Chapter Seventeen

❧   ❧   ❧   ❧   ❧

Before my drive out to the Landing, I stop by Haley's and find her alone. It's the beginning of spring break, and she's taken a half day off from school to get Abbie and Zach's suitcases and toys packed up. As soon as Austin can get away, he's picking up the kids and heading for Huntsville, where they'll spend a week with his parents. Haley was in a quandary, disgusted at Austin because he hadn't told his parents that he was leaving her for another woman. When they called to express their sorrow and regret over the divorce, she longed to tell them but restrained herself. "Austin's dad will *kill* him when he finds out," she bemoaned in disgust. "And I wanted to tell him so bad! How come doing the right thing doesn't feel nearly as good as retribution?"

During spring break, Haley will be alone in a way she hasn't been before. The kids will be gone; I was considering going away for a few days; and Jasmine and Tommy are celebrating their engagement with a trip to New Orleans. As I'd hoped, Tommy's promotion to dockmaster went a long way in helping her family come around. It's also helped that Jasmine has kept her big mouth shut and been more sensitive to her dad's concerns about interracial marriage. Etta tells me that R.J. is still not keen on the idea, but he's getting used to it. Haley's having to get used to it as well. The loneliness that follows a divorce has shocked her with its ferocity, and the week of spring break is a test. Turning down invitations from friends to go to the beach, she insists she's got to learn to be alone, and by God, the upcoming week will be a true test.

"Why don't you come with me this weekend?" I ask her when I arrive. "We can share the sofa bed in my office. Or you could stay with Gramma Zoe and sit in on the parts of the retreat that interest you."

It distresses me to find her going through her wedding pictures. A half-filled box is nearby; she's been packing away the photo albums from their wedding but stopped to look through them one last time. I try to lighten her mood by telling her of a client who took her wedding photos and cut off the head of the groom in every picture, then placed them back in the albums, and Haley smiles wanly. More evidence of the ups and downs: Last time I was here, I found her writing in the journal she's kept since Austin left, which I'd urged her to do as a crucial part of the healing process. Reading a section to me, she was laughing and lighthearted, and my throat tightened as I watched her. When she first came to live with Mack and me, she was a shy, jumpy young girl with a hang-dog expression and a poor self-image. At times during the breakup, I've seen reflections of that girl for the first time in years, and it worries me.

When Haley doesn't respond to my suggestion about coming to the retreat, I try another tactic. "You could sign the participants' copies of *The Lighter Side of Divorce* now that it's out in print."

Her smile is bitter. "I'm letting Jasmine do all that, because none of it seems funny anymore. Can't imagine why, can you?"

"Oh, sweetheart, it doesn't seem like it now, but you'll be happy again one day, I swear. And it will sneak up on you when you're least expecting it."

She shrugs. "I need a little more time before I can think like that."

"I know you do, and I'm not going to push you about the retreats. You'll know when you're ready."

She chews her bottom lip, pensive. "I did tell Dory that I'd come out tomorrow evening to watch the ceremony at the labyrinth. Is that okay? I mean, I'll stay out of everybody's way."

I hesitate, then choose my words carefully. "It's okay as long as you listen to me instead of Dory about the way the ceremony affects the participants. It's difficult to watch, especially for someone who's where you are in the process. I don't object to your coming, but it's liable to be harder than you think."

"Oh, I understand that. Main reason Dory wants me there is for something Gramma Zoe has planned. Oops—I don't think I'm supposed to tell you that."

"Oh, God, why does that make my blood run cold? Your gramma Zoe and Jasmine made a dangerous combination, but Zoe and Dory might be even worse. And guess who's the common denominator in both?" We smile at each other, and I get to my feet to give her a goodbye hug. "Look what time it is! I've got to run."

She stops me at the door with a sly grin, and I see a spark of the old Haley for the first time since I arrived. "Mom? Dory told me you and Lex were seeing a lot of each other now."

I turn away quickly so she won't see my expression. "I'm sure whatever Dory told you wasn't something one wants to hear about one's mother."

Haley laughs lightly. "Don't worry, I wouldn't let her tell me the good parts. I've teased you about him in the past, but I couldn't be more pleased. You've had a rough time since Daddy died, and you deserve a little happiness."

"I dreaded telling you," I admit, "since you love Rye so much."

Her response surprises me. "And I know that you do, too. But he would always remind you of Daddy, wouldn't he?"

I nod and say, "And the sad thing is, it's not Rye's fault. Guess Dory would say it wasn't meant to be."

"You've been so mysterious about being gone during spring break," she says, grinning. "Now I know why. You're going away with Lex, aren't you?"

"We'd planned to, but . . . I'm not sure now." Instead of telling her of Lex's ultimatum, I give her another quick hug and say, "I'll see you tomorrow evening, okay?"

She shrugs and gives me a small smile. "I'll be there, but you might not see me. Most likely I'll be hiding behind one of the oak trees."

≫

The dreary clouds have lifted; the sun is out; and the day is suddenly one of heart-stopping, dazzling perfection. When I park my car behind the retreat center at Wayfarer's Landing, recalling my early-morning prayer humbles me and fills me with an awed gratitude, and not just for the weather. Since the day I met with George Johnson, this place has undergone miraculous transformation. The newly redone building has an inviting ambiance that no one could've put into it; it had to spring from the Landing itself: the protective palms standing sentinel, the oaks waving welcome banners of moss, and the caressing breezes of Folly Creek. Dory's work in the gardens is the perfect touch: The hundreds of azalea plants she set out have exploded into scarlet blooms, and their brilliance is a lovely contrast to the greens and browns and silver-grays of the wetlands. Impulsively I hop out of the car, leaving all my material inside for the time being, and take off. Before being assaulted by the demands of the weekend, I need to seek out a quiet place for a few minutes of reflection. Fortunately no one else is in sight. Zoe's pickup is parked in its usual place by one of the outbuildings, but there's no telling where she is.

I'm not sure where my wanderings will take me; I'm thinking

vaguely of the labyrinth, which I've yet to walk. But I pause at the edge of the creek instead. Putting up a hand to shield my face, I walk out on the weather-beaten old dock and scan the distance for Zoe, fishing in one of her canoes. Beneath me, in a ribbon stretching all the way to the dark swamp on the other bank, the black-green waters of Folly Creek ripple and shimmer in the sun. A breeze stirs the yellow-tipped marshes, pauses to give my face a caress, then moves on to playfully rattle the brittle brown fronds of the palms on the shoreline. After throwing my arms wide in a salute of sheer joy, I sink down to sit on the sun-warmed wood of the dock, worn as smooth as marble. Leaning against a post, I think it's only fitting that the retreat center is now here; the Landing has always been a sanctuary for the wounded. I can't imagine the retreat center being anywhere else. A dozen or so of Zoe's ducks are floating atop the undulating rolls of the creek without a single quack to disturb the late-morning stillness. I watch them bobble one by one under the sun-sparkled water, then reappear to shake themselves off. It's unusually quiet on the creek, except for the hum of insects and the plop or splash of a fish and the distant rustle of wings and cooing and squawks from Zoe's aviaries. I close my eyes to feel the delicious warmth of the sun on my face, savoring the almost erotic sensation. With a deep breath, I inhale the briny smell of the creek, fish and fern and swamp lilies and rich black mud. In spite of having slept in this morning, I would find it easy to doze off, and I'm dangerously close to doing so. I'm determined not to think about Lex and the comfort I found nestled in his arms; nor am I ready to explore the desolation I felt when he yanked that comfort away. Instead, I allow myself to doze until I feel a peck-peck-peck on the hand I've let slide off my lap in my stupor.

Any other day I would've jumped up or even shrieked in fear; but, drunk with sunlight, I open my eyes halfway and peer at my

attacker. I'm surprised to see one of the mousy brown peahens regarding me with beady eyes, her head with its little tufted crown
cocked curiously to the side. "Catherine the Great," I murmur.
"What are you doing, old girl?"

The peahen is motionless except for the swaying of her head,
and I watch in surprise as she bends forward to peck at my hand
again. She doesn't hurt me, and I wonder what it could be on my
hand that attracts her. Perhaps it's the lingering scent of the apple I
had on my drive out here, or even my peach-scented hand lotion.
I've seen Zoe feed them dried fruit enough to know they love the
taste.

"You hungry?" I ask her, wriggling my fingers her way. Hoping
no one's around to see me talking to a peahen, I pull myself up,
brushing the dirt from the dock off my linen pants and matching
jacket. So much for the professional look I strive for on the first day
of the retreat. Everyone else will be in sweats or jeans, anyway, so
it matters only to me.

I should ignore Catherine the Great—getting up to feed her will
spoil her even more—but she's watching me with her funny little
eyes so hopefully, or so I tell myself, that I can't resist. "Come on,
Your Majesty," I say. "If you won't tell on me, I'll sneak into Zoe's
kitchen and get you some fruit, okay?"

But Catherine the Great doesn't follow me when we reach the
side of Zoe's house and I start toward the door off the kitchen. Instead, she startles me by spreading her mottled brown wings and
beating them heavily, then rising at a sharp angle to glide off toward
the back of the house, where the other peafowl roost in the tall trees
clustered there, behind the pens and aviaries. I stand with my hands
on my hips and watch her, bemused. If she doesn't want food, what,
then? If it weren't so ludicrous, I'd think she meant for me to come
with her. Glancing over my shoulder to make sure no volunteers
have arrived at the retreat center to catch me in such a flight of

fancy, I shrug and take off after the peahen. As soon as I reach the back of the house and pass the numerous cages—which are quieter now, almost ominously so—I come to the clearing where a copse of mimosa, dogwood, and redbud trees provides the roosts for the peacocks. With a gasp, I see immediately why I've been summoned, and I take off running.

Under a huge, spreading mimosa, Zoe is down on her knees, bent over the long, inert body of Genghis Khan. With a loud clamor of rapid wingbeats, Catherine the Great lands gracefully near them, cocking her head from side to side as she regards the lifeless form of her mate. Kneeling next to Zoe, I place a hand on her shoulder. "Oh, God. Is he dead?" It's a stupid question: His stare is sightless, and his white four-pronged feet are stiff and tightly furled under him.

Rather than answering me, Zoe reaches down and strokes the back of Genghis's head behind the magnificent crown, letting her fingers trace a trail down his long curved back. "Poor old thing," she mutters. "Guess he was just plumb worn out."

"Had he been sick?" I ask inanely, and Zoe wipes her eyes with the back of her free hand while she rubs Genghis with the other.

"He had a weak heart, but it was mainly old age," she says with a sniff. She raises her head and looks at me for the first time, her black eyes dull with grief. Then she inclines her head toward the woods. "I'd been in there working on . . . something for the retreat, and I heard Catherine the Great carrying on like everything. I didn't think much about it, just figured her and Genghis were fighting again. Had to get all my stuff put up before I could come see what was going on, and that took a while."

"It must've been before I arrived, because I noticed how quiet everything was when I got here," I tell her. "Now that I think of it, it's never been so quiet." I don't add that only a few seconds ago, the quiet turned ominous, and I felt a shiver of dread.

Zoe nods. "That's what made me suspicious, how quiet all the birds got after Catherine went on like she did. Usually when one of them screeches, every blame one of them will join in. The next thing I know, here comes Catherine, flying around looking for me. That's when I knew for sure that something was wrong. She's so blame fat and lazy she don't ever fly, except to follow Genghis to roost at night."

"That's right," I say. "I knew something was even odder than her coming after me and pecking my hand. I've never seen her fly before, not even to roost. It's weird, isn't it?"

"Naw, not really. Birds know things. How come they got so quiet when Genghis died? They all knew. I can promise you that, they all knew." Zoe lowers her head to look at Genghis again. "Poor old thing," she repeats, and now she's tenderly stroking the great long sweep of tail feathers lying in a train behind him.

"You're really going to miss him." I slip an arm around her and lean my head to touch hers. "He's been with you forever, hasn't he?"

"Yep, he sure has, since I came out here. I'll miss this old fellow for sure," she says with a nod. "The place won't be the same without Genghis." She turns to look at Catherine the Great, who stands frozen in the same place, still as a statue except for the curious movement of her head, side to side. She's staring at Genghis, but she won't come any closer. It's as though she's allowing Zoe her time to say goodbye to him. "We're all gonna miss Genghis, ain't we, old girl?" Zoe says to the peahen.

We're silent as we look down at the body of Genghis. I give Zoe a squeeze and say gently, "What do you need me to do?"

She sighs wearily. For the first time since I've known her, she looks old and tired, and her voice is shaky. "Reckon you can call Cooter for me, if you don't mind. I'd 'preciate it if you'd do that. Ask him if he'll come out here and help me bury this old fellow, okay?"

I get to my feet but keep my hand on her shoulder. "I'll have to go to your house or the retreat center, since I left my cell in the car. But I'll run and make the call, then come back and stay with you till Cooter gets here, okay?"

Zoe looks up at me and shakes her head, her eyes bright and watery. She hasn't cried, and knowing Zoe, she won't. She'll hold her grief inside, as she always does. "No, ma'am," she says sharply. "You've got a retreat to run, and you've got no business fooling with a silly old woman. Go on to your office to call Cooter, and stay there, you hear me?" When I open my mouth to protest, she wags a finger at me. "Hush up and listen to me," she says in a firm voice. "You know how Cooter carries on. When he gets here, he's liable to cry like a baby. He loved old Genghis, even though the two of them fought all the time, and Cooter got on Genghis's nerves so bad. You might not think this of Cooter, but he's a lot more sensitive than he acts. So he wouldn't want you to see him grieving over Genghis. You understand what I'm saying, don't you?"

"I do, but I'll be glad to stay with you, or to help you and Cooter bury—"

But Zoe won't let me finish, waving me away furiously. "Go on, now. I mean it!"

It hits me that it's not Cooter's grief she's concerned about. I lean over and kiss the top of her head, then leave her to her silent mourning. When I reach the still-silent aviaries, I pick up my pace, hurrying to call Cooter so she won't be alone. When I turn to look back, Zoe hasn't moved from her pose, kneeling over Genghis and petting his lifeless body. The stillness is shattered by a sound that sends a shiver down my spine: Catherine the Great's unearthly scream, shrill and piercing and, somehow, heartbreaking. This time her cry stirs up the other peafowl, and they join her, the unnatural silence of the morning broken by an unmelodic chorus of raucous bird cries, echoing over and over through the woods and the swamp lands beyond the creek.

❧

Late Saturday afternoon, on the day of the spring equinox, they begin to arrive. After a light, early supper alone, I'm in my office, having turned the program over to a yoga instructor from Gulfport who's leading a session on relaxation techniques. From the window, I see what looks like dozens of cars, more than the meager parking spaces we've provided can possibly hold. I leave the office as quietly as possible to skirt behind the group of women in the main meeting room, trying not to disturb them. They're sitting cross-legged on floor cushions, eyes closed and humming along with the instructor, and they wouldn't notice me if I were an elephant charging through the room. On the porch, I go to Etta, who's setting up a table with the hot cider we normally serve before dinner in lieu of cocktails; we call it the cider-and-sunset hour. This evening it is coming after dinner and following the yoga session, while the women watch the sunset and wait for dusk. Having to alter our orderly schedule for the ceremony at the labyrinth has me in a dither. Everything went so beautifully yesterday that I keep expecting the ax to fall today.

"Etta!" I screech. "Are these people who I think they are?" Evidently the arriving cars belong to the former participants whom Dory talked me into allowing to attend the Asunder Ceremony, and they're arriving in droves.

Etta nods, beaming. "Yep. Told you everybody would want to be here for this."

"And I told you and Dory it'd be okay for a few of them to return, but we couldn't handle this kind of crowd! What are we going to do?" Fighting a rising panic, I try to keep my voice from sounding so shrill, but not very successfully.

"It's all taken care of." Etta is calm as a clam. "Look, if you don't believe me."

Following the direction of her pointing finger, I see that someone is directing traffic, instructing the drivers to park along the
road leading into the Landing, since the parking area around our
building has filled up. Shading my eyes, I ask, "Who is that?"

She laughs and rolls her eyes. "Put your glasses on, Clare. It's
Son Rodgers."

"Son! But where is Dory?" Yesterday the White Rings spent
hours filling hundreds of brown paper sacks with sand and candles,
which will be used to line the pathway through the woods leading
to the labyrinth. Since all of the White Rings have assigned chores
at the retreat, Dory brought in Son for the task of placing the sacks
on the path, which has taken him all afternoon. And now she has
him directing traffic. Laughing, I told her if she's not careful, she'll
turn Son into a decent human being yet.

Again Etta points, and I see a slim figure in the distance whom
I assume is Dory. "We have it all worked out," Etta says serenely.
"We figured the former participants would start arriving about this
time, and what would we do with them while we were finishing our
supper? Well, since Zoe Catherine wasn't able to, Dory's taking
them through the nature preserve while we're getting set up here.
Then everyone will join us on the porch for the cider. After that,
time for the ceremony."

I nod, recalling that Dory had told me the plan already. She'd finally gotten Zoe involved by agreeing to show the participants
around the nature preserve, but since the death of Genghis, Zoe
has disappeared. She'll probably stay hidden away in her cabin or
on the creek until the retreat is over tomorrow. None of us has seen
her, at the nature preserve or anywhere else.

"Okay, okay!" I cry, throwing my hands up. "You women are
phenomenal as usual, and I'm properly chastised." Glancing at my
watch to avoid Etta's gloating look, I say, "Let's ring the bell—
time for the cider!"

The plan is, I'm to meet Dory at the labyrinth right after the cider-and-sunset hour while Etta and the White Rings are assembling everyone in preparation for the ceremony. I make my way anxiously, barely glancing at the candles burning in their paper sacks and lining the pathway through the woods. Except from a distance, I haven't seen Dory all day; everything has been so hectic. I'm not sure why Dory and the White Rings insisted on having the ceremony at dusk, and I don't dare ask, afraid it might have something to do with the equinox or the goddess or the bird with the frozen wings.

When I arrive at the labyrinth, Dory is placing a little twig chair of Zoe's under one of the oak trees, and I assume it's where she's seating Margo. A classical guitarist, Margo Slaton plays background music for the Asunder Ceremony. Hearing me approach, Dory puts down the chair, then heads my way. Seeing her outfit, I cry, "Dory! What on earth do you have on?"

Holding her arms out, she prances around and models the long white tunic of loosely woven material that she's wearing over her jeans and T-shirt. "It's my equinox ceremonial dress," she says, eyes glittering. "I made one for each of the White Rings."

"Oh, no." I groan. "Please tell me you didn't! You look like an extra in *The Lord of the Rings*."

Dory throws her arms around me and kisses my cheek, hugging me hard. "And you look like you're going to your execution! I swear, you'll never change, will you? Still the same uptight nerd you've always been."

"And you're the same weirdo," I say, "with your crazy magic circles and symbols and crap. Did you see how many folks we have? How are we going to handle this?"

Repeating Etta's speech about having everything under control, Dory takes my arm and drags me to a low twig table that came from Zoe's yard, which she's placed near the opening of the labyrinth. "Okay," she commands, standing me in place as though I'm a mannequin. "You and I will be here. You stand by the table, and I'm gonna sit on this little stool, see? Sorry you'll have to stand the whole time, but no one will be able to hear you otherwise."

When I see the arrangement on the table, my hand goes to my throat, and I feel the unexpected sting of tears behind my eyes. "Well, we know where those came from, don't we?" I say, and Dory nods. The wedding candle we use is a huge white pillar, and Dory usually surrounds it with flowers from her gardens. Today, though, she's woven a small strand of ivy around it, which is all it needs because it's centered on a spectacular spray of peacock feathers.

"I've never seen anything so lovely," she says, "but looks like it will be Zoe's only contribution to the retreat. She'd worked so hard to present something else, but she's hidden herself away grieving for Genghis."

"This is more than enough."

"I know, but Zoe had her heart set on the other thing because it was to be her gift to you. Oh, well," she adds with a shrug. "I told her that Genghis's donation would be more than enough. Now, wait here. I'll go to the porch and tell everyone we're ready, okay?"

I nod, nervous and jumpy again, and Dory gives me an encouraging hug before heading down the pathway to fetch the others. Too fidgety to stand by the table and wait for her, I step to the opening of the labyrinth and bend down to read Dory's sign. In her welcoming remarks, Dory has told the participants that the myth of Theseus, Ariadne, and the Minotaur is so much a part of the labyrinth walk that it's impossible to separate them. Reading it again, I see that she's right.

Startled out of my thoughts by the sound of voices in the woods, I return to take my place by the table as the participants enter. When the hushed whispers of the crowd have died down and the women stand grouped together in front of my table, I hold a hand high to get their attention. Looking over the group of about fifty women, I smile in recognition when I spot the previous attendees Dory invited back. So many stories within this crowd! My eyes linger on Helen Murray, the woman from my Saturday-morning group whom I've worried about for almost a year and never expected to see here. The histories of the participants are as different as they are alike, but all of them share a desperate longing to leave their heartbreak behind them and move toward recovery, and that's why they are here.

"If you're participating in the Asunder Ceremony and have asked someone to walk the labyrinth with you, that's fine," I say in a loud voice. "We couldn't have made it this far without the support of others, and it's the major idea behind the retreats. But I do ask that you enter the center on your own. Some things we have to do by ourselves, and this is one of them. Is everyone ready?"

After murmurs of assent and much head nodding, a hushed expectancy falls over the group. "Okay!" I begin with what I hope is a reassuring smile. "Let me tell you how this will work. On the table here, Dory and I have placed the Asunder vows, if you want to take a copy with you. In addition, we have the wedding candle and a basket of tapers." At her cue, Dory lights the giant white candle in the center, a replica of the pillar candles popular at many weddings nowadays, usually sitting on a satin-draped table and used by the bride and groom as part of the ceremony.

I pause when I spot Haley in the crowd but standing at the edge, away from everyone. When her eyes meet mine, she gives me a weak smile and a wave, and I smile back at her. Just being here is an important step for her. When she's ready, I tell myself, then turn my attention back to the participants. Scattered among them are several of the White Rings in their white tunics, with the necklaces Dory made them hanging around their necks. Even Etta is sporting a tunic, and I suppress a smile at the strange sight. How Dory talked her into wearing one, I can only imagine.

I go on, "The wedding candle represents the vows you and your spouse made the day you married. Please take one of the tapers and light it from the wedding candle. You might have done something similar on your wedding day, maybe taking a taper to your parents. But for our purposes, I want you to think of the lit taper as a symbol of the two of you *after* your wedding vows, when you were joined together and became one." I hold one of the tapers high so everyone can see it.

"With the taper in hand, start your journey into the labyrinth. As you walk the circling paths, take the time to reflect on your married life. Don't think only of the bad times; remember the good ones as well. Sometimes the good ones can be more painful because they make us realize what we've lost. Once you reach the center, please hold on to your candle until you're able to say goodbye to your marriage partner. Do this in whatever way feels right to you; the vows I've provided are only a guide, and some of you have brought farewell letters. Once again, let me remind you that if you're not ready to take this step, please don't force it. Do it only if it feels right for you at this time, okay?

"When you've said what you needed to say, blow out the candle and leave it on the center stone. If you brought a letter, leave it with the candle. You've symbolically acknowledged that your marriage is over, and your vows are no longer valid because you've taken a new set of vows. You've vowed not to look back and not to mourn or grieve again. Your old life is over, and you're ready to put it behind you."

I pause to hold up the piece of paper with the vows on them. "If you'll look on the front of the Asunder vows, you'll read the familiar words of Wordsworth: 'What although the radiance which was once so bright / Be now for ever taken from my sight . . . We will grieve not, rather find / Strength in what remains behind.' Here's what I want you to take from these words: *You* are the strength that remains behind. You've been through a lot of pain, but you've come away a stronger person. You've walked through the fire, and it has left scars, but you came out on the other side. You can't go back to where you were, and most of us wouldn't even if we could. But we can find our strength in what remains behind. Once you acknowledge that—once you really believe it—you're free to walk out of the labyrinth and into a new life."

After a hushed pause, they start coming forward. The first ones to step boldly up to the table are the women from the previous retreats, and I touch their hands in greeting as they take a copy of the vows and reach for a taper. The first woman is shaking so badly that Dory has to hold her hand steady as she lights her taper, but she gives a satisfied nod when it flares, and Dory releases her. Hesitating for a brief moment, she straightens her shoulders with resolution, then steps onto the path of the labyrinth. Once she has entered, the others begin to flow into it, one by one. A few walk in pairs, but most of them make the journey alone, holding the slender, glowing tapers in front of them.

Once the paths of the labyrinth fill up with participants, some coming in, others going out, the whispered vows and sobs of those in the center become lost in the soft guitar music playing in the background, and the shuffle of feet against the dirt path. Hearing them is almost more than I can bear, and Dory turns her head to swipe furiously at her eyes, trying not to let the ones who are waiting to enter the labyrinth see her tears. We've discovered from the previous ceremonies how devastating they are to witness, and those ceremonies have been on a much smaller scale, in a sterile rented conference room. It hits me that this might be too much for Haley, and I lean over to whisper to Dory, "That seems to be the last one, so hold down the fort until I get back, okay? I'd better go see about Haley."

Pushing through the group of women left standing outside the labyrinth, I make my way to the spot where I saw Haley. She's moved farther away, standing under one of the five oaks, her back to me and her hand against the trunk as though to hold it up. I come behind her and place my hands on her shoulders, and she whirls around, her eyes stricken. "You were right, Mom," she says, and her voice catches in a sob. "Guess I shouldn't have come."

I pull her close and stroke her silken hair. "I thought the only problem about having the ceremony out here would be the logistics," I tell her. "It's always the most difficult part of the retreats, but in this setting, it's pretty hard to watch."

Haley hugs herself, shivering as though an icy wind has blown through the oaks. "My God! I can't imagine myself ever going through with it. Most of the time I hate Austin's guts, but still . . . It's like a funeral service, isn't it, held for a love who's dead and gone?"

"You're nowhere near ready, honey. After you've been divorced for a while, and when you attend one of the retreats in a few months, I imagine you'll see it differently."

She studies me for a long moment, then says, "You know, I can see how it can be a good thing, hard as it is. To have a way of saying goodbye and to move on with your life—that's the right thing to do, isn't it? Or maybe I should say it's the only thing to do. I'm proud of you for coming up with this. It's a good thing you've done, and I'll be glad when I get to the point where I can do it."

"Me, too." I reach for her again, hugging her close. "I've got to get back now, but I hope you'll stay for the dancing. You'll be surprised at how the mood changes. It's a catharsis, after the sadness of the ceremony."

Haley inclines her head toward the table where Dory sits perched on her stool. "Oh, I am. I promised Dory I'd stay and dance. And I'll try to bring Gramma Zoe. She might not dance, but she can watch, and it'll help get her mind off Genghis. Matter of fact, I need to go look for her again. I haven't seen her since I got here, and I can't find her anywhere."

"I hope you find her. If she's on the creek, she'll be back when it gets dark, so maybe you should go to the dock and wait for her. So I'll see you, and hopefully Zoe, at the dance."

I've taken a few steps back to where the ceremony still goes on when Haley stops me. "Mom?"

Glancing over my shoulder, I raise my eyebrows. "Yes?"

She regards me quizzically. "You've never done the ceremony, have you?"

I turn back to face her and shake my head. "No, of course not, honey. It's not intended for women like me, who lost someone like I did your father. That's what a funeral service is for. You said the Asunder Ceremony was like a funeral, and it is, in a way, because it offers a ritualistic way to say goodbye to a marriage that's ended. That's the idea behind it." I shrug and add, "The Asunder Ceremony isn't for everybody, and I never intended it to be. But a lot of the participants like the idea because it helps provide them with closure in a way that nothing else has been able to do."

Haley nods, then says thoughtfully, "Yeah, but maybe that's what you need. Some kind of closure. Even though there was a funeral service, I don't think you've let go of Daddy, have you?"

I stare at her for such a long moment that she tilts her head to the side and says, "Mom?"

"No, you're right," I say faintly. "Dory, and Rye, and Lex— they've all tried to tell me that, but I haven't wanted to hear it."

Haley regards me with compassion, and her eyes shine with tears. "I can't blame you for not wanting to let go of Daddy, the way you loved him. I don't want to let go of him, either."

"Of course you don't, and you shouldn't. Both of us have wonderful memories of him and of our time together." Staring off into the darkening woods, I add, "But the truth is, it's not those memories I want, or need, to let go of." Shaking my head, I admit, "Oh, Haley, it's the guilt I've carried all these years that I haven't been able to turn loose of, not your daddy! I've felt so responsible for his death—"

"You know better than that, Mom," she says sharply. "I loved Daddy—idolized him, really—but he was the most self-destructive man I've ever known. I didn't know it at the time, but I can see it now that I'm older. Daddy and my biological mother both, they were beautiful and lovable and charming, but they were also needy and constantly looking for someone, or something, to lean on, whether it was drugs or booze or other people. You've never liked me saying this, but it's the truth: Daddy got his strength from you because he didn't have much of his own. When he used yours up, you ended up feeling guilty because you didn't have any more to give him. Am I right?"

We regard each other for a long moment, and finally I nod. "That shows a lot of perception on your part, sweetheart, and yeah, you're right about most of it. I just haven't been able to face it."

Haley moves to stand beside me and reaches for my hand. "Come on, Mom. Take a dose of your own medicine and do the ceremony. I'll come with you."

"Absolutely not. I won't have you getting upset—"

The blaze of her eyes stops me in midsentence. "You've got to stop treating me like I'm going to fall apart the minute you let go of me," she cries. "You've been a big help, and I appreciate it, I really do, but Jesus H. Christ! You act like I'm so fragile, I can't do anything on my own, and it drives me crazy. You're going to do this, and I'm coming with you!"

"If you're trying to say that I've coddled you long enough," I say with a shaky smile, "then spit it out. Tell me how you really feel."

"Very funny," she says as she grabs my hand, hard. "Now, quit arguing and let's go. And all that stuff you told everybody about not doing it until you're ready? Don't listen to yourself. Because if you're not ready now, you won't ever be."

Dory opens her mouth to question me when Haley drags me to the table, but when I pick up the taper, she doesn't say a word, just looks over at Haley in surprise. I fit the cardboard protector in place, and as with the first participant, my hand trembles when I light the taper from the wedding candle set on the spray of peacock feathers. Dory says, "I'm coming, too, Clare." I start to protest, but after Haley's outburst, I think better of it and keep my mouth shut.

Cupping my hand around the taper, I start the walk, and with each turn of the circle, Dory and Haley stay a step or two behind me. When we reach the center, both of them move close enough to me so Haley can give me a push forward. I'm not really surprised that Haley and I are dry-eyed while Dory sobs loudly, having given up her brave front and leaned against Haley for support. Before Haley can give me another push, I step up to the flat stone in the center of the labyrinth and look down at all of the slender tapers with blackened wicks that are piled up there.

I've gotten this far, though not very willingly, so I force myself to shut out the noises of the woods and the participants and the lovely sound of the guitar music, and I tell myself that I've fought this long enough. Lex was right yesterday morning, and Dory's been right on target, too, though I wouldn't allow myself to listen to either of them. Lex . . . God, he was so right! I should stop the ceremony right now, wave my arms in the air, and tell the participants what a coward I've been. When I leave here, I ought to get out my Rolodex and call every one of my clients whom I've so piously given my little speech to, telling them they're not ready and they need to work harder before they can attend the retreats. I've been guiltier than any of them, and I've been the worst kind of hypocrite. It takes more courage to stand up here than I ever imagined, and so many of the women here, distraught and traumatized by things no one should ever have to endure, have bravely walked up and taken a new set of vows without flinching. Unlike me, the ones who've come up here have been willing to do whatever they have to in order to put the past behind them and start a new life. It hits me how much easier it is to cling to the past. No matter how miserable and wretched and heartbreaking it might be, at least it's familiar. It's the coward's way out, and even though I knew better, it's the one I took.

Funny, I had to get here before I was able to see why it took me so long. In saying goodbye to Mack, I'll not only be giving up the man whose memory I've clung to all these years; I'll be forced to give up some things about myself as well. Haley doesn't know that I've secretly cherished the notion of myself as strong and brave and together, but in truth, I'm none of those things. Since the day Mack died, I've tormented and tortured myself for letting him down, and for all the mistakes I made with him. How could I possibly save Mack when I couldn't even save myself? I saw so clearly that Mack's demons came from his regrets, his bitterness with his father, the way he shut his mother out of his life, and his guilt about Haley and her mother. But I wasn't able to see how I, too, have been paralyzed by my own regrets. I've come to the center of the labyrinth and face-to-face with the Minotaur; now the question is, am I strong enough to slay the monster and find the path that will take me in the right direction? There's only one way to find out.

I blow out the candle and place it on top of the others. Turning around, I nod at Dory and Haley. Both of them reach for me at the same time, and the three of us cling together. Hugging me, Haley whispers in my ear, "Way to go, Mom. I knew you could do it."

In my other ear, Dory says, "Well, I sure as hell didn't! I'm still in a state of shock."

"I'm glad you two came with me," I say when we pull apart, smiling our watery smiles at each other. "You wouldn't believe how much harder that walk is than it looks! It's amazing to me that all these women have done it. It takes a lot of guts."

Dory wipes her eyes and says, "Not only that, they're ready to dance now."

With a nod, I say, "Then let's get out of here so they can, okay?"

"You and Haley go on," Dory says. "I've got the basket on my arm, so I'm going to gather up the tapers while I'm here. Then no one will have to come back later and do it."

Haley and I step back and wait for her until we realize she's purposefully stalling, taking forever to bundle up the stack of burned-out tapers and wadded-up papers on the rock and put them in the small basket hanging over her arm. She keeps glancing around, pretending to be casual, and Haley nudges me.

"What's Dory up to, Mom?"

"Damned if I know," I mutter. The labyrinth paths have almost cleared, and some of the women are leaving the site, heading down the candlelit path in the woods. "Dory!" I say impatiently. "Leave those things alone and come on. We've got to get back and get everything set up for the dance."

Her arms cradling the basket, Dory gives another look into the woods, then sighs and shrugs. When Haley and I start on the path, Dory shuffles behind us, muttering to herself. We've taken only a few steps when Dory lets out such a whoop that I stop and whirl around. The women still on the path ahead of us stop dead in their tracks, as though someone yelled *"Freeze."*

Haley cries, "Mom—look!"

She points upward but doesn't need to, because by then I've heard them. Over our heads are the rustle of wings and the soft coo of two dozen doves, flitting and swooping, shining gloriously white against the falling darkness like the shadows of angels. Haley, Dory, and I stumble backward, out of their way, as they make their spectacular landing in the center of the labyrinth, some on the stone and others scattered about the ground surrounding it. Zoe's white wedding doves have arrived, and it hits me with a jolt of understanding that Zoe has had to retrain them for this occasion. I cannot imagine how she managed it. I know how long it took her to train them to fly away and return here after she released them at weddings. She must have been working for weeks on end to get them to do this. It's no wonder none of us has seen her lately; in spite of her grief for Genghis, she's been preparing them so they would arrive at this moment, just as the ceremony is over. This is her gift to me, this reverse landing of the wedding doves, and I put a hand over my mouth as I blink back my tears.

After a stunned silence, the crowd bursts into applause, and I scan the sea of faces for Zoe's. Dory has dropped her basket of candles and is hopping from one foot to the other as she applauds and whoops and laughs, hugging first Haley and then Etta, who has appeared out of the crowd and hopped over the rock-edged paths to join them. Etta raises her big, jiggling arms above her head to clap her hands as a grin splits her face from ear to ear. With loud cries and cheers, the rest of the White Rings come forward to stand behind Etta, all of them decked out in their ridiculous equinox tunics. Evidently they were all in on this, Zoe's contribution to the ceremony. Now I know why none of us has seen her all evening. I recall the time she first trained the doves, and I know she has to be close enough to them in order to give them her commands. Where on earth could she have released the doves from? I wonder.

From the distance comes a sharp whistle, and at the sound, the doves cock their heads in attention and cease their cooing sounds. As suddenly as they appeared, they lift their pearl-white wings, and one by one they begin to float upward, heading back the way they came, over the dark points of the leafy treetops etched against the blue-gray dusk.

Then I know where she is, where she has to be. I turn my head toward the oak tree that Zoe and Dory and I climbed the day we spied on Lex walking the labyrinth, and I see her. Sitting halfway up the tree like some giant, long-limbed bird is Zoe Catherine, her fingers in the sides of her mouth, whistling her white doves home.